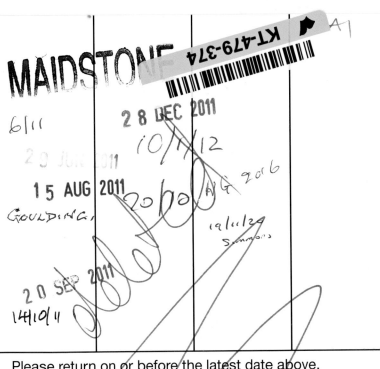

Please return on or before the latest date above.
You can renew online at *www.kent.gov.uk/libs*
or by telephone 08458 247 200

CUSTOMER SERVICE EXCELLENCE

Libraries & Archives

Kent
County
Council

00884\DTP\RN\07.07 LIB 7

C155309305

REVENGE

The McHarg family may be unconventional but Millicent, an eccentric and forthright novelist, is adored by her three granddaughters and her daughter-in-law, Maria. With Millicent's son working abroad, the three generations are very close and the girls, from quiet, talented Plumpet to her adopted sister Maya, are protected and happy. Then on Christmas morning, Plumpet is found assaulted and dazed in her own bed. In one night the McHargs' lives are irrevocably changed, and as memories and old secrets reveal more about the mystery of that night, Millicent prepares to take revenge...

REVENGE

For Roger Latham,
much missed

REVENGE

by

Mary Stanley

Magna Large Print Books
Long Preston, North Yorkshire,
BD23 4ND, England.

British Library Cataloguing in Publication Data.

Stanley, Mary
   Revenge.

A catalogue record of this book is
available from the British Library

ISBN   0-7505-2150-3

First published in Great Britain in 2003 by Headline Book Publishing

Published in Large Print 2004 by arrangement with
Headline Book Publishing Ltd.

Magna Large Print is an imprint of Library Magna Books Ltd.

Printed and bound in Great Britain by
T.J. (International) Ltd., Cornwall, PL28 8RW

Thanks to Flora Rees, editor and friend

The LORD said:
   'Because the daughters of Zion are haughty
   and walk with outstretched necks,
   glancing wantonly with their eyes,
   mincing along as they go,
   tinkling with their feet;
   the LORD will smite with a scab
   the heads of the daughters of Zion,
   and the LORD will lay bare their secret parts.

ISAIAH Ch. 3, v. 16–17

Prologue

Millicent McHarg sat on an iron chair on the patio in the back garden where the Buddha with its green lights resided. She was wearing her winter coat, her grandmother's furs and her felt hat with an ostrich feather. As she said herself, she only wore that particular feather when she was feeling triumphant. Nonetheless she was in a thoughtful mood. Her height, her elegance, her fine-boned features were apparent even in repose.

The funeral was over and she was planning on how to proceed. She looked up at the house with her apartment attached at the side. The lights were already on and the warmth from inside almost drew her in. Then she turned and looked down at the orchard. For a moment she thought there was movement among the trees, but not being given to fanciful thinking she quickly dismissed the possibility of a ghost. She had other things on her mind. She thought of her granddaughters in the main part of the house and she considered the options.

She would write the synopsis of a new book, she thought. She would call it *Divine Justice*, or maybe *Retribution*. No, she thought. I will call it *Revenge*. I will never have it published, but I will use it. My God, but I will give it to him, and watch him read it, and then he'll know. I will people it with real characters, and she ran through the list in her mind:

Millicent McHarg grandmother and author, known as Grammer to the children
Maria McHarg her daughter-in-law, known as Mum
Prunella McHarg eldest granddaughter aged seventeen at the start of the story, known as Plumpet
Daphne McHarg middle granddaughter aged fourteen and known as Daffers
Maya McHarg youngest granddaughter, adopted, aged between four and five, known as the Dumpling

I'll let them tell the story, Millicent decided. And I'll include Theresa Carmody. She can tell her story too.

It was very cold on the patio and the plan was forming nicely. The door from her apartment into the garden opened, and Waldorf appeared on the step.

'Millie,' he called, 'are you really sitting out there in this weather? Is that really you?'

'The one and only,' she said, which observation pretty much summed her up.

'I thought I saw a ghost,' he commented lightly, 'down among the trees.'

'I think not,' said Millicent McHarg. 'I doubt that a ghost would dare to hover here.'

'Too right,' Waldorf replied. A tall thin humorous man, slightly older than Millicent, he talked with a plum in his mouth and was given to

14

wearing a buttonhole, swinging an umbrella and talking in riddles.

'I'm going in to the girls,' he told her.

'I'll follow in a moment,' she replied. 'I'm just putting the finishing touches to a new book.'

'I should think you've done enough for one day,' he said dryly.

We'll see about that, she thought.

The door closed behind Waldorf and she lifted her head. For a moment she thought she could hear the laughter of her granddaughters coming from the house. She sighed, knowing that she had not heard them laugh like that all Christmas, and that it would be a long time before she could hope to hear them laugh like that again.

Chapter One

The story of Prunella McHarg

I am one of three. I am the eldest. And I am the one in whom so much hope was invested. That's what happens with eldest children. Middle children fluctuate between fury at not being the eldest, and despair at not being the youngest. The baby in the family does its own thing. They tell me not to think this way. That this is a misconception. They tell me that we are all the same and yet that we are all different. They tell me that the same aspirations were there for each of us, that we were brought up the same, and that the

15

same love was given to each of us. And although I know that these are facts in other people's eyes, and that on some level this is the truth, I am no longer sure of most things. I only know that I am one of three.

I am one of three.

And I am Plumpet.

What defines me? Grammer, my grandmother, says that we are defined by moments in our lives which change us and which make us what we are. There are moments like when the Dumpling arrived. There is Daffers's arrival too, but I only really remember being brought in to see her in the hospital and she looked at me and screamed. I don't really remember a time when she was not there. Oh, I remember life before her, but I don't remember her not being part of it.

Until last Christmas there was really nothing momentous in my life. We live in comfort in Dublin in a large house, and Grammer lives in the adjoining apartment, which was built on before I was born. Grammer says we have choices in life all along the way. But sometimes we don't have choice – things happen to us and our lives are changed for ever.

They tell me not to think so much, but how do you close down the human mind and think of nothing? Pablo Picasso was born in 1881. I recite these dates to myself all the time. Auguste Rodin was born in 1840. This year is 2003 and I was born eighteen years ago although I was only seventeen last Christmas. Daffers was born in 1987. We don't know when the Dumpling was born but her papers say 1998. Daffers and the

16

Dumpling are my sisters. We named each other. Not with care but by chance.

Names. They come from our forefathers and foremothers down through the centuries. We carry one name with us until our line ceases. The other name – our first name – is given to us, usually by those who bring us into the world. Sometimes those names are badly chosen. We can change them, discard them, twist them around – but in a sense they define us.

I was christened Prunella. What does it make you think of? It didn't make me think of anything, until I started school. Apparently it made other children think of prunes.

'Mum,' I said to my mother after one of those agonising days at school...

Prunella McHarg isn't cool.
Prunella, Prunella, you're a fool!

'Mum,' I said. 'Why did you call me Prunella?'

'Because you looked just like a Prunella when you were lying in my arms in the hospital,' Mum replied. She was sitting at the kitchen table with Daffers, my younger sister – real name Daphne, but renamed by me at an early age, as I couldn't get my three-year-old mouth around the tricky bit in the middle of her name. I think it was the *n* that posed the problem.

I sat beside them at the table. Mum was making a fruit salad – oranges, apples, plums, pears, one banana, and a tin of strawberries were to hand. The tin of strawberries was there because of my fondness for the sugared syrupy fruit. As Mum chopped up the fruit and put it in a large bowl, Daffers, blonde curly hair bouncing as her head moved from side to side, big blue eyes staring at me, was surreptitiously removing the slices of banana from the salad and popping them into her mouth. She was so busy listening to our conversation that she forgot to swallow, and her cheeks were getting bigger and bigger with the stored fruit.

'But Mum,' I said. 'What does a Prunella look like?'

'Why,' said Mum, unabashed and with that logic that adults sometimes have when they are asked to explain something to a child. 'Why, a Prunella looks just like you.'

I thought of the rhyme my classmates had sung as I came into the hall:

Prunella McHarg is a prune.
Eat her with a teaspoon!

It didn't scan, but at the age of six, scansion was not high on my list of priorities.

'Mum,' I tried again. 'What's a prune?'

Mum's eyes narrowed slightly, but when she looked up at me her face was as kind and friendly as it had been before I asked the question.

'A prune is a dried plum,' she said. 'Quite delicious.' She picked up a plum off the table, and started to cut it into pieces. 'Would you like a piece of plum, pet?' she asked.

Daffers had now discovered that her mouth was overfull, and so she swallowed its contents quickly, gulping to get some air and then she said, 'Plum pet.'

It is unclear whether she was asking for some plum, which seemed to me to be the most likely thing as she was a determined eater, or whether she thought that Mum had just addressed me as Plumpet.

Either way it stuck. And by nightfall I was known as Plumpet.

'You can't call her Plumpet,' Grammer said at dinner that evening. Grammer was Millicent McHarg, mother-in-law to Mum, bestselling author of romantic fiction of a unique sort, to the nation. She had been described in the papers as such, but as she said, she wrote about the soap operas of other people's lives. As well as being a writer, she was and is grandmother to Daffers and me. And of course to the Dumpling. But back then the Dumpling was not even born.

'What's wrong with it, Grammer?' I asked, thinking about the name Plumpet.

'Plumpet,' said Daffers, large blue eyes rolling from one person to the next, blonde curls bouncing, mouth full of chicken. Under the table, one of her legs was swinging backwards and forwards, possibly trying to kick me.

'Don't talk with your mouth full, Daphne,' said Grammer.

'Daphne called her Plumpet,' Mum said. I could see her trying to catch Grammer's eye – discreetly, but not discreetly enough for me.

'What's wrong with it, Grammer?' I asked again.

'Why nothing, darling,' Grammer said, reaching out for a baked potato with the bashed silver

19

serving spoon. 'I just thought it was a little unusual, that's all.'

'She's a very slender child,' Mum said vaguely addressing no one in particular except for the string beans in the vegetable dish. 'And she quite likes it.'

'Indeed,' said Grammer. 'Daphne, sit up straight and pass the butter.'

And so I was re-christened, and Daffers passed the butter.

Of course I didn't tell them in school that I was now Plumpet. I just thought it inside my head when they sang the *Prunella McHarg* song. After a few days, I think because I ignored them, they stopped singing the song. In my heart it didn't hurt any more because I was now Plumpet McHarg.

Grammer says that surnames come from your forefathers, and that our name goes back to long before the Ulster Plantation to the Highlands and the Lowlands of Bonnie Scotland, and that we must never forget that. She says that Daffers and I must never change our name when we get married. She says we must carry our surname with pride.

Daffers asked her if she had changed her name when she got married.

Mum was sewing nametags on to our school skirts when Daffers asked, and she smiled. She said, 'Grammer is a law unto herself, girls. Never forget that.'

Grammer said, 'Hrrumph,' or something like that.

That was all a long time ago. A lot of water has flowed under the bridge since then, or, as Grammer says, a lot has been flushed down the loo. Daffers and I were just little girls back then when I was renamed Plumpet, and fortunately for me I stayed quite thin so that the *plump* part of my name was not relevant. I stayed taller than Daffers and my final spurt in growth at around the age of fifteen ensured that Daffers would not catch up on me. Needless to say, this was one more thing for her to complain about.

'If you had only been taller,' she moaned to Mum.

'I'm so sorry,' Mum said. No trace of irony in her voice: she doesn't do irony. Mum is not small though, she has long legs like mine, and she is quite slim – she just is not quite the same height as I am.

'Dad was tall, wasn't he?' Daffers said, with her face screwed up as she contemplated our absent father.

'*Is* tall,' Grammer replied from her armchair at the window.

'It's so long since I've seen him,' said Daffers, 'that I don't remember.'

Grammer says that men are a mystery. You give them soil to plant seeds in, but they never grow long enough roots. 'It doesn't mean they don't love you,' she always adds. 'There isn't anyone better than your father.'

Daffers said that of course Grammer would say that, seeing as our father is her son. Daffers did not say that in front of Grammer though.

21

Mum went on holidays with Dad sometimes. He worked abroad – still does, in fact – and she flew out to meet him. When they went away while we were really young, she brought home the most amazing things. We were all very taken with the four-foot-high Buddha, which subsequently resided in the garden, between the patio and the orchard. An electrician installed green flood-lighting, which comes up from the ground making the Buddha look like a place of worship at night. However the most exciting parcel she ever brought home was the Dumpling.

'Don't ask,' Mum said. 'Just don't ask,' as we stood there, openmouthed, gazing at the blanketed child in Dad's arms. Mum also brought Dad back that time. Mum looked so worried, except when she gazed at the wrapped-up bundle. Then her eyes softened, as she took in the large black eyes of the child, and the smooth, almost translucent golden skin.

'What's its name?' Daffers asked.

'Her papers say that her name is Maya,' Mum said cryptically.

'Wrapped up like that she looks like a dumpling in the soup we had in Switzerland,' Daffers said, unwittingly giving her a name.

The Dumpling had a prominent upper lip.

'She won't need collagen implants,' Grammer said thoughtfully, as she took the bundle, suddenly named the Dumpling, from Dad.

From the word go, the Dumpling made no noise at all. She seldom cried, but when she did, her tears were silent.

'She'll keep us awake at night,' said Daffers, clearly livid that someone might outdo her noise levels. But the Dumpling didn't keep us awake. Placid, good-natured, silent Dumpling.

Down came the boxes of baby toys from the attic, and one by one their contents were fed to the Dumpling. Where Daffers and I had placed building blocks on top of each other, the Dumpling placed them in rows. At first it was difficult to see if there was a system or pattern to her way of playing, but then it became clear. The Dumpling placed one block, then two blocks, then three blocks, then four, neatly flat on the floor so that they looked like a side view of a staircase. She had a pink pig, a furry fellow with a curly-wee tail, which Dad had bought her on the way home in an airport along the way. Daffers, who has always gone for the obvious, christened this pig Pink Pig. The Dumpling guided it along the building blocks. I got the impression then, and I still carry the same view now, that the Dumpling views the world in a different way to the rest of us. Grammer says it is as if her perspective is randomly lateral or aerial. The Dumpling had a tape of nursery rhymes; her favourite was 'This Little Piggy Went to Market', although she was also very fond of 'Tom Tom the Piper's Son'. She played it on the family stereo system and knew how to rewind and fast forward until she found the rhymes she liked the best. Sometimes when she was listening to 'This Little Piggy', she took off her socks and shoes and she pointed at her toes. It used to break my heart.

She also listened to her tape on Theresa Carmody's tape recorder in the house next door.

The Dumpling and Theresa Carmody took to each other like a duck to water, as Theresa was fond of telling everyone. In fact the Dumpling took to most people like a duck to water, except for Daffers. Which was pretty smart of the Dumpling. You know the expression, beware of Greeks bearing gifts? Well, beware of Daffers who most certainly did not bear gifts. At least, not back then. And the Dumpling copped on to this fairly fast. Not about the gift thing, because the Dumpling had no concept of gifts. If she saw something she liked the look of, she simply pointed to it. If it was passed to her she considered it hers. Grammer said we could give her the clock in the drawing room for Christmas, as it would be a great way to get rid of the clock and the Dumpling would be delighted.

Grammer didn't like the clock in the drawing room. But Mum did, and so it stayed on the mantelpiece. I think it must have belonged to Mum's mother sometime in the past.

Grammer said, 'Get attached to nothing. We have to leave it all behind one day.'

The Dumpling would have taken the kitchen sink with her if she could carry it when she was going out in her buggy. She travelled most places in her buggy because Mum said she was frail. Grammer usually made her walk because she said that would strengthen her legs. Except when Grammer was on a mission, and then she popped the Dumpling in her buggy and off they went.

Theresa Carmody's tape recorder had a little

microphone and you could talk into it and be recorded. The Dumpling clipped the microphone on to her sweater or dungarees or whatever, and pretended to talk into it.

Except she made no noise.

The Dumpling was silent.

When Theresa Carmody moved in next door a couple of years before the Dumpling arrived, she bought the house with 'sausage money'. That's what she said.

'What does she mean, Grammer?' Daffers and I asked as one, after we had been in for a housewarming bash, which went on until two in the morning.

Grammer brought the pair of us home at eleven o'clock because she said it wasn't New Year's Eve, and girls of our age needed our beauty sleep. 'And so do I,' she added firmly when we objected.

Grammer was a beauty in her day, but Mum says never use the past tense if happening to mention this. Grammer is probably the most beautiful-looking woman of her age, whom I know anyway. She is tall with good bones. Grammer says that good bones last, but that we must drink milk for the calcium in order to develop the bones in question.

'What does "sausage money" mean?' we girls asked.

It transpired that Theresa Carmody was related to Wallace the butchers, once prize-winning sausage makers, but who had recently had some scandal attached to them. Grammer said some people have no ethical sense whatsoever and that you could not go around just butchering anything and everything in sight.

'Discretion and conscience,' she said firmly. 'Always use both.'

I did.

But Daffers didn't. I don't think Grammer did either.

Theresa Carmody had dozens of people at her housewarming. She wore her hair pinned up with masses of tiny shiny clips, and she wore the prettiest of earrings. She passed around sausages on plates, with little cocktail sticks in them. Very few people ate them, although there was a big rush on the cubes of cheese, the nacho chips, the gherkins and the chocolate-covered strawberries. I liked the black chocolate strawberries best, and Daffers liked the white ones.

In all families, people, especially children, have different heights and different tastes. Grammer said that is what makes the world go round. Daffers said the world spins on its axis and in her opinion we were bloody lucky we hadn't all been spun off it. She didn't say that in front of Grammer though.

Daffers likes geography, geology and meteorology. Or she used to anyway. Theresa Carmody liked Grammer. She said that Grammer was her icon. This was because Grammer wrote books and was published, and that was Theresa's aim. She recorded into her tape recorder and then transcribed it all later on to her laptop. Grammer wrote with a pen straight on to lined paper.

26

Mum went out to work every morning at eight o'clock. After the Dumpling arrived, Mum took three months off work – accumulated sick leave, she said – and she didn't go back to work until Grammer said to her that she should maintain her career. It helped that Grammer was based at home, and that the Dumpling was usually delighted to sit on the floor with her blocks and anything else she could line up.

When Daffers was doing her maths homework at the table, the Dumpling sat beside her and watched. Daffers had recently started geometry and was wailing about the meaning of all three angles in a triangle equalling two right angles or one hundred and eighty degrees. The Dumpling got a big plastic triangle out of her box of secrets, which she kept behind the sofa, and took a sheet of paper from Grammer's writing block. She drew a straight line across the page, and taking the plastic triangle, marked on the line each of the angles of the triangle. At first I couldn't believe what she was doing. Daffers, needless to say, was ignoring her. I looked over at Grammer who was painting a bookmark for her friend Waldorf for his birthday, and I saw her eyes were widening by the minute. She glanced at me and we exchanged a look of disbelief, before we both looked back at the Dumpling sitting with her triangle, pencil and sheet of paper.

I said, 'Einstein.'

Grammer said, 'Euclid.'

'I don't understand,' wailed Daffers at the table, staring at her open textbook.

Grammer got up and went over to the table, and

she said, 'Let me show you.' She took a triangle from Daffers's geometry set, and like the Dumpling she marked each of the angles on a line.

'Oh,' said Daffers. 'I see. And does every triangle's angles fit like that, or is it just this one?'

'Every triangle,' Grammer said.

After that we watched the Dumpling with even greater care, if that is possible. Sometimes she went into the kitchen and pointed at a cupboard where the pasta was kept. She liked the bags with the small shapes in them. She laid them out in patterns we didn't always understand. One day she laid them out on the floor like this:

X
Xx
Xxx
Xxxxx
Xxxxxxx
Xxxxxxxxxxx
Xxxxxxxxxxxxx
Xxxxxxxxxxxxxxxxx
Xxxxxxxxxxxxxxxxxxx
Xxxxxxxxxxxxxxxxxxxxxxx

Grammar and I stared at them for ages. They were butterfly pasta shapes. We wondered at first if the fact they were butterflies was important.

'I don't get the sequence,' Grammer murmured. 'One, two, three, five, seven, eleven, thirteen, seventeen, nineteen, twenty-three. Nine is missing.'

'And so is fifteen,' I said, frantically trying to see the pattern. 'And twenty-one.'

Then Daffers moaned at the table, 'What is a

prime number? Someone tell me what a prime number is.'

And Grammer and I looked at each other and then at the prime numbers in pasta lying out on the floor.

'A prime number,' Grammer said slowly, 'is a number that can only be divided by itself or by one.'

The Dumpling cleared her pasta away. She put it in her treasure box.

We are all born with gifts, Grammer says. 'Sometimes it is unclear what those gifts are – but they are there, hidden in each of us.'

'I can't do nothing,' Daffers said.

'It's *can't do anything*,' Grammer corrected her. 'And yes, you can. It's just that you haven't identified yet what it is you do best. But I know.'

Daffers rolled her blue eyes at Grammer, and waited for more to come. More invariably did come.

'I didn't start writing until I was plenty-nine,' said Grammer. 'I didn't even know I could write until I gave it a go.'

'But you said you know what *I* can do,' Daffers wailed. Daffers mostly talked in a wail.

'Yes,' Grammer said. 'But if I just tell you, you mightn't bother to develop it. You have to find it out for yourself. It's part of you.'

Daffers was good at causing rows, being mean to the Dumpling, and whinging.

Theresa Carmody sang 'Silence is Golden' to the Dumpling. In the summer she put a rug on the grass in her garden. She lay on the rug dressed in a pink bikini. Her black hair was wound up on top of her head so that the sun could tan her neck, as well as the rest of her. She unclipped the straps of her bikini bra, and rubbed in suntan lotion – factor four because she has skin that tans easily. Daffers's skin is very fair, and mine is sort of middle. Grammer said we had to wear sunhats and sunglasses so that we didn't get wrinkles on our faces.

'Boring,' said Daffers.

'Essential,' said Grammer.

'Mum, do I have to?' whinged Daffers.

'Grammer is right,' Mum said. 'A thing of beauty is a joy for ever,' she smiled at Daffers. 'You'll be glad when you're older.'

Daffers did her own thing. Grammer's genes are strong in her, and when she went to the sea for a week with Samson and Delilah (real names Sam and Delia, one known for his brawn, the other for her beauty) and Daffers's pal Daisy, their only daughter, she lay out in the sun until her pale skin turned red and her eyes puffed up and she ended up in hospital. Burned to a crisp as Grammer described her.

'You can bring a horse to water,' as Grammer said.

Theresa Carmody had a sister named Polo. She had shortish straight blonde hair. Daffers said it had been hacked, not cut. It was very uneven all right.

'Talk about androgynous,' Grammer said to Mum.

'What's a drogynous?' asked Daffers, echoing my own query.

Grammer opened her mouth to reply, as she believed all questions should be answered, but Mum had a coughing fit and sent Daffers for a glass of water and shook her head frantically at Grammer.

When Mum went to the laundry room to put clothes in the washing machine, and Grammer was crushing lavender for her dressing-table, Grammer said to Daffers and me, 'All I'm saying, girls, is that femininity is meant for females, and masculinity is meant for males. Decide what you want to be – whether gay or straight, it really doesn't matter – and then go with it. Never ever have people looking at you and not being sure whether you're male or female or what it is you're after.'

Daffers looked at me. I looked at Daffers. Now, homophobic Grammer was not, and neither were we. We had sort of bypassed the sniggering at sexuality stage which seemed rampant among our peers from time to time. Grammer was very open and clear cut about the equality of human beings regardless of their background and their station in life as she called it. But now she seemed to be giving us some kind of advice that was not quite clear.

Later I heard Mum saying to Grammer, 'They're bound to bump into that Polo person again. Better to say nothing about androgynes.'

Later I asked Grammer more about this, but she had developed a certain vagueness, which I could not penetrate.

31

The Polo person did indeed visit her sister, Theresa Carmody. Theresa's gentle femininity was certainly counterbalanced by the horse-like features and dumpiness of Polo.

'Why do you think she's called Polo?' Daffers asked me as we looked out of my bedroom window into Theresa Carmody's back garden where Theresa was sitting on a chair in a pretty summer dress, and Polo was dressed in large check shorts and was sitting with her legs apart. Both women were small and slim and Polo would probably have looked all right if she had bothered to do something with herself. She always had a sort of sneer on her face.

'Something to do with polo-horses?' I suggested.

'What are they?'

'Polo is a sport. A bit like hockey, but on horse-back. I suppose that's why she's called Polo.'

'She's certainly sitting as if she were on a horse,' Daffers agreed, and tried a few neighs.

'For God's sake, Daffers,' I said. 'The window is open.'

Polo had been living abroad and had only recently moved back home. She became a regular visitor at her sister's next door to us. I don't know where she herself lived in Dublin, but I think it was an apartment somewhere so you couldn't blame her for constantly visiting Theresa as we all had such nice gardens in our secluded cul de sac, each with patios, lawns, an orchard and raspberry canes.

Theresa told us later that her name was

Mintalla – at least, that's what it sounded like, so the arrival at the name Polo was immediately clear to us McHargs.

By the time we had that conversation the Dumpling had arrived to live with us. I remember that afternoon so well. Across the hedge in Theresa Carmody's garden, the two sisters sat. And in our garden Mum was shelling peas. I think it must have been the weekend, or else Mum was on holidays, because she never shelled peas on a working day. There was never time. Anyway, there was Mum at the garden table, and the Dumpling was sitting on the lawn. The Dumpling was laying blades of grass out on her thigh in a row. I saw Mum look at her and then look back to the peas. I glanced around at Daffers who was about to leave the bedroom. And when I looked again the Dumpling was gone. I stood at the window wondering where she could have got to.

Maybe Grammer came and called her, I thought, in that minute when I had looked around to see Daffers leave the room.

Then suddenly I saw her sitting on the grass behind Theresa Carmody in the next garden. Theresa was lying flat on a sunbed with her eyes closed, but Polo was sitting looking at the Dumpling. I surmised that she had gone through the hedge, although I wouldn't have thought that possible. At that moment Mum looked around again and saw that the Dumpling was gone. I could see the puzzlement in her face, as her head swivelled from left to right as she tried to find our missing baby. We thought of her as our baby because she was so little, but she was well past toddler stage by then.

I didn't like to yell down where she had gone because I would be heard next door, so I scooted downstairs and out to the garden where Mum was now looking among the raspberry canes. We checked the hedge to see how the Dumpling could have got into the other garden so quickly, and indeed we found the way she must have gone. There, down low in the privet there was the equivalent of a tiny pathway leading through from our garden to the drop to the next garden.

'Theresa,' Mum called through the hedge. 'Is the Dumpling in your garden?' She didn't like to say I'd seen her, in case it looked like I'd been spying.

'No,' called Theresa through the hedge.

Mum and I looked at each other.

'We think she wormed her way through the hedge,' Mum called.

'No sign of her,' Theresa called back. 'And we've been sitting out here all the time.'

'Could you just check the house to see if she has gone inside?' Mum asked.

'What if they don't find her?' I said aghast.

'I'm coming round the front,' Mum called through the hedge. 'Plumpet saw her from the window. She must have gone through the hedge. I'll be right around.'

The peas were abandoned as Mum and I hared around to Theresa Carmody's front door. Theresa opened the door with the Dumpling sitting on her hip.

'She was in the kitchen,' Theresa said. 'She

must have slipped past Polo and me – neither of us saw her. We were lying in the sun.'

Mum reached out and took the Dumpling back. The Dumpling clung to whoever held her, like a baby koala holding its parent. That was the Dumpling. Sometimes when you were just standing thinking about what you were going to do next, she came and stood in front of you and put her arms around your legs. I always picked her up and hugged her. She buried her face in your neck. She breathed hot little breaths on to your cheek. Her eyes were dark and her hair was spiky straight. Sometimes when she was asleep, I used to go in to look at her. She crumpled up her little hands with her thumbs sticking out, and she slept uneasily. She moved from side to side in her cot, sometimes thrashing out with her fists; her eyelids never seemed to be totally still. It was as if her eyes were active all the time she was asleep.

I just wanted to hug her and hug her.

She collected things – claiming them as her own. Grammer said we had to be very careful in the shops as the Dumpling just acquired items at will. Grammer said that maybe there were no shops where she came from, and perhaps that was why she was missing the basic concept. As she did not like giving things back it was easier to make sure she didn't get them to start with.

Mum said that the Dumpling had to learn and that we must put our foot down.

Grammer said, 'Feet down, Maria?'

'You know what I mean,' Mum said.

But the Dumpling was so good and sweet that

35

it was very difficult to be firm with her.

'It's for her own good,' Mum said. 'It's for her safety. It's one way of protecting her. I'm always afraid that she'll wander off...'

I didn't think the Dumpling would wander off. I mean to say, I knew that she sometimes went into Theresa Carmody's garden, and I knew that sometimes we couldn't find her because she seemed to disappear, but I thought the Dumpling was anchored with us. I thought she knew that we had all the love in the world for her, and as Grammer says, 'Love makes the world go round.'

Grammer also says that diversity and coincidence make the world go round too.

Chapter Two

Daffers's Tale

Grammer and Waldorf took us to the pantomime at Christmas. Waldorf is Grammer's companion. He is very tall and Grammer always says he looks like Leslie Phillips except that he is even funnier. She also says that he talks like Leslie Phillips, but as I didn't know who Leslie Phillips was back then when Waldorf appeared on the scene, I couldn't judge the comparison. All I knew was that he was very funny. Anyway, I thought Plumpet would say she was too old for the panto, but she didn't, so I didn't have to either. They took a box in the Upper Circle. First of all I thought we were so high up that no one would be able to see us, then I was glad that no one could see us, because when Waldorf arrived he was carrying a picnic hamper and a cooler box. I kid you not.

Grammer wasn't too keen on us girls having champagne – Waldorf called it 'champers' – but he said, 'They have to start living sometime, Millie.'

Millie – that's what he called Grammer. It says Millicent McHarg on her books, all forty-eight of them and translated into fourteen different languages. Her name looks great in Japanese. Squiggle-squiff and a hieroglyph. Grammer refused point blank to allow the Dumpling to even sniff the champagne. I'd have sulked if I'd been the Dumpling. But the Dumpling being the Dumpling, she just sucked her thumb and looked at Grammer and then at the champagne and said nothing.

When Grammer went to the loo, the Dumpling checked her champagne glass carefully. There was only a drop left in it, and so she tasted that. Waldorf laughed and said, 'Girls will be girls,' and the Dumpling beamed up at him and wriggled her little nose. By the time Grammer returned, the Dumpling had settled down and was peering over the edge of the box, and the curtain went up before Grammer could say anything at all. I hate the safety curtain on the stage at the pantomime, which is always there before the show starts. It makes me wonder, Is it to keep the actors safe, or the audience? And safe from what? Or from whom? To keep the actors safe from marauding onlookers? I love the word marauding. If the safety curtain wasn't there I don't think anyone in the audience would even think of jumping up on the stage and accosting anyone. Not that I was in a position to do anything like that because we were up so high. The nice thing about a box in the theatre is that you are sort of secluded, while the downside is that the view isn't great. Grammer said I had the best seat and to stop making a noise.

The Dumpling sat on Plumpet's knee and waved at the audience and at the actors and actresses on the stage. A large white goose descended from behind the lifted curtains, but because we were so high up we could only see its enormous orange webbed feet for about ten minutes. These feet remained suspended just below the curtain line while the Dumpling pointed in fascination at them. I thought she might actually be about to say something because she kept one finger in their direction and turned her head from Grammer to Waldorf and back again while jabbing the air with one small digit.

Plumpet whispered, 'It's a goose, Dumpling. Just wait a minute and you'll see more of it.' The reason Plumpet had cottoned on to it being a large white fowl was because the show was called *Mother Goose*, which rather gave the game away.

Grammer doesn't whisper, so she said loudly, 'It's a goose, Dumpling.'

The Dumpling jabbed the air frantically as the two feet hung at our eye-level.

I had a chocolate and waited to see what would develop. Waldorf filled up the champagne glasses and said cryptically, 'Has anyone seen my yo-yo?'

Meantime the Dumpling was jigging up and down on Plumpet's knee frantically pointing at the orange feet.

Plumpet was whispering, 'It's all right, Dumpling. More goose in a minute,' sounding like Mum on Christmas Day.

The Dumpling got down off Plumpet's knees and tried to climb over the edge of the box. I looked over and down to see who she would have landed on had Plumpet not grabbed her. She would have squashed at least three children down below.

Plumpet was starting to look frazzled, while Waldorf rooted in the picnic hamper and surprisingly pulled out crayons and paper.

The Dumpling grabbed the paper and one orange crayon, sketched the webbed feet but put the body of a man above them. From where I was sitting it looked like a hanged man because his head was definitely suspended from a rope. Meantime the goose started its slow descent to the boards of the stage. An uglier-looking creature I never did see. As it landed on the stage it squatted and dumped a large golden egg on the ground. While the audience were busy gazing at this apparition, members of the cast unhooked the creature from the wires by which it had descended. A trapdoor opened in the throat of the bird, and a face peered out.

Well, if the Dumpling had been surprised at the bird's descent and by its golden turd, it was nothing to the surprise she got when the neck opened. She dropped to her feet from Plumpet's restraining grip, and she leaned on the edge of the box, her almond eyes opened wider than you could imagine. She was now so excited that she didn't know how to react, and the finger which had been pointing at the bird now started to point at herself and then at Waldorf and then at me.

'There's a man inside the goose,' Plumpet explained to her.

The Dumpling's lips quivered and tears appeared. It was only then I realised that this was not excitement on the Dumpling's part, but serious agitation and real distress.

'It's all right,' Plumpet whispered. 'It's a friendly goose.'

Friendly my foot! No wonder the child was distraught. This was not *Mother Goose* as I had been told the tale. This was one lethal creature and it was armed with a bow and arrow. I'm sure someone had mixed up the stories. It bore more resemblance to the sheriff out of *Robin Hood* than it did to *Mother Goose*.

Plumpet soothed the weeping Dumpling, while Grammer had some more champagne. I took the nicest chocolate out of the box and while Plumpet wasn't looking, I slipped it to the Dumpling.

Well. I didn't like seeing her cry.

Anyway, I ate half of it first. It was white chocolate – my favourite. And the chocolate must have done the trick, because the Dumpling settled back on Plumpet's knee and buried her face in Plumpet's sweater and held on tight for a while. When she finally let go there was mushed-up white chocolate on Plumpet's woolly and the Dumpling finally got into the swing of the pantomime, pointing with excitement at various happenings and almost chuckling out loud when the audience yelled, 'Oh yes he is!' in response to the goose's, 'Oh, no he isn't!'

I always find that bit boring, so I nabbed another chocolate. I needed a distraction because chocolate always makes me think of being in hospital. And hospital makes me think of pain.

Five days I had to spend in hospital when I got burned at the sea – *and* everyone seemed to think it was my fault. I just wanted a tan like Theresa Carmody's. That's all. You'd think that was too much to ask. None of the family actually said, 'I told you so,' but you know that look, disguised as concern.

Mum saying, 'Darling, how did this happen?'

And it hurt like anything. Even my lips were blistered. Plumpet brought me in a bar of white chocolate. I could smell it and I wanted to taste it, but my lips were so sore that I actually could not even bear the thought of opening my mouth. She said that when I got home she'd buy me white chocolate ice cream. I couldn't open my eyes because they were so puffed.

One of the nurses asked my mother if I had a sight problem. A sight problem! What did she bloody well think – that I was pretending my eyelids were so burned so that I didn't have to look? I certainly didn't want to look at *her*. She sounded as if she'd been brought up on a cattle farm – and I'm not talking *in* the farmhouse, if you get my drift.

'Moo,' I said to Mum, knowing that *she* would get my drift. I was referring to the nurse, but Mum, who knew perfectly well what I was getting at, said, 'Don't worry, darling. You'll soon be as pretty as anything again.'

I'd seen myself in the mirror in Samson and Delilah's mobile home at Brittas Bay, just before I had passed out, and what I saw made me terrified that I was going to look like a blistered tomato for the rest of my life.

I howled, and they came and gave me another injection.

Samson and Delilah were as worried as anything, probably afraid that Mum and Grammer would sue them. Samson was a litigation barrister and he constantly expected the worst.

Daisy came in with them, and peering into my face, she asked, 'Is Daffers going to die?' She asked this in a tone of voice that made me wonder if she were actually encouraging me to pop my clogs. (Popping one's clogs was an expression of Grammer's and repeatedly used when she was reading the death notices in the papers. 'Good Lord,' she'd say. 'I see so-and-so has popped her clogs.' It always made me think of someone's feet suddenly growing too big.)

Later Daisy said they were all afraid that I was going to die, but that she knew I would pull through. She also said that Delilah felt guilty as anything. Delilah kept saying to Mum, 'Factor 30 – that's what it said on the bottle – Factor 30.' And Mum said, 'I know, Delia. I know. I don't

42

know how this could have happened.'

Huh. Well, I know how it happened. If Mum had only bought me a decent low factor like everyone else used, I wouldn't have had to have poured the contents of the Factor 30 into the measuring jug, replaced it with Theresa Carmody's Factor 4, and then filled her bottle up with the Factor 30. I mean, what was I supposed to do?

Grammer said, 'No foal, no fee.'

Grammer said she would be writing to the manufacturers of the suntan lotion. So maybe Samson would get some litigation work out of this after all, I thought.

Everything hurt me. Even the sheets on the bed hurt. They put me on a water mattress but it still hurt. The only time it was okay was after the injections that made me sleep. Mum said she was never letting me out of her sight again. The thought of that was awful.

Plumpet brought the Dumpling in to see me, but the Dumpling looked out of the window and sucked her thumb. I could see that through my eyelashes. By that stage I could open my eyes, but I couldn't be bothered.

They gave me drinks through a straw. I always quite liked straws up until then. However, if you're thirsty and your lips are burned it's a very slow way to drink. Grammer always said, 'Give me a bottle of wine and a straw and I'm happy.'

Waldorf was much the same. He would drink anything. Grammer met Waldorf at a literary lunch. Mum thought he was a very bad influence on Grammer, but I thought it was the other way

43

around. Mum used to say they were a lethal combination but that it was nice to see Grammer so happy.

Grammer was happy anyway – anyone could see that. But it was quite good fun going out with Grammer and Waldorf. There was a sense of the unexpected happening, be it a shopping spree or lunch, or going to the pantomime. Grammer said if you don't know joy you haven't lived. But I suppose that joy is different things to different people. She said, 'Take pleasure and happiness where you can find it. Life is short.' I was just trying to take pleasure and be happy, and look where it got me. Floating on a water mattress in a hospital, unable to eat white chocolate.

I remember how Grammer swept into the hospital with her most magnificent feather stuck in her felt hat. 'Maria,' she said to Mum, 'home you go and get some sleep. I'll stay with Daphne. You'll be no good to man nor beast if you don't get some shut-eye, not to mention the bags you'll develop beneath your eyes.'

Grammer had been a beauty in her day, so Mum told us, but Grammer always said that beauty is something you have to work at. She also said that it is in the eye of the beholder, which always struck me as being a contradiction. If someone thought you were beautiful, what was the point in working at your looks because they already thought you were perfect? While if they did not perceive you as being beautiful then you were wasting your time in trying to beautify yourself for them.

'Goodness shows through,' was another thing

44

Grammer used to say while she looked at Plumpet, the Dumpling and me. I always felt she was getting at me, but that could have been feelings of guilt on my part.

So Grammer stayed with me in the hospital.

'It'll give me plenty of time to work on my new book,' she said. She always had a book on the go, and as she said, half of the writing of a book is the working of it in your head. Mum often wasn't there when a mother might be most needed, but Grammer was the perfect grandmother so we didn't miss out on anything.

Mum didn't come with us that night to the pantomime. Dad was due home for Christmas. I always pretend that it is top secret and very hush hush, what he does abroad. Actually I don't have a clue what he does, but occasionally you see him on the television, somewhere where there is a drought, or maybe where there isn't. I don't remember.

Anyway Mum didn't come with us to the theatre because he was due home and she was busy getting things ready. It was supposed to be a surprise – Dad coming home, I mean, but I had guessed what was going on. It was ten thirty by the time we left the theatre, and Waldorf came in the taxi with us, to drop us off home and then to go on to wherever he goes. Grammer says he lives in a hotel, but I think he probably has a place somewhere and just meets Grammer in a hotel.

As we pulled up outside our house there was great activity. Theresa Carmody looked like she was having a party in her place, as there were cars everywhere and her front door was open. People were dancing on the grass in her front garden, even though it was freezing. In our house there were no lights on at all. Then in the next house which had been up for sale for about six months and the SOLD sign had gone up the previous week – well, golly gosh, but every light was on in it, and there was an enormous removal van parked outside. The streetlights only seem to work in summer when they're not needed, so the road was in darkness bar the lighting in the houses, and the removal men were busy trundling in and out of the house in the darkness carrying what presumably was a family's possessions.

We poured out of the taxi and Waldorf said he'd come in and see us safely inside, have a glass of bubbly and then get another taxi home later. Theresa Carmody appeared out of her front garden and said we all had to come in and have Christmas drinks with her. 'Come in, come in,' she insisted.

'We should settle the girls down for the night,' said Grammer.

'Aw, Grammer,' I wailed. It's so unfair. Just because the Dumpling is only a baby, Grammer lumps us all in together.

'Nonsense,' said Theresa Carmody. 'Sure the Dumpling can sit on the sofa and look at the tree.'

Theresa Carmody was sounding more like Grammer by the day. Grammer being the only person I know who can say 'nonsense' like that.

Then I saw Plumpet moving in the most extraordinary way. She's so clean and well-behaved and good. Her hair was neatly tied back like always, and she was holding the Dumpling in her arms, which is quite difficult to do getting out of a taxi. Grammer was busy with Theresa Carmody, and Waldorf was lifting the picnic hamper and the cooler box out of the boot – well, he'd brought them, it was only fair he should carry them into the house. I was standing there looking at the furniture van, listening to Grammer cut a deal with Theresa Carmody, when suddenly Plumpet thrust the Dumpling at me, knowing full well that I find her awkward to carry.

Then, Plumpet pulled the elastic bobbin from behind her head, and let her hair swing loose. I was standing there open-mouthed. Grammer and Theresa Carmody were now agreeing that we'd all come in for half an hour. Waldorf was fishing in Grammer's bag for the house key, and there was Plumpet looking like Nicole Kidman in *Eyes Wide Shut* or whatever it was called. (Seriously over-rated, me and my friends said – Madonna in *Body of Evidence* was great, and the sex was better. Well, so Daisy, daughter of Samson and Delilah said. I haven't actually seen either.)

Then I saw what had caught Plumpet's attention. There was a boy leaning against the wall watching the furniture being lifted out of the van. He was tall, and he had neatly cut fair hair. He was dressed in dark trousers and a sweater with the collar of his shirt sticking out. Plumpet was almost twirling with excitement. She took

47

the Dumpling back from me and shot over to the van like an escaped convict.

'Hiya,' she said.

'Hey,' he replied.

Golly, I thought. I'd hardly have had the nerve, but Plumpet just went up to him.

'You moving in?' she asked.

Well, he was either moving in or he was waiting to hijack the lorry, I thought.

'Sure am,' he said.

Clearly he'd been watching too much American television. But then who doesn't?

'We live in there,' Plumpet said, gesticulating at our place.

The Dumpling, who had been almost asleep, now had both eyes wide open, and her thumb was suspended in mid-air. She was clearly as surprised as I was.

'Haven't seen you in ages,' said the boy.

The penny finally dropped. They were acquainted already, as Grammer would say. Grammer uses words like 'acquainted' which is sometimes really annoying because you would think there was a smaller, easier word to use, but at other times you'd think, What a clever word. Anyway I should have known they were already acquainted. Plumpet would never have approached a stranger like that.

'These are my sisters,' Plumpet said.

God, she's so polite.

'Hello,' he said to the Dumpling and me.

Clearly he was as polite as she. Grammer says that like attracts like. In which case if I ever grow up and get married, and I'm not in a rush to do

48

either, I'll marry someone with no concentration who wonders about sex all the time and likes to play cricket and tennis.

'This is Dumpling.'

The Dumpling, introduced, waved her little hand. I couldn't see her face, but I knew from the way she was waving that she was beaming. The Dumpling loves males.

Samson and Delilah have a dog called Poppy. Funny that they called their daughter Daisy and the dog Poppy, now that I think about it. I bet Grammer would say that they wanted flowers in their lives. Anyway, Delilah says that Poppy prefers males to females. It drives Delilah mad as she feeds Poppy and takes her to the vet and those kinds of things, but the minute Samson walks into the room Poppy is reduced to a quivering mass of jelly and drools and slobbers with excitement at the look of him. Can't think why.

Having dealt with Theresa Carmody, Grammer came over to see what was going on.

'Grammer,' said Plumpet with excitement. If it had been me I'd have shifted myself and the boy into the shadows. That's what you do with boys, Daisy says. 'Grammer, you have to meet Ronnie. Ronnie, this is my grandmother.'

I could see Grammer eyeing him with interest, but she must have seen something she liked because she said, 'Lovely to meet you. Are you moving in?'

People say these kinds of things. Self-evident. Overly obvious. But that's what they do. Like, 'Wet, isn't it?' when it's been raining for days and

49

people are thinking of emailing Noah and asking for a cabin, preferably portside, on his ark. I know about portside because Grammer explained to me about the meaning of the word 'posh' and how people going to India by boat would travel port out starboard home. I don't know why anyone would want to go to India by boat. It would take so long. It would be quicker to walk. Even Hannibal worked that out.

Anyway, before Ronnie could answer, Grammer launched forth on how it was a happy house he was moving into. She didn't mention that she had almost run over the previous owner.

'It's a wonderful home for a family,' she said. 'A happy home, I would call it. And are your parents inside, Ronnie?' she asked.

Sometimes Grammer uses these phrases, and next thing you know they're either in a book or adorning the cover of one. I can just see *The Happy House* in pink italics on the front of her next novel. Though, come to think of it, that may be the title of her last one, which is why I can see the pink italics so clearly.

'Ronnie,' said Grammer, 'your parents will probably need a drink at this point. We're all going into Theresa Carmody's, so why not ask them to join us.'

If *we* had asked people into someone else's house, Grammer would have grounded us for a month. It was called different rules for different generations, she said. Anyway, she was right about asking them into Theresa Carmody's because Theresa Carmody hated living alone and filled her house up with all sorts. Including her sister Polo who looked like a small horse.

Into our house we went, so Waldorf could drop
the hamper and the freezer bag. There was a loud
clunking of empty bottles as the containers
touched the floor. And then it was off to Theresa
Carmody's. Polo was propping up one of the
pillars in the porch. She was wearing – wait for it
– tartan shorts. I swear to God. Tartan shorts.
And socks and runners. At a party. Imagine!
When God handed out good taste, Grammer
said, He didn't give it to everyone. She also said,
when in doubt, don't. She said this advice applied
to everything, but specifically to clothing.

'But what if you're not in doubt?' I sometimes
asked her. 'What if you're absolutely sure that
you look good in say, tartan shorts?'

'No granddaughter of mine would ever imagine
that she would look good in tartan shorts,' she
replied, straightening her back and elongating
her neck. 'Doubt is when you try on a frock and
you're just not sure about the colour. That's
doubt. That's when you go away and think about
it, or ask someone you can trust for their opinion.
Never ask the assistant...' This was a favourite
theme. Clearly Grammer must have had a bad
experience from a dubious assistant at some
point in her life. She had even written a book
called *The Double Life of Dorothy Dea*. In this
book, Dorothy Dea made her husband breakfast
in the morning and waited until he went out to
work. She then shot across the city where she was
a secret sales assistant in a fancy boutique where
she was paid by the sale. Because she was

51

working on a percentage basis, she pushed the most awful garments on to her unsuspecting customers who apparently always asked her for advice. It all sounded a bit unlikely to me. I mean, if you went into a boutique and came out dressed like Homer Simpson on the advice of the assistant, would you really go back and ask her advice again? Well in her book, customers came back time after time, and Dorothy Dea earned enough money to take her husband on the cruise of a lifetime when he retired early. Which worked out very well for Dorothy Dea because her husband dropped dead halfway through the cruise while eating dinner with the Captain, and Dorothy Dea ended up with the First Officer and had the best sex she'd ever had in her whole life.

Actually I might be mixing up *The Double Life of Dorothy Dea* with *A Lifetime of Love*. Either way, there is a little tragedy, some heartstrings being tugged, and a happy-ever-after ending. Grammer says that's the formula for a successful life. 'Avoid blood,' she says when we're doing essays for school. 'You can lure your teacher into a pleasant frame of mind when she's marking your work, if you've given her satisfaction.'

Nothing would have satisfied Miss McCracken, my English teacher. Daisy (of Samson and Delilah) said that you'd need a rugby team to satisfy *her*.

So, in we went to Theresa Carmody's house, passing Polo in her tartan shorts, who looked down her nose at us. Polo is Theresa's sister. You'd never guess by looking. 'Fancy a dance?' Waldorf asked her. Polo did not bother to answer him. She just raised her chin and stared up at the sky.

Waldorf and Grammer did the tango in the hall while me and Plumpet and Dumpling went into the kitchen. There was a lovely smell of sausages, but Grammer had warned us off them, so I had to wait until Plumpet and Dumpling went on through before I could stab a few with a cocktail stick. Polo Carmody came in and stood there looking at me with a drink in her hand.

There was something about Polo Carmody which would give you the willies. She sort of stared and you didn't know what she was looking at, and then after a bit you thought she must be looking at you but you couldn't think why.

Well, Grammer wasn't there to pull me up on my manners, so I took another sausage on its little stick and was about to walk out into the hall, when she suddenly said, 'You. Where do you think you're going?'

Honestly, that's what she said. I thought of saying to the loo, and then I thought of saying to find my sisters, and then I thought of telling her to mind her own bloody business. I mean, it wasn't her house. It belonged to her sister, and if you ask me, Polo Carmody spent too much time in it.

I stuffed the sausage into my mouth so that I couldn't speak without spitting all over her, and I pointed at my mouth, gave a sort of a sausagey-smile, shrugged and went out the other door into the dining-room end of the double rooms. I saw no one there whom I knew because Plumpet and the Dumpling had disappeared and I was afraid of Polo coming after me – I didn't know what she wanted. So I just went and stood behind the curtains at the back bay window.

The floodlights were on and I could see into Theresa Carmody's conservatory, which was behind the kitchen to the left of where I was hidden behind the curtains. I could also see across her patio and clear down her garden as she had all the floodlights on. I sat on the windowsill just staring out and then I saw that Polo had gone into the conservatory. She must have gone straight through from the kitchen. There was a man sitting on a wicker chair and Polo went up to him and stood in front of him. I could see her quite clearly. And the man just sitting there put one hand up the baggy legs of her tartan shorts.

Honestly.

I couldn't see who he was, but I could see the sleeve of his jacket. He was wearing a sort of greenish velvety thing, and Polo just stood there looking out of the conservatory window while he fiddled around under her shorts.

I wondered what Grammer would say if she could see them. Then I suddenly thought that if I could see them, maybe they could see me. And while I knew they hadn't yet seen me, I was really afraid that they would. I was afraid to move in case I drew attention to myself. I tried not to look at what they were doing. It struck me that it might be the sort of thing you'd do in a bedroom, but certainly not in someone else's conservatory at a party.

Daisy – she was my best friend – said that the first time she has sex it is going to be in a lift – or

54

an elevator as the Americans call them. She had read somewhere that if the elevator was going up, it lasted twice as long and that was better.

I didn't know though. I think I was afraid of the doors opening or something. I mean, I would have hated someone to see me doing something like those two were doing. I knew I didn't look one bit like Polo Carmody, but I was pretty sure that if someone had their hand up my knickers I'd be making some kind of a face and not just staring out of the window looking like I was thinking about my homework or what I'd just had for dinner. Polo looked like she was thinking of the price of sausages in Dow Jones. Dow Jones is the name of a butcher, I think.

I couldn't take my eyes off the man's hand or the way Polo was just standing there, and I kept hoping the reflection of the different window-panes would make me invisible. Polo Carmody then pulled back her lips so that I could see her teeth – they were very small and pointed, more like a child's. She opened her mouth and leaned towards the man and he put one finger into her mouth and she looked like she was sucking it or biting it. Then Polo closed her eyes and she seemed to shudder.

It sort of made her look like she wasn't really enjoying herself, so I don't know why she was letting him do that to her. I always thought that two people kind of did it together, sort of as a pair – I hadn't really thought it could be like that. I made a mental note to mention it to Daisy.

Daisy says that the perfect human orgasm can

shatter glass.

'You reach such a pitch,' she explained to me and Joan Kennedy. I looked at Joan, and Joan looked at me. I think Joan and I were thinking the same thing – like how come no one had mentioned this before, and surely beds would be in broom cupboards rather than in a bedroom with a window if this were the case, but I didn't like to ask this as Daisy had a way of making you feel like you hadn't lived yet.

Joan Kennedy chewed her bottom lip but she didn't say anything.

'Most elevators have mirrors in them,' I said thoughtfully.

'What's that got to do with the price of sliced bread?' Daisy snapped.

'Well, you said that you're going to do it for the first time in a lift,' I said.

'So?' said Daisy.

'Well, mirrors are made of glass,' I said. I really wasn't trying to score a point. I just wanted to get my facts straight.

'Oh,' said Daisy. 'Don't worry about that. The silver bit they stick on the glass to turn it into a mirror holds it together so that it can't shatter.'

I hoped she was right. I couldn't think of anything worse than being hauled out of a lift with my knickers down and splinters of mirrored glass sticking out of me.

Well, there was Polo Carmody shuddering away goodo in Theresa Carmody's conservatory and the glass didn't shatter. I wondered what Daisy would make of *that*.

56

Chapter Three

Theresa Carmody's Tale

I threw a party just a few days before Christmas and I think that that is when it all started. Of course, back then I did not know that I was letting trouble loose on the world. On the world of the McHargs, of all people. If I had known ... if it had ever occurred to me, I would bypass that night and never throw a party again.

I have never thrown a party since.

I loved laughing and chatting and having dinners and dancing. When I moved back to Dublin I bought this large house that had too many rooms and the place was silent unless I had friends around. I loved people. I just loved them. And I loved the McHargs. Who could not have loved them? They were the most exciting, exhilarating people I had ever met. Millicent McHarg became my friend when I moved in next door. They had been living there for ever. Millicent had moved into her house when she got married and had stayed there when her marriage ended. Her daughter-in-law Maria moved in when she got married and it was from there that she had Plumpet and Daffers. A few years after I moved in, the Dumpling arrived. I was one of very few people who knew the true story of the Dumpling. Millicent had told me one afternoon.

We used to sit and drink piña coladas in my back garden with the sun beating down on us. Millicent wore her hair tied up in a bandana. We lay in the sun and Millicent told me that something had happened and that Maria was going out to join George; when they came back, there would be an addition to their family. George, of course, was Millicent's son, and Maria's husband.

I listened in amazement as this story unfolded – a horrifying story of a child, a little girl with one foot, who had been found by George and his cameraman lying beneath a gibbet on the edge of a village.

'Retribution,' Millicent said.

'For what? Retribution for what?' I asked.

'God knows,' she said. 'Not my God or yours maybe. But someone's God.'

The helicopter had been flying in low over the village when they saw something and decided to take a closer look. Apparently George lifted the child from the ground and they took off immediately. A woman – presumably the child's mother – had been hanged and the little girl had been left beneath the gibbet.

I remember sitting there in the garden and the heat of the day seemed to evaporate as I listened to this horrifying tale.

Maria McHarg had a friend, a Swedish woman who looked very like her. This Swedish woman, Pia Somebody, had adopted a child from that same country two years earlier and she had the child on her passport. Maria was going out with two passports, her own and the Swedish woman's, to take this rescued baby back home.

'It'll never work,' I said to Millicent. 'For heaven's sake, Millie, if she's caught think what will happen.'

'It'll work,' Millicent said. 'George will see to it.'

As it happened they didn't have to use the false passport, because George and the crew took the child to the next province where money changed hands and papers were produced.

'For thirty pieces of silver,' Millicent said. 'The best spent thirty pieces of silver ever.'

I always thought of thirty pieces of silver as being to do with betrayal. But this time it seemed to be to do with the opposite of treachery – because it gave life and it offered hope. And so the Dumpling, as she became known, came to live at the McHargs' and she and I took to each other like ducks to water.

The McHargs seemed to be able to take things on, to expand when needed, to cope with events in a very calm way. I think it must have come from Millicent, who really was the most amazing of women. She was an icon to the nation, a successful novelist of romantic fiction that always had an unusual twist. If there is such a thing as an Agony Aunt novelist, then that describes Millicent to a T.

I had aspirations to write a novel, but short unpublished stories were the best I could come up with so far. I could never think of a long enough story, or else I only knew how to tell them short!

And Millicent tried to help me. She always

said, 'Stick with it, Theresa. If it gives you pleasure to write, just do it.'

'Maybe I should write fact rather than fiction,' I said to her. 'History might be easier.'

'I imagine it is much the same,' she said to me. 'Don't forget, history is something that never happened told by someone who wasn't there.'

I thought that was a Millicent McHarg original, but she assured me that it was said by Ramon Gomez de la Serna, whoever he was.

'Write anything,' she advised me. 'It doesn't matter if it isn't published. Of course, it is a joy to be published, but it's not as if you need the money.'

She was right about that. My sister Polo and I were born rich, and as a result the pair of us have never done anything other than to dabble. We dabbled at school – no ordinary schooling, I might add. We were sent to the best private school in Switzerland, and when Polo got expelled for deviant behaviour with a girl on her floor, we were simply sent to another one. And from there we went to the States to a private college where we went on dabbling and having fun.

Fun for me was partying, burning the midnight oil, dancing on the streets, punting on the river. For Polo – well, for Polo I'm not so sure what she found fun. It was never so clear. Polo had a habit of watching people and I used to say to her, 'For heaven's sake, stop looking like you're sneering.'

It was the expression on her face that I think was offputting. She was my sister and I loved her because we had shared everything – our upbringing, our schooling, the endless flights back and forwards to school, all that growing-up stuff – but she was difficult to get close to. I used to tell her things but she would seldom tell me things back. Actually when she did tell me things I wasn't always sure I wanted to hear them. I mean, we all had crushes on other girls at school – it's part of growing up, but it's not everyone who actually does something about those crushes. Anyway she had been having a consensual encounter with this girl on her floor, and one night the two of them did something to this other girl. And the other girl didn't play stumm. Instead she spilled the beans. Oh, it was all hushed up and Daddy had to come over and pay money out left right and centre to keep it quiet. Polo said she was drunk and couldn't remember what had happened. In fact, she said they were all drunk and they were all participating and that there had not been any violence involved, but the girl who screamed 'foul play' was a bit bruised and was quite vociferous in her complaint.

Daddy was furious, but he paid up, bought silence and we switched schools. He said it would be easier for me in another school and anyway he wanted me to keep an eye on Polo – which I did. But it wasn't easy. Polo did her own thing and she had this ability to be standing there beside me one minute and gone the next.

She got into a bit of trouble in the States. I tried telling Daddy that it might be better if she didn't have so much money, because she started dabbling in drugs, but Daddy had a heart attack on the plane coming home from the States after that row and the next thing, we had inherited the whole family fortune.

I thought Polo might feel bad about that, but she didn't. We stayed on in the States doing our own thing. She moved up to Manhattan and started doing a bit of editing and journalism. I took writing classes in Boston and went on partying. And somehow the years just slipped past.

When I bought the house next door to the McHargs, having finally come home to roost, it was with the most incredible joy I found I had this readymade family beside me. I was almost the same age as Maria and we quite enjoyed each other, although I didn't see that much of her as she was out at work most of the time. Millicent was like a friend, mother and grandmother all rolled into one. And there were these little girls. First Plumpet and Daffers, both of whom were fascinating as they were so opposite, both in looks and in behaviour. And then the Dumpling came along. She was so adorable – jet-black short hair, and the sweetest brown eyes, and very plump lips. And she was such a courageous little thing. Oh, I know she knew nothing else, but sometimes you'd look into her eyes and you'd wonder. I mean, I know that she was not really likely to remember her past, and yet I know I remember things from before I was two years old – not many things, but a few. Oh, I spent hours in the garden with the Dumpling, reading to her and singing to her and just enjoying her. It wasn't altruism. I'm not given to altruism at all. I just loved the company and I loved watching these children grow up. Plumpet was the gentlest, most

62

polite child ever, and she grew quite tall. She was both compliant and introverted and Millicent would tell me how much it worried both her and Maria, because Plumpet didn't mix with the girls at school. She had no real friends, unlike Daffers who did have friends – a whole entourage, in fact, but a particular one named Daisy. Millicent told me how Daisy's parents were good friends of Maria's, but that Daisy was a bit precocious for a child of her age. I loved hearing all the bits of gossip.

Sometimes Daffers would ask me things – extraordinary things, and it always transpired that Daisy was behind the particular suggestion or idea.

'Theresa,' she once said to me, 'is it true that if you French-kiss under a gooseberry bush, you get pregnant?' She was quite young when she asked that. I thought it was so sweet that I said yes.

Such are the misconceptions of children. But then they are not the only ones who misconceive things. There I was throwing yet another party, oblivious to what might or might not be going on. My only concern was that there was enough food and drink, good music for dancing, and lots of laughter. All the ingredients were there. And I produced the goods as I always did. It was a great party. I had only planned it at the last minute and by the time I rang the McHargs there was no answer, just their voicemail. So I kept an eye on the window, and in due course when I saw a taxi pull up, I went out and coerced them into coming in.

Millicent was not that keen as she said the girls were tired; something had happened at the pantomime and she was a little concerned about the Dumpling. The Dumpling's real name was Maya, which Daffers amusingly said was written with two dashes and a squiggle, but certainly 'the Dumpling' suited her better. It might not, when she was older, but they could always revert later. I convinced Millicent to come in. She and Waldorf were a great asset to a party, and I always loved the girls being around. I think it made me feel that I could span all age groups.

Christian and Gervaise Holt were at my party. Gervaise was over from the States for Christmas. He was quite smooth like his brother, but oily in a way that Christian was not. I've known Christian for ever. We're like brother and sister – well, we were then, but way back when I was about nineteen we had had a brief fling. My first, actually. I had wanted to do something unique. Although Polo was a year younger than me, she always seemed light years ahead, and I knew about some of her sexual escapades – I couldn't *but* know seeing as I had had to move school because of her – and I thought, what better way to lose one's virginity than in an aeroplane. So our first trip to the States alone – Polo and me, that is – I was sitting beside Christian Holt. Need I say more? Even Polo was impressed. It was one of the few times that I ever saw her really laughing. 'The Mile High Club and your virginity all in one go,' she hooted.

'Lower it,' I said. 'People will hear you.'

'What's the point of doing something like that, if you don't let people know?' she chortled.

I didn't quite see it like that. And it seemed a bit rich coming from her who was quite reticent about what *she* was up to in that department. Anyway, I had my first penetrative sexual encounter on that flight. How Millicent loved that story too.

'Standing in the loo?' she asked. 'Wasn't that a bit uncomfortable?'

She loved details, and I must admit I enjoyed telling her. She wrote about it in one of her novels maybe a year later, but I was well disguised. No one would have recognised the naïve rich kid as me. And the sex she described was really excellent. She has such a way with words. After all, it was a bit wham bam in the toilet – there wasn't much room for foreplay, although Christian and I had done a bit of that already while we were sitting beside each other in our seats, with Polo asleep on my left.

Millicent was delighted when she met Christian a short time afterwards, and in fact they became so friendly that on one occasion when she was doing a tour in the States she stayed with him in his brother's apartment in Manhattan, although Gervaise wasn't there at the time.

I danced with everyone and I just loved showing my friends off to each other. People are always so impressed with Millicent, and with Waldorf in tow, they make such an amazing couple. I've never seen anyone – even in Argentina – doing the tango like they do. They would take your breath away. After the tango, they did a foxtrot. Then Waldorf sang 'Don't cry for Me, Millie McHarg', to the tune of 'Don't Cry for Me, Argentina'.

Millicent assured him that she wouldn't.

They didn't stay that late. And I didn't see anything amiss. I really didn't. If I had, I would have done something about it. I know I would have.

Chapter Four

Maria's Tale

For some reason that night reminded me of the night Plumpet was born, and I have no idea why. It was real December, with the lights on Christmas trees twinkling in the windows of all the houses on the way to the airport. Our own house was looking particularly interesting. Plumpet had used a snow spray around the corners of the windows, and with her customary artistic flair had made a stencil of a snowman. Using the stencil she sprayed the snowman right on to the centre of the large sitting-room window. She had window paints and she did an excellent job of decorating him with a white hat, black eyes and an orange nose. However, after she had finished, Daphne must have decided that there was something missing because she got a carrot and superglued it to the outside of the window in the middle of the snowman's face. By night it could not be seen, but by day there was this long carrot stuck on to the middle of the window. How we were going to get it off I could not imagine, but Grammer told me not even to think about it, that there was time enough to worry about that after Christmas.

On that particular night Grammer and Waldorf had taken the girls into town to the pantomime. She and I had pretended that I had things to organise for Christmas and for their father who was due home. In fact, he was due in that night. We did not say anything to the girls because Grammer and I thought it would be such a surprise for them to come home and find him there.

As it turned out, it was just as well we had said nothing to them.

On the way to the airport I was running through checklists in my mind of the various things still needing to be done in the last days before Christmas. The presents had all been bought and were carefully stashed in the top of my wardrobe, and Grammer had organised wine and other drinks which had been delivered earlier in the day. The goose was on order, to be collected on Christmas Eve. I was trying to keep myself distracted from the main event of the evening – which was of course the return of my husband.

Grammer has always said that men are a mystery, and for a joke I have often called George *Myster Man*. He thought I meant Mister Man when I first said it, and when I explained that it was a sort of a pun and that I really meant 'mystery man', he laughed. 'We're simple folk really,' he said to me. 'Not a mystery at all. We need our homes and our work, and the love of a good woman.' This he said in a drawl, teasing me as he always did.

'But if you need a home,' I asked him tentatively, 'how come you're never in it?'

He didn't answer.

For a while, in the early days of courtship, I wondered if it was me he was running away from. Later I wondered if it was his mother. Then I realised it was neither – it was simply the way he functioned or something else that I didn't understand. We went out there on our honeymoon and it was then that he told me the truth and everything fell into place. That was the first of many trips I made there over the subsequent years.

There was a song in the 1970s that said something about some man being on every picket line, but not being there for the woman who loved him. It could have been written about George – except, of course, he did not see himself in that light. He thought he was there for me and for the girls.

And in time I adapted. Grammer once said to me, after Daffers had been born and George had arrived too late for the birth, that it was better surely to have a man in one's life who really loved one but was seldom there, than to have a man who was there but who didn't love one. At the time I didn't agree, but you get used to things. A full life and a busy schedule meant that I sometimes wondered how I would have fitted him in if he had been living permanently at home.

The night that Plumpet was born I felt this rush of excitement mixed with nervousness all the way to the hospital, just as I did that night going to the airport. Grammer still had a driving licence in those days – it was before she wrote off our car and the neighbour's front door. I've never worked out quite how she got away with that. The driveway up to the neighbour's house did not even look like ours, so her claiming that she thought it was our driveway didn't wash with me, although the police seemed to buy it. Then the neighbour sold up so Grammer got what she wanted even if she did lose her licence.

Grammer drove to the hospital, with George and me sitting in the back of the car because the seat belt in the front put too much pressure on my swollen stomach. 'No need to be afraid,' Grammer called to me from the front of the car, as she took the corner too tightly and went over the kerb as we left the cul de sac. The front left wing of that car was bashed so many times that we stopped getting it beaten out – it was simply a waste of money. And I wasn't afraid. Not of the forthcoming childbirth anyway, not with George holding my hand and Grammer supervising operations both at home and in the hospital.

'God is good,' Grammer said, when Plumpet was born in the Rotunda Hospital. That's how I felt driving over the East Link Bridge to the airport that night – that God was good and I was safe. The tide was coming in and the River Liffey

69

was high, the lights on the banks reflected in the quivering water as I crossed the bridge.

We do our best, we mothers, in the cycle of life. We learn from the mistakes of the past, and then we make other ones as we progress on our journey, and I thought that night that God was good and that I was safe. And for me to be safe, that meant that those I loved were safe too.

Later, of course, I have gone over and over this in my mind. I've done every 'If only', and 'Why did this have to happen?' I have even attacked Grammer, in my mind. I've asked her repeatedly, 'Why?' I've attacked George: 'Where were you? Why weren't you here when we needed you?' I've quizzed Waldorf a hundred times: 'You, you of all people – you were outside the family, surely you could see?'

And in the end, of course, I blamed myself.

When I was leaving the house I noticed that Theresa Carmody was throwing another party, and I knew that when I returned she would undoubtedly pop in, or there would be a note in the letterbox saying *Come in for a drink*. Theresa Carmody liked company, and when she asked you in, even if she had a hundred people in the house, she meant it. She wanted to fill the house with music and laughter and boozy people. I also noticed that there was a lorry outside the house on the other side of us. That was the house that Grammer had practically demolished with the car the previous summer. Shortly afterwards the owner had moved out, and the house had been

70

standing empty since then with a *For Sale* sign on the pillar at the gate. Just last week, up had gone a *Sold* sign, and we thought that come the New Year, we would have new neighbours. But someone was clearly moving in, just in time for Christmas.

I was early at the airport, with time for coffee before going to meet George's flight. The place was lit up like a winter wonderland with welcome signs and dancing snowmen. The flight arrived, but no George emerged. I was not that surprised, knowing from experience just to wait for the next flight or the one after that. There had been one occasion when I had driven back home, only to get a call two hours later asking me where I was, and why wasn't I waiting for him at the airport. He was in the bar having a drink and should he get a taxi on home?

Grammer says regularly to the girls, 'Never scowl, you'll get wrinkles.' I have learned never to scowl – I mean, what is the point? It changes nothing, and as Grammer says, 'You'll end up with lines on your face.' She also advises pragmatism and stoicism in the face of the mystery of the male.

I went and bought a packet of cigarettes. I only smoke when George is around. He smokes heavily when abroad, and lightly at home. I keep him company.

As I sat in the bar, nursing a mineral water and puffing on the first cigarette I'd had in five or six months, I contemplated Grammer and George. For a woman who had a view on everything, it was interesting how my mother-in-law claimed to have no comprehension about the male species, least of all about her own offspring. The male characters in her books are strong determined men who sweep the fairer sex off their feet and carry them into sunsets on tropical islands or windswept coastlines. Her own husband did indeed sweep a girl off her feet and carry her into another sunset, but the girl wasn't Grammer, and the last sunset she saw was as her plane headed into the sea. Grammer got the house, the money and, of course, George, her son. Hidden between the lines of her novels with male passion and female swooning predominating, there is a certain amount of advice on not getting caught out by pregnancy or sexually transmitted diseases and, of late, Grammer's books were showing certain tendencies towards advising the woman of the day on how to lead a successful double life which would keep the males in her life happy while she herself found fulfilment.

I waited an hour and a half, getting up to check the arrivals of different flights, returning to whatever spare seat I could find to sit on, and gazing absently at the large television screen in the corner of the room. Because of the noise I could not hear a word that was being said, but it offered a distraction while I waited. There was that expectant buzz that you always get in airports, the buzz of love, I suppose. People waiting for others, hoping, wanting, full of expectation ... I was starting to feel very excluded from it. Eventually I decided to call home and listen to our voicemail. Sure enough, there was a message on it from

George to say he would not be getting in that day after all, but that he would phone the following day. I don't know why he did not phone me on the mobile. It would have saved me a lot of time.

As I was about to leave the bar to head home I suddenly saw him on the television. Because of the noise around me it was impossible to hear what he was saying, but it seemed that some tidal wave had caused a whole village to be swept away somewhere hot. I could see palm trees, and thatched roofs being swept out to sea, and there was George, flak-jacketed and harnessed in the helicopter above, observing or commenting.

I buttoned my coat and headed out into the bitter night. Bitter? *I* felt bitter. He seemed to be on everyone else's picket line and battlefront but mine.

If George had come home that night, the course of our history would be different. If we had told the girls he was due in, they would have stayed at home, and events might have been somewhat diverted. If George had caught the flight... If Theresa Carmody had not thrown yet another party... If the new neighbours had not moved in... If a tidal wave had not destroyed a coastline and villages... If, if, if...

I drove home slowly. I felt not just disappointed, but also angry. You cannot change other people, so you try to compromise and to take them on their terms. But there are times when George's terms are so ungiving that it's difficult. And that particular night was one of those times. The chances of his actually making it home for

Christmas Day were dwindling by the minute, and I was really glad that Grammer and I had said nothing to the girls about him being due in that particular night.

Theresa Carmody's party was in full swing when I got home. There were traces of Grammer and the girls' return in the hall, including a cooler box with two empty champagne bottles, and hamper with glasses encased in tea towels, sandwiches and an empty chocolate box.

It smacked of Waldorf, and I found myself laughing. I mean to say, if George ever disappeared into someone else's sunset, there lay the evidence that one could pick up the pieces and still have fun. Grammer must have picked up George's message from our voicemail, because there was a note from her saying to join her next door. It read as follows: *Abandon ship. Head for Theresa Carmody's. The night is young. And so are you.*

I didn't feel like Theresa Carmody's, so I poured myself a drink and went upstairs to draw the curtains and to change out of my high heels. Looking out of the window I saw the removal van pulling down the road out of the cul de sac, and I wondered what kind of bedlam the new neighbours were facing that night. As I stood there at the window, with the curtain in my hand ready to pull it closed, I noticed three people coming out of the neighbour's house. From that angle I thought at first they were three adults, but as they passed our drive I identified them as a man, a woman and a youth. For a moment I thought they were going for a walk. Then they turned into Theresa Carmody's and I realised they were calling in on her. I was surprised, because if I had just moved in to a new home I would never have had the energy on the first night to go to a party with people whom I didn't know. What motivated them? Was their new house not in a state of chaos? I'm sure I'd have been trying to find the sheets and bedding so that we would at least have somewhere to sleep. Had I been in a more sociable mood I would have followed them. After all, I had been invited, and it would have been a perfectly normal thing to do, but the truth was I was tired, let down, and also keeping an eye on the clock in the hope of picking up the late-night news and maybe seeing exactly where George was that night.

How I wish I could put the clock back to that moment in time, and somehow find the energy to put my high heels back on and head into Theresa Carmody's.

As it was I drew the curtains in my room, and one by one I went into the girls' bedrooms at the back of the house and pulled their curtains and turned down the tops of their quilts. Plumpet's curtains I left open, as she liked to sleep with the moon and the stars accessible, as she once put it. Sometimes I would put a chocolate in its silver or gold paper on Plumpet's and Daphne's pillow. Once when we were staying in an exceptionally nice hotel in Switzerland, they had gone to their rooms and found their nightdresses laid out on their beds and a chocolate on their pillows.

Occasionally for fun I do the same for them. That night I did. But not for the Dumpling – she was too little.

Downstairs I settled in front of the dying embers of the fire and watched the news. One more tidal wave, one more flood – it would be history by tomorrow. Life and death for some people, and tomorrow it would be forgotten.

Archived? I've no idea. I just caught the same few seconds of George in the helicopter. I wondered, as I often did, how a cameraman had captured him. Was his helicopter being filmed from another helicopter? Or was the cameraman hanging out on a trapeze and swinging the camera back in on those on board? It wasn't clear. A panoramic view swept across the screen and again I saw the swell of water carrying huts, trees and animals. And presumably human beings – but fortunately I couldn't see them.

My few seconds of contact with George were quickly over and I was left feeling even emptier. Then I was sorry I had not made the effort and gone into Theresa Carmody's, but if I hadn't felt like it earlier, I felt even less like making the effort now. It would have involved rousing myself off the sofa, and that seemed beyond me. It started to rain, and I could hear it hammering against the window. When I was a child I had, at some point, believed that the rain was God crying for His children. Putting my drink down, I curled up on the sofa and half-dozed, safe with the knowledge that Plumpet, Daffers and the Dumpling were with Grammer in Theresa Carmody's house.

If this were a Millicent McHarg novel, George would appear at the window – possibly on a white horse – and I would be rescued before the house was washed away. Instead, as I lay there knowing there would be no white horse and no George outside the window, I thought of him as I had just seen him on the television; his dark curly hair was tousled on his forehead, presumably he was sweating heavily in the tropical heat although he always managed to look untouched by the weather, the hint of a five o'clock shadow was on his chin and above his lip, and that look was on his face as his eyes searched the water.

I had fallen in love with that look a long time ago. It initially gave the impression of extreme confidence, as though nothing could faze him, and yet later if I happened to catch him looking at something else, I thought I could see the depths of his humanity portrayed in his eyes. It was that look and that humanity which had lifted the Dumpling from where he had found her and taken her to safety nearly two years earlier. I won't begin to describe the time between him rescuing her from a nightmare situation – the urgent phone call to me in Dublin, me hastily borrowing a passport which I eventually didn't need as I was able to use my own, then my arrival in the house he had rented, to find him and others caring for this completely silent little girl. Through my disbelief at the turn of events, he remained totally calm and completely focused on his plan to bring her home. And home he brought her. It was then that he became agitated. He paced the garden that night – the night we arrived back – up and down through our orchard, up and down, until eventually he settled in a chair on the patio, lighting up his umpteenth cigarette.

'Maria,' he said, 'what have we done?'

I didn't answer him at first, not knowing what he meant. I mean, the deed was done, the papers had been bought and there was no going back. The Dumpling was sleeping in our house in a country far from where she had been born, far from where she had been abandoned, if abandoned is the word you use for a child whose mother has been hanged and who has been left on the ground beneath the gibbet.

'What have we done?' he asked again.

'You rescued a tiny child,' I replied tentatively. 'You risked your life to save her. And you succeeded.'

'But should we have done it?' he asked.

'How can you doubt it?' I thought of the sleeping Dumpling, clean, warm, smelling sweetly of baby talc and baby cream, with her shock of black hair lying in the cot upstairs. 'How can you doubt it?' I repeated.

But I knew both how and why he doubted it. Long ago we had seen *Superman* – the first film, and afterwards I had ranted and raged about how Superman had turned the world backwards so as to rewind time so that he could save Lois Lane. 'He had no right,' I remember saying. 'No right at all. We have no right to interfere in the course of events.' I was young and idealistic, and I think it seemed unfair to me that just because Superman loved Lois Lane, and just because he had superhuman powers, he was in a position to save his love.

Later George had said to me that he often thought of that when he was at work. He was there as an observer, and an observer only, with no right to warn one guerrilla group that another was behind the next mountain, or to leap in front of a bullet, as if one could, to save the life of a child. The role of the observer is to observe. And to observe only.

'To lift a bundle of rags from the ground,' I said gently. 'And to give it life ... surely the gods must smile.'

Grammer says to the girls that we must not see things in a small way. Presumably Grammer had brought him up with the same observation.

'What if someone else came looking for her later?' he asked, and then he shook his head.

I knew he was just thinking aloud as he worked through the nightmare of the discovery of the Dumpling. I took a cigarette from his packet on the table.

'Another night lying there ... do you really think she would have survived?'

Of course there is no answer to such a question. In some places on our planet life and death are very close – or so it seems to me. But when my mother died, then it seemed as if her life was extending on and on into a terrible place where there were only times of pain and of no pain, and when death finally came, it came so quick I could not believe my eyes. And then when my eyes took her death in, my brain could not understand it.

Grammer, who was visiting a woman in the

next bed in the ward in the hospital, and whom I had seen most days while with my mother, came to my side and held my hand. That was how I came into the McHarg family.

I was dreaming. I woke to hear the children in the hall, and Grammer and Waldorf laughing. They burst into the sitting room.

'Try and get a taxi on St Stephen's Green at night!' Grammer mouthed.

'Plumpet danced with the boy next door,' Daphne said, that teasing edge to her voice, even though she should have known by then that Plumpet did not respond to teasing and was upfront about everything. To my surprise Plumpet blushed.

The Dumpling came in and climbed on the sofa beside me and surveyed her shoes. She flapped her arms then and looked at me.

'She enjoyed the pantomime,' Grammer said.

We all filled in for the Dumpling, giving the words we thought she would have used to describe or explain what she saw.

'She sipped Grammer's champagne,' Daphne said. Daphne always told tales – an unpleasant streak but nonetheless one that gave me insight into what was going on. I raised my eyebrows at the Dumpling.

'She did not, Daphne,' Grammer said.

'Did too,' said Daphne.

'Don't contradict me,' Grammer said.

'Tell her, Waldorf.' Daphne addressed Waldorf as he put his head around the door.

'Tell her what?' asked Waldorf, smiling at me

and adding, 'Good evening, m'dear,' in his wonderful rich voice.

'About the champers,' said Daphne.

'What, what?' said Waldorf. 'Is there more champagne? Oh goody.'

Daphne gave up. The Dumpling leaned back against me and flickered her eyelids – a sure sign that she was more than ready for bed.

'I'll bring you to bed, Dumpling,' I said as I touched her black hair and looked into her dark, dark eyes.

'You look all in,' Grammer said, eyeing me. 'I'll take her up for you, Maria.'

Grammer was good to me. Friends sometimes used to ask me how did I cope living with my mother-in-law, but it was seldom a problem. When George and I got married I was more than aware that his work was going to keep him overseas for long periods of time, and Grammer said, 'Look, I'm virtually alone in that enormous house. We could keep each other company. We'll build an apartment on at the side – the planning permission is already there...'

Delia, one of my friends, said that Grammer was suggesting this so that she could keep tabs on me when George was away, but I didn't think that was the case. Grammer was unique – yes, she did interfere, but I've never had cause to complain about her interference. It's always been practical, or amusing, always been caring, and for someone like me whose parents were dead, well ... I liked it. I listened to Delia because she was already married and I thought she might be right even though my gut feeling told me otherwise, but in the end I went with my instincts. Grammer built the apartment – with style, flair and panache – suggesting that she would have no entrance to the house other than through the front door.

'For God's sake,' Delia said, 'don't have an interconnecting door,' but George and I thought that it might be nice both for Grammer and me if there was a door between her kitchen and what was about to become my kitchen. And I never regretted it. Friend, confidante, mother-in-law and mother – that's what Grammer became for me between the time I met her in the hospital and now.

'Upsa-daisy-doodle,' said Waldorf, lifting the Dumpling from the sofa where she lay snuggled in beside me. 'Kiss your Mum and let's get you up to sleepy lands.'

The Dumpling smiled and I kissed her smooth forehead. Grammer and he headed upstairs with the Dumpling who had decided to go limp in his arms. She waved at Plumpet and Daphne on her way out.

'Plumpet danced with the boy next door,' Daphne tried again.

'There's a new family moved in,' Plumpet said, taking the Dumpling's place on the sofa beside me.

'I saw them from the window,' I said, encouraging her for more information.

'Ronald, Maureen and Ronnie Fielding,' said Daphne informatively.

'Fields,' corrected Plumpet.

'And Plumpet danced with Ronnie. She already knew him.'

'Tell me more,' I said to Plumpet. She was pink in the face again.

'I met him at Daisy's in the summer,' she said.

'He's quite tall,' Daphne contributed helpfully. 'Past the spotty stage hopefully.' For a moment she sounded like Grammer.

'Nice?' I asked.

Plumpet nodded.

'There were loads of people in Theresa Carmody's,' Daphne said. 'Grammer and Waldorf did their tango, and I met Christian Holt.' Christian Holt was a writer Grammer sometimes talked about – one of Theresa Carmody's entourage. 'And his brother Gervaise. And Polo Carmody,' she added.

'There was no one young there,' Plumpet said, 'except for us.'

Youth sees 'young' in such a specific way.

'There was dancing in the garden until it rained,' Daphne said. 'And lots of food.'

'They played Elvis Presley,' Plumpet said. 'And Grammer says that's what she wants played at her funeral.'

'How morbid,' I said, but I was smiling. Grammer was known for her theatrical plans for her post-death celebrations. When she saw *Apocalypse Now* she was very keen on Wagner for a while. Then when she saw *Live and Let Die* that became her theme tune for nearly two months. George said to her that he wasn't sure it would be that great at a cremation, but Grammer was

83

adamant at the time.

'Any particular song of Elvis's?' I asked.

'Wooden Heart', I was told.

'Polo is peculiar,' Daffers said out of the blue.

Grammer and Waldorf appeared at that moment and Waldorf said, 'Has anyone seen my *Beano*?' as he settled into an armchair.

'That's the Dumpling tucked up,' Grammer said. 'She got a bit upset at the pantomime, but I think it's over and done with.' There was a slight edge to her voice and she emphasised the word *think*.

'Upset?' I asked.

'When the goose descended on to the stage, all we could see up in the gods were his feet hanging there. It ... it agitated her.'

I could feel Grammer looking at me and I knew that she was telling me something.

'She got a fright,' Plumpet said. 'All she could see was the feet. That would upset anyone – seeing a pair of feet hanging there like that.'

I thought about the image they were describing and I suddenly knew exactly what Grammer was talking about. Of course the girls knew nothing of how the Dumpling had actually been found, or of the randomness of the helicopter flight that day, which had brought George and the others to that particular village. Although I must admit I did wonder if it was random. Sometimes I felt that George was hinting at something else. But he was like that so I never pursued it. If he wanted to tell me he would; if he didn't then he would not. Either way, the Dumpling was old enough to remember what she had seen, and perhaps, even more terrifyingly, old enough to have been aware of what was going on, perhaps not in words, but certainly in emotions – whatever it was that left the woman hanged, and herself lying on the ground. I couldn't bear thinking about it myself, and of course we couldn't talk to the Dumpling about it or get her to talk to us because she was completely silent. I sighed.

'I should go up and kiss her again,' I remarked, getting up and slipping my feet into my shoes.

'Plumpet, will you get some champagne from my fridge?' Grammer asked.

On my return, the girls were drinking cocoa, and there were glasses and champagne out.

'To Christmas,' Waldorf said to me, raising his glass and handing me mine.

'To Christmas and safe returns,' I replied, thinking of George in the helicopter, even though I knew that that was now several hours earlier. By now, with any luck he was somewhere safe, in a hotel, probably in the bath – or maybe in the bar having a nightcap. I seldom thought in terms of time differences. The reality was that he was probably already up for the start of a new day.

'There was a man with purple eyes,' Daphne said suddenly.

'Gervaise Holt,' Grammer contributed, by way of explanation.

'I saw that too,' Plumpet said. 'I never saw anyone with purple eyes before.'

'The Japanese,' said Waldorf, looking at the ceiling.

'What do you mean, the Japanese?' Daphne asked.

'Purple, green – you name it,' he said.

Both girls were looking at him with interest. Grammer looked like she was about to get out her notebook and pen and interview him.

'It's a fact,' he said. 'They henna their hair – or use some kind of dye, I don't know what. And they all wear contact lenses.'

'They do?' asked Grammer, alert on her chair.

'Indeed they do,' he affirmed.

'But Gervaise isn't Japanese,' Daphne said carefully.

'No,' he smiled at her, 'but he does have purple eyes.'

'Contacts?' Daphne said. 'But why?'

'Why does anyone do anything to change themselves?' Waldorf asked.

'For beauty,' suggested Grammer.

'Not to look ordinary,' said Daphne.

'To hide what they really look like,' said Plumpet.

Good answer, I thought. Wasn't beautification a form of hiding what one really looked like? I know that Grammer would see all forms of cosmetics as being an enhancement. But I was not so sure.

'Why on earth would someone want purple eyes?' Daphne continued.

'Presumably they think that purple eyes look better or more interesting than their own ones,' I said.

'And if Gervaise Holt had his own eyes in tonight,' Grammer said, 'we wouldn't be sitting around drinking champagne and talking about them. Therefore, his wearing purple contacts has achieved what he wanted.'

'Have you ever seen his own eyes, Grammer?' Daphne asked.

'I never met him before tonight,' she said. 'Of course I know his brother Christian – and on my last trip to New York I actually stayed in Gervaise's apartment, but he wasn't there. Though come to think of it,' she added, 'there was a photo of him and he had pale eyes. I had forgotten. No wonder he prefers purple ones.'

'I'd quite like purple ones,' Daphne said.

'Nonsense,' said Grammer. 'You've wonderful blue eyes.'

Daphne smiled. She had got the compliment she was looking for. I sometimes wondered how I could have three such different children. There was Plumpet, self-contained, generous, diligent, obedient and polite – there was so much more I could say about her, but those would have been her main characteristics. The Dumpling – well, how could she be anything but different to the other two? And yet one might have thought that because she came to us at such a young age, they would have influenced her in some way. However, to date I had seen very little evidence of it. Strangely, when she is concentrating, our little Dumpling looks remarkably like Plumpet. Then there is Daphne, as pretty as a picture but full of hang-ups and angst – in many senses a typical middle child, even though she was the youngest up until two years earlier. Spoilt, I suppose, like the youngest often is, self-indulged and self-indulgent. As Grammer said, Daphne was an enigma. She needed constant reassurance about herself and her abilities, and yet had a funny self-confidence that seemed to belie that.

Plumpet on the other hand appeared to have confidence, but it wasn't to do with herself. She did not make friends easily and yet her peers often sought her company. But it was as if she related better to those older or younger than herself, and she mostly sought out people of completely different ages to herself – which is why I was so interested in her pink-faced reaction to Ronnie Fields next door.

At her age I would have been uncomfortable at Theresa Carmody's parties, and probably in Theresa Carmody's company, but not Plumpet. Though that may say more about Theresa Carmody than Plumpet, as all three, Plumpet, Daffers and the Dumpling loved going in next door. I wondered would Plumpet become more interested in the neighbours on the other side now.

'Polo is very odd, isn't she?' Daffers said. Looking back, I think she had already mentioned this, but at the time I was more concerned about the Dumpling and I wanted to be sure she had dropped off to sleep.

'I'm just going to check on the Dumpling again,' I said. Maternal instincts are very strong but sometimes we miss things. Sometimes we get waylaid.

Chapter Five

Dumpling's Tale

Red leather shoes with tiny hearts. Tiny red shoes with a leather heart. Shiny hearts with... I lay in my cot. All the words in the world to use in silence. They danced in my head. Grammer taught me words that twirl. That dance and prance. That sing and spring. They sprang up and down like in musical bumps. Bumpical muses. Rumpling bumpling dumpling.

I was the Dumpling.

Dumpling with dimples. Dimples on Dumpling. Hap a tap. Rap a tap. Nap. Nap-nap. Time for a nap. Climb on a lap.

Climb from the slime. Climb from the earth. Never look down. Always look up. Sky and beyond. Clouds. Air. Space. A God-sky – that's what Waldorf said. When the clouds were low and then they separated... When Mum came to kiss me good night and to tuck me in, tuck, no muck, lots of luck, she said as she looked at me, 'God is good.' Good was God with an extra o. Grammer said, 'In the beginning was the word, and the word was with God, and the word was God.'

Mum said Grammer was a law unto herself. Law. Flaw. Flawless. Lawless. Grammer wrote books with pictures on the front of men with black hair and women with blonde tresses –

that's what Grammer called the women's hair. Grammer had a blue felt hat. Helt fat. Fat felt. Flat hat.

When you ran your fingernails over her felt hat, it made you want to bite the hat because your nails sort of shivered. Once I bit the felt hat because I wanted to know what it tasted like, but the felt made my teeth shiver. I never bit it again.

Grammer had a drawer of feathers and she chose which one she was going to wear with care. Sometimes she lifted the drawer out off its runners and placed it on the bed and then she said I could preen her feathers. That's what you do with feathers. You preen them. If you were a bird you would peck at them and straighten them with your beak. I sat on the bed and I took them out carefully and laid them out in rows. My favourite one was the peacock feather she picked up for a song in Hong Kong. I was brought out through Hong Kong. I think.

She had thirty-three different feathers. Some were artificial like the silver one with the long pin attached, which neatly pierced the hat. Grammer said it was a good weapon in times of need. Needy times. Stymied indeed. Chinchilla coque feather, half-bronze coque feather, Lady Amhurst tail feather from a pheasant, ringneck feather, an eagle feather for hunting, a feather for all weather.

But that day, going to the pantomime she wore her fourteen-inch bleached and dyed pink ostrich feather. I didn't know if it really was an ostrich feather, but that's what she called it. The fastest non-flying bird. That was Grammer. It was secured on her hat with a hatpin – another lethal weapon, according to Grammer. She wore purple leather trousers. Mum said only certain women could wear leather. Red leather. Purple leather. Apparently you need leg length, but as Grammer was a law unto herself she could wear purple ones.

I lay in bed after the pantomime and thought about the journey. Grammer said we're all on a journey and we must each make our own journey as wonderful and as special as possible without hurting other people.

Special. Especial. Especially special.

The Mystery Man had fair skin and dark hair with grey in it. He said, 'You're special.' I understood nothing, but I held the word to play with later.

'Special'.

It had the sound of a soft cheese. He had a birthmark on his forehead, and brown eyes. His hair was curly. My hair was straight.

I knew that some day soon Mum would say, 'Revenge.' Grammer would say, 'Revenge is best served cold.' They would look at each other, and Grammer would say, 'Leave it to me.'

They didn't know that then. Sometimes I knew things before they happened. It was as if past and future were mixed. Sometimes I was cold when the room was warm, and sometimes I was warm when the room was cold.

Ice cream was cold. I liked ice cream with jelly – we had that at my arrival party. Plumpet made the jelly and the Mystery Man carried me into the house. When I touched his chin it was slightly rough, but earlier when I sat on his knee on one of the planes and he fell asleep, his chin rested on my forehead and it was smooth. My forehead was smooth and my hair was very soft – Grammer said it was the colour of a raven's wing, and that when my hair was long enough she would cut a lock and have it woven onto a hatpin to wear with her felt hat. She would call it her raven's feather. Faven reather. Heather. All weather. Sever.

Daffers's hair was blonde and curly and she wore it short. Plumpet's hair was brown and she tied it in a ponytail. When my hair grew and Grammer had cut the lock off for her hatpin, if there was enough left I wanted to wear it like Plumpet's.

Plumpet and Daffers are my sisters. Borrowed on the journey through time, as Grammer says.

Daffers said in the beginning there was Mum and Dad, and then there was Plumpet and then herself, and on a bad day when the wind blew from the East, I arrived. Grammer said that in the beginning was the word and the word was with God, but just as there were many words, there were many gods. She said that sometimes she looked at a bird in the sky and she could see the mark of God, and sometimes she looked at me and she knew that gods came in many guises. Guise. Disguise. The skies.

Plumpet said Daffers got out of bed on the wrong side. Daffers's bed was up against the wall. Fall. Wall. Not at all.

Plumpet said, *'One, two, buckle my shoe,'* when

she put on my shoes. Daffers didn't open the buckles to take my shoes off. She just pulled. My shoes were red. In the leather around the toes there were tiny little hearts on each shoe. The hearts were stitched onto the leather. Leathery hearts. Hearty leather. My tights were white. Tight. Light. Very white. Except when I went through the hedge in the hole.

One two was twelve when you wrote the figures beside each other. They were three when you added them together. They were one when you subtracted the one from the two, and they were less than nothing when you subtracted the two from the one. One was a prime number. There was very little you could do with it. But it was special. Special. Especial. Especially special. Like me. The Dumpling.

Between our garden and Theresa Carmody's garden there is a hedge. Theresa Carmody's garden is lower than ours. There was a hole in the hedge – or in the hole there was a hedge. I didn't know which. When I scrambled through the hole I lowered myself down into Theresa Carmody's garden. Theresa Carmody had a cat. His name was Cat. He was grey with a white throat and a white tip on his very long tail.

There was a robin in our garden. Grammer said, 'Look, there is Robin Redbreast.'

In my book of nursery rhymes, Cock Robin had a red waistcoat with pockets in it. Who killed Cock Robin? It was a mystery.

Our robin had an orange breast and no pockets. Theresa Carmody put a little collar with a bell on it around Cat's neck, because Grammer

93

told her I was afraid Cat would catch our orange-breasted robin. Theresa Carmody had jellies in her kitchen drawer in a bag in with her cutlery. 'One for Theresa,' she said. 'And one for Dumpling.' It was our secret because Grammer and Mum said that sweets rot your teeth. 'Sure it's only a wee jelly,' Theresa said.

Some people don't know when to stop. There are people like that all over the world. Grammer said all people are replicated. Somewhere. And if you put a group of replications together you get trouble doubled. Trouble multiplied. People who don't know how to stop.

Theresa Carmody had a tape recorder. 'When I die and go to heaven,' she said, 'I'll leave my tape recorder to you, Dumpling.' Her tape recorder was small with a microphone, which you could clip onto your sweater. She talked into it, and it recorded everything she said. Then she played it back and typed it up. Grammer said there were many ways to write a book, and that different ways suited different people.

Theresa Carmody's hair was black. She said it came out of a box. In the supermarket you could see rows and rows of little boxes with coloured hair inside them in bottles. Grammer said, 'Don't be fooled, it's only the hair and not the face that you're buying.' Theresa Carmody's hair looked too big to fit in one of those little boxes. She wore it pinned up in a bun.

What fun.

The bars of my cot – not a lot, what a lot – went

94

round and round. Ten bars, five bars, ten bars, headboard. Ten bars, five bars, ten bars, headboard... Between the bars there were spaces. Each space was a bar apart. Each bar was a space apart. Mum says I'm too big for my cot. I'm not. I'm the right size for my cot, and my cot is the right size for me. Mum says, 'You're too old to be in a cot,' but Grammer says, 'Leave her be, Maria. She's just a little tot.' A little tot in a cot.

I slept in bed with Mum. Every night she put me in my cot, but when we woke in the morning I was lying beside her in her big bed. She said I have the skills of a miniature Houdini. Grammer said that where the head could fit, the body would follow. Mum said that might be true if you were as little as me, but that Grammer shouldn't try it. What she actually said was, 'At plenty-nine, Grammer, I wouldn't try it if I were you.'

Grammer laughed.

What *is* plenty-nine? Mum says that Grammer is plenty-nine. It's a Grammer word. Daffers says that Grammer is seventy-six. Grammer says she is sixty-six. If Grammer is seventy-six, and knowing Daffers's interest in finding out the facts, she is, then Grammer is eight nines plus four. Does *plenty* mean a specific number? Numerically specified. Or does it have a meaning of its own? Is it nine times eight plus four? Is it always nine times eight plus four, or just this time? Next year could it mean nine times eight plus five?

Three times twenty-two is sixty-six. Of these only three is a prime number. But the other numbers are interesting because one reads two

two, and the other six six. Grammer was six six. That's what she said. Daffers said, 'Knock me over with an eagle's feather. Grammer is seventy-six.' That is six six plus ten. If you write the numbers six six upside down, they read as ninety-nine.

Grammer wore a corset. She said, 'Every enhancement should be tried at least once.'

Waldorf said, 'Woof.'

Woof from a dog was a bark. Many different barks. Hello bark. Postman at door bark. Santa on top of chimney bark. Samson and Delilah and Daisy had a dog. Woof woof.

Waldorf's woof was full of throaty plums. Plummy throats. He put his hands on Grammer's curves and said, 'I think I've found my yo-yo.'

Grammer giggled. Grammer's giggle was like a box of chocolates at the pantomime. The chocolate melted across your tongue and touched all your taste buds. Buds that taste. Tasty buds. Her laugh went into your ears and it tickled until you giggled too. Inside your head.

Theresa Carmody tickled me once. She said to Grammer that she would make me laugh out loud. I closed down my ears and my taste buds, my sight of her dark hair from a bottle on her head, my smell of her perfume, my thought of the jellies in the cutlery drawer, my feel of fingers on my skin. I closed them all.

Back on the journey I went – back, back, far back to the shapes and the cries and the first and last silence.

Grammer shouted, 'STOP!'

Theresa Carmody made tea.

'Dumpling pie,' Grammer said. She held me on her lap. Close. Bosomy warm. Warmly bosomy. Wosomy.

I found I was in the garden on Theresa Carmody's tartan rug. Pre-war rug, Grammer said.

'It's all right, Dumpling,' Grammer said, gentle, close and soft into my ear. I heard the words tickle inside my head. Like Grammer's laugh, they eased their way along the hairs inside my ears until I remembered how to smile.

'Is she all right?' Theresa Carmody asked. 'I'm so sorry. I didn't mean–'

'We won't have tea,' Grammer said. 'I think we'll just go home.'

Adult looks exchanged between them. No annoyance. Just Grammer knew best.

Grammer is a law unto herself, and Grammer knows best. Mum knows best too. It is maternal instinct, Grammer says, but it is not unique to females. Daffers said that female spiders eat their babies. Spidery females. Babies male and female. Equal rights. Daffers saw a film in which Garibaldi fish cleaned their nest, seduced a female, then chased her away so that she couldn't eat the eggs she had laid. Grammer said there are men with this instinct. And Grammer said there are women without it. We should beware of the women without it.

Robin Orange-breast was brought up with maternal instinct. His mother doted on him. Brought him worms to her nest in the hedge.

Cat's mother taught him to hunt. This could be bad training or could be good maternal instinct. Difficult to know.

In my cot I listened to the downstairs noises. Through the open door I could hear Grammer and Waldorf going to Grammer's home next door through the kitchen. Waldorf's throaty plummy voice said, 'Where's my yo-yo?'

Under Grammer's corsets, I thought.

No corsets on Maureen Fields. Daffers thought Fielding. Plumpet said Fields. But they were definitely Ronald and Maureen and wee Ronnie Fields. Maureen Fields's hands were like a butterfly's. I thought she was a butterfly. She turned her head from left to right. She had poise. Poise. Not poison. Perfect poise. Ronald Fields was hard. Under his jacket his muscles were packed. Tight packed. Packed tight.

He danced with his butterfly in Theresa Carmody's house. She floated when she danced. He had to use his muscles to contain her. When he opened his arms she looked to spin away.

He was a detective. Hard pushed. Hard pressed. Stressed. His eyes devoured her. He turned towards the sofa where Plumpet had placed me. Grammer and Waldorf were tangoing in the hall. Hangoing in the tall. Talldorf near the wall.

'What a little person!' said Ronald Fields, looking at me. He leaned down so that his face was close to mine. He had a big face. Big neck. Heart of love for the butterfly. Plumpet was dancing with long-legged Ronnie. Clear-skinned

98

Ronnie. She smiling Ronnie. Ronnie pretending he was the coolest dude in the room. The doodest cool, the rudest dull, the ruddiest...

Plumpet left the white-toothed Ronnie and was beside me in an instant when she saw Ronald Fields leaning down to me.

'This is Dumpling,' she said. Protectively.

I looked down at my red leather shoes and I pointed my toes. Two shoes. Five toes to point.

'Would you like to dance?' Detective Ronald Fields asked me.

I looked at Plumpet. We were heading into unknown territory. But he loved the Butterfly. And Plumpet liked their offspring, wee Ronnie Fields.

Plumpet smiled at me. 'Dance, Dumpling?' she asked.

I raised my arms, and Ronald Fields lifted me like the Mystery Man so that I sat in the crook of his arm while he danced with the Butterfly.

Could he be the Mystery Man? It was a long time since I'd seen him. Ronald Fields smelled of man. Like the Mystery Man. Chin a little rough – or so my fingers discovered. No tiny birthmark on his forehead. No mark on his head. But eyes as dark as the Mystery Man's.

The Butterfly touched his arm so I was included in their dance. He met her eyes and I was excluded. I stared him in the eyes and brought them back to mine. When his eyes made complete contact with mine, I smiled so that he could see all my tiny white teeth. He smiled too.

'What a dumpling,' said the Butterfly.

99

I pointed my toes so they would be like hers.

The detective said, 'Two ballerinas. I didn't think I could strike it quite so rich.'

Plumpet smiled and waved at me. I waved at her with the hand that was on Detective Ronald Fields'ss shoulder. When I put my hand back down after waving, I touched his hair.

Different feel to the Mystery Man. Detective Man and Mystery Man were two different people.

I was glad for Mum. She wouldn't have liked the Mystery Man to fly away with the Butterfly. To flutter by and by.

Time to sleep. Time to leap.

'Wee Ronnie,' said the Butterfly to Detective Man while they danced, me in his arms, 'he looks well happy.' Her voice and the sounds she made were different. They had the overtones that Grammer has. From another place. Another country. Northwards where they sing. Their voices lilted and lifted.

Wee Ronnie didn't look so wee to me. He was nearly as tall as his father. Wee must have another meaning. And not pee-wee, another meaning altogether. Wee Ronnie knew how to dance. Much better than Plumpet. He didn't seem to notice or to mind Plumpet's shuffling.

'Like a drink?' he asked her.

'You all right, Dumpling?' Plumpet asked me.

I nodded my head. I was busy. So much to see. A man with purple eyes came and looked at the Butterfly. Then he turned his eyes to me. Behind

100

the purple there was something else.

Grammer came into the room with Waldorf. I heard her say, 'So many people we don't know. What fun.'

Grammer loved meeting people. She said to us, her girls, that in observing human nature you see the oddest contradictions. And every contradiction makes a story.

'Why,' said the Butterfly to Detective Man, who was holding me on his arm, 'isn't that Millicent McHarg?'

Grammer came over to say hello. 'Hello, I'm Millicent McHarg.'

They were delighted. People loved meeting Grammer. And Grammer loved meeting people.

Grammer took precious Dumpling from Detective Man. Introductions all round. All round ductions intro. She held me close to her so that I was wrapped in her perfume.

Purple Eyes moved in and said, 'You once stayed in my apartment in New York, Ms McHarg.' He was addressing Grammer.

'Millie to my friends,' said Grammer.

'I'm Gervaise Holt,' said Purple Eyes.

'Christian's brother?' asked Grammer.

Butterfly said, 'We are Ronald and Maureen Fields. We're new neighbours of Theresa Carmody's.'

'And we're old neighbours,' said Grammer, hugging her Dumpling tight. Tugging her Dumpling to a height. 'So nice to meet you.'

These were the things that people said when they first met. Now we would all live side by side. No hole in the wall into the Fields'ss. Yet.

'Will we dance?' asked Gervaise Holt.

'Time for my Dumpling to go to her bed,' said Grammer.

Purple Eyes touched my hand with one dry finger. His finger had tiny marks on it, and a bead of blood on one of them. I looked at the blood and I shivered. Purple Eyes followed my gaze and saw it. He pulled a face and took a white handkerchief from his pocket and dabbed the blood off. Dab. Bad. It just spouted again. His eyes narrowed and he wrapped the handkerchief around the wound. I wrapped my arms around Grammer's neck and sighed. Bed calling. Calling all beds.

Waldorf came to take Grammer's bundle from her. That was me.

Plumpet was summoned from her drink in the kitchen with wee Ronnie Fields.

Daffers emerged from her hiding-place behind the curtain. Daffers had seen something. It was in her eyes. She stayed close to Grammer.

Butterfly and Detective Man met the other granddaughters. So did Purple Eyes. Daffers did not look Purple Eyes in the face. She stared at his hands. He removed the handkerchief. The bleeding had stopped and so he put the white square back in his pocket. He looked at Daffers. Daffers looked at the mark, and she pulled closer to Grammer and me. Purple Eyes didn't blink. Like a snake. He looked at Plumpet, the side of one lip turned up. Plumpet did not see. She was looking at wee Ronnie.

'Time to go,' said Grammer. I held on tight to Waldorf. Time to go sometimes means more talk.

Chatter. Chatter. Like frozen teeth.

But it was definitely time to go. Grammer's face said it. Ronnie Fields looked at Daffers. He did not smile. Ronnie Fields looked at Plumpet. His mouth turned into a laugh. Wee Ronnie liked my Plumpet.

Good night. Good night. Good night.

Around and around go the bars of my cot. Ten bars, five bars, ten bars, headboard. Ten bars, five bars, ten bars, headboard.

Sleep. Peels. It was time to sleep. Leap into sleep. Safe behind bars.

Chapter Six

Millicent's Tale

I was furious with George for not turning up that night. He was his father's son in many ways. I sometimes felt that the other side of the world was not far enough away for him. At least Maria and I had not told the girls he was due home. He had not been home since the previous Christmas, although Maria had been briefly out to see him. Waiting for a man to return is not how a woman should spend her life and I'd always said that to Maria. 'Do your own thing, Maria,' I said. 'Have your own life. Fulfil yourself.'

When George's father went off the face of the earth via the ocean with his girlfriend in tow, I had the female version of every Tom, Dick and Harry commiserating with me over man's ingratitude to woman, over how humiliated I must feel, and how brave I was. I sat on a chair on the patio and contemplated human nature. I sat there, ankles crossed, looking up at the sky and wondering what I was supposed to feel.

No one had ever told me what to do when one discovers one's partner for life is sticking his whatnot into one's best friend. I had not known how to handle that. I pretended it was not happening, pretended I did not know what was going on. My best friend, Jeannie O'Brien, sat with me. I wanted to tell her to take a flying fuck at herself, but being so well brought up I sat there sipping coffee and trying not to listen to her.

What was really going on was that *she* felt betrayed but she didn't know that I knew that. At least I had known that Dirk McHarg couldn't keep his whatnot inside his zipper. Jeannie O'Brien hadn't realised that. She thought that she was the only one for whom he took it out. Therefore, while I was knocked off my perch trying to take on board that Dirk McHarg was gone, this time for good, Jeannie O'Brien was all in a stew as she had lost her weekly banger.

I didn't know these words then, or if I did, I certainly would never have uttered them aloud, nor written them down. But the advantage of age is that I don't need to give a fuck about the fuckers any more, and certainly that day as widowhood was born, I started to realise that I could rise to any occasion.

'Poor, poor you,' said Jeannie O'Brien, with her

red-rimmed eyes, and her tissue balled in her hand. 'Oh, poor, poor you.'

Poor, poor me, I thought. My arse. I was brought up to be polite, so Jeannie O'Brien sat on my patio and bemoaned my lot while all I could think was, Fuck off, you stupid cow. Not the language of a lady, and certainly not the kind of language I would ever have used aloud.

All I really knew that particular day was that my world had been turned upside down. I, who had so carefully pretended not to know who Dirk was balling – yes, balling, a great word when you're angry – was forced to accept that everyone knew that he had gone down into the sea with a woman. And if they didn't know it yet, they would when the news was announced that evening and, if not then, when the papers came out the following morning. And if not then, then word of mouth would carry it.

I wished Jeannie O'Brien would shut up so that I could think straight, because the truth was I was in a terrible muddle. I was fourteen years married, and for six of those years I had been aware that Dirk's éclair and doughnuts (as he liked to call them) had been doing the rounds.

There were several ways forwards, but because of the mixture of my feelings and the awareness that my humiliation was about to become public property, I was frantically trying to collect my thoughts.

I could come out and say it. I could say, 'Jeannie, I know you're terribly hurt, dear. Believe me, I know. After all, you hurt me when you started having your affair with Dirk.' But as

Dirk would say, if he could, if he wasn't swimming with the fishes that is, 'It meant nothing. You are everything.'

I wanted to hurt Jeannie O'Brien and I knew how to do it, but there were several restraining factors. The first was that as long as I didn't give the game away, I was actually in a stronger position. The second was that it was interesting in a sense watching her grieve for herself while pretending that she was grieving for me. And the third was that I was aware that I didn't yet know what I felt about Dirk's demise, and that until I could get that clear in my head, I was better off saying nothing.

'Don't weep so, Jeannie,' I said to Jeannie O'Brien as she sat on one of my patio chairs on her miserably skinny bottom. How many times had Dirk fondled that scrawny backside of hers? A lot. What a bastard, what a bitch. 'Weeping dulls the senses, clogs the nose, reddens the eyes, and puts lines on your face.'

Oh, I surprised myself all right at how sensible I sounded. I thought that might be a good way to play things for a while.

'You're so brave, Millie,' said Jeannie O'Brien to me as she held one delicate hand against her heart or, as I suddenly thought to myself, as she held one bony fist to her undersized chest.

Fascinating, I thought. Absolutely fascinating, how things could be perceived. It is all in the eye of the beholder. Is it to do with projection or perception? Is it the way Jeannie is projecting herself, or is it the way I perceive her? Or the way I *choose* to perceive her? If I were writing a book about her, how would I tell the tale? Would she be beating her poor heart with a fragile hand, or clawing at her size thirty-two AAs with scrawny fingers?

I quite surprised myself with this thought. And apart from anything else I had actually forgotten Dirk, the patisserie he kept in his trousers, the floozy who had sunk with him, and the fact that everyone was going to know I had been betrayed. If Jeannie O'Brien had been in an Elizabethan tragedy she would have been saying, 'Woe is me.' As it was, she was making similar if more modern utterances, and I started to see things a little more clearly. I knew I had a way to go, and I couldn't really see the way forward, but I also knew that while I was observing my 'best' friend and her behaviour, I was most definitely not thinking about Dirk McHarg. And that was good.

Distraction, I reasoned, was the way forward. So, from wanting Jeannie O'Brien to disappear up her own arsehole, I suddenly wanted her to stay sitting on my patio so that I could take in how she was behaving. And the more I watched her, the more I saw how I did not want to be. Tragedy queen was unpleasant, I thought. Stoic, stalwart, courageous seemed a better option. I tilted my chin a little upwards, and continued to watch the tragedy queen as she shifted uncomfortably on her scraggy arse on the hard patio chair. I crossed my legs. I did not feel uncomfortable, though Jeannie clearly did. I thought at first this could be because my bottom was bigger, firmer, with better padding. Then of course I realised that I had brought a cushion out with myself and so it was no wonder I was more comfortable. I made a mental note, 'Millicent,' or so I addressed myself, 'always bring a cushion with you.'

'What will you do, poor, poor Millie?' asked Jeannie O'Brien.

Well, thought I to myself, I rather fancy a Scotch.

But I didn't say this aloud as a) I didn't want to have one with Jeannie, and b) I didn't want people hearing that poor Millicent McHarg had hit the bottle, and I was pretty sure that was what would do the rounds within twenty-four hours.

I tilted my chin upwards a little more. 'I shall grieve for my beloved husband, and then I shall assess the future,' I said with courage and conviction. Wow, I was surprising myself.

'Oh, Millie,' said Jeannie O'Brien, 'you're so brave. You're so, so brave. Aren't you destroyed by the thought that Anne Pollock went down with him?'

'Anne Pollock?' I said, keeping a steady hand as I picked up my coffee cup and thought of the double Scotch I would have later.

'You know,' said my best friend. 'The other woman. The one in the plane.'

'Who?' I asked with what I hoped was sufficient interest and curiosity.

'Anne Pollock,' said the best friend, who was determined now to spare me nothing.

'Why,' I said sadly, 'poor Anne. And her poor family. How they will grieve for such a wonderful girl.'

Jeannie's mouth opened and closed a bit like a fish – possibly a bit like a fish that was nibbling the flesh off poor Anne Pollock even as we spoke. A large fish, I imagined, with teeth, and a nice fin. At first I imagined the fish with big teeth, and then I decided small teeth would be better. Dozens and dozens of them in multiple rows. Nibbling away.

'Such a great assistant she was. Why, I nearly said I don't know what poor Dirk will do without her...' I almost giggled aloud. 'But of course, he won't need her any more, will he?' Nor, I continued on my internal dialogue, will you, my dear friend Jeannie, get to nibble on his éclair, or squeeze his doughnuts any more.

I smiled courageously. 'I suppose I ought to phone Anne Pollock's parents,' I said. 'Show them my support. They must be grief-stricken.'

'I think you're in a state of shock,' said Jeannie O'Brien as she mangled the tissue in her hand.

'I dare say I am,' I admitted in a brave little voice. 'But then, who wouldn't be? It's not every day one loses one's darling husband.'

Of course inside my head I was not as blunt as I am implying. I didn't know back then some of the expressions I have used in the telling, as these belong to more modern phraseology, but I did surprise myself with my vehemence and the clarity with which my mind was progressing.

I was beginning to realise that I needed occupation as a distraction, that I did not need or want the 'sympathy' of friends, because ultimately I only had myself to fall back on.

Up in his bedroom, my son George – I found

myself already thinking in terms of 'I' and 'my' instead of the 'we' and 'our' I had been used to – was busy dismantling or destroying the model planes he had so painstakingly constructed. It suddenly occurred to me that I was going to have to deal with him finding out about the other woman. Human nature being what it is, people would be quick to tell him. I wondered what was the best line to take.

If I told him the truth he might, possibly correctly, believe that all men take mistresses. Now if he learned this at such an early stage in his life – being a mere twelve years old on the day in question – it might harden him, and make him callous. He would progress into adulthood with the wrong approach to relationships. On the other hand, I might be doing him a favour by just telling him the truth. 'Nothing is sacred,' I could tell him, 'so go for it, my boy.'

If I did tell him the truth about his father, then what would I say to my friends? I could hardly deny it to them, since he would undoubtedly tell their sons. Or perhaps not. My experience was that men did not talk to men; they preferred to talk to women.

There was an awful lot to think about, and there was Jeannie O'Brien still sitting on the patio talking about a wake.

'A wake?' I asked in surprise.

'Well, yes,' she said. 'I mean – you know, prayers.'

'Prayers?' I reiterated. 'For whom?'

'For Dirk, I suppose,' she said.

'For Dirk?' I couldn't for the life of me think

why Dirk might suddenly want a prayer said for him. 'Jeannie,' I said gently, 'Dirk is dead. He's not coming back.'

She looked at me in total bewilderment, and it occurred to me that maybe I was missing something.

'Funeral service, I meant,' she said.

'Oh, I see,' I said after a moment's thought. 'But Jeannie – if they find the plane, and the nice man who came out to see me didn't seem to think that was very likely – something to do with miles below the sea and statistics showing et cetera, et cetera ... I don't think there will be much left of Dirk or anyone else.'

'I was thinking more of a memorial service,' Jeannie said.

'Oh, I see.' I hadn't thought of that. I realised that I might be in a state of shock after all. 'A memorial service,' I repeated. I couldn't think of anything worse. All of the women Dirk had known would be there – oh dear, what a thought.

'It's what people usually do,' Jeannie said.

'People?' I wondered aloud. 'You mean, women whose husbands go down in the sea?'

Jeannie nodded. I suddenly knew she was thinking that she wanted to pray for him in public, to say her goodbyes. Oh well, if that's what everyone expected, maybe I would have to go with it.

'Yes,' I said. 'A memorial service. That's what we'll have. Something memorable,' I added.

Something very memorable.

Oh, I have learned to love parties. Parties are

111

where you can shine. I used to be a modest soul – brought up to be seen and not heard. Actually, I was probably brought up not even to be seen. Victorian parents were very repressive. My parents had dinner either with friends, or alone together in the dining room, and I had supper in the kitchen. I was briefly aired when they had guests in, my hair quickly and sharply brushed by my mother, and I would be brought in to say good night. As a child I wondered why I was allowed in for two or three minutes only. I learned to thrust my small hand out to shake hands with Mr and Mrs So and So, and I soon learned that I didn't like sitting on Uncle Todd's knee for a 'cuddle', as he had a hard thing in his trousers and he jiggled me up and down against it while he chatted. At an early age children do learn what they like and what they don't, even if they have no idea how to express it.

Within my own marriage, and I married young before I was fully formed – mentally and emotionally, I mean – I was the wonderful wife. As I now say, 'Behind every great man is an even greater woman' – well, that took a while for me to realise, and it was not until Dirk was really gone that I had the chance to come into my own.

Widowhood does not necessarily mean liberation, but for someone like me who had been living a lie, hiding from the knowledge of Dirk's relationships, pretending that all was well in our large and comfortable home, vacuuming and dusting so that the place was sparkling … well, widowhood meant the opportunity of dropping the lie. I needed to decide what parts of it I

112

wanted to drop, or if I just wanted to grow into myself, to re-invent myself, to become someone inside whose skin I could feel fulfilled.

'We'll have to contact the church,' Jeannie O'Brien said.

'Why?' I asked. Really, she was being very interfering.

'For the memorial service.'

'I will look after that with the undertakers,' I said.

'But you won't need undertakers,' said Jeannie O'Brien in a tragic if informative way. 'No body,' she added, as I looked a little blank.

Corpseless, I thought. Wasn't that the name of a book – *Corpseless in Gaza? Corpseless in Dublin 4*, I thought. It had a different ring to it. Not quite as flamboyant as Gaza. Why I should think of Gaza as being glitzy I have no idea.

'No body,' I repeated. 'But then there is no soul, so why would I want someone from the church?'

'Because the soul is separate from the body,' said Jeannie O'Brien.

'Is it?' I asked. 'Are you sure?'

'Of course I'm sure, dear Millie,' she said. 'The body gets buried and the soul goes to...' She paused. And no wonder. She could hardly say the soul goes to heaven considering the circumstances of Dirk McHarg's demise. It was not a case of ashes to ashes and dust to dust. It was more like flesh to fish, and fish to market. My God, I thought, I might end up making fish stock with him.

Eventually she went home, as she had to get dinner for her husband and children.

'Will you be all right?' she asked.

'I will,' I reassured her in my new brave voice. 'I have a lot to think about, and this is a good time to do it.'

'Don't think too much,' she advised. Really, there seemed no limit to her knowledge on how to deal with a dead husband.

She let herself out and I stayed there on the patio chair and thought about the best way to handle my mother and to give darling Dirk a good send-off.

Now I had loved Dirk McHarg. I married him for love and because I wanted to honour and obey. And I had done those things and look where they had got me. I weighed up the balance. I had lost my partner for life. I was probably going to have to deal with a quantity of humiliation, and a lot of pity. On the plus side, I had a wonderful son, a nice house, a fair amount of money, and I no longer had to pretend that Dirk was a good and faithful husband.

How to move forward, I wondered. I did not want pity, and whereas I was going to get sympathy whether I liked it or not, I needed to make sure that I could deflect the humiliation at least publicly.

I phoned my mother before I started to prepare dinner, and I told her what had happened. After an initial silence there came a peculiar question. 'Are you sure, dear?'

'Sure of what?' I asked.

'That Dirk is dead. I mean, are you absolutely sure?'

Of course I was absolutely sure. It was not the kind of thing you made up. 'His plane went down, Mother,' I said. 'It's going to be on the news tonight. It's a fact.' Unalterable. Unchangeable. Terminal.

'Did you have anything to do with it?' she asked. Really, that woman seemed to think there was no end to my capabilities.

'I wouldn't know how to tamper with a plane, even if it were sitting in my back garden and I had a spanner handy.' Actually I don't think I said that aloud. My mother was not the kind of person on whom one practised one's irony.

'I need your support, Mother,' I said. Support and my mother did not always go hand in hand.

'Hmmm,' she said.

'George,' I said as I peeled the potatoes. We were in the kitchen – just the two of us. Nothing unusual in that. Dirk was away so often that we had our own comfortable ways when we were alone. George was laying the table. 'Put wine glasses out,' I said. 'We're going to open a bottle.'

'But Dad wouldn't like me to drink,' George said aghast.

Dad won't know, I thought, but I didn't say that aloud.

'I think your dad would see you as the man of the house now,' I said, 'and a sip of wine will do you no harm. There is an especially good bottle of Châteauneuf-du-Pape on the wine rack in your father's den. He was keeping it for something

115

special. Open it, will you, and let it breathe.' Such a lovely wine. Made from thirteen different varieties of grape. Or so Dirk used to pontificate. I knowingly use the word *pontificate* here – it's a little pun on the word *pape* or pope. Mediterranean sunshine and stony soil, or so he used to say. It always sounded a little hot and dusty to me – the weather, I mean of course. Not the wine.

And yes – Dirk had a den, wouldn't you know it? He seldom used it but he occupied it totally. When I wanted to use my sewing machine, I would have to haul it into the kitchen, set it up on the kitchen table, use it, and have it put away by the time Dirk came home, as he disliked clutter. He didn't even like it in one of the spare rooms. On occasion I had rebelled against this – but never aloud. Just little things in my head like, 'It's not fair.' Then it occurred to me that I could empty his study, put the sewing machine on his desk and leave it there for years and years and never use it.

'Now George,' I said. 'We need to talk.' At this stage the news had not officially broken, but I knew from the nice man who had come out to the house that there was going to be an item on both the radio and the television that evening. I had the phone off the hook, as I didn't want to have to deal with any calls.

George and I were settled at the table with our lamb chops, mashed potatoes, peas and carrots. And our glasses of Châteauneuf-du-Pape. I briefly wondered if that meant nine castles of the Pope, or if it was the pontiff's ninth castle. We were taught French so badly at school. For years I thought *savoir-faire* meant knowing how to do it, as in how to have sex.

'When people die tragically,' I said carefully, forcing myself to stop thinking about the papacy and its properties, 'all kinds of suggestions and innuendoes are made. You know, if someone dies in a car accident, people are quick to suggest alcohol. Or if there is someone in the car who was just getting a lift home from the pub, people will suggest they were having an affair ... it's human nature. It's gossipy and it's unpleasant.'

George put a bite of lamb into his mouth and chewed it and I wondered what he was thinking. I also wondered how explicit I was going to have to be as his face was completely impassive.

'The meat is nice,' he said.

I took that to be his way of saying that he didn't want the conversation to continue the way I was leading it. I sipped my wine and we ate in silence for a while.

'Who was in the plane with Dad?' he asked after a bit.

'Oh, the pilot,' I said. 'And his assistant Anne, a nice girl. I've always liked her.'

'The pilot's assistant?'

'No, your dad's.'

Another silence.

'His business often took him abroad,' announced my twelve-year-old son.

'It did,' I said. 'And he was lucky to have such a good assistant. She went everywhere with him of late. So sad for her family.'

George nodded.

117

We watched the nine o'clock news where Dirk McHarg's death got the opening slot. First there was a photograph of Dirk McHarg with his high forehead and his dark curly hair, his tiny birthmark carefully camouflaged for the publicity shot he had had taken a few years earlier. Then there was an image of a small plane in a field which was presumably meant to be similar to the one in which he, Anne Pollock and their pilot descended into the water. A picture of the water followed this image, but as I said to myself, it could have been anywhere.

George looked at me and said, 'Do you think if we went looking for him, we might find him?'

I shook my head. What a thought! 'It's a large sea,' I said. 'And it's very deep.'

He nodded.

'We'll have a great send-off party for him,' I said to George. 'Maybe a few prayers in the church and then something in the church hall.'

'When?'

'Tomorrow I'll start making the arrangements,' I said. I wanted to put this as far behind me as possible, but I needed to take George into consideration.

'Dad liked cakes,' George said.

He sure did, I thought. 'He did, didn't he?' I commented. 'We'll do him proud.'

And proud we did him. There was a great turn-out the following week. The service was short, just with prayers for those lost at sea. I refused a eulogy – I didn't want any irony, and I didn't want to feel weepy. It was a head-held-high day. Afterwards George and I received all the supporters and mourners in the church hall. I avoided my mother as much as possible. There was tea and coffee, and tables laid out with chocolate éclairs and doughnuts. The local cake shop had made the little doughnut balls in what I would call half-sizes, while the éclairs came in two different lengths – tiny bite-size ones, and longer ones. It looked lovely, and I think Dirk would have enjoyed my wit. Certainly it was interesting to see some of the women's faces. Jeannie O'Brien's mouth fell open when she saw how I had laid out the food. And so did Marjorie Whelan who lived next door to us. Until the moment when she gasped, 'His patisserie,' I hadn't realised she was another one who had had her fill of my husband.

'What did you say, Marjorie?' I asked her sweetly, and with my new dignity wrapped around me.

'N ... nothing,' Marjorie replied, eyeing the delicacies.

And Josephine Holland who kept sucking the end of her thumb – well, well, I thought, that's all you'll be sucking for a while. There were other women whom I knew and who looked at the cakes with dismay. The men tucked in, clearly not getting the joke at all. And George and his friends had a feast.

I had bought a hat for the occasion, with a little bit of black net, which came down over my eyes. I had gone into town on the Monday and got a facial and, although I was perfectly well aware

119

how to put on make-up, I went and had a demonstration if that is the right word. Then I bought a load of very good products and practised. Smooth skin, youth, and dignity – I was arming myself well. A couple of little black numbers and I had a style I hadn't hitherto aspired to. Millicent McHarg, I thought, you're on your way.

'What do you think, Jeannie?' I asked my so-called best friend.

'Think?' she asked, rather parrot-like I thought.

'About the do.'

'The do?'

'This.' I gestured around the room. 'Dirk's send-off. Lots of people have turned up – from his business, family and friends. Lots of friends. He was so well liked,' I said. We were standing near a table and Jeannie was holding a cup of tea, as was the priest. 'And he had so many women friends. It's wonderful,' I continued. 'It makes me feel so much less alone.'

Jeannie swallowed uncomfortably. I think she must have got a bit of a shock.

'Maybe I should have organised a string quartet,' I mused to Jeannie and the clergyman. 'Dirk loved to dance.'

'Dance?' she said.

'Oh, we often danced in the bedroom before going to bed,' I lied.

'D-d-did you?' she stuttered.

The clergyman was distracted by someone at his elbow trying to get his attention.

'Yes,' I said. 'Oh yes. Dirk loved a foxtrot,' I

120

giggled a little. 'And then of course he would pretend to be a hound and chase me – "his little fox" he called me. I'll miss those hunts and how they always ended up.'

Jeannie's husband, Hugh, came over. 'Millie,' he said. 'You look wonderful.'

'You're supposed to be commiserating with her,' Jeannie hissed.

'Well, she does look wonderful,' Hugh said. 'In fact, I've never seen you look so well, Millie.'

'I'm trying to cover my grief for George's sake,' I said.

'You must feel so betrayed,' said Marjorie from next door, joining our group.

You little bitch, I thought. You go to bed with my husband, come to his farewell bash, and the best you can come up with is to make a nasty comment. Marjorie Whelan was a good twelve years younger than me. I have never understood men who have affairs with or who marry girls that much younger than them. I mean, what do they find to talk about? Their perspectives are more than a decade apart.

Hugh was looking uncomfortable at Marjorie's observation.

'Betrayed?' I said. 'Yes. Yes, of course. There is the feeling that God has betrayed me by letting my darling Dirk die at such an early age. But I have so much to fall back on. You see, I have wonderful memories. We shared so much. There is nothing he didn't tell me, nothing I didn't know about what he did both at work and for fun. He loved telling me things. Sharing is such an aphrodisiac.' I looked her squarely in the face

121

and smiled encouragingly. I'll deal with you later, I thought.

'I'll miss the things we shared,' I continued. 'I'll miss how we used to laugh over his observations on other human beings. He loved imitating people ... especially women. He was very naughty.' I beamed. 'Ah well. Those times are over, aren't they? And now I have my memories – joyous memories – and all that insurance money, so I'm safe. And poor Dirk is dead. Marjorie, you *must* have an éclair,' I said, putting one on a small plate with two tiny doughnuts. 'They're just scrumptious. And there's plenty to go around.'

Marjorie's husband Gerald, who had moved out of their house some two months earlier – and I now knew why – came over and, lifting the netting on my hat, he kissed me.

'It's great to see you looking so glowing,' he said.

'Thank you, Gerald,' I said bravely. 'I'm doing my best – such difficult times.'

'I've to leave now to get back to the office,' he said, 'but maybe I could give you a call next week, and if you're up to going out for a spot of dinner...?'

A spot? A spot? I felt like more than a spot of dinner.

'Thank you, Gerald,' I said. 'Do call. I know that I'm going to need my friends – and you certainly learn who your friends are at a time like this.'

As Gerald left, I turned to Marjorie and said, 'I suppose this is a bit like when Gerald left you and

I rallied around – I do so appreciate your being here for me.'

I made sure there wasn't a single trace of irony in my voice. I liked this new role. I felt I could grow into it, given half a chance, although there were still gaps to be filled, gaps both in my knowledge and in my character. My generation were well formed in some respects but left wanting in others.

With regards to my knowledge, I'm referring to assessing my friends and acquaintances. Earlier that day I had only known of a couple of women who had slept with Dirk, and that knowledge was attained by careful observation of how he watched the women among our friends when we were in their company. A lingering look, a bedroom smile ... give-away glances. But by the time his memorial service and party were over I had identified at least half a dozen others. True friends look you in the eyes and you know that they mean it when they offer you condolences. You know that they are sad for themselves because they have lost a friend, but more than that – for you they project themselves and their sympathy is sincere. Friends who have been laying your husband can't quite meet your eye. I learned a lot that day.

My own mother hovered, a bit too close for my liking, eyeing me from a small distance with her lips pursed every time she looked at the confectionery. I am not sure if she got the joke at all. I tried to keep well away from her as she had this ability to undermine me and make me feel truly inadequate.

George was wonderful – he was going to grow into a fine man. I just knew it. I do admit that at that particular time I was not sure what a 'fine man' meant, but I had the notion that there was such a thing, and that with a bit of luck George was going to be such.

And indeed he did grow into a fine man – down there, somewhere in Southeast Asia on a helicopter as Waldorf and I saw that night when we turned on the midnight news. I sometimes thought he was looking for his father as he searched and observed from on high. I could safely say that I did my best with him – he was solid and dependable, interesting and intriguing, but always at a distance.

'I wonder will he get here in time for Christmas?' I mused aloud. My irritation had eased somewhat after I had seen him hanging from his trapeze or whatever it is in the helicopter.

Waldorf ran his hand over my leather-clad thigh. 'God, but I love you in leather,' he said huskily.

I know, I thought. He was the only reason I was wearing purple leather trousers. I could write a book or two about men and their fetishes. Indeed, I have.

I smiled at him. 'I've such a nice surprise for you for Christmas,' I said.

He chuckled throatily. 'As I have for you,' he said.

'Maria is going to be devastated if George doesn't get here.' I continued my earlier train of thought, and an image of my daughter-in-law endlessly waiting flashed into my mind.

'That girl needs a right good...' Waldorf left the end of the sentence unspoken.

'Bonk?' I suggested.

He nodded as he elongated his thumb and forefinger to open the zip on my leather trousers.

'We need to give her something to distract her,' I observed, as I shifted a little on the sofa to give him easier access.

'Let me guess what colour corset you have on,' he said. He was such a single-minded man. There was little to distract him once he got going.

'Well, well, well,' he said. 'Is this new?' as he fingered the thin lacy Lycra in which I was encased.

'It is,' I said. 'But it's not your Christmas present.'

He groaned in excitement. 'This will do just fine for now, Millie, m'dear.'

Right, I thought, I'll think about Maria and distractions tomorrow...

Chapter Seven

Plumpet's Tale

When we got out of the taxi after the pantomime and I saw Ronnie Fields standing on the far side of the removal van I simply couldn't believe my eyes. I'd met him at Daisy's house during the summer. Daisy lives out Foxrock way. She is a friend of my sister Daffers but I was over in their place too as Samson and Delilah, Daisy's parents, were having a garden party, and the McHargs were invited en masse.

Ronnie Fields was a cousin of a cousin of Daisy's and he was just gorgeous. He lay on the grass with his long brown legs and his white shorts. Blond hair was sprinkled on his arms and he wore a navy-blue T-shirt. His eyes were the colour of the T-shirt. He had a perfectly straight nose and white-blond hair, cut very short except for a small peak which stuck out in front.

I only met him that once, but when we went back to school after the holidays Daisy said to Daffers that her cousin said that Ronnie had said that he'd like to meet me again. I didn't know whether to believe Daffers when she told me that because Daffers doesn't usually tell the truth, but it was nice to think that he might like to meet me again, and I thought about that on and off all term.

When the *Sold* sign went up on the house next door, needless to say, it never occurred to me that Ronnie Fields's parents might have bought it, and that by Christmas Ronnie himself would be ensconced on my doorstep.

When we went in to Theresa Carmody's for the first of her many pre-Christmas parties, I was so excited about the Fields being in the house on the other side of us. I never expected them to turn up at her party that very same night. Apparently, Theresa Carmody had seen the removal van while we were at the pantomime and so she had hurried over to say hello and to find more people to fill her house.

Ronnie told me much later that his parents had wanted to get the beds made up, but that he had put it to them that it wasn't often one got invited to a neighbour's party on the night you were moving into your new house – and that really they ought to go. He said to them that it might help him to make friends, as it was awkward at his age moving into a new area.

And so there we were in Theresa Carmody's, and I put the Dumpling down on the sofa because when she's tired she seems to get heavier, though maybe it's really that when I get tired, I feel her weight more, I'm not sure. But I didn't feel tired, I just felt excited. Then in he walked. Ronnie Fields with his long legs and his peaked blond hair.

And he wasn't shy. He just came over – as I had done when I'd seen him outside on the road.

Later I watched his dad and I saw exactly where Ronnie got his mannerisms from. He really wasn't shy at all. He did things like putting his hand on my arm. 'Let's dance,' he said, and we did. A hand on my shoulder. 'Thirsty? Let's get a drink, I saw lots of different bottles in the kitchen.' Then later, when he'd poured us each a Coke, he said, 'I'm sure our hostess won't mind if I get some ice.' He opened the fridge and took some ice out. He had been like that at Daisy's during the summer. 'Like a drink?' he had asked and then had just gone and got me one.

Theresa Carmody's house was full of people all dressed up. Grammer and Waldorf danced in the hall. Theresa's house is completely different from ours. When she moved in she removed the wall between the sitting room and dining room and put bay windows in the back of the house to match those in the front. 'Sausage money goes far,' Grammer said.

Theresa Carmody also removed the wall into the room that is a study in our house so her hall is about five times as big as ours – long enough for the tango and big enough for the people dancing in the front garden to pour into when it started to rain. Waldorf was wearing a black jacket made of a very soft material. The Dumpling loved that jacket – she petted it with her little hands, stroked it like you would a kitten. If she could purr I am sure she would have. Waldorf wore a seasonal bloom in his buttonhole – holly and berries coming up to Christmas. Daffers said he had mistletoe in it last New Year, but I did not really remember.

Daffers 'did a Dumpling' as we say in our house. At the party, I mean. She just seemed to disappear, although later she emerged from behind the curtains around the bay windows at the back, so maybe she was there all the time.

Ronnie pulled chairs out at the bar in Theresa's kitchen and we sat there drinking our Coke through straws and eating nuts and dates. There was loads of lovely-looking food but I wasn't hungry. I think it was the excitement.

Ronnie said, 'We can walk to school together.'

I was startled. 'How do you mean?' I asked.

'School ... side by side ... down the road ... on our feet,' he explained.

'Oh. What school are you going to?' I asked. In the summer when we had talked at Samson and Delilah's garden party, he had mentioned a school on the other side of the city.

'I'm moving school,' he told me. 'I'm going to the square block that is presumably modern architecture at its worst which is just past yours.'

Daffers and I went to an all girls' school and down the road – a good mile away actually – there was a school where the boys wore grey trousers and navy blazers.

'Oh,' I said again.

'Unless you'd prefer to walk by yourself,' he said, looking at me squarely.

Oh no, I thought. I'd pay to walk to school with you. I'd be over the moon at the very idea of walking to school with you.

'I'd love to walk to school with you,' I said, hoping I didn't sound too enthusiastic. The girls in my class always go on about playing it cool and being more in control and stuff. But I don't know much about that.

'Do you ever wear your hair out loose?' he asked.

I fingered my ponytail and nodded my head, even though I didn't ever wear it down. I had let it out when I saw him on the road outside, but then I had tied it back up again. I don't know why.

'Let it down now,' he said, tilting his head to one side as he watched me.

Oh, I was putty in his manly youthful hands. I pulled the scrunchy from my hair and it fell down onto my shoulders. I shook my head slightly to release it from the way it had been pulled so tightly.

'It really suits you like that,' he said.

My hair is dark brown and very wavy, and having it pulled back and tied up keeps it out of my way. I slipped my hand through the scrunchy so that it sat on my wrist, and then because I thought it looked silly like that I pushed it up under the sleeve of my sweater until it disappeared from view.

I wanted to say to him, 'I love your hair. I love the way it just sits on your head, and the way your eyes are dark, dark blue, and the way your neck goes down into your collar. I love the way your ankles look, the way your wrists are strong and your nails are all neat and tidy.' Instead I said in my best Mum voice, 'So are there just you and your mother and father?'

'In here tonight?' he said. 'Yes. The others stayed at home.'

'The others?' Now I was surprised. My silly comment had simply been to cover up my silence and to stop me from saying something like 'I love your nose,' which might just as easily have come out.

'Yes, my brother and the dog.'

'Oh.' A brother and a dog. 'What's he like?' I asked.

'The brother or the dog?'

'Well, both. Either.' I didn't mind, I just wanted him to go on talking and not to decide that I was too boring to sit with in Theresa Carmody's kitchen, or to walk with to school.

'They're both fairly lethal,' he said with a laugh.

Gosh – when he laughed, his eyes crinkled at the corners. He had the whitest teeth, and I could see his tongue.

His tongue.

Stop it, Plumpet, I said to myself. Stop, stop, stop. But I couldn't. His tongue was a dark pink.

'How old are they?' I asked as I looked at his mouth.

One, it turned out, was the same age as Daffers – a walking companion for Daffers, I wondered. The other was eighty-four – in canine years.

'I wonder will he have a problem settling in,' I said.

Ronnie smiled. 'I don't think either of them will settle in as quickly as I have.'

Could he mean because of me?

'I've always fancied having a girl next door,' he said.

What did he mean? I didn't know what to say again. I looked at him, and then I sipped my Coke frantically and didn't know where to look.

'Where we lived before,' he said, 'was way out – a lonely sort of place. My mother is going to love being closer to the city. She's a ballet teacher and she has to travel miles at the moment. So it'll be easier for her and for my father for going to work. The new school is close by, and the best part...' he paused. I watched him with the straw firmly stuck in my mouth.

'The best part is that there is a girl next door.'

My heart sang a little song. I wished I were called Alice. I knew that if I were called Alice I would have a theme tune – remember that song 'Living Next Door to Alice'? Dad used to play that every time he came home.

Ronnie was just so at ease, it was unbelievable. I knew that I was blushing. A bit of my brain was thinking that he could mean Daffers or the Dumpling as being the girl next door, but I knew in my heart that he meant me.

Me, Plumpet. Ponytailed. Neat. Tidy. Ordinary.

There – I've said it! I was ordinary. Grammer says no one is ordinary. She says we are each unique and we each have special attributes but I look very ordinary.

Ronnie Field was the first boy who seemed to want to talk to me. And I wanted to talk to him. I just had to work out how to do it.

'Which bedroom is yours?' I asked. Then I nearly bit my tongue off. It sounded so ... I don't know – so forward or something. I couldn't even think straight I was so embarrassed.

Now let me explain the positioning of the houses. As you came up the road, Theresa Carmody's was just before ours, and then came ours, and then the Fields's. They were double-fronted houses in their own grounds, ours being the most different as Grammer had her apartment attached on to the far side of the house, on the Fields's side. The bedrooms upstairs were all in the same position as ours, so far as I knew, and in our house, mine was the first bedroom at the rear of the house; from the window I could just see into Theresa Carmody's back garden. The Dumpling's bedroom was situated in the centre of the back of the house with a view out on to our extended kitchen, and Daffers's room came next just before Grammer's apartment. From Daffers's window you could see our back garden clearer than from any other room. You could also see Grammer's patio, which was really an extension of ours, and the wall that separated us from Ronnie Fields's garden.

My bedroom was the largest of the three at the back, though Mum's room at the front was way bigger. It transpired that Ronnie Field was sleeping in the equivalent of my room in his house.

'Oh,' I said, now unsure what to say next.

'Which room do you have?' he asked.

'The same one,' I mumbled.

'I can see into your back garden from mine,' Ronnie said as he reached for a cocktail sausage.

'I wouldn't have one of those,' I advised. 'Grammer says that you can't be sure what's in Wallace's sausages as they butcher everything.'

Ronnie Fields laughed. It's funny how something sounds so normal when your grandmother says it, but when it comes out of your own mouth it sounds outlandish.

'Then I don't think I'll risk it,' he said, which I thought was very nice of him, because he could have scoffed at Grammer and at me but he didn't.

'Pity your bedroom isn't the one closest to mine,' he said.

I wanted to say, 'Why is it a pity?' but I was afraid to because I couldn't imagine what he might come out with. So I sucked at my straw and kept my eyes on my glass.

A man with purple eyes came into the kitchen and looked at us. 'Misbehaving?' he asked. I had a feeling he was trying to sound roguish, but instead he sounded slightly creepy.

'No,' Ronnie said, quick as a flash. 'This is Ms McHarg.' It sounded like Miss McHarg the way he said it. 'And I'm Ronald Fields Junior.'

I laughed, and the man looked very intently at Ronnie for a moment, before turning and leaving the room.

'Talk about sinister,' Ronnie said, and I agreed.

Then Polo, Theresa Carmody's sister, came in and took a look at us both.

'I haven't met you before,' she said to Ronnie. 'Have I?'

He got up and introduced himself. 'I take it you know Plumpet,' he said to Polo.

She nodded. She seldom smiled. When Daffers was little, she drew a picture of an orchard and in it she had all different kinds of fruit trees. One of the trees she called a Polo-tree because she said it was full of nasty fruit. She doesn't remember that, but I do. I knew what she meant even though Grammer and Mum didn't.

'Like lemons,' Daffers said when Grammer asked her to explain. 'With insects inside them,' she added.

Grammer and Mum looked at each other, but they didn't say anything.

Polo sat down at the table just beside us and reached for a sausage.

'I wouldn't have one of those if I were you,' started Ronnie Field.

I quickly interrupted him. 'They're cold, Polo,' I said. 'Oh Ronnie, Polo is Theresa Carmody's sister,' I explained. I was quite proud of myself for my quick reaction.

'How nice,' said Ronnie Field, copping on quickly to the sausage situation and covering for it wonderfully. He pushed a plate of gherkins and cheese over to Polo. 'You might prefer one of these,' he suggested.

'No,' she said icily. 'I'll have a sausage. I like them – even when they're cold.' Her eyes turned to me and I tried to smile. 'So what are you two doing?' she asked.

I couldn't think what she meant, because it was fairly obvious that we were drinking Coke and talking. And that we did not want her sitting there looking at us.

'Drinking Coke and chatting,' Ronnie said. His voice was even, unruffled, but I sensed something – maybe a slight irritation, maybe puzzlement at her question. 'Now, we're going to dance,' he went on. 'So please excuse us.' And just like that he took my hand and we left Polo sitting at the table.

In the hall he looked at me and whispered, 'We certainly don't need her on our case, do we?'

I would never have had the nerve.

Like Daffers I didn't like Polo but I was not really sure why. You know with some people you feel they think a bit like you do – girls and women, I mean. They have periods and you know that they have optimism and that if they saw the Dumpling, they'd just love her. I suppose that loving the Dumpling is my parameter – is that the word? I mean that people would just have to love the Dumpling, and if they didn't, then I'd

135

know that I just couldn't like them. That there was something missing. Polo didn't like the Dumpling. She had no interest in her at all.

Then we got called inside because Grammer said it was time we girls went home. The man with the purple eyes touched the Dumpling and she threw her arms around Grammer's neck, and I wanted to shout at him to leave her alone. But of course I did not.

'Pity you have to go,' Ronnie said to me.

'Will you stay much longer?' I asked.

He laughed again, but I don't know why, and he said, 'No. We only came in to say hello. My parents might stay on, I'm not sure. But I'm off now.'

I was glad.

Polo said, 'Goodbye, Plumpet,' and I looked at her in surprise because I didn't know she even knew my name. She had certainly never used it before.

I said, 'Good night, Polo.' Daffers put her hand into Grammer's, and Grammer swept us out of the room. Ronnie came after us. I thought I'd lost him in the crowd. He put his hand on my shoulder. I wanted to say, 'Will I see you tomorrow?'

'See you tomorrow, right?' he said.

I knew I had a beam on my face – from ear to ear and we went home.

Mum was lying on the sofa. She looked awful – tired maybe, and sort of sad, as if she had run out of steam. The Dumpling was tired too but she was busy with her hands telling about the goose in the panto, and the dancing at the party.

I couldn't wait to go to bed because I wanted to think about Ronnie Fields, about sitting with him in Theresa Carmody's kitchen and dancing with him in her hall. And I wanted to think about him in the very next house in the same bedroom as I was in. I wondered was his bed in the same position in his room, and if he had a similar view to the one I had, proportionate I mean to the positioning of the houses, and what colour his walls were painted. I wanted to know all these little details – and I didn't have a clue how to ask them.

The houses are old, with washbasins in the bedrooms, and that night, after I had done my teeth and brushed out my hair, I stood in front of the mirror and wondered if I should leave my hair down the following day. Or would it just get in the way? I peered at my eyebrows and eyelashes. Daffers always complains that mine are so dark and hers so light and that that is not fair. Now, looking in the mirror, for the first time I was glad they were so dark – they gave my face a certain intensity, I thought. They outlined it. And with my dark hair down, sweeping on to my shoulders and framing my face I thought that maybe I didn't look too terribly ordinary. I mean, not that I thought I looked great – but maybe not too ordinary. And I couldn't stop smiling. I kept thinking about how Ronnie had just put a hand on mine and said, 'Let's drink,' or 'Let's dance,' or 'Let's whatever.'

Let's whatever ... now there was a thought. I

pulled on clean pyjamas – pale pink fleece ones with little white clouds on them and looked at myself again in the mirror. I felt a pang of lust. Not lust for me, but lust *at* me. Can I explain that? Lust at the fact that I was young and healthy and my body was lithe and slim, and that in the same bedroom in the next house was Ronnie Fields with his white-blond hair, and his dark-blue eyes. I ran my hands over myself and I thought how I would like him to touch me.

It was then that I saw the chocolate on the pillow. Mum puts a chocolate on our pillow when she's worried about something. I wondered what was going on.

I put it on my bedside table to keep for the following day. Normally I'd have opened it and devoured it immediately, but the way I was feeling, chocolate wasn't what I wanted. And anyway, my mouth felt all minty from the toothpaste.

I was about to get into bed when I realised I had left the main light on in my room, so I started towards the door where the switch was, and somehow got distracted. I wondered if there was any way I could see any of Ronnie Fields's garden from my window.

At the window I leaned as far to the left as possible and peered over towards their garden, but nothing was visible in the darkness. So I stood there staring down into our own garden. The floodlights were on in Theresa Carmody's back garden and they lit up some of ours, so that I could see part of the patio, and the garden swing, and the outline of our Buddha and the first trees in the orchard. I wondered when Dad was going to get home. There were only a couple of days left until Christmas.

I thought I saw a movement in our garden and leaned towards the glass only to see that it was Cat, Theresa Carmody's grey pet. Then I glanced over at Theresa's garden and to my horror, realised that I was being watched from her patio. Two people were standing there side by side looking up at my window – my light being on showed me up clearly. I stepped back immediately and went and turned it off. I kept thinking, So what? What does it matter if someone saw you standing at your window? But it did matter. I felt really uncomfortable and uneasy. I knew who they were and I knew that they had been watching me. And I did not like the feeling at all. All the lovely thoughts and feelings I had been having about Ronnie Fields seemed to evaporate.

I clambered quickly into bed and sat there shivering, feeling ... I don't know what words to use. Shaken – I think that may describe it best. You see, when Polo Carmody had come into the kitchen earlier and asked Ronnie and me what we were doing, I had had the feeling at the time that the man with the purple eyes had told her to come in and find out. And there they were – the two of them in Theresa Carmody's back garden, looking up at my window.

Then I thought, Don't be silly. They didn't go out there to look up at your window. You went to the window with the light on and they happened to be there, and they naturally enough looked up at the light. But I kept hoping they had not been able to see my undressing, even though I had not done that right in front of the window.

After a couple of minutes, I slipped out of bed again and went back to take another look out. This time with my room in darkness I knew I would not be visible to them. I think I just wanted to reassure myself that they were gone.

But they weren't.

They were standing in the same place, still looking up at my window. And even though I was almost convinced that they couldn't see me, I moved away from the window and got back into bed, telling myself not to think about them but to think about Ronnie.

Why would they still be there, I wondered. I mean, it was dark and cold and quite unpleasant outside. Okay the rain had stopped, but it was not a nice night. Then reason washed in and I thought they must have come out for some air. Or he fancied her (though I couldn't imagine how or why) and had lured her out by turning on the floodlights. Or she fancied him (again I couldn't for the life of me think how she could) and had enticed him out to dance on the patio.

And once they were out there, maybe they couldn't think of anything to say or do and just stood there staring up at our house. Or something like that.

I was glad to hear Mum's footsteps on the stairs, glad we were all safely at home, and wishing Dad back soon as down, down I drifted into the sleeping place where Grammer says dreams come true, where Ronnie Fields walked in the orchard holding my hand, and the Dumpling had two feet and could talk.

But suddenly the trees in the orchard were all lemon trees, and the Dumpling was crying aloud and it was unbearable. I woke. There was no sound, but I knew that if the landing were not carpeted, I would hear her little shuffle as she crossed to Mum's bed.

I felt really disturbed, and started thinking things that I knew I should avoid, because once I thought about them I would not be able to get back to sleep. Why are we born? What is it all for? Grammer says it's an enormous opportunity and it's ours for the taking. Seize the day, she says. She also says that this generation will be known for fornication and reading newspapers. It's a quote from Albert Camus and she says he's dead right. She also said it was the generation that would be known for abandoning basic manners, and that it was an era that would be recalled for the death of chivalry. Waldorf was chivalrous. So was Ronnie Fields.

I was neither a tosser nor a turner in the bed, but that night I lay there after waking, unable to get back to sleep. Eventually, I got up and put on my dressing-gown and slippers. I had no idea what time it was, but I found myself sneaking around my bedroom in the dark, afraid to draw any attention from outside to my room. I could see from the lighting outside, without actually going to the window, that Theresa Carmody's floodlights were still on. I didn't look out – instead, I slipped out of the bedroom door and went downstairs to the kitchen, where I closed the blinds before turning on the light down there. I made hot milk and honey in the microwave and I was going to turn on the radio and put on some music, when Grammer's door opened from her kitchen and she put her head through the door.

'You okay, Plumpet?' she asked.

She looked so nice, not like other people's grandmothers – but like mine. Like the only one I've ever known. She was wearing scarlet Chinese-type satin pyjamas, and purple mules on her feet with little heels, and a lot of fluff on the front, and her face was covered in night-cream. As she always said, she was a slave to her routines – and night-cream was one of them.

'Is Waldorf still there?' I asked.

'Now do you think I'd let him see me looking like a vampire?' she asked. I took her point, because I wouldn't have let anyone see me the way she looked right then. I don't mean the red jammies or the purple mules, but I do mean the thick white face cream. She said that's what kept Doris Day looking so young and if it worked for Doris Day in downtown LA, it would work for Millicent McHarg in Dublin 4. She always said that she wouldn't dream of letting Waldorf stay over, but I'm pretty sure he did. She said that she had to set an example to us girls, but Daffers said it would be a much better example if she admitted that she did let him stay over. She did not say that in front of Grammer, though.

Grammer came into our kitchen and looked around. 'It's cold in here,' she said. 'Come on into my place.'

It was cosy in there because she has an Aga. She

142

made herself a cup of tea and we sat on her sofa, and when I had finished my milk and honey I lay against her and she kept her arm around me.

'Did you ever think of writing a book about Daffers, Dumpling and me?' I asked.

I could feel the smile in her voice as she answered, 'There's time enough when I see how your stories go. When I do write one, it will be one that rocks the core of the planet.'

'Do you think Dad will be home in time for Christmas?' I asked next.

'There are no guarantees,' she said, 'but if I've anything to do with it – then watch this space.'

It was my turn to smile. If I was Dad I would have been afraid not to come home.

'Was he good when he was little?' I asked.

'Now that's another story,' she said. 'I think we'd better get you back to bed.' She said she would come up with me and tuck me up – honestly, she's the best. But I said I would be okay going up by myself.

She kissed me good night.

There was no one on Theresa Carmody's patio when I went up, and the floodlights were off.

And this time I slept soundly.

Chapter Eight

Dumpling's Tale

Daffers put the eggs on the breakfast-table. Break the fast. Fast-breaking soft-boiled eggs. Boiled softly until the clear was white, and the yellow was runny but not raw. Grammer said Polo Carmody was hardboiled.

Mum said, 'Sssshhhh, pas devant les enfants.' Mum had gone to work, 'To tidy up the office,' she said.

'No brooding,' said Grammer to Mum.

'But what if...' said Mum.

'Don't do *what if*,' said Grammer. '*What if* goes nowhere slowly.'

Three girls kissed and Mum was gone. Late start for Mum that day. Three girls gone and Mum was kissed. Mum left in her car. Sound of revving in the front garden. Rrrrrrrrrrrrr-rrrrrrrrrrr. Rrrrrrrrrrrrrrrrrrrrrrrrr.

Grammer said every day, 'She should get that seen to.' Grammer used to drive a car, but she didn't have a licence any more because she drove the car up the neighbour's drive and straight at their front door. Daffers told me that. Daffers said that Grammer did not like the neighbour whose name was Marjorie Whelan. I could recognise every sound on the road outside. Each car. Different noise.

The eggs sat in their little cups on the table. Daffers stood looking at them and rubbing sleep from her eyes.

'I don't know why I should have to get up so early,' she complained.

'Early?' said Grammer. 'Ten o'clock isn't early. Early is when the milkman comes. Early is when the first bird sings.'

'Well, no bird has sung yet today,' said Daffers, correctly.

'That's because it's wet,' said Grammer.

'It's because it's cold and dark and the middle of the night,' said Daffers.

Plumpet winked at me. Me winked by Plumpet. When I winked, both my eyes blinked. I didn't know how Plumpet learned to wink. I practised in front of the mirror, but when I was trying to wink it was difficult to see if I was winking.

'Ten o'clock is almost the middle of the day, Daffers,' said Grammer.

Twelve o'clock was the middle of the day if twelve o'clock was the middle of the night in Grammer's world. Two o'clock to three o'clock was the middle of the night for me.

Daffers scowls. Slwocs. That was the sound of Grammer's hand coming down on the table.

'Don't ... look ... at ... me ... like ... that!' Grammer said.

Down from my chair, and across the floor I pulled myself – much quicker. I turned on the stereo system. The radio came on before I could turn on my music. 'Here is the ten o'clock news. A tidal wave–'

145

Press buttons. Buttons pressed. 'Georgy, Porgy, pudding and pie...'

Grammer laughed. Plumpet came over and hugged Dumpling. Even Daffers smiled. Nursery rhymes were played through the eating of the eggs. Daffers was in pale-blue jammies.

'What's happening today, Grammer?' she asked

'All kinds of things,' Grammer said. She was still in jammies too, even though it was the middle of her day. When she came close to pour my hot chocolate into my cup with D U M P L I N G written on it, I smelled Waldorf.

'Did you sleep, Plumpet?' she asked Plumpet. Plumpet was dressed. The only one of us. All clean and showered and hair washed. Hair loose around her face.

'Slept fine, thank you, Grammer.' Plumpet smiled dreamily into her teacup. Plumpet was thinking of something nice.

Brrrrr. Brrrrr. Phone ringing.

'Me, me,' said Daffers.

Plumpet spun around on her chair.

'I'm answering it,' said Grammer. Her hand reached out and picked up the phone. 'Helllllllooo. Millicent McHarg here,' said Grammer in a booming voice, sounding like she was talking all the way to the North Pole, as Daffers said.

'George? You get home here this instant.' Grammer put a hand over the mouthpiece. 'Girls, go upstairs and get dressed.'

Plumpet and Daffers looked at each other. Daffers opened her mouth to argue. Grammer said that Daffers's mouth was a cupid's bow. Grammer uses wonderful words – each word

146

with a different meaning. Plumpet picked me up, turned off my nursery rhymes and said, 'C' mon, Daffers.'

Grammer eyed us grimly. The grim eye. Down the phone line.

Daffers left the door open.

'I don't care if hell freezes over, George,' said Grammer. Hell was hot. Fiery red and yellow, like a barbecue. A place for devils. George was Dad. Never seen. Ever unseen. 'If you managed to get a plane out there yesterday, you can get a plane back here today... I don't care if you went there by helicopter. Then come here by one too.'

Pause on the stairs. Plumpet, Daffers and me. Six ears straining towards Grammer' s voice.

'DO YOU WANT ME TO COME AND GET YOU?'

Daffers looked at Plumpet. Plumpet looked at Daffers. Both made a wide-eyed face, pulled down the corners of their mouths. Both looked the same. Both looks were the same.

'Haaaaaaaaaaaah!' said Grammer.

Plumpet nearly dropped me. I held on tight.

'It's okay, Dumpling,' Daffers said.

This surprised Plumpet and me too.

Up the stairs we went. Daffers and me to get up and dressed. Plumpet washed my face with a pale-blue facecloth. She called it baby-blue. She was wearing her baby-blue hoodie and white trousers. Plumpet washed my hands with soap and water. Dried carefully between my fingers.

'Nice clean tights,' said Plumpet. She had put me sitting in the armchair in my room. She had forgotten to clean my teeth. And Grammer would check. Grammer said your gnashers were your best friends. I waited until she turned to show me the clothes she was taking from my wardrobe, then I opened my mouth and I made a big smile with my teeth together.

'We never cleaned your tootles,' said Plumpet. Grammer said gnashers. Plumpet said tootles. Daffers had just learned the word incisors. 'Off to clean my incisors,' she said, and Mum grimaced. Mum played bridge on Tuesday nights. No grim aces then. Four aces. Black red red black. Hearts are nicest. All red and loving. Inside Plumpet there was a smiling heart with beating pulse. Pulsing beat. So neat. So sweet. I wondered if Ronnie Fields was awake.

'WOOF. WOOF.'

Plumpet and I looked at each other. My tootles were full of toothpaste.

'Here, rinse quickly,' said Plumpet. 'Stay here for a minute, Dumpling.' Where would I have gone just in my tights and vest and knickers?

Plumpet went out of the door and listened on the landing. The sound was like a dog barking.

'What is that?' we heard Grammer saying, still making contact with the North Pole but not using a telephone.

'It's our dog,' said a boy's voice.

'Are you sure? Are you absolutely sure? It looks more like a baby elephant,' shouted Grammer to the North Pole.

Plumpet came running back in to me. 'Dumpling, can you stay here for a moment? I'll be right back. Don't go and do anything,' she said. Plumpet all excitement. Plumpet all panic.

Grammer on full throttle. Plumpet racing to the stairs.

'Is that you, Ronnie?' said Plumpet's voice.

I looked around my room. Lovely yellow. Primrose, said Plumpet. But now it would be more interesting to be on the landing. I scooted across and sat at the top of the stairs. I called there 'the bus'. Sitting on the bus I could hear but not see the elephant.

Woof. Woof. Woof.

'Oh,' said Plumpet, 'he's gorgeous. Ooooh. Oooh. Aaaaaaaaaaaaagh.'

'Oh, I'm so sorry,' said Boy Voice. Ronnie Fields was a-visiting. Dropping in his calling card as Grammer would say. 'Down, boy. Down! I'm so sorry. Are you all right, Plumpet?'

I peeped out of the windows upstairs on the bus, through the banisters and what did I see but Plumpet in her baby-blue fleece lying on her back. Small elephant was licking her face.

'Is this a circus act?' asked Grammer loudly enough to waken the hibernating polar bears.

'Sorry, Mrs McHarg,' said Ronnie Fields. Grammer always said first impressions were vital. I hoped he made a better first impression yesterday.

'For God's sake,' said Grammer. 'Take that animal back to the zoo, and next time bring a bunch of flowers.'

Daffers was beside me on the bus, her big blue eyes peeping out of the window. Daffers was shaking. I looked to see. Daffers was laughing.

Oh dear. This did not look good. Plumpet was like a pale-blue beetle on her back, white legs in the air. Elephant was refusing to let go. Ronnie Fields, big enough to be on a rugby team, was trying to pull the elephant off. Grammer was standing in red silk Chinese pyjamas with angry blue dragons embroidered with golden eyes, and purple fluff balls on her feet. The dragons were furious.

'Grammer,' squealed Plumpet. 'Please...'

I was unclear whether this was a plea for assistance or for Grammer to stop teasing Ronnie Fields. Because Grammer was teasing but Ronnie Fields did not know this.

'What is his name?' asked Grammer.

'He's Ronnie Fields,' said Plumpet, misunderstanding as she was being licked to death. 'You met him yesterday,' she continued.

'I mean the animal,' said Grammer in a very distinct voice, as Plumpet struggled to find her feet.

The Mahout pulled his elephant off my Plumpet and said, 'WC.'

'WC?' said Grammer in disbelief, or so it sounded at the top of the bus.

'After W.C. Fields,' said the Mahout.

Plumpet stood up all pale blue with a very pink face and her neatly brushed hair all every which way. The elephant reared enthusiastically on hind legs. He had fallen for Plumpet.

Grammer still had the phone in her hand and she now said into it, 'Goodness, George, you'd better get home at once.'

Only one side of the conversation was audible to Dumpling's ears.

'Of course you can.'

'Don't be ridiculous.'

'An elephant called Water Closet.'

'No, of course we haven't got an elephant.'

'What do you mean, you wouldn't put it past me?'

'No, Plumpet's new friend has one.'

'Oh, just come home and make everyone's Christmas and see for yourself.'

Plumpet, the Mahout and the elephant were all looking at each other with affection. I tapped on the window of my bus with tiny silver nails. Plumpet remembered me.

'Oh, my darling Dumpling,' she called. 'I'm coming. Ronnie, come into the sitting room...'

'You can't take that animal in there,' Grammer said. 'Unless you promise to break the clock on the mantelpiece.'

'I'll go back home,' the Mahout said. 'I'll be next door. Come in when you're ready, Plumpet.'

'I'll bring the Dumpling,' Plumpet said. She loved her Dumpling. She dumpled her loving. Thumb in mouth I waited.

Grammer went back to the kitchen with the phone in her hand calling to Southeast Asia via the North Pole.

'Since the day your father died,' she shouted so that the polar bears at the North Pole could hear – they must have shivered in the snow in terror – 'I have never taken no for an answer, and I'm not starting now.'

I was dressed in clean white tights, and a denim pinafore with pink sweatshirt. Plumpet said powder pink. 'Where's your jacket?' she asked me. She tidied my cot while I got my shoes, which she had forgotten. Plumpet's mind was somewhere else.

I looked in my wardrobe for my red leather shoes which Grammer put in there last night. In among my secrets. Shoe boxes neatly at the back. So back and neat. Such secrets. In my boxes. I sat on the floor for Plumpet to buckle my shoes. *One two, buckle my shoe* – shuckle my boo, one and two.

'And up you come,' said Plumpet as she lifted her Dumpling to sit on her hip.

I pointed to the stairs and we went that way. Down, down, down to the hall where the lime-green waterproof jacket with the Eskimo fur around the hood was hanging. Grammer said bright colours were good, especially on an island that was engulfed in water. And when Grammer said that, she said she was not talking about the sea.

Plumpet said that you should not say Eskimo, that the word was 'Inuit'. Grammer said Eskimo-Inuit-Inuit-Eskimo, who cared? Plumpet said that the Inuit cared.

Lime-green jacket zipped on Dumpling, Plumpet zipped in snow-white jacket. 'Goodbye, Grammer,' called Plumpet. 'Dumpling is with me, back soon.'

The Mahout and the elephant were waiting – porch door open – in the house next door. Their front door was open too. The elephant was basking in the damp porch with condensation on the windows. Drip drip went the water on the window. Drip drip slobbered the elephant.

'It is hectic inside,' said Ronnie Fields by way of greeting.

A head appeared around the front door.

'Well, hello,' said Ronald Fields, muscles bursting beneath his T-shirt and a smile breaking his face in two. 'Maureen,' he called. 'We have visitors.'

The Butterfly appeared. 'Girls, come in, come in.'

'You must be up to your eyes,' said my Plumpet politely. 'We won't disturb you.'

'Come in, come in, we're delighted to stop for ten minutes.'

Note that, Plumpet. We may go in for ten minutes. Tick tock. Tick tock.

'We've been up since six.'

'Exhausted.'

'But excited.'

'Want it nice for Christmas.'

'Do you drink coffee? Dumpling, would you like a glass of milk?'

'Dumpling can't drink ordinary milk,' said Plumpet. 'Dairy intolerance, you know.' She was very grown-up, minding her Dumpling.

Intolerant cows kicked Dumpling's tiny tum. Soy for Dumpling. Goat for Dumpling. Nothing that moos.

There were boxes everywhere. Piled up. Piled high. The house was plied with boxes.

The Butterfly took me from my Plumpet. Plumpet smiled at her Mahout. The elephant flopped on top of a very large cushion. His head and front paws were on the hill of it, his body sloping down on to the hard kitchen floor. He

153

snored. Like Grammer in front of the television.

I pointed my finger at the elephant.

'Would you like to sit beside him?' asked the Butterfly. She was wearing a grey jogging suit. Plumpet would say silver-grey. The Butterfly flitted with Dumpling to the snoring elephant, and crouching she put me beside his hot body. I could feel his heart beat. He opened one enormous black eye and looked at a possible dinner. Then he wagged his tail. Tailing his wag it thumped on the floor – one, two, then snore. For a moment I thought that he might see me as his next meal, but his heartbeat was regular, and I smiled.

'Oh, you smile so sweetly,' said the Butterfly. 'Ronald, look at how her little face lights up. So gorgeous.'

'Let's get that warm anorak off you,' said Ronald with his muscling bulges. Unzip, slip off, large chocolate chip cookie put into Dumpling's hand.

Chomp.

The elephant had eaten it and was snoring again before I could blink.

The hot wafty smell of coffee circled the room as the Butterfly flitted around her kitchen, twirling in silver-grey almost on tippy toe. She made me want to point my feet. I watched as she moved like a ballerina. Ronald Fields watched too.

'Will we get it all done?' asked the Butterfly.

'We will,' he said. 'We'll have the Christmas tree up by tomorrow and we'll be so settled in that Dumpling will think we've always lived here.'

In came Daffers's double. When Dolly the sheep was cloned, her offspring sprung off the same sex. Plumpet told me that. Daffers's clone was male. He had a mop of blond uncombed hair and an it's-not-fair face. Grammer would have said, indeed would say, 'He's of an age. Give him space. Give him time – there may yet be hope.'

Garrrrumphwarrrrumph. So he seemed to say. I didn't know what this meant, but the Butterfly did.

She said, 'Yes, darling. I'm just making coffee now.'

The elephant beat his enormous tail on the lino-covered kitchen floor. Thwack. Thwack. Thwack.

'Where's my favourite WC?' said the mop-head clone with quantities of affection in his voice. This Dumpling was well surprised. 'Christ Almighty,' said the mop-head. 'Who the hell is this?'

'Darling, language,' said the Butterfly. It sounded like a gentle rebuke, the kind a colourful butterfly might make when it saw a bee landing on the flower it was going to sit on. 'This is Dumpling. She lives next door. She's our new neighbour.'

'My God,' said the mop-head. 'Isn't she a bit young to be living in that house all by herself?' Chuckle. Chuckle. Chuckle. This was mop-head wit.

The Butterfly did not follow his thought-pattern and said with maternal seriousness, 'Darling, say hello to Dumpling. Of course she

155

doesn't live by herself. She has two sisters and all kinds of other people.'

I knew that the Butterfly was thinking of Grammer and Waldorf and suddenly wondering who else might be living in the house and the apartment next door.

'She's Millicent McHarg's granddaughter. Aren't you, Dumpling?'

I nodded and smiled at the mop-head carefully. It was a difficult age. Hormonally active but under repression by society, Grammer said. It was unclear what Grammer meant, but she was usually right.

'Who's Millicent McHarg when she's at home?' asked the mop-head.

'Darling,' said the Butterfly, 'she's the novelist. You know. *The* Millicent McHarg.'

Darling Mop-head leaned down to rub the large tummy of the elephant whose tail was still thwacking on the floor. 'Who's a lovely big boy, then?' he said, forgetting about novels and novelists.

His face was close to mine. He looked into my eyes. 'Do you like WC?' he asked.

The Dumpling nodded.

'How long have you lived here?' he asked.

I felt the kitchen was very quiet. The Butterfly was listening. Ronald was the detective. He listened too. I looked at the mop-head and I stuck out one finger on one hand, and then I stuck out another finger and bent it over in half.

'A year and a half?' he asked.

The Dumpling nodded. It was more than a year and a half but it was difficult to show a year and

156

three-quarters with my fingers.

'Don't you talk?' he asked.

The Dumpling shook her head.

'No rush,' said Ronald, the detective.

'Girls say too much anyway,' said the mop-head.

The Dumpling laughed. My laugh. Inside my head. Big smile on my face. There was a sigh in the kitchen. The coffee machine started to bubble and frubble. The steam burst out. Cups clattered on to the table and Plumpet and the Mahout came in.

'So, is our house like yours?' asked the Detective.

'In some ways,' Plumpet said.

'Except theirs isn't full of boxes,' said the Mahout.

My wardrobe was. All my boxes. Full of secrets. No one knew what was in my boxes. Except me.

In the afternoon – after the middle of Grammer's day, she put me in my buggy. A buggied-Dumpling. Usually Grammer made me walk. She said it was good for me. But on that day to conserve both her and my energy she took me into town in the buggy on the bus. The buggy folded quite neatly down into a flattish umbrella-like shape. It was white with red hearts on it. Daffers said it would be totally unsuitable for a boy. But I was not a boy. I'm a little girl. Such a pearl.

Grammer said little girls should make as much noise as possible, but not when she was minding them.

I stood beside Grammer while she was dismantling the buggy. She lifted me and the buggy on to the bus, waved her pensioner's pass at the bus driver and then she ensconced me on her knee on a seat. Ensconce is a Grammer word. It might be difficult to say out loud. When you're little.

The bus was good for serious contact with the proletariat, said Grammer. She chatted to everyone. They were her fans. She said they were fantastic. Fanstastic.

We had to go on an escalator up and up when we got into town. It said on the front of the escalator that buggies and wheelchairs were not allowed, but as Grammer was a law unto herself I found myself virtually horizontal in the buggy as we ascended smoothly with my face looking up at the ceiling. I held Pink Pig by the tail, and Grammer said not to drop him because he would become bacterially infected from touching the ground where the underside of people's shoes had walked. Pink Pig had a curly tail and he was squishy with blue button eyes. Plumpet said that he was as sacred to me as the cow was sacred in India. Daffers sometimes hid him. Once she put him in the toilet, but unfortunately for her Grammer found him. He washed up well and came out from the washing machine and tumble-dryer smelling of roses – that was what Grammer said. Actually he smelt of spring fragrance conditioner. Now when she washed him, she put him in a pillowcase so that his little hard nose did not get caught on the rim near the door of the machine. Once it got caught, and he went round and round, but his nose didn't. His nose stayed in the rim near the door. I was sitting on my little red chair in front of the door watching him. When Grammer took him out, she said, 'Oh, no.' She kept saying *oh no* while she pulled and pushed him back into shape. His nose was so wriggly it looked more piggy than his tail. Then she said he would have to be washed all over again. And dried. And that it could take a day or more for that to work properly. When I got him back two days later he looked completely better. No one would ever have known that he had had a nose job. In fact he looked completely new – even the missing stitch on his tail was fixed. He was a clone of my first pink pig. Different but the same. Like Dolly the sheep's baby clone. The same. But with weak kidneys. Weak bits. Pink pig was the first perfect clone. No weaknesses. Re-strengthened. Pink Pig's blue eyes looked like Daffers's eyes, except he didn't roll them round and round like she did, nor did he turn one in slowly and then out again while Grammer or Mum said, 'Daphne, stop that this minute.'

When I lay back in my buggy I always thought of aeroplanes. Plumpet said that aeroplanes are one of man's ways of defying gravity. Grammer said they are the quickest way to get from A to B especially if you lived on an island engulfed in water. You need papers to travel from watery places to other places. I had papers.

Dumpling papers. Bought with money, in a place far away.

Grammer tried on hats in a shop. None were as

nice as her felt hat with the feathers. She tried hats on me too and said, 'Dumpling, you're blessed with a face that will always look wonderful in hats. Fur, frills, lace, calico – a born hat beauty.' She checked her watch. Time to go. Time for her meeting.

The doorman took my buggy – *whish* and it was gone. Doors were opened and Grammer and Dumpling entered the hotel. Chandeliers hung from the ceiling. Smell of polish and the pine of Christmas tree. Gold baubles. Red bows. Tiny twinkling lights. People turned to look. Fanstastic.

Grammer held my hand. 'No rush, Dumpling,' she said as we walked down the lobby.

'Millicent, Millicent. How wonderful you look.' And there they were. Her publishers. Her agent. Travelled in from across the water to our island. And – surprise – Purple Eyes. His lips pulled into a smile. His eyes ... his eyes, they did not smile. Behind the purple was something else...

I could not see behind the purple.

On the mezzanine, there were chairs and tables all arranged. Grammer would have Scotch with soda. 'Better keep it watered down,' said Grammer. 'I have a bus journey home with my granddaughter.'

'Take a taxi. Take a taxi. Don't water anything down. It's Christmas time. It's a great day. Your forty-ninth novel. We are delighted. Delighted.'

Everything was repeated. Not once. Not twice. But more and with joy. And success. Grammer produced the goods. And the goods were very good indeed, as her publisher said.

I watched Purple Eyes's shoes. His name was

Gervaise. Gervaise Holt. His shoes had buttoned-down socks over them. White on black leather. Later Grammer said to Mum, 'Spats. Would you believe it, in this day and age? Spats.'

His mouth was thin. But he had fat lips. The smile did not come easily to him. Grammer's feather had a hatpin. A lethal weapon. At the ready. Not ready enough.

'I'm part of the US team now,' said Purple Eyes.

'Good,' said Grammer.

Not so good. God was good with only one 'o'.

I had orange juice and crisps. The orange juice had a cherry, a slice of orange and an umbrella in it. Around the rim of the glass were tiny sugar crystals. The crisps came in a cut-glass bowl. I held the umbrella over them in case it rained on them. Then I held it over Pink Pig and he and I ate the crisps.

Grammer drank whisky, and everyone laughed with her. Her stories twisted and turned, but the others listened and followed them with care. Inside my head I told Pink Pig a story about a little girl who had a primrose bedroom and a farm where her piggy lived. In her wardrobe she had boxes of exciting things that she had collected. I had boxes in my wardrobe but they were full of secrets that only I could see. Each box had a different memory. When I opened one of the boxes, the words danced like musical notes in the air, and I could read them and listen to them.

Not too often. Better to keep the boxes closed in case their secrets escaped.

Chapter Nine

Millicent's Tale

I took the Dumpling with me for the meeting with my publishers. I thought it would do her good – lots of lights and atmosphere in the city, and the hotel was at its best, as good hotels are when they're preparing for Christmas. Their Christmas tree was up in the lobby and the fire was burning brightly. There was lots of bustle.

That peculiar man Gervaise Holt was there. He had joined the team, and had invited me back to New York – this time when he's there. Last time I went, I think it must have been before I met Waldorf, Christian Holt, Gervaise's brother was staying there. We painted Manhattan every night, Christian and I.

Not having any siblings myself, I was always fascinated at how different they could be. I saw it in my granddaughters, and it was certainly there in Christian and Gervaise. Difference, I mean.

Christian must have been Maria's age, or thereabouts, and he was just an easygoing, relaxed man – good-looking, I should add, and fun to be with. But Gervaise was a different kettle of fish altogether. I felt when he had finished a sentence that either I had not been listening or that I had missed the point. I suppose I just didn't relate to him. Like Christian, he was a

162

well-built man, but the similarity ended there. In his face there was something too lived in, as if he had been around the block – and not just once.

There was great bonhomie among the crowd over from the publishers. Well, fair enough, I'd made them a mint. Just as they had made me a mint. But all the time while we were drinking and chatting, I felt that Gervaise Holt was watching. And I was not even sure whom he was watching.

'Fiddle dee dee, Gervaise,' I said. 'Do you never laugh?' This was after a particularly good joke to do with a pair of knickers and a bottle of champagne; the content of the joke escapes me now, but it was so funny that three of us had to wipe the tears from our eyes.

Not Gervaise though.

Dumpling was sitting in a rather plush armchair with a cucumber sandwich which she was studiously ignoring, and a bowl of crisps, which she most definitely was not, and she was smiling – but I assumed at the sandwich or her pink pig or something else, as she would hardly have got the joke.

Gervaise looked up at me. 'I enjoy a joke, Millicent,' he said. 'But I seldom laugh aloud.'

Your loss, you smooth pompous bastard, I thought. I was about to say that my friends call me Millie, when I suddenly realised that I would not want to include him in that category. As the party started to break up, because they were all heading back to the airport, including Jasper, my agent, Gervaise asked where I was going. Until that moment I had been planning on going straight home with the Dumpling, but the insinuating way he enquired seemed to imply that he was going to come with me wherever I was heading, so I said, 'I'm off to visit my mother.'

This brought a certain amount of surprise from everyone. I couldn't think why.

'Where is she?' asked Jasper after what I can only describe as a stunned silence.

'In a nursing home,' I said. 'A very good one, thanks to all of you.' I waved happily at the latest contract, which I had just signed.

'Is she all right?' Jasper asked. I got the feeling he didn't really know what to say. I couldn't think why. Everyone was entitled to have a mother.

'She's fine – for someone in her late nineties,' I said. And that was true. 'Not what you'd call mobile,' I added, 'but her quality of life is as good as can be expected.' I don't know what I sounded like. Spokeswoman for the Anti-Euthanasia Society, probably.

'Are you here for Christmas, Gervaise?' Jasper asked him. 'Or are you going back to the Big Apple?'

'I'm staying around,' he said.

I wondered where but I did not ask, as I didn't want him to think I was remotely interested. But he had all the makings of a character in one of my novels – and I'm not talking a hero.

The Dumpling and I left them all on the steps of the hotel. There was a lot of hand-shaking and Christmas greetings, and messages of affection being sent by me to people in their offices, together with promises of future meetings early in the New Year. The taxi driver put the Dumpling's buggy in his boot, and I settled on the back seat with the child beside me, her little hand holding on tightly to mine.

We took the taxi straight to the nursing home. I had been planning on going the following day anyway, so a day early made no difference. My mother might or might not recognise me, and she certainly wouldn't know what day it was.

I got the taxi to wait as the staff at the nursing home were always busy, and hanging around in reception for a taxi to come back was not an agreeable prospect.

'Mother,' I said, leaning to kiss my elderly parent who was sitting in a wheelchair in front of the window.

'Where have you been, Millicent?' she demanded. Her voice was surprisingly strong for one so frail.

'I had to go into town,' I said. 'A publishers' meeting.' I was unsure if that would mean anything to her this time.

It did.

'Well, did you get the new contract?' she asked.

'I did indeed,' I replied. It was a bit like fishing in the dark for a while to find out what wavelength she was on.

'Lawyers? Did you have legal representation?'

I reassured her that my agent was there.

'New terminology,' she said grumpily. 'Always new terminology. So, have they found the body?'

We were now in old territory. She was presumably talking about Dirk's body. I thought of telling her that his body had finally been found, but it might have opened up a whole new series of enquiries, so I stuck to the truth.

'No, no sign of the body yet,' I admitted. And forty-odd years on I didn't think there would be.

'Much better,' she said. 'Much better. Less chance that they will connect you with the murder. This DNA business could mean that they would find your fingerprints all over him.'

Oh dear. She was back to thinking that I had murdered Dirk. On an aeroplane in the South Seas. Not very likely, but it was one of her many trains of thought, or should I say planes of thought.

'And who have you brought with you today?' she asked, peering at the Dumpling who was sitting in her buggy clutching her furry pink pig.

'It's Dumpling,' I said. 'Do you remember Dumpling?'

'We never get any of those in here,' said my aged parent, pulling her rug closer over her knees.

Dumpling looked at me. I looked at Dumpling. Dumpling waved her pig at her great-grandmother.

'Roast beef,' said my mother. 'Never a Yorkshire pud. Never a decent potato. Mind your teeth,' she added to me. She has always had a thing about teeth. 'Clean them before you go to bed, when you get up in the morning, and before using contraception. And don't tell me you don't use contraception. At your age you should know better.'

I could see this was going to be a cheery half-hour.

'Did I ever tell you about the night your father

166

and I conceived you?' she asked.

Oh, great. New territory. Any curiosity I might once have felt about my conception was gone, and anyway her facts were mixed with fantasy, illusion, and the novels she had read – some of which I had written.

'In a coffin,' she said firmly. 'That's where I conceived you, on the night your father died.'

This bit of misinformation was being shared with another three elderly people, and their guests. I hoped they couldn't hear. My mother's ability to embarrass me had, I thought, reached a peak when I was seventeen.

Wrong.

Thank goodness it was the Dumpling, and not Daffers or Plumpet who was with me.

'Holy Jerusalem,' said my mother suddenly, and very distinctly. 'Don't tell me you forgot your contraception.' She was eyeing the Dumpling as if she was only just seeing her for the first time. 'Vinegar and a sponge – it's the only way. And don't tell me I didn't give you good advice. A mother's work is never done. Never. Who is that child?' she asked.

'It's Dumpling,' I tried again.

'None of that in here,' my mother said. 'I haven't seen a Yorkshire pudding in ... I don't know how long. Why, I'd give my eyeteeth for a Yorkshire pudding.'

You did, Mother, you did, I thought. It was true, she had. Well, one eyetooth, not both. A mere accident. I had made Yorkshire puddings one winter's night, and invited both my parents to dinner – long ago, in the Dirk days, before

George was born. My wedding ring came off my finger during the preparation – obviously an accident, but my mother seemed to think I had deliberately placed it in her Yorkshire pudding. I paid for the loss of that tooth for many a day. I had thought she had forgotten, but old age does stir up the oddest things, and I could only hope she would not dig that one out now. Not that I minded for me, but I did for her. I try, each time when I depart, to leave her on the best of terms. Or at least, the best possible terms.

'Who are you?' she suddenly said, looking at me in amazement. 'You look very like my daughter. Her name was Millicent. I've no idea what happened to her.'

I thought of saying, 'I am Millicent,' but what was the point? She only perceived things in a particular way at a particular time.

'What was she like?' I asked, instantly regretting the question as I suspected the response might be entertaining for the other occupants of the room, but might not be so cheering for me.

'A lovely child,' she said, smiling at the Dumpling.

I didn't know whether she was referring to me in my childhood, or to the Dumpling sitting there in her buggy with her dark eyelashes flickering on her little cheeks. It seemed a good note to depart on. She appeared to be asleep when I leaned over to kiss her. Her forehead was parchment dry, her skin thin and almost translucent. The bones of her face were outlined like a death mask. I touched her hand.

'Goodbye,' I whispered.

Dumpling waved her pink pig as I turned the buggy and headed for the door.

Maria was at home when we got back.

'Waldorf was looking for you,' she said.

Good, I thought. I could do with a bit of cheering up. 'What did he say?' I asked.

'Oh, just wanted to know if any of us had seen his yo-yo,' Maria said.

We both smiled.

'George called,' I said. 'I didn't leave you a note. I preferred to tell you myself.'

She didn't say anything. I could see the hurt in her face. And I couldn't make any promises, even though I felt sure he would make it home for Christmas. Well, I felt that at the very least he would try.

'He sounded well,' I continued. 'He's doing his best to get home.'

She nodded. 'We lunched out at the office,' she said. 'It's great to be done and finished for the next ten days.'

'I think we should have a drinks party tomorrow evening,' I said. 'Just a couple of hours. Neighbours, friends, a quick phone around and see who we can muster. What do you think?'

I knew that Maria knew I was just trying to fill in the time until Christmas Day – and that if I was confident that George would make it home I wouldn't be talking about a party.

'That'd be fine,' she said. She's great that way. She's pragmatic and strong when she has to be. She really knows when to make the best of a situation.

'We'll defrost things from the freezer, and there is enough booze in the house to keep Napoleon's army going for a month.' What more do you need for a party?

Plumpet appeared with her new friend Ronnie Fields. Thank God they had abandoned his elephant somewhere else – possibly in a Big Top where it would be best suited.

'Mum,' said Plumpet, all beaming with happiness, 'this is Ronnie Fields who has just moved in next door.'

I left them to it while I went to my own apartment to contact Waldorf, and to ring around about the party. At my connecting door through the kitchen I looked back. The image is etched in my mind – Maria helping the Dumpling up on to a chair at the table where paper and colouring pencils were laid out. Ronnie Fields was standing watching, and Plumpet, usually so calm, with this big smile on her face as she talked to her mother. She had her hair loose, and it was very soft around her face, and her green eyes were sparkling. It was just one moment, and then I was through the door, but for some reason it was the one moment I could clearly remember later: Plumpet looking so happy.

We set up the party in record time. Plumpet and Daffers asked the neighbours, and Maria and I each phoned half a dozen people. Everyone seemed to be delighted, as Christmas Eve can be very dull. We made it for early that evening: 'Come between six and seven,' we said. Some of the people had children, and they would have

170

wanted to get them to bed at a reasonable time, and who wanted to be flattened on Christmas Day anyway? A couple of hours was plenty, and it would keep Maria occupied.

As it turned out, at twenty to seven, just when everyone was there, from Samson and Delilah and the pithy Daisy, to the new neighbours and a dozen others, including a few old friends from the past, who should arrive but George! The girls fell over each other trying to leap into his arms. Plumpet clutching his right arm, Daffers jumping up and down in front of him like a Jack-in-the-box, or should I be politically correct and say Jill-in-the-box? Or is that sort of political correctness out of the window nowadays? Who knows? Anyway, there was Maria with a half-smile on her face.

'Gosh,' said Waldorf. 'Who needs my *Beano* anyway?'

'Why didn't you phone?' Maria said. But not crossly, just puzzled. 'I'd have come to the airport.'

'I was afraid something might go wrong again,' he said. 'Wouldn't want to let you down twice in forty-eight hours.'

He looked much the same. Tanned. A bit crumpled, but then he had been travelling for over twenty hours at that stage. When he managed to detach Plumpet, and sidestep Daffers, he hugged Maria until she squealed.

'Can't breathe,' she said.

'Good,' was the reply.

'Gosh,' said Waldorf. 'Has anyone seen my yo-yo?'

'Has anyone seen the Dumpling?' asked Plumpet.

Not a sign of the darling.

She emerged in due course when the sausage rolls were brought in. There must be a hideaway inside the sofa because I know we looked behind it in our search for her. When she came out, she sat on the floor and looked at George. Just stared and stared. As if she had never seen him before.

But it had been a whole year, I suppose.

'Is it my little Dumpling?' he asked. 'The tiniest McHarg of all.'

He knelt down on the ground in front of her and held out his arms to her. I've never seen her move so fast. Up and into them she was in less than two seconds. People who had been milling around moved back to watch.

The Dumpling has a number of expressions – they are smiling, tearful, impassive, sleepy ... I think that covers them all. But now she had a totally new look on her face. I think it was wonderment.

When they stopped hugging she touched his chin, running her tiny fingertips over his stubble – presumably he hadn't shaved in the last two days. Then she ran her fingers over his forehead – I must say he has a good forehead. He got that from my side of the family, a nice high smooth forehead, with a slightly receding hairline. Very attractive on a man. The Dumpling touched every square millimetre of it, peering slightly at the tiny birthmark on his temple. His father had one in exactly the same place. Some genetic flaw on the McHarg side, I suppose. Anyway the

Dumpling checked the outline of his ears, ran a finger over his nose. And then she kissed him. And that was that.

Dumpling refused point blank to let him go. In due course he tried to detach himself from her, but she simply sat on one of his shoes and held on to his leg, with both arms and legs wrapped around him. He discovered he could walk like that which brought a lot of laughter, including from the Dumpling. But he picked her up then, and she sat in close straddling his hip, and she stroked his face all the time.

Plumpet was circulating with both Ronnie, whose mother Maureen seemed to call 'wee Ronnie', and a tray of canapés. Wee was a most inappropriate adjective for the lad. Daffers in the meantime had met this extraordinary-looking boy who had an absolute mop of untidy blond hair and who, in due course, was introduced to me as yet another new neighbour. We now had Ronald and Maureen, a detective and a ballet-teacher, wee Ronnie who was six foot if he was an inch, an elephant called WC whom they were trying to pass off as a dog, and a boy disguised as a blond mop called Raleigh.

'Raleigh?' I repeated, just to be sure I'd got it right.

'Like Walter,' he said. Daffers looked puzzled, which was hardly surprising. That girl reads nothing and pays no attention to anything unless it's to do with the earth's crust, or crusts on the table.

'Who's Walter?' she asked.

173

'A blighter with a cloak and a sack of potatoes,' Waldorf said obligingly. His sprig of holly in his buttonhole looked very fresh – I do like his attention to detail. I knew that if George had not been there, he would have had the Dumpling like a limpet fiddling with the holly, and pretending to nibble the berries, just to get him all worried. She loves the way he says, 'Oh, Dumpling, m'dearest, don't.' Always makes her laugh. Not out loud of course.

Theresa Carmody came over, all black flowing dress with a black and silver boa. 'Millie, Millie.' She was sparkling, as if someone had just put a new light bulb in her. 'You have to meet Tony.'

One look at Tony and I saw who had just put a new bulb in her. Theresa Carmody goes for the oddest people. Give them the whisper of a limp wrist and she's in there. It's as if she feels she can give them a particular exercise to do to strengthen their wrist. It's called 'bring-me-to-orgasm-with-your-fingertips'. She had that glow off her this evening, and Tony Fonzetti – I think that was his name – stuck out his hand on the same limp wrist to shake mine.

'Delighted,' he said.

His trousers were too short – not on the leg length, but at the waist. They sort of came to halfway up his hips, and were far too tight, so tight in fact that you could make out the outline of everything he had tucked into them. And he was wearing a white shirt through which I could see his body hair, all over his chest and down and down. Very thick and dark. Some of it was sticking through gaps between the buttons.

Extraordinary. His face was smooth-shaven and the hair on his head was slightly too long.

I couldn't keep my eyes off his chest, and lower down too, although I tried to look elsewhere. He glanced down to see what was attracting my attention.

'Aaargh!' he went, and appeared to nearly jump out of his skin.

'Darling, what is it?' said Theresa Carmody.

I've always suspected she is very short-sighted, and this certainly proved it. Like me, he too stared at his white shirt with a look of total horror on his face. 'God, what is it?' he said. He seemed frozen and just stood there saying, 'God, what is it?' over and over.

'What is what?' asked Theresa Carmody.

By this stage I realised that there really was something amiss. I mean, only a gorilla would have gone around with a chest and body of hair like that pouring out between his buttonholes.

'Something you fed him, Theresa?' I asked.

'What are you talking about?' Theresa said, peering at Tony Fonzetti.

With shaking fingers he opened a couple of the buttons on his shirt and more of the hair fell out.

By now Theresa could see that there was something odd going on, and she reached out towards the hair, saying, 'What on earth? My goodness,' she said, pulling what appeared to be the best part of a wig out of his shirt. 'My hairpiece – I couldn't find it earlier. What on earth is it doing there?'

I must say, Tony Fonzetti looked an awful lot better without that tucked in behind his white shirt, but he did seem awfully embarrassed. Everyone was laughing, and Theresa was delighted – not so much about her hairpiece being public knowledge, but about the fact that Tony having it inside his shirt seemed to hint at some strange intimacy. Personally, I think he had stuck it on his chest to see what it would look like, and then forgotten to remove it.

Daphne and Raleigh were laughing so hard that I had to tell them to stop. Daphne looked like she was going to wet herself, doubled over with her knees tightly together.

'Anyway, Millie darling,' said Theresa Carmody as she kissed the hairpiece and stuffed it into her handbag, 'I wanted to ask you if one of the girls wouldn't mind letting Cat in later and topping up his bowl if it's empty. Tony and I are spending the night in a hotel – just for fun, and for room service on Christmas morning. I should be back tomorrow night. But if I'm not, would they mind awfully ... you know, just letting Cat in and out until I reappear?'

Daphne, who had been hanging around shrieking with laughter, suddenly disappeared, and it was Plumpet I addressed, asking her if she wouldn't mind helping Theresa out. Theresa gave her a key.

'Help yourself to anything you want,' she said to Plumpet. 'There's food in the fridge, and drinks and things. There are also some choccies open in a box in the dining room. I've left the lights on – so just enjoy yourself in there. Cat will sit on the back patio until you let him in. And will you let him out in the morning? Anytime that 'suits you.'

'I'll go with her,' said Ronnie Fields. I watched him. He wasn't proprietorial – it wasn't that. It was something else. A funny confidence beyond his years.

Plumpet smiled at him.

'Well,' said Theresa. 'Just be sure to make yourselves at home.'

And off she went with Tony Fonzetti and his smooth chest to enjoy room service in some hotel.

The party was still going strong when I heard Plumpet saying to Maria that she and Ronnie Fields were going in next door to look after Cat, and then they'd take WC for a walk. Or maybe the other way around. I may not have been listening properly, or they may have been vague.

'Will you be late?' Maria asked.

'Not really, Mum,' Plumpet said.

'I'll bring her straight back as soon as we've done the rounds,' said Ronnie.

'Well, if we've gone to bed,' Maria said, 'be sure to put your head around the door so that I know you're home.'

George came over with the Dumpling still attached to him. 'I've a little coming home present for you,' he said to Plumpet.

'Dad,' I heard her say, 'shouldn't you keep it until tomorrow?'

'No,' he said, fishing in his pocket. 'This is for today.' He took out three little packages each tied with a different coloured ribbon. The one with the green ribbon he gave to Plumpet.

'And I'm to open it today?' she asked.

He kissed her forehead and said yes. The Dumpling took the opportunity to kiss his cheek while he was leaning down to Plumpet.

'I've a present for you too, Dumpling,' he said to her. 'I'm going to give it to you when I take you up to bed.'

'If Dad gives you a present, Dumpling,' Maria said, 'will you sleep in your own bed tonight?'

The Dumpling nodded.

Plumpet meantime had opened her tiny package and inside was a ring – with a green stone to match her eyes.

'It's lovely,' she said. Her eyes were shiny and sparkling. She put it on the middle finger of her left hand and stood there looking at it with her arm and hand outstretched in front of her. Then she thanked him, kissed him and left with Ronnie Fields.

Chapter Ten

Maria's Tale

I couldn't believe it when George walked in on Christmas Eve. I had nearly, so nearly, had sex with a colleague in the office at lunchtime the previous day. This had been coming for quite some time. All the ingredients were there.

I was lonely and I was let down. Lonely because George only came home every six months or so. And this time he hadn't been home for a year. Yes,

I used to go and join him for a weekend in some odd place, usually halfway between home and whatever Third World country he was in. And let down? Well, George not appearing for Christmas was like the last straw. That evening waiting at the airport and he, typically I suppose, leaving a message on the voicemail at home, rather than on my mobile which added well over an hour to my wait ... it all just left me feeling really fed up.

Martin Garner, my office colleague, was very attractive – broad-shouldered, intelligent, wry and droll. We had flirted hugely at our Christmas party the previous week. In fact, we had flirted hugely at the last three or four Christmas parties, and after them there was always a day or two of looking at each other in the office, he finding reasons to come to my desk and to lean close to me while he showed me something.

But reason always prevailed. On my side anyway. And I thought on his. It was merely a flirtation between two people who clearly liked each other. I suspect he was bored at home, and as I said, I was lonely.

I'm not trying to diminish the attraction, which was definitely mutual, because there were certain spices mixed in with the basic ingredients. He had habits which I found attractive – like winking at me when the office bore got going, or blowing a kiss on his fingertips and following the kiss with his eyes until it invariably landed on my desk. He also smelt stunning. Sandalwood soap, I think.

On the day in question, Martin came over to my desk to ask did I feel like a last pre-Christmas drink.

'Well, a pre-Christmas drink certainly,' I said with the pedantic correctness for which I was known. 'But I doubt if it will be my last drink before the feast day.'

'You know perfectly well what I mean,' he said. 'I meant a last pre-Christmas drink with me.'

I hid my smile. I loved teasing him, but I would never let him know this.

'You know, Maria McHarg,' he said, 'sometimes you give the impression of wearing starched knickers.'

This was the first time he had ever referred to my underwear, and for some unknown reason all I could think of saying was, 'I do love that stiff feeling.'

There was a pause as our eyes met. And I suddenly heard what I'd said. 'I mean, you know, starch in my knickers. I mean...' Oh God, what was I now saying? Starch in my knickers! As if I actually put starch in them. Oh God.

'I know perfectly well what you mean,' he said. And his voice was suddenly lower and slightly thicker.

Well, I didn't know what I had meant. I kept thinking, Was that a Freudian slip? Was I really trying to say I want to be ... you know. I couldn't even find the words.

'What are your knickers like?' he whispered into my ear.

I pretended not to hear and started tidying things on my desk for the Christmas break. I did like to leave everything just so, just right, so that when I came back after the holidays everything would be nice and neat and easy to find. I tried to give the impression of busy competent me who hadn't heard what was going on.

'Hey Maria, Martin,' it was Tessa and Joe at the door. 'Will you catch us up down in the pub?'

'I'll be along in a bit,' I said. That had been my chance to say, 'Hold on, I'm coming with you now,' but instead I said, 'I'll be along in a bit.'

The door closed as they left.

'So, what are they like?' Martin said again, no longer in a whisper.

I looked up into his face. I didn't answer for a minute.

'Tell me,' he said.

'Tell you what?' I tried to sound brisk.

'Tell me what your knickers are like.'

I wasn't sure I knew how to tell him. Apart from anything else I couldn't actually remember at first which type or colour I'd put on that morning. I opened my mouth, and then I closed it again. He really was so attractive, and the verbal thing was terribly exciting.

'As your boss,' he continued, 'I think I ought to know.'

'You're not actually my boss,' I corrected him, even though he was above me on the office Richter scale of salaries.

'Right this minute, I think I am your boss,' he said. I liked the way his eyelids seemed to have gone all bedroomy.

'So as my boss you feel you ought to know what knickers all the members of your staff are wearing?' I asked. Oh God, why had I used the word 'member'.

'No,' he said. 'Just specific ones. Ones I'm

181

especially interested in.'

'Oh,' was my contribution to this observation.

'So, let's start with the colour,' he said.

I suddenly remembered pulling a pair from my drawer that morning. Black lace French knickers. Oh no, I had stay-up stockings on. I could only think, He's going to think I'm a slut. Why, I don't know, but that's what I thought.

'Black,' I whispered.

'Indeed,' he said. 'I think we should lock up in here, and then go into my office. I want to see them.' His voice was pleasantly firm, it was deep, and there was this incredible huskiness in it, and I couldn't imagine not doing what he was telling me to do. I could hardly stand up. I was so aroused I was almost shaking.

He went over to the main door and clicked the lock down, and then he headed for his own office, where he stood in the entrance for a moment looking at me. I was wearing very high heels and a smart black skirt with a V-necked black sweater and a thin red silk scarf – to give it a Christmassy feel. Martin waited at his door until I started to move from my desk and then he went on into his room. He was sitting behind his desk when I got to the door.

'Come in,' he said. 'And close the door behind you.'

This was like walking into a whole new territory. At the office party when we danced my breasts rubbed against his chest. The first time was an accident, the second time he engineered it, and the third time I pulled back. But this was him summoning, and me obeying, and I felt caught in the atmosphere. Not trapped – I mean, a willing prisoner.

I closed the door behind me and stood there on the carpet between the door and his desk.

'Well?' he said. 'I'm waiting to see those black knickers.'

It was broad daylight and the lights were on in his office – it was as bright as it could be, and there I was totally unsure whether to unzip my black skirt and step out of it, or to lift it up. At no point did I think, What are you contemplating, Maria McHarg? At the back of my brain something was saying to me, 'Maria, you've gone mad.' But I didn't care. I was hurt and alone, and I wanted some excitement in my life.

I decided to pull the skirt up. God, it was tight. It was one of those skirts that you usually unzip and lower with your knickers when you're going to the loo because it's quicker and easier. I eased it slowly up my thighs, wondering if the knicker-legs would go up with it. But they didn't. With my fingertips I could just feel the lace on the legs of them lying neatly against my thighs.

Martin's eyes were focused on mine, until I had my skirt up, then he looked down at what he had asked to see. I heard him inhale sharply, and I didn't know where to look. It was intensely erotic but I had no idea what to do next. Out of practice, I suppose. Not that I had ever been in this specific situation before.

He stood up and came around the desk. 'I think you should take them off,' he said. He propped himself on the edge of the desk just in front of me.

'Off?' I whispered.

'Yes,' he imitated my whisper. 'You know – remove them.'

Well, I'd gone that far, I'd lifted my skirt for him and I really didn't want to stop at this point. I felt incredibly sexy, and also intensely involved. It was as if the atmosphere in his office was building by the second. I started to ease the French knickers down, forcing myself to focus on his face. It was the not knowing what to do with my eyes that was so difficult. I kept wanting to look at his fly to see if there was any obvious reaction – I don't know why. I mean, his voice was telling me that there certainly was. I really wanted to look but I felt it would be quite rude. Once I thought of the word *rude* I found I was totally intrigued by it. *Rude* to look at his fly, when I was busily dropping my knickers for him? How could that be *rude?* And yet that's what I felt.

The satin slid down my legs and I glanced down to see the little pool of black material lying around my feet. I stepped out of them. He was breathing quite quickly now.

'Jesus,' he said, 'do you always wear stockings?' I realised that the lace on the French cami-knickers must have been covering the stocking tops so he had thought I'd been wearing tights.

Actually I don't always wear stockings. I do wear them when dressing up for something, but also when I'm feeling low as they boost my morale in some obscure way, but I thought I'd just say, 'Yes,' rather than try to explain all of that. I would not have been capable of the explanation at all.

'Yes,' I said. My voice was as thick as his own.

'Jesus Christ,' he said. 'Turn around.'

Well – in for a penny, I thought. I turned around slowly.

I felt incredibly wanton, standing there in his office, with my back to him, my bottom bared, in black stockings and high heels, and my skirt up around my waist. He came at me from behind, pulling me back towards the desk where he propped himself again; then with one hand he held my breasts, and with the other he briefly held my bare stomach. Then, with his fingers spread apart, I felt his hand slipping down until one finger found what he was looking for.

He only had to touch it and I was over the edge. I had an immediate and very intense orgasm.

'Someone needed that rather badly,' he said into my ear as shockwaves turned my knees to jelly.

I just let myself go. A bit of me felt very defensive. I wanted to say, 'It has been six months since I've seen my husband,' but I reckoned it was better to leave George out of it. I might have sounded ridiculously prudish and self-righteous. And anyway I didn't want the distraction of my thoughts.

He held me until I stopped quivering in his arms, and then he brought me around the desk and bent me across his blotter. I could feel him fumbling with his zip and as he got himself ready he brought one hand around and sought to arouse me yet again. I jerked in surprise and, at the same moment as the phone started to ring, I

185

accidentally hit it with my hand and it went on to loudspeaker.

We both heard his wife loudly and clearly saying, 'Is that you, Martin? Don't forget to pick up the fucking turkey on the way home. Oh, and Martin, for God's sake tell them to remove its gizzard and whatever other bits they usually leave in it. I don't care if your fucking mother likes them for the gravy, I don't want them in my kitchen. Are you there, Martin?'

Bent right over his desk, with Martin on top of me, just about to enter me, both our mouths were right beside the loudspeaker. I tried not to breathe.

'Yes, yes, I'm here,' he said.

'You're being very quiet. Anyway, I've just had a brilliant idea. Ask them to pack the gizzard and testicles separately and I'll wrap them up and give them to your mother as a Christmas present.'

I started to giggle. I couldn't help it. It was just awful – the ludicrousness of the situation! The heavy sexy atmosphere in his office had evaporated with the words *fucking turkey* and *gizzard*. And at the idea of a turkey's testicles – well, I almost collapsed, except I was face down on the desk. The notion of anyone wrapping them up and giving them to their mother-in-law as a surprise present was more than I could countenance.

'I don't think they're testicles,' Martin said with that pedantic correctness that I thought was peculiarly mine.

'I don't care what they are. Heart, liver, whatever

– the poor fucking turkey was probably a helluva lot nicer than your mother.'

I started to choke. I was trapped under Martin and I couldn't even get my hand to my mouth.

'What's that noise, Martin?'

Martin coughed loudly. 'Sorry,' he said. 'I'd been drinking coffee and it went down the wrong way.' He had one hand over my mouth now. 'See you later,' he said to the loudspeaker.

'Goodbye,' she said. 'And don't forget the fucking turkey.' And we were disconnected.

My desire to laugh ended immediately, as did my desire to be shagged on my so-called boss's desk. We both scrambled back up, he pulling up his trousers and tucking in his shirt, and I frantically trying to smooth down my skirt. I didn't even bother to put my knickers back on. I rolled them up in a ball and let myself out of his office, putting them in my bag when I got to my desk.

'Jesus, Maria,' he said. 'I'm sorry.' He was standing in his office doorway. 'You okay?' he asked.

I was probably feeling a lot better than he was. After all, I had had an orgasm, which had certainly offered me some relief.

'I'm going to consider this unfinished business,' he said.

'I promise I'll think of you while we're eating our turkey,' I said, inwardly grinning at the fact that we were having goose.

I was torn between feelings of guilt and of excitement. The guilt was because of this wife of his, possibly stuck at home with a mother-in-law whom she clearly hated, and who probably hated her, while I was in this wonderful position of having a mother-in-law who was unique to man and to womankind, and without whom I would not be able to go to work and leave my children safely. I had met Martin's wife at some do sometime in the past – I couldn't remember where – and she had seemed a nice enough woman. I certainly did not wish her any harm. And yet, if you don't wish a woman harm, how could you indulge in what I had just done? Isn't marriage for life? Doesn't it involve commitment and monogamy – isn't that what it's all about? In sickness and in health. In loneliness and in lust. You are committed to one person and you have no right to do something with someone else. No matter what.

I was in a turmoil as I cleared up and got my coat.

I had to go down to the pub and have a drink with my colleagues and pretend that everything was fine. But it wasn't fine, not by a long shot. I was facing a lonely Christmas – not lonely in the sense that I would not be surrounded by most of my loved ones – but lonely in that my husband would not be there, and that I was increasingly wondering how committed he was to his family. A year is a long time not to visit your mother, your wife and your children. And I knew that if I had not gone out to see George during that period, we simply would not have had any physical contact in that time. It was not that I blamed George. I knew how tough a year he had had. But I felt I had been truly understanding, and given him the recovery time he needed away from home. And there was Martin, with his wife at home, and Christmas looming and yet he was lusting after me. Lonely people, I thought. People apart who should be together. People together who should be apart. Fortunately, Martin did not turn up in the pub. I say fortunately, but I'm not sure if I even mean that. I did want to see him again, even though every cell in my brain was telling me that I should look for another job immediately, and should never be alone with him again. Halfway through the drink I realised that I had forgotten to put my knickers back on, which made it very difficult to put aside what had taken place at work.

Needless to say this had been on my mind all the previous evening and on and off during the day, so when George walked in just as the party was getting underway, I felt this incredible sense of relief that Martin and I had not actually had penetrative sex. I also kept thinking that George would know that someone else had touched me, but he was kept so busy with the three girls, each of whom wanted more than a third of him, that I had time to recover from his surprise arrival.

He had brought us back presents. Plumpet and Daffers got a ring with a stone the colour of their eyes, though the way Plumpet was behaving that evening, her eyes sparkled more than her stone. The Dumpling got a tiny silver teddy with an amethyst in its navel. The teddy was on a chain and she put it with her dress for Christmas Day, carefully placing it over the hanger that held her party gear. Her new black patent shoes she put on the floor in front of the hanger. She's such a careful child, with a neatness and precision which is totally belied when she goes to the shops and tucks all kinds of objects under herself either in the supermarket trolley or in her buggy.

She could hardly bear to let George leave her in her cot in her room. Usually she lay down and in went her thumb, but that evening, she kept standing back up and looking at him beseechingly.

'I'm just going to have a drink with Mum downstairs,' he said. 'Then I'll be back up to check on you. And you'll have to be asleep because Santa is coming later.'

The notion of Santa, which had hitherto entertained her hugely, was of no interest by comparison with George's presence.

Plumpet had gone off with Ronnie Fields to walk his dog, which Grammer said bore more resemblance to something in the circus, and then to feed Theresa Carmody's cat. Plumpet said something about it being politically incorrect to imagine that animals should belong in a circus, but Grammer ignored her. Daphne had been bribed with hard cash to stack the dishwasher and to run the vacuum cleaner over the living-room floor. In the event she had found a very house-trained boy called Raleigh to assist her. It transpired that he was one of the Fields, a fact that I had somehow or other missed earlier on. He had the most amazing amount of hair – thick, blond and curly, unlike the short spikes on Ronnie's head. And he was a bit like Daphne in that he appeared unruly and a little wild, yet when push came to shove, he pulled out the vacuum cleaner, and carried glasses and plates into the kitchen, picked up paper napkins and cocktail sticks and binned them.

Ronnie and Raleigh's parents, Maureen and Ronald Fields, had only come into the party for an hour or so as they were trying to empty the last boxes before the morrow. My immediate reaction to them was one of pleasure. They were nice people. I thought it would be great having them as neighbours.

Grammer and Waldorf disappeared at about eleven thirty, and George and I headed for bed. Our usual routine would be to have sex on the night he came home, but because Plumpet was due back in we were taking it very slowly, both of us aware of the interruption that could take place at any minute.

It was eleven fifty when George's right hand was exploring my left breast that the door opened, and Plumpet said, 'Hope I haven't woken you. Just telling you I'm home.'

George said, 'Good night, Plumpet. See you in the morning.'

I murmured, 'Good night,' too, and listened until the door closed. I'm sure her voice sounded normal. I'm as sure as can be that I didn't pick up anything amiss.

I'm sure I heard her footsteps on the landing. I'm sure I heard the loo flush, but by then George's mouth was nuzzling my nipples, going from one to the other and a slow steady rhythm was building up as we properly reacquainted ourselves with each other's bodies. Sometime during the evening he had shaved, and his face was smooth as it went hunting around my body, searching for the places where I most liked being nibbled.

I realised that night for the first time that George had sex with other women.

I'm not altogether sure how it dawned on me, but certainly it was related to the experience I had had the previous day, and the fact that I had more restraint than I would usually have after six months' absenteeism and celibacy. And somehow I could identify these effects in George and his behaviour in bed, his control, his patience, his unhurried deftness. What amazed me most was the fact that I hadn't considered this before.

For the first time in my life I felt obliged to feign an orgasm, simply so that he wouldn't realise that I too had been up to mischief.

Because of what had happened at work I was not quite in the same form I would normally have been in. And I felt that I didn't have time to think clearly. None of this really matters – none of it is important, but it was at the time. It was important within those minutes while we were making love, and I didn't want him to realise that I wasn't in quite the state of arousal I would usually be in when he returned. So I wrapped my legs around his hips and gave an Oscar-award winning rendition of an orgasm, trying to keep my mind off Martin Garner and the turkey's gizzard.

'Was that good?' George asked.

'Oh, yes,' I said. And it wasn't really a lie.

We did a lot of catching up that night in bed – on the girls, on his travels and on Grammer and Waldorf. He had met Waldorf a number of times before but always seemed surprised that he was still around. He wanted to know about the new neighbours whom we had both only just met, but I wasn't able to tell him anything really on that front. A detective, a ballet-teacher, two pleasant boys and a dog. And then he asked where the previous neighbour, Marjorie Whelan had gone, but again I didn't know.

I wanted to say to him that I'd had enough, that I couldn't bear this marriage as it stood any more, that I wanted him either here, or not here, but not this continual coming and going. I wanted to tell him that he was like a ghost in my life and that I had no freedom.

But I said nothing. I knew that I needed to think. Now that I knew that he was not being faithful to me while abroad I needed to assess this. I needed time. The oddest thing was that I suspected it would be Grammer I would talk to about this. In many ways she was my closest friend. She was certainly my closest confidante.

Round and around my mind went, as we whispered in the dark. And eventually we fell asleep.

Sometime during the night we woke together and carefully and silently we pulled the girls' presents from Santa from inside the wardrobe where I had neatly lined them up. In our house the girls leave their stockings hanging from their door handles and Santa leaves the presents outside their bedroom doors – so there was no reason to go into their rooms and possibly waken them. In the Dumpling's case we were really concerned about waking her even as we laid her gifts gently outside the door. As things stood, I was surprised that she hadn't yet appeared in our bedroom, as her routine is fairly rigid.

When we had originally come up to bed, George had gone in to her. He said she was still standing where he had last seen her, in the corner of the cot staring at the door. He kissed her again, and got her to lie down so that he could tuck her in. He left her with promises that morning would come faster if she slept and that they would spend all of Christmas Day together.

We left their Christmas stockings outside their doors, and slipped quietly back to bed. I was cold when we climbed back in and he held me in his arms and we fell asleep like that, safe and warm and close.

That is the way you think you are, inside your own house. You think that it is the safest place. You take so much for granted. Well, I did anyway. Grammer had told me long before about her husband, Dirk, George's father and his womanising. She told it to me as facts – something she had learned about, and then had digested and learned to live with. But she did say that when he was finally gone, it was only then that she felt secure in her own house. Prior to that there had been a feeling of not really belonging, or of there being something amiss. She said that she had had to exorcise quite a lot of ghosts before she found both equilibrium and a sense of serenity.

I have never thought of Grammer as being serene, but I think I had some idea of what she was talking about. She told me that it was years and years before she fully came to terms with what had happened. After Dirk went down in the sea she held a memorial service, and that seemed to have given her some strength. Then during that period, she said that she started to watch people and their behaviour, and started to work out what she admired and what she despised, and then she started writing. She wrote the stories, which she would have liked to have been her life. Or so she said. In a sense they are banal soap-opera type of tales, where true love wins through after having to climb over a couple of hurdles. But she said that she worked out then that that was what people wanted, and while real life just is not like that, to read her books was the next best thing. In her case, to write that kind of story seemed to have been sufficient.

Sometimes she would say to me, 'Maria, I have unfinished business to attend to.' It wasn't until that summer when she finally ran her car up Marjorie Whelan's drive that she said she had found peace at last. And the fact that Marjorie Whelan then sold up and moved gave her immense pleasure.

'What did Marjorie Whelan do?' I asked her. I knew it had to be something pretty extreme for Grammer to go to such lengths. Marjorie's porch was demolished as was Marjorie's car, which had been parked to the side of it. And by all accounts Marjorie was jolly lucky herself to have scampered into the porch and on into the house at Grammer's approach.

'A long time ago,' Grammer said, 'when Dirk went down in the sea and I finally realised how many of my friends had been having affairs with him...' There was a long pause – quite unlike Grammer who usually has something to say on every topic. 'You see, Maria – it is a fact that men have affairs. I know that. I didn't when I got married, but I realised it soon enough. It's just a fact. It's in the nature of the beast. But what I didn't realise was that they have them with one's friends. I didn't mind the idea of him having affairs I didn't have to know about, but when I could see it in my friends' eyes, when they dined in my house, and it wasn't just my food they were eating – it was that that I couldn't stomach.'

Lying there beside George in the early morning I thought of Grammer saying that. I thought of the fact that George undoubtedly did have affairs. I thought of Martin Garner and it occurred to me that I should not feel guilt over what had and had not happened.

'Sexual appetite is part of human nature,' Grammer had said.

So why should my desires and interests be any different? Who was I hurting by being felt up by Martin Garner? It was all innocuous, enjoyable, unthreatening, immediate... Presumably he went home with the gizzardless turkey and got on with his Christmas, just as George came home from his other life in Asia, and I came home and played my role of mother.

I was so busy thinking about me. Me. Me. Me. As if I didn't know that a mother should never put herself at the top of her agenda.

Chapter Eleven

Plumpet's Tale

Every girl in my class had been kissed at least once. I'm under-exaggerating. Every girl in my class had been kissed dozens of times. But not me. I wasn't a great mixer. I knew half of them lied their heads off just to get attention or to imply how popular they were, but Grammer says lies catch you out in the end, so what was the point? I think I'm trying to say that I had thought about pretending to have a boyfriend in the past just so that I could get on with my life and have them leave me alone. But then I saw that once you started to lie, the lie would sort of grow and you'd have to back it up and give it substance with other lies. So I didn't bother.

Grammer says that all things come to those who wait. She also says if you want something, you should go out and get it. A lot of her observations are at complete variance with each other, but I think it means you can choose what you want to do at a particular time.

I didn't go looking for Ronnie Fields. I couldn't believe my luck when he turned up next door. And I certainly couldn't believe my luck the way he seemed to want my company in those two days coming up to Christmas. We spent every spare minute together, either walking WC, or in each other's houses. I liked him so much, and a bit of me was afraid that he just liked me as a sister. Having no experience to back up the feelings I was having, I wasn't sure what was going on.

At the Christmas Eve drinks party in our house, Theresa Carmody came and asked if I'd let Cat in and out of her place as she was going away, and while she was doing the asking I could see Ronnie's face just beside her and he was nodding at me, as if willing me to say yes.

I would have done it anyway because Theresa Carmody was nice. She was a good neighbour as Grammer said, and she was very obliging to us. She was kind to all of us, especially the Dumpling, so there would have been no hesitation on my part about agreeing to go in and look after Cat. But the nod from Ronnie suddenly spoke volumes and I felt myself going slightly pink. Several times during the day I had thought he was going to kiss me.

I had helped to unpack boxes in his house, and the two of us would be working on a box and our faces would be so close that I could breathe his breath, and I kept thinking that we were getting closer and closer. But then nothing would happen and that was why I thought that maybe he saw me as a sort of sister. I mean, he seemed very competent, and gave the impression that he knew what he was doing all the time, so the fact that he had not kissed me seemed to say that he was not going to. But I still felt on edge the whole day, sort of on fire, and terribly excited.

He was such fun. He made me want to laugh all the time. And when he wasn't making me laugh he made me feel like I was the most important person in the room. Okay, I know I was the only other person in the room most of the time, but it was all so real and exciting and such wonderful, wonderful fun.

Then Dad came home and that just added to everything. It was as if there was nothing more I needed. My whole family there in our house. Waldorf too. And next door, all the Fields, especially Ronnie. And they were all so lovely. I remembered reading somewhere 'my cup runneth over', and I knew exactly what that meant.

Theresa Carmody gave me a key to her place, but we left going there for a while after she had gone. Then Ronnie said, 'Shouldn't we see to that cat of hers?' And I agreed. 'I ought to come with you,' he said. 'It's a big dark house and I wouldn't like you in there alone.'

I didn't say that I had been in there alone before and that it hadn't frightened me. In fact, I'd been in there simply loads of times alone. There was the time Theresa Carmody had gone on holidays for two weeks and taken Cat with her – I can't remember where she'd gone, but she phoned late the first night to say she was convinced she had left the iron plugged in. And so I had gone in to check. I had gone in the dark and looked under the special stone in the front garden to find her spare key, and sure enough she had left the iron on, so I just unplugged it. Sometimes she was a bit careless about how she left the place, but that was the only time I think she had done something dangerous – and at least she had remembered. And there had been other times I had gone in to take in her milk and to cancel the milkman because she had forgotten – those kinds of things. I really didn't mind going in by myself, but I definitely wasn't telling Ronnie that.

Then Dad gave me a lovely ring with a green stone and that delayed us a bit, and then Ronnie said to our parents that we'd walk WC as well – this was to buy us a bit more time, and Mum and Dad both said that was fine. So off we went.

We walked WC first – the shortest walk he ever got, I'd say. Once around the block at high speed and Ronnie put him back in their kitchen, and then we walked down to Theresa Carmody's. She had left a light on in the hall and we let ourselves in with the key in my pocket.

'I'll see if Cat is ready to come in,' I said, as we went through to the kitchen.

'Shall I pour us a Coke?' Ronnie asked. 'She did say we should help ourselves.'

I agreed readily even though I didn't feel like a fizzy drink at all, but it seemed to make sense that we should have a glass in our hands and then we would have a reason to sit down and make ourselves comfortable while we drank.

There was no sign of Cat on the patio. When I came back in from the extension, Ronnie had disappeared.

'Where are you?' I called.

He'd gone through to the living room, and he was putting our drinks down on the coffee-table. There was a bowl with salted almonds in it which he picked up and, sitting down on the sofa, he placed them on his knee. He patted the space beside him. 'Come and sit,' he said.

I felt slightly gauche, as if I didn't really know what to do. A bit of me was reading things into his movements and his gestures, and another bit of me was saying, 'This is brotherly-sisterly stuff, so stop imagining things, Plumpet.'

I perched awkwardly on the edge of the sofa, and he put the bowl of almonds back on the table and turned towards me... I have a book on body language which Grammer gave me. She said it was a font of knowledge but that ultimately you should also trust your own instincts.

His legs were crossed and were sort of pointing in my direction, which according to the book is a sign of the person being interested in you, though I've always thought that if someone has one foot pointing towards you it looks more like they want to kick you. Anyway, this was clearly a case for believing the book and not going with my own instincts.

'I really like your hair like that,' he said.

My hair was loose. It had been all day. It suddenly occurred to me that for all his worldly ways and the comfortable way he comported himself that maybe he was a little shy too.

'Thank you,' I said. I thought that if I appeared shyer than him, then he might just take control. But I think he was totally in control anyway; he was just biding his time. He sat forward to pick up his drink, but instead of reaching for it, he put his hand under my hair and lifted it off one shoulder.

Our eyes met, and I just smiled at him. Shyly. Coyly. I don't know what word. Just a smile.

He moved a little closer, and then he kissed me gently on the corner of my mouth. It was the loveliest, most wonderful feeling in the whole world. I thought of Grammer saying to us girls that you only get one first kiss in the whole of your life so make damned sure it's with someone you really want to kiss so that you can enjoy it, and that it's worth remembering.

I was so lucky. It was with the one person I really wanted to give me my first kiss. It seemed that we had everything. There we were living next door to each other. There was no rush. It was all so real and so genuine. It was like being passed a plate full of perfectly prepared chocolate-covered strawberries, which wouldn't go off, and you could taste one whenever you wanted it. That might sound silly, but that's what I thought. Time, space, everything was on our side.

We kissed a bit more. It was like melting. I was so glad I had never lied in school about being kissed. So glad that even my conscience was clean – it made it all the more exciting, all the more real. And I had no doubt that I was the luckiest person alive. As well as feeling lucky, I felt like sparks of electricity were shooting through my veins when our lips met.

After a while Ronnie said, 'Maybe we should see if that cat has returned.' I was about to get up to go and check, when he placed two fingers on my arm, and said, 'You stay here. I'll be right back.' He got up and went down the length of the two rooms and out into the kitchen. I could hear doors opening and shutting and I heard him say, 'C'mon puss.'

After that, I remember absolutely nothing.

I woke on what turned out to be Christmas morning, in my own bed, feeling really unwell. Not just sick, but sore and hurt and bruised. I had never felt like that before. It was different from having the flu when you're all blocked up and just ill. This was as if someone had battered me. I lay there in the winter morning's darkness, hearing Dad and Mum calling Merry Christmas from their room, and bit by bit I started to realise that I had no recollection of coming home, no memory whatsoever of getting undressed and climbing into bed. I felt ill and I started to feel really frightened. I reached to turn on the bedside light, but I had a problem getting my hands to move and in the early morning light coming in through the open curtains I could see my clothes lying on the floor beside the bed. My body felt peculiar, as if it wasn't attached to my mind. At first I couldn't get my hands to move, but when I did, I touched myself and found I was wearing my bra and knickers. The feeling of fear increased until it reached what could only be called terror.

It was like looking into a room that was completely full of cobwebs and trying to see some way through them. The last thing I could clearly remember was looking at a bowl of salted almonds on Theresa Carmody's coffee-table. Then I recalled hearing Ronnie saying something. But that was all.

'Santa's been,' called Mum.

I wanted her to come into me. I wanted her to hold me and to make it all right. I wanted to call out to her but my tongue seemed stuck in my mouth and the feeling of real terror just got larger and more immense until I could feel nothing, only all-consuming fear.

I could hear Daffers on the landing getting her stocking from her door, and I wondered if the Dumpling was already up but all I wanted was Mum to come into me.

The door opened and the Dumpling's face peered round it. She padded slowly across the floor to my bed where she stood and looked into my face. I didn't want her to see me like that. I wanted her to go away. I wanted Mum or Grammer to come and help me. My eyes met the Dumpling's eyes and I tried to look away, but I also tried to plead with her through them, trying to get her to understand that something was wrong, even though I didn't want to frighten her. The Dumpling looked at me and then she scurried across the floor and out of the door. I could hear her on the landing and I knew she'd gone for help.

Mum came, pushed and pulled by the

204

Dumpling. She switched the light on as she came into the room. The moment I saw her face I knew that she knew there was something wrong. I could see it in her eyes.

'All right, Dumpling,' she said to my sister. 'You go back into Dad now, and look at your presents again. Climb into the bed. Plumpet and I ... we'll be in shortly.'

The Dumpling's little wise face looked at me. So impenetrable. And yet I knew that she was assessing the situation, and then she left the room.

Mum sat on the bed beside me. She lifted my chin. Her eyes seemed to be taking something in, but I didn't know what. Then she slowly pulled down the bedclothes – just as far as my waist.

'Who did this to you, darling?' she asked. Her voice was soft but I knew she was covering something up. 'It's all right, precious,' she said. 'I'm here. It's all right now.'

I could feel tears on my cheeks but I wasn't sure they were mine.

Chapter Twelve

Daffers's Tale

Raleigh Fields and I cleaned up downstairs on Christmas Eve.

'We'll get brownie points,' he said. 'Someone else will have to clean up on Christmas Day. We do the work now and we'll get to sit after the plum pudding has been served and eaten.'

He seemed to have family life fairly well sussed out. Admittedly he didn't live in a house with so many females – in fact, there was only Maureen his mum on the girl side of things. Even their dog was a boy. I quite liked the way he seemed so sure of himself. I didn't have to pretend – not like with Daisy. With Daisy I sometimes had to lie. She was allowed to see any film she wanted to, and I was not. She used to tell me to just hire a video, or sneak out to the cinema or something, but Grammer would have gone mad if she had found out – and Grammer *would* have found out. Grammer bloody well found out everything.

Grammer would have said that Raleigh was house-trained. He was quite good at stacking the dishwasher, and he was nice to the Dumpling. 'Want a piece of cheese?' he said to her.

She took the cube of cheese and put it in her pocket and then went back to sitting on Dad's foot. The Dumpling can't eat cheese because it comes from a cow but I reckoned she'd just keep it stored in her pocket so it wouldn't do her any harm. She's allowed goat and sheep's cheese and they keep her happy enough.

Dad brought Plumpet and me each back a ring. Plumpet's had some kind of green stone. Mine was really, really beautiful with a sparking blue stone. Raleigh's brother Ronnie said that it was the same colour as my eyes. But I thought it looked more like Raleigh's eyes. Raleigh said we could play tennis on Christmas Day – we could climb over the walls of my school, as the caretaker would probably be ossified. That means drunk. Daisy said her parents got scuttered on a Friday night and ossified on a Saturday.

I didn't think Dad or Mum would let me disappear on Christmas Day but the day after seemed like a good option. Raleigh said we could go down on our bicycles. He was to start in the boys' school just down from ours right after Christmas.

Anyway, Raleigh helped me clean up and then just as I thought Mum was going to say, 'I think it's time you went home, Raleigh,' he said it. He just upped and said, 'I think it's time I went home. What with Santa, and all that lark.'

I saw Dad smile before he turned his head away.

Grammer and Waldorf were hitting the brandy mixed with champagne. Waldorf said it was the best thing for a decent night's sleep.

Grammer said, 'We should leave all these young people, Waldorf.'

He just said, 'Mmmm. And where's my yo-yo?'

Raleigh laughed and said, 'I'm off. See ya tomorrow, Daffers,' and he disappeared. So I went to bed.

I text-messaged Daisy on my mobile. She and her parents had only stayed until nine. I say *only* but actually I was thrilled when she left. She was big into innuendo. Innuendo means insinuating and hinting at things. And usually it was very funny, but I didn't like it when Raleigh was around. I mean, he had only just moved in next door. And I was hoping he might be a good tennis partner.

Oh, all right, I don't play much tennis. But I would, if I had half the chance. I used to really like it, but Daisy said it wasn't cool. She said, who would want to run around a rectangle trying to swipe a ball the size of an onion. That was the problem with Daisy: she was so busy being cool that she forgot how to have fun. I used to love playing tennis, but Daisy had talked me out of it. No, not really talked me out of it, more like sneered me out of it. I also loved Christmas but I had to hide it when Daisy was around as Christmas wasn't cool.

I woke on Christmas morning with that nice feeling you get when you know there are presents and fun ahead. I lay for a moment listening to the Dumpling on the landing and Mum and Dad calling cheery greetings around the place. Then I fetched my stocking from the door and as I took it off the handle the Dumpling came across the landing and pushed open Plumpet's door. Her stocking was still hanging on it.

'Morning Dumples,' I called to her. Well, it was Christmas Day after all.

I brought my stocking back to bed and started going through it. There were lots of things in it, some things I had really been wanting, and some surprises. I could hear Mum going into Plumpet's bedroom. Typical, I thought. Typical that Plumpet would get her attention first. That's the way it is with the firstborn. They get all the attention.

It was a while later before I got the feeling there was something wrong. It came in slowly – it was a feeling of something being topsy-turvy. Getting up again I went across to Plumpet's room; a bit of me was surprised to see that her stocking was still hanging on the door. I pushed the door open and went in.

'Morning Plumpet, morning Mum,' I said. 'Happy Christmas stockings to you both.'

Mum turned her face and looked at me and there was something like horror in her eyes.

'Get your dad,' she said to me. 'Quickly, go and get your dad.'

Plumpet was lying there in her bed. She was really pale – like almost completely white and there were marks on her. She bruises really easily, always has – and there were purple and red marks on her neck and on her chest. And she was crying silently.

I was reminded of the Dumpling crying, and I felt really afraid.

'Get your dad, and stay with Dumpling,' Mum said.

I couldn't take my eyes off my sister. I was really shocked. She looked awful. 'Plumpet,' I said. 'Oh, Plumpet.'

I couldn't move and Mum yelled at me, 'Daphne, just go and get your dad!' at the top of her voice. Then I moved. I backed out of the door with my eyes locked on Plumpet's body until I was on the landing. Dad, of course, had heard Mum's yell and he was out of the bed by the time I got to his room.

I climbed into his and Mum's bed and sat with the Dumpling looking at the contents of her stocking. She had got lots of cute things and was busy lining them up across the duvet.

There were all kinds of things happening outside the door. Dad had fetched Grammer and then he called for a doctor but could only get an answering machine where they asked him to leave his number. I could hear Mum saying, 'Should we take her to the hospital?' And Grammer's voice saying gently, in a most un-Grammerlike way, 'I'm going to talk to her, Maria. I want you to make a pot of tea, George. Just go and do it.'

And Dad said, 'What do you mean, make tea?'

Then Grammer, sounding a bit more like Grammer, said, 'George, go downstairs and make tea. Maria, you have a shower and get dressed. We need to start getting this show on the road. N ... O ... W.'

Waldorf's voice sounded clearly from the staircase. I think he must have been standing there listening. He said, 'George, come and give me a hand in the kitchen.' He didn't really sound like Waldorf at all. He's usually going on about something else, like, you know, looking for his yo-yo or his *Beano* or something, but now he sounded terribly ... I don't know, in control maybe.

I could hear Mum in the shower and then she came back into the bedroom and asked me to get the Dumpling up.

I opened my mouth to ask how Plumpet was, and to ask what had happened, and she said, 'For goodness' sake, Daphne, for once in your life, don't argue. Just do what you're told.'

It was totally unfair, as I didn't argue. I wasn't

the arguing type. But I could see she was really, really upset, so I didn't say anything. I just lifted the Dumpling up, and told her to leave her presents, that we'd get them when she was dressed. She waved at them lying on Mum's and Dad's bed. I could already see that she was forming an attachment to a small furry orang-utan, which slipped from her grasp when I took her up.

'Come on, Dumples,' I said. 'Let's bring it with you.'

She reached down and grabbed it when I lowered her back towards the bed, and she hugged it really close. I thought that was a good thing, as I really wanted to hug someone or to have someone hug me.

I gave her a quick kiss while she wasn't looking.

We could hear Grammer talking in Plumpet's bedroom, but the door was closed and the words were muffled. I dressed the Dumpling – she'd laid everything out the previous day; even the present Dad had given her was hanging over her dress. I suddenly wondered if Mum had meant her to dress like this. It's just that it didn't seem much like Christmas Day, and these were clearly her best clothes. I dressed her in them anyway as I didn't know what else to do.

When the Dumpling was dressed, I fetched all her presents from Mum's and Dad's bed and settled her on the floor in her room and told her to stay busy. Then I went and showered and got myself ready.

Ready for what? This was totally unclear.

By the time I was dressed, so were Dad and

211

Waldorf. We all seemed to be congregating down-stairs. Grammer was now downstairs too, so I supposed Mum was in with Plumpet. I heard Grammer saying, 'We have to get a doctor.'

Dad said, 'Hospital?'

Grammer said, 'No, not yet. A doctor first and we work from there.'

'Why not hospital?'

'Plumpet doesn't want hospital,' Grammer said. 'She's most adamant about that.'

Waldorf interrupted, 'Where does your doctor live? Isn't he supposed to be a friend of the family? So – I'll drive around and get him.'

I'd never heard Waldorf sounding so normal.

'Shall we take Plumpet with us?' Dad said.

'No,' Waldorf said. 'The last thing she needs is to be paraded in front of someone else's family. I'll drive over, find the good doctor and bring him back here.'

And he did.

Dr Fairbrother, Richie to my parents, arrived back with Waldorf about thirty minutes later.

There was none of our usual big fried breakfast for Christmas. Dumpling and I sat and ate cereal together, and when I poured her soya milk on hers, I didn't even pull a face. She had her pink pig and her new furry toy with her. I told her the orang-utan was called Gunkey. I don't know why, but he sort of looked like a Gunkey. She patted his head and pretended to feed him some of her cereal. And then she pulled a face just like I usually make, and I knew that Gunkey didn't like soya milk. It made me smile.

I was glad to smile at something.

Dr Fairbrother was upstairs for simply ages. When he came down I listened at the door. Waldorf must have remained with Plumpet because Mum, Dad and Grammer were now all downstairs. I knew from the sounds Mum was making that she was either crying or trying not to.

'You're going to have to bring the police in,' Dr Fairbrother said. 'I've taken a blood test, but there is a special unit down in the hospital, and I'd really like her to be taken there.'

'She doesn't want to go to hospital,' Grammer said.

'I know. And we have to take everything into account, because she is going to need all the support we can muster.'

Dad's voice said, 'Exactly what are we talking about? Exactly what has been done to her?'

The blood was pounding in my head. I think I knew in some way what was coming next. 'Drugged and sexually assaulted.'

Dad got it out of him. Dr Fairbrother said it looked like rape.

Drugged and raped.

That didn't happen to people like us. It couldn't. We were safe in our big house with people who love us. Plumpet, Dumpling and me.

It seemed that they needed the experts in. There were people who dealt with this every day. There were people out there who held the hands of victims like Plumpet, who knew what to say and what to do. People who knew what tests to take, what to do with those tests, people who

213

knew how to find the perpetrator, people who would make Plumpet better.

'I'll kill him,' Dad said.

'I think it would be a lot more helpful, George,' said Dr Fairbrother, 'if at this stage you just put Plumpet first. Forget about everything else and concentrate on her.'

The hospital was phoned. The Dumpling and I pretended to be busy while this was going on. Then Dad and Mum went off with Plumpet and Dr Fairbrother.

Waldorf and Grammer came in to talk to Dumpling and me.

Grammer said, 'Daphne, I don't know how much of that you've picked up on, but your antennae are usually pretty good. So, ask if you want to know something. Otherwise, can I ask you a few things?'

I didn't say anything. I just wanted it all to go away. I shrugged.

'Did you hear Plumpet coming in last night?' she asked.

I half nodded, half shook my head. I really wasn't sure.

'Now, think,' she said.

'Gently, Millie,' said Waldorf. 'How about some coffee, m'dear?'

Surprisingly, Grammer went and put on the percolator. Waldorf and I sat down on the easy chairs in the kitchen.

'You all right, m'dear?' he asked me.

I said that yes, I was.

'Good,' he said. 'Now the sooner all the pieces

of the jigsaw are got out of the box and laid out neatly, the sooner we can get the whole puzzle done.'

The Dumpling went to her treasure box and took out a jigsaw puzzle and started laying it out on the floor. Plumpet would have smiled at her, and said something like, 'You adorable darling.'

I started to cry. I have no idea why. But there I sat on one of our big squishy kitchen chairs on Christmas morning, and the floodgates opened and I was blubbering like an eight year old.

'It'll be all right,' Waldorf said, taking a large freshly ironed white handkerchief out of his jacket pocket and passing it to me. 'It'll be all right once it's all been pieced together.'

The Dumpling worked away busily, and I snorted and snuffled a bit as I tried to stop crying.

'Why are you crying?' Grammer asked, coming over to us. She hadn't been that far away in the kitchen that she hadn't heard everything that had been said to date, so I suppose she was just trying to work out what had set me off.

'The bruises,' I sniffled.

She nodded. 'I know,' she said. 'I know.'

'Daffers,' said Waldorf, 'just try again. Do you think you heard Plumpet coming in last night?'

Yes, I told them. I had heard her. I had heard her on the stairs. I had heard her saying good night to Mum and Dad. And that was it. I had been really sleepy and I only heard those things in the far distance. And then I'd fallen asleep.

'Nothing else?' Waldorf asked.

I shook my head.

'How did she sound?'

'Dunno. Like Plumpet, I suppose,' I said. I meant, if she had sounded like someone else I'd have thought that at the time. So would Mum and Dad. Or if her voice were all shocked or whatever, we'd have picked up on it. That was clear.

The Dumpling was already finishing putting the edges of the jigsaw together. She looked up at us to see what was happening.

'Well done, Dumples,' I said. 'You're very fast.'

She seemed to look suspiciously at me. Okay, I didn't usually have much time for her, but Plumpet did, and Plumpet wasn't there, and so she needed someone to give her a little extra attention.

Waldorf sipped his coffee and watched the Dumpling as she moved in on the centre of her jigsaw. 'I suppose you slept the night through, Dumpling?' he said. It was more a question than a statement.

She abandoned her jigsaw and started to suck her thumb. I got up and retrieved her pink pig and Gunkey off the breakfast-table.

'I'm going in to have a shower,' Grammer said. It was only then I realised that she was still in her pyjamas. She dresses so exotically most of the time anyway, that it's sometimes difficult to know what clothes are for daytime and what for nighttime wear.

Grammer had no sooner disappeared through the connecting door into her kitchen, than our hall doorbell rang. I went out to answer it. It was

Ronnie Fields with WC. He said, 'Happy Christmas, Daffers. Is Plumpet around?'

I just looked at him. I didn't know what to say.

Waldorf appeared beside me, carrying the Dumpling. 'Who's been reading my *Beano*?' he said in the general direction of Ronnie.

Ronnie said hello.

'Hi, Ronnie,' Waldorf said to him.

They did the Happy Christmas thing, and all the time I could feel Waldorf's hand on my shoulder and I knew he didn't want me to say anything.

'I'm just checking if Plumpet would like to come for a quick walk,' Ronnie said.

'What, walk off the plum pudding in advance?' Waldorf laughed. For a minute there he sounded just like he usually sounded, but then his voice changed and became more formal. 'I'm sorry to say she's gone out with her parents. We'll tell her you dropped by,' he said. 'Won't we, Daffers?' he added. His hand was firmly on my shoulder.

I just nodded.

'OK,' Ronnie Fields said. 'We'll see you later,' and he and WC bounded off down the path.

Waldorf stood there with me beside him and the Dumpling on one arm, and the three of us watched Ronnie Fields until he disappeared behind the hedge.

'Did he do that to her?' I said. I was watching Waldorf's face now, trying to read his expression.

He patted me on the shoulder. 'Listen to me, Daffers m'dear,' he said. 'I have no idea who has done this terrible thing, and I must admit that I personally would have a problem in believing that that young man did it. But there are going to be a lot of questions asked, and I think it's best if we say nothing to anyone – that way people don't have the opportunity to start thinking up alibis. Let the truth come out.'

I didn't really know what he meant. 'What'll we do now?' I asked him.

'We'll be helpful,' he said. 'We'll lay the table, and make things nice for when your parents return.'

I wished he had said, 'For when Plumpet and your parents return.' It would have made me feel better.

I went upstairs. I thought I might put Plumpet's stocking on her bed for when she got back. In her room her clothes were lying on the floor, and her bed was a mess, so I went to tidy things up and then I saw that there was blood on the sheet. I stood there looking at it. I didn't know what to do. Her period, I thought. It has to be her period. She got her period. I kept saying that in my head. I couldn't bear the idea that someone had hurt her and had made her bleed. Bruising was bad enough. Bleeding was unbearable.

Waldorf suddenly appeared in the room. He was alone – he must have left the Dumpling with Grammer. He came up beside me and put his hand on my shoulder. He seemed to be doing a lot of that today.

'Come, m'dear,' he said. 'We'll leave this for now.'

'I want to tidy it,' I said. 'I want to put a clean sheet on her bed and put away her clothes.' My voice was all wobbly again.

'Not now,' he said. 'Later. I think for now we should just leave it.'

'But why?' I said. 'Why? They're going to come back from the hospital and Plumpet may want to lie down for a bit and ... and ... and...'

I was crying again. He guided me out of the room.

'This is dreadfully upsetting,' he said, 'for anyone, let alone for her dear sister.'

This was jolly nice of him as he knew that Plumpet and I went at it like cat and dog half the time. Well, *I* went at *her* like a cat or a dog.

'I think,' he said, very gently – this was a whole new Waldorf voice – 'I think we're going to have Forensics in here shortly and they'll want to take some of this clothing and bedding away.'

'Waldorf,' I said hoarsely. 'Waldorf, do you think this happened to her here in bed?'

He shook his head. 'I have no idea,' he said. 'I don't have a clue.'

'It couldn't have,' I said. 'One of us would have heard. We would have,' I insisted.

'I don't think,' said Waldorf, 'that you're going to do any good either for Plumpet or for yourself getting upset like this. The best thing you can do is to keep both of these feet of yours as firmly on the ground as possible. That's how you'll help your Mum and Dad the best. And it's how you'll help yourself,' he added.

I didn't know what he meant. And I'm not sure I cared.

'Come on, m'dear,' he said to me. 'Grammer is going to need some help with the stuffing, and your Mum isn't here to do it.'

When he'd ushered me out, he closed the bedroom door firmly. 'You're not to go back in there for the moment,' he said. 'Do you understand?'

I nodded. I went to fetch some of the Dumpling's stocking fillers to bring down to her. Waldorf came with me and he refilled her stocking with everything and carried it downstairs.

'You're a good girl,' he said to me, which rather surprised me. It's not a term that usually comes my way.

I can't tell you how awful the rest of that day was.

Grammer gave me apricots and celery and things to chop for the stuffing. I got a bit carried away with the herbs but she said not to worry. 'Herbs are good,' she said. Then she added, 'That might make a good title for a book.'

Grammer has a terrible hang-up about titles for books. Every time she names one of her new books, the publishers change it. They say that it either needs a more obvious or a more subtle approach – I can't remember which.

'I don't know, Millie m'dear,' contributed Waldorf, 'that I'd be that inclined to buy a book called *Herbs are Good*. Unless it were a cookbook, of course.'

'Goodness me no,' said Grammer. 'I was thinkng more about two men, both called Herb. It could be called *Herbs are Good*. If you see what I mean.'

I looked at Waldorf. He winked at me. I could see why the publishers changed the titles of her books.

'And what would these Herbs get up to?' Waldorf asked.

I got the feeling they were just talking to fill the time.

The Dumpling got pasta shapes from the cupboard and she laid them out in a funny pattern. Plumpet always watched her when she did that. She and Grammer said that we could learn from the Dumpling if we could just tap into her way of thinking. I cut the apricots with scissors, and I kept an eye on the Dumpling, just in case Waldorf and Grammer weren't.

She used to sit on the floor in such a funny way, but she was always really busy. She placed the pasta quills in an odd shape, side on side – not end to end. They went like this – three quills side on side, then a break. Then at right angles to the last of the first three quills she laid a further three, then a break. Then she placed fourteen quills side by side, the first one coming at a right angle to the last of the second three. Then another break, followed by a further seven quills, again starting at a right angle. The pattern sort of reminded me of something, but I couldn't think what. Then she started laying quills out end to end. By this stage I was busy mixing the ingredients into the bread-crumbs for Grammer so I didn't really watch. But when she had finished she went to her box of secrets – that's what Plumpet called it – and she got out one of her little cars. She would have been better off doing a jigsaw for all the sense her little game was making. But I didn't say anything because it was Christmas Day and things were looking bad enough.

Dad phoned in the early afternoon and he talked to Grammer. The Dumpling was having a nap on the sofa with her head on Waldorf's lap, and he and Grammer had been drinking champers. He said I could have a glass. Grammer said, 'Make it just a wee one.'

When the phone rang, the Dumpling stirred but then went back to sleep.

Grammer said into the phone, 'Of course it's me, George. Who did you think it was?' Then she said, 'Sorry.' Well, it was a bit snappy, and presumably Dad and Mum weren't having a great day down in the hospital. When she hung up she said to Waldorf and me that a couple of detectives would be over.

About ten minutes later the doorbell rang, and when Grammer came back she had Ronald Fields with her. He had brought over an enormous bunch of flowers, which apparently they had bought for the party the previous evening, but in all the hassle of unpacking and sorting, Maureen and he had simply forgotten about them.

Grammer looked at Waldorf, and Waldorf looked at Grammer, and Ronald Fields looked at each of us in turn. He was wearing a suit and tie and he was smiling around as if it was the happiest day of his life.

'They're quite lovely,' said Grammer, standing there swathed in lilies and holly and green fronds and things.

'Delightful,' said Waldorf. 'Can't get up old chap, sorry,' he said to Ronald, pointing at the Dumpling's spiky head which was keeping him on the sofa.

'Was she up early for Santa?' Ronald asked.

'Don't know, old chap,' Waldorf said. 'Haven't a clue. I slept like a submarine.'

Sometimes Waldorf said things that didn't make sense to people who hadn't been in, say, a submarine. That particular sentence always makes me think of a long grey steel tube resting on the ocean's floor – fast asleep. But how could a steel tube be asleep? See? It doesn't make any sense.

Then the bell rang again, and Grammer went out of the room, while Ronald Fields stood there. I could see he was puzzled at his reception; we'd all been as friendly as anything the previous day and the day before that, and now the atmosphere was as chilly as inside the deep-freeze.

The next moment, Grammer came in and said, nice as pie to Ronald Fields, that we had visitors and would he mind excusing us. Go away, is what she was saying.

I felt a bit embarrassed and started twiddling the ring on my finger as Ronald Fields looked around at us all. Waldorf gave him a little wave, then Ronald Fields wished us all a Happy Christmas. As he was about to go out of the door, he came face to face with the two visitors. If Grammer had been thinking clearly she'd have realised in advance that if one detective is visiting you with flowers, and two more walk in, they may well recognise each other. Which of course is what happened.

'Ronald.'

'Joe.'

'Margaret.'

As Grammer said to Dad later, it was like being at a meeting of the Masonic lodge. I wondered how she would know. Joe was Joe Malone and Margaret was Margaret McGregor, and they had neat little identification cards with photos of themselves. The Dumpling woke up in the middle of this, saw Ronald Fields and wanted to be picked up by him. He obliged. She wrapped her arms around his neck. We all got to meet Joe and Margaret who, if they were disappointed not to be at home eating turkey or goose with their own families, hid it quite well.

They introduced themselves to each of us, and then Joe said to Ronald, 'I didn't realise you'd been called in.'

And Ronald said, 'I live next door. I just dropped in with flowers.'

And Margaret said, 'For the girl?'

And Ronald said, 'Well, for the family really.' Then he looked carefully at both Margaret and Joe, and then he turned and looked at us. 'What has happened?' he said. His voice was hard and the Dumpling buried her face in his neck.

Grammer put one hand to her forehead.

Waldorf said, 'Millie, sit at once. You look like you're going to faint.'

Grammer is not the type of person to faint. It's much more likely that someone else would faint because of her, but I must admit she didn't look great. Her face was very pale. Joe and Waldorf helped her to a chair. Margaret went and got her a glass of water. And Ronald Fields stood there with the Dumpling clamped on to him.

'Not water. Champers, champers,' said Waldorf. 'It'll keep her blood pressure and her spirits up.'

The Dumpling petted Ronald Fields's hair, and he turned to me and said, 'Please tell me what's going on.'

'Someone raped Plumpet,' I said.

Ronald Fields looked from each of us to the next as if he didn't know where he was. Then he said to Margaret or Joe or someone, 'Is this true?'

'It looks like it,' Margaret said. 'We're waiting for confirmation from the hospital. But she's definitely been seriously assaulted. That's why we're here.'

I didn't like the word 'seriously'. It scared me. It sounded worse than rape, but I didn't really understand the meaning of that word either.

'When?' snapped Ronald Fields.

'Last night,' I said.

'I want in on this,' he said to Joe.

But Grammer, looking all pale and grey, said, 'I don't think you can be. It's a bit too close to home.'

Ronald Fields passed the Dumpling to me and she wrapped herself around me. I could suddenly see why Plumpet liked holding her so much.

'Then let me help at least,' said Ronald Fields.

Chapter Thirteen

Millicent's Tale

When Dirk McHarg hit the ocean at two hundred miles per hour, or whatever speed it was, I thought that was the most difficult thing I was ever going to have to face. Looking back on it from a distance I can see that I handled it with a certain amount of cynicism, mixed with pragmatism and the need to survive with dignity.

Sitting beside Plumpet on her bed that Christmas morning I knew that Dirk's departure was nothing compared with this. If I could have swapped places with Plumpet I would have done so.

Plumpet has an inbuilt goodness, a sweetness of nature, a seriousness, a gentle compliance – very like her mother, in fact – and whatever had happened to her, I felt that the anguish and pain she was in had destroyed her. At first she couldn't speak at all, but as the words came to her it became clear that she actually had no idea what had happened. I think in a sense that was a relief for me.

When we said to her, 'Who did this to you?' I thought her silence was covering for Ronnie Fields. But as time went on it was obvious that she had no idea either what had happened to her or how she had got into her bed.

I couldn't believe it of Ronnie Fields – it just didn't make sense, but George and Maria were both adamant that she had come in the previous evening and had said good night, and that she sounded normal. So it had to have happened after that. But Ronnie Fields was the last person known to have been with her.

'Do you remember saying good night to your parents?' I asked her.

Tears rolled slowly down her cheeks and she shook her head.

'You took that dog for a walk,' I prompted her, referring to the elephant living next door.

I wanted George to ring for an ambulance but I felt that she needed us close to her at this stage, that there would be time enough later for ambulances and doctors. Whatever chance there was of accessing her mind, it would be most possible while she was safe with us.

Safe! What does the word mean? Lying in your bed in your own home you should be safe, and clearly Plumpet wasn't.

'Did Ronnie do this to you?' I asked her as gently as I could.

She shook her head. When she spoke it was as if her tongue were thickened in her mouth. 'He couldn't,' she mumbled. 'He wouldn't.'

It was then I felt that she really didn't know what had happened to her. I think she was terrified. She could hardly move her hands at all. It took a while for me to realise that she might not even have known that she had been assaulted.

I got her a glass of water hoping it would help her to speak more easily because her mouth sounded so dry and cracked. Her pupils were dilated. I held one of her hands in mine and I stroked her and talked gently to her, trying to help her refocus.

'What do you remember?' I asked her.

'Dad came home,' she said. There was a long pause.

'And then what happened?'

'Ronnie and I walked the dog, then we went into Theresa's house, and Cat wasn't on the patio, so we sat and had a drink.'

'What did you drink?'

She seemed to think for ages. 'He poured us each a Coke.'

'Did you drink yours?'

She did not remember. She seemed to remember absolutely nothing else. I wondered if he had slipped something into the Coke.

I recalled Maria telling me that on her last day of school, the Principal had said to them all, 'Never sit on a boy's knee, and never have a drink that you haven't opened yourself.' Maria told me that she and her classmates had nearly had convulsions trying not to laugh, but that in hindsight the second part of the advice had become very good sense.

After they left for the hospital, Richie Fairbrother, the family doctor, going with them, I took Waldorf aside and said to him, 'It all points to Ronnie Fields, and yet I find it hard to believe.'

Waldorf chooses to hide behind a façade, which amuses him. It amuses me too. He pretends to have schoolboy things on his mind all the time –

it's very droll, but behind the plummy utterances and the m'darlings and m'dears, there is a very astute mind at work.

'It's way too early to say to whom it points,' he said.

'But she was out with Ronnie,' I argued.

'If you ask me,' he remarked, 'Ronnie had no need to attack her – unless, of course, that's what turns him on.'

'What do you mean?'

'She was so sweet with him. I got the impression that she adored him. Where was his rush? He's an intelligent boy. They've just moved in next door. Why would he assault the girl in the next house a couple of days after he'd moved in? He was loving what he was getting – anyone could see that. He liked knocking at the door. He liked asking her to go out for a walk. And she liked it too. There was no reason for him to do something like this.'

'But what if he did do it?'

'Softly softly catchee monkey,' Waldorf said, returning to his more obscure way of speech.

'What do you mean?' I asked. The funny thing about Waldorf is that he never, ever irritates me – if someone else was that obtuse I would be seething, but with Waldorf it is not like that.

'Don't rush this,' he said. 'All that matters at the moment is Plumpet.'

When the detectives arrived, Ronald Fields was here dropping in flowers. Ronald tuned in very quickly to what was going on, although there was, perhaps understandably, a sense of disbelief on his part. From a distance I can see that he was being friendly – just a decent neighbour, I suppose, who was delivering a gift that he and his wife had forgotten the previous evening. And he walked into a minefield. He was astute enough to realise immediately who the prime suspect was likely to be. His insistence on being included in the 'team' was probably because of the fact that his son's head was on the chopping block. And yet, a bit of me suspected that he just wanted to help the neighbours who had made his family feel welcome that Christmas. I still feel that.

But I was first and foremost a grandmother, and the thought of Plumpet being hurt by anyone in any shape or form, being bruised and worse ... it was absolutely unbearable.

Oh, I had done the busy-busy thing – organising the dinner, parboiling potatoes for roasting, cleaning the celery – which, I might add, is a tedious job. I don't understand why string-free celery hasn't yet been produced. We can put men on the moon, and genetically modify straw-berries, but we haven't yet sorted the celery problem. It is probably because men don't have to scrape celery. Yes, I know. There are women scientists, but they are clearly not working in the department of celery modification.

Anyway, all the time I was doing these things my mind was being tortured by the memory of Plumpet's bruises, and the blood in her bed.

I was very polite to Ronald Fields at first but then suddenly I needed him out of the house.

'You'll have to leave,' I said. 'These people,' I

gesticulated in the direction of Joe and Margaret, 'have a job to do, and we need it done now.'

Bugger off my mind was saying. And yet at the same time I didn't want him racing off home to rig up some alibi with his son. Once that thought occurred to me, I felt that keeping him in the house with us might be a better option. I was torn between needing his departure and wanting him present.

'Margaret,' I said, 'may I speak to you privately for a moment?'

I took the female detective or forensic specialist or whatever she was, back into the hall and laid the situation out clearly to her. I explained that the last person Plumpet had been with was Ronald Fields's son, and I felt that he should be interviewed as quickly as possible.

'It's all right,' she said.

Though it bloody well wasn't, no matter what she might say.

'Someone has already been sent next door to the Fields's house to see the son. They're probably there right now. We got the name when we were down in the hospital. We just hadn't connected Ronnie Fields with Detective Inspector Ronald Fields. The address didn't ring any bells because the Fields used to live somewhere else. I think they only just moved here?' Her voice had a question mark in it, and I agreed that they had literally only just moved in.

With that the phone rang. Waldorf took it. It was Maureen Fields ringing to ask Ronald to come home immediately as their son Ronnie was about to be taken down to the police station for questioning.

I am not hugely into sympathy. I might have been once upon a time, but Dirk's demise put paid to that. There are too many levels of sympathy which are loaded. 'Millie darling, I really feel for you,' was a constant line in my life back then. And you knew your husband had felt up the bitch. When friends of mine – and few real friends turned out to be women – went through grief or trauma, I pulled out the practical stops only. I never said, 'You poor thing,' in case it left them waking in a sweat at night wondering if I knew something they didn't know. Instead I brought around smoked salmon, or sent them a case of champagne – something that would give them a little comfort or a pleasant distraction, and if they did wake in the night in a sweat because of some bit of bitchery, they could always go down to the fridge and nibble the salmon, or have a glass of bubbly.

That said, I did feel something when I saw Ronald Fields's face after Maureen called. How could I not? I have a son too.

The man did not seem to know what to say. He kept looking at us.

'Go on home,' Joe said to him.

Ronald looked at me. He reached out to take my hands but I pulled them away from him.

'God help us all,' he said. His face was white and taut.

Waldorf explained to Joe and Margaret – I am not really sure how we all got on to first names so quickly, though Waldorf has this theory that because I'm so often interviewed and people have read my books, they feel they know me, so first names come naturally (he also says that I am the equivalent of a national treasure) – anyway, Waldorf explained to Joe and Margaret that we had all been in and out of Plumpet's bedroom and might have contaminated it. They said we should not worry. Then they asked what downstairs had looked like this morning.

'What do you mean?' I asked.

'Was there any trace of a scuffle down here? Any sign of blood? Anything out of the ordinary – anything at all?'

I looked at Waldorf. Waldorf looked at me. We both looked at Daphne. We all shook our heads.

'Do you have any reason to think this happened downstairs?' Waldorf asked.

This was after the two officers had dressed in white clothing from head to foot, and had been in Plumpet's room from where they removed her bedclothes and the clothing on the floor, and they were looking around downstairs, going through each room.

'Well,' Margaret said, 'it doesn't look like it happened upstairs – so we need to work out where it *did* happen. None of it fits together. We'll be back later and we'll talk to you and Plumpet's parents then.'

'Shouldn't you check next door?' Waldorf asked.

'With the Fields? No, there's someone else in there at the moment.'

'I didn't mean the Fields,' Waldorf said. 'I

meant in the house on the other side – Theresa Carmody's. She's away at the moment and Plumpet and Ronnie Fields went in there to let the cat in or out, I don't know which.'

'To let it in,' Daffers said.

In – out. Out – in. Bloody Cat was probably howling to be let out at this stage.

'We'd have to get permission to enter the house,' Joe said.

'Millie m'dear,' Waldorf remarked, 'I should go in and check that the cat is all right. Why don't Margaret or Joe come with me to give me a hand?'

'Maybe I should go in,' I said.

'Under the circumstances I wouldn't like you to go in by yourself, and I think Daffers and the Dumpling would like you to stay with them.'

He could be so clear-thinking when he wanted to. Joe said that if Waldorf were going in next door he would go with him just so that they could continue their conversation. Everyone was talking between the lines, if you follow me. Clearly Joe could not go in and take a look, but if he were accompanying Waldorf and it was just to let the cat out, well, then it was a different matter.

Waldorf said later that there didn't appear to be anything out of the ordinary. 'Millie,' he said, 'the place looked tidy. No mess of any kind.'

'They had a drink,' I said to him. Plumpet had said that she and Ronnie Fields had had a Coke.

'Well, they'd cleaned up after themselves,' he said. 'There were no dirty glasses.'

The dishwasher was full but it had been run. The cat was sitting inside the conservatory and wanted breakfast or whatever cats want in the morning, so Waldorf had given it a bowl of milk. He was going to boot it out, when Joe said to leave it in.

'We've to go back to the hospital now,' he said, 'but we'll come back later, and if the cat is in and you need to let it out, I can go with you. We need to talk to Plumpet again. She hadn't said earlier that she'd been in Ms Carmody's.'

Poor Plumpet. I knew instinctively that she hadn't told them because she did not want them thinking that Ronnie had hurt her, and saying that she had been in Theresa Carmody's would have been the same as saying that he had had every opportunity...

They asked us about Theresa Carmody. I once described her to Waldorf as a wannabe-writer, but I could afford to be generous because of my success. I knew that she was fascinated by what she saw as the formula I had found for writing a bestseller, but part of my secret for success I would not give away, even to the most ardent of fans. It was a fact that to do something properly, to write something that touches people's hearts, you have to have been in that place yourself. As they say, all fiction is based on fact.

My marriage had never been idyllic, even though I naïvely thought it was, and it wasn't until it really fell apart that I saw all the flaws. So many flaws indeed that it looked like a moth-eaten net curtain, and I wondered how it had held together at all for even a month, let alone for years.

But I also saw, when it had ended by my darling

Dirk dying of a dunking, that tragedy worn on one's sleeve has no appeal at all – either for oneself or for the onlooker. It occurred to me that ordinary people like me – all right, I know that people say I'm not that ordinary, that I am a walking eccentric, but in fact I was blandness personified, and I just chose to attach a few eccentricities on to myself, or maybe, as Waldorf once remarked, I grew into the embodiment of an eccentric ... ah, who knows or cares? Anyway, it occurred to me that ordinary people like a happy ending. I know I did. I knew that I had wanted Dirk to love me as I loved him; the fact that he was not the ideal partner, or that we were not remotely suited was neither here nor there. But I had the formula there for writing a novel: take a woman, push her to the edge, maybe break her heart, but then give her love, heal her, rescue her... It didn't have to be the heartbreaker who finally spent the rest of his life with her. Give her someone else, someone with broader shoulders, a more handsome face, a kinder heart or a bigger willy. Or even a smaller one.

It didn't matter. Just give her someone who would love her, as she deserved to be loved.

But you couldn't tell that to Theresa Carmody. Theresa was born with a silver spoon of sausagemeat in her precocious mouth, or maybe it was a silken condom encasing the sausage meat. She lived a life that was full of people and laughter and money, and she had never lived on the edge. Or maybe it was that she had never had to look over the edge, down that precipice to total blackness. I did not doubt that she had cried

236

from sadness, felt the pangs of loneliness, hurt from rejection – hadn't we all? But I didn't think that she had known or ever would know huge grief.

It is shock that changes us.

If we need to reinvent ourselves later in our lives, shock certainly helps.

'What do you want?' Dirk McHarg had once asked me. It was probably for a birthday or a Christmas present. And the answer had been that I wanted for nothing. I had everything, or so I thought. But the shock of loss changed all that. It brought me up short. I didn't want for money. I didn't want for a roof over my head. But I was so badly hit that my taking to writing was my way of rebuilding my self-esteem and repairing some of the damage.

Waldorf came much later – he was the icing on my latest cake. No jam doughnuts or chocolate éclairs in *his* cake shop. It was all yo-yos and more interesting fetishes. And he had left his partner to come to me.

'Are you sure you want to?' I asked him. Even then, with all that success and money behind me, some forty-plus books on, I put so little value on myself that I couldn't imagine someone would actually want to leave someone else to be with me.

'Do you doubt me?' he asked.

Well, yes, I did. But I was proved wrong.

Theresa Carmody flittered from boyfriend to boyfriend. She partied heavily. She was a fun neighbour. And as such I described her to

Margaret and Joe.

'She has a new boyfriend – they went off somewhere last night, to a hotel somewhere, she didn't say which one. But she should be back either tonight or tomorrow. That's the way I understood it,' I explained.

'And the boyfriend?'

'Tony something. Fonsetti or Fonzetti – I'm not sure. I only met him the once, and that was yesterday.'

'What does Theresa do for a living?' asked Margaret.

'She's a sort of heiress,' I said. 'The sausage empire – Wallace, you know. She and her sister dabble in writing.'

'Would we know the sister?' Margaret asked.

'Polo Carmody? Possibly. She covers sport in one of the tabloids.'

'Polo Carmody?' Joe said. 'Yes. I know the name.'

Shortly after that they left us alone, Daphne, the Dumpling, Waldorf and me. We moved into the sitting room, and Daphne pointed out that we had forgotten to turn on the Christmas tree lights. I forced myself to ignore the carrot Daphne had stuck on the window. It looked like an extraordinary phallus. Just as well the child had stuck it on the snowman's face.

We hadn't even lit the fire. We did so then. At least Waldorf did, and I put the goose in the oven while Daphne laid the table. The Dumpling stayed with Waldorf to help him. Then he called us in to join him and the Dumpling. He thought that he and I should give the girls their presents. And he was right. It was Christmas, and we needed to do our best to keep their spirits up.

Every so often an image of Plumpet came into my mind. She bruised so easily. I tried to think no further than the bruises. I had no doubt that she had been a virgin, and I had very little doubt that she now no longer was. I had to close my mind to the image of the blood on the sheets.

Too much blood. Way too much blood.

Unbearable.

The Dumpling was delighted with the small farm I had bought her. She already had a Lego farm or one of those building-block ones. This one was different. It came with a variety of livestock and a farmer and his wife. But she was most taken with the extra pigs purchased by Waldorf. She lined up all the animals in rows, beaming happily at them. But every so often she would get up and shuffle over to look out of the window, and I knew she was missing the others. I presumed the whole business was passing over her head, so I did my best to reassure her that Dad and Mum and Plumpet would be back soon.

'Should I put fresh bedding on Plumpet's bed?' I wondered aloud.

'We should have asked those two while they were here,' Waldorf said. 'I'll go and phone them and check that they are finished in her room,' he added, taking a card from his pocket.

When he returned from using the phone, he said that yes, it was all right to go ahead and put fresh bedclothes on the bed, and that according to Joe, they were just about finishing up in the hospital and should be back soon.

I left him with the Dumpling while Daphne came upstairs to help me. I wanted to give her a bit of time alone with me in case she needed to talk. Not that I really knew anything more than she did, but just in case.

'Will this affect things with Raleigh?' she asked me. She sounded very grown-up all of a sudden.

'How do you mean?' I said as I raided the airing cupboard.

'Well, Ronnie being his brother,' she said.

I wanted to be fair. I wanted to be reasonable. I wanted to say that we didn't know who had done this. We must not judge until we did. But I also wanted to protect her. If this was the work of Ronnie Fields, where did that leave poor Daphne? Where did it leave poor any of us?

'Do you think Ronnie did it?' I asked her, as I handed her the pillowcases.

She was silent for ages. I just went on sorting out items, as I knew that we required a blanket for under the sheets as they had even taken away the mattress cover and the quilt.

'Grammer, I just don't believe he could have done it,' she said.

'Why not?' I asked her. I did say it gently because I wanted to encourage her to talk.

'Because...' another long pause. 'Because he's Raleigh's brother. He's Ronald and Maureen's son. Because he's too like them. They're like a parcel.'

I knew what she meant. They were too intact. That was it. And I felt that she was right.

'Daphne,' I said, 'I don't believe he did it either. And until it's proven otherwise then you should feel very free to go with your own instincts.'

'But if he did do it?' she asked.

'Why go down that road unless we have to?'

'Raleigh must be feeling awful,' she said.

They all must be, I thought. For a moment I was able to move outside of myself, and the pain I was feeling for my family. What with George just home after a long absence, and Maria ... it didn't bear thinking about. As parents they must be in agony. But so must Ronald and Maureen Fields. They must be rueing the day they moved in next to us.

'Do you think I could call in to see him?' she asked. 'Raleigh, I mean.'

'Tell you what, Daphne,' I said, 'I think you should wait until your dad and mum come home. There'll be time enough to go next door – just leave it for now.'

I did try, especially when George was around, not to interfere too much. Men like to feel they run their own houses, and it was important to let George think he did. It suited Maria to let me run the show on a day-to-day basis; we had talked about it and she had reassured me that my input was vital.

'When you and George are away,' she said, 'I get the full brunt of it, so I'm happy for what you call interference.'

Well, it gave me carte blanche.

Daphne and I made up the bed for Plumpet. There was a spare duvet in the top of the airing cupboard, and Daphne surprised me by how she rejected the first cover I chose. 'It needs to match Plumpet's room,' she said. 'You know how she likes colours to ... you know.'

'Coordinate?' I asked.

'That's it,' she said. 'Coordinate. That's the word.'

This may sound like nothing in the retelling, but the Daphne of yesterday would not have taken a new word or a correct word on board. Yet here she was, colour coordinating her sister's bedclothes, and agreeably using a word when it was offered to her. It was very gratifying, because if there is one thing I've tried to give my granddaughters, it's a full vocabulary.

I looked around Plumpet's room.

'Tidier than mine, huh, Grammer?' Daphne said.

'I wouldn't know,' I replied. 'I have not been in there in a month of Sundays.'

She grinned. I did too. We were both recalling Daphne and a bad head cold about six weeks earlier. Maria had gone to work, and I was playing Matron or Head Nurse or whatever.

I brought the child up a bowl of soup and I dropped the soup spoon on the floor. Bending down to pick it up I accidentally saw under her bed from where an extraordinary cider-like smell was emanating. I looked in closer to discover that she must have eaten every apple from the orchard and just put the cores under the bed.

'Are you trying to grow penicillin?' I had asked her.

She leaned out of the bed and peered

underneath it. 'So that's where they went,' she said.

Cheeky monkey. As if you could put a couple of hundred apple cores under your bed and not know it.

'The minute you're better,' I admonished her, 'you will get out of that bed and pick up every one of those furry rotten lumps.'

'I can't,' she wailed, hanging upside down over the side of the bed with her hair trailing on the ground and her bottom in the air. 'They look disgusting – I can't touch them. I bet I didn't put them there anyway.'

I gave her upturned bottom a wallop, which brought on a wail of fury.

'I mean it,' I said. 'Every single one of them.'

'Did you ever get rid of those apple cores?' I asked her now as she plumped up the pillows on her sister's bed.

She shook her head so that her blonde curls bounced up and down. 'I forgot all about them,' she said, adding in a most un-Daphne like way, 'I must do that tomorrow.'

I didn't say anything. Another time I would have, but there was something about her that had changed or shifted in the last eight hours. She went to Plumpet's wardrobe and took out clean pyjamas and put them on the bed, arranging them neatly on the pillow.

'There,' she said. 'That looks better, doesn't it?'

Chapter Fourteen

Plumpet's Tale

Time. It drifted. Then sped. Then it was stationary. I saw the concern in their eyes. I was afraid they would think I had taken something. I needed them to get me out of this. I needed to be me again. To feel my hands and feet. I could hear the questions before they were asked. *Where were you? What happened? Did you take something? Smoke something? Inhale something? Swallow something? Tell us, we can only help you if we know. Who did this to you? My God, who did this to you?*

My arms were disembodied. My head was full of matter that was not mine. Mum's eyes were full of fear. Grammer's voice was full of understanding. She reassured. Mum's words reassured; her voice did not. Dad's eyes moved from worry to fury.

Ronnie would not have done this to me.

Cat was outside and Ronnie went to let him in. My drink was on the table. Then there was a blank. My voice, furry and thick, started to return. When I looked down at my body I could see marks on my chest. My upper arms were bruised. This was terror that I was feeling. Did I fall? My head felt woolly, not like it had banged off something, just strange as though I was disembodied.

I wanted to sleep but I was afraid to.

Dr Fairbrother came. He shone a light into my eyes. His voice came and went. I wondered if I could have had a stroke, because I had no notion of what had happened to me. Great-grand-mother had a stroke and was paralysed down one side for a while. Could that be what had happened to me?

Dr Fairbrother reassured me. He said that I would be all right. Would be. Not was, but would be. When? When the bruises faded? When memory returned? When I could talk clearly? When I could forget, even though I had no memory?

In the hospital I was put in a small room by myself, where I was examined again. I had never been in hospital before, other than visiting, and I wanted to go home. It was Christmas Day, and there were presents to be given, and the fire to be lit in the sitting room with the pine cones Daffers and the Dumpling and I had collected a few weeks back and kept to burn on Christmas Day, and then we would open our Christmas presents and...

I looked at my hand to see the ring Dad gave me the previous day. Its little green stone was shining.

They did unspeakable things to me in the hospital; they checked bits of me which had never been checked before. 'There are procedures which we have to go through,' said this nurse. She was kindly but brusque. I wanted Mum with me, but I didn't want her to know what they were doing to me. Another woman held my hand. She explained slowly and carefully as if I didn't quite understand English, 'We're looking for traces of whoever did this to you. Sperm. A hair. Anything. We're taking swabs and samples.'

By now I knew I had been raped.

I knew the word rape. I knew the meaning of the word, but I did not know what rape actually was, even though I had, apparently, been raped. I thought it was something brutal. I thought it was the taking of something from you. I thought it was penetration by force.

And it was all those things. But I knew none of them. I had no memory.

'Please,' I asked the woman. She had come from somewhere which deals with this all the time. 'Please,' I said, 'does this mean that I participated?'

She looked at me as though she didn't understand. 'What do you mean?' she asked.

'Because I don't remember,' I said. 'Because I remember nothing, what does that mean?'

'They think you were drugged before this happened to you. That's what the blood tests are about.'

Drugged.

Raped.

Words I couldn't really understand. What I knew was that my memory was gone, and that my body hurt. My neck and breasts hurt. It hurt between my legs.

'Can I bath or shower?' I asked.

'As soon as we're finished,' they explained to me. 'You can bath then, and shower too if you like.'

They looked at each other as they proceeded

246

with a comb, and other instruments.

'Are you very sore, pet?' the doctor asked.

I nodded. I wasn't crying any more. Grammer always said it was better not to cry, that it didn't make you feel any better.

'Do you remember getting into bed last night?' the doctor asked.

'No.'

'What's the last thing you remember?'

I explained about being in the neighbour's house, and then the blank. 'My ring is gone from my finger,' I told them.

'When did you last see it?'

'Last night. My father gave it to me as a coming home present – he's been away for months. I was wearing it. It's gone.' For some reason that made me start to cry. I didn't know why. I just wanted my ring back. I was afraid Dad would think I'd been careless with it, and I didn't want to hurt him.

I looked down at my hand and the ring was there, and then I remembered looking at it a few minutes earlier and it had been there.

'But it's there,' I said. 'I...' I didn't understand. I thought it wasn't there.

'It's all right,' the woman said. 'Your memory is coming and going in flashes. It is there. It's on your finger. So don't worry about it.'

But I was worried. I didn't understand.

'Why don't I remember properly?' I asked.

'It's a side-effect of the particular drug we think you were given,' someone explained.

It was so intrusive. I knew what they were saying. I knew that they were doing their job, and that part of their job was to patch me up, and also to gather information. There are words to explain what they did to me, but those words didn't reach anywhere near the depths of me which were being unveiled. And yet they were doing their best. I could recognise their kindness. There was kindness in the hand that held mine. And in the words, 'I'll be as quick as I can,' 'I'm being as gentle as I can,' 'I'm sorry, pet, nearly done.'

I lay there as they did their work, and I wondered if I would ever recover. Indeed, I wondered if I would ever find out what I had to recover from.

'It wasn't Ronnie,' I said to the policewoman. 'He wouldn't do this.'

'You're not to worry,' she said to me. 'We'll look into this. What you need to do is to concentrate on recovering. And anything you remember, anything else, no matter how small or how trivial it seems, you can contact me.'

Ronnie would not have done this. I knew that. I knew it like I knew that something terrible had once happened to the Dumpling. Long ago before she came to us. Like an instinct. Indefinable.

'Did they find traces – the DNA thing they were talking about?' I asked.

She shook her head.

'But there must have been something?'

'It looks as if there is nothing. They've taken swabs, but they're not hopeful. It is as if you had already bathed,' she said.

Of course, I could have had a swim in the sea for all I remembered.

They let me rest. Mum came in with Dad. She held my hand and he went and stood at the window. He kept turning and looking at me, and then turning away. After a while he left the room. With Mum holding my hand I tried to sleep. I lay there, but the void that was the previous night was larger than my mind and I couldn't escape from it into sleep.

'Can you give her something?' Mum asked a doctor.

No, they couldn't. They still hadn't identified what drug I had taken and they were afraid to give me anything.

'Even something to relax her?'

'Maybe later. But not yet,' was the response.

We had read *Hamlet* in school. You know that bit about when he is contemplating death and he fears what dreams may come – that is what sleep seemed like to me. I feared it. But I also feared being awake. I craved unconsciousness. Mum held my hand and stroked my fingers. I must have dozed because the hands on the clock had moved on when I next looked at it.

She drank tea and made me drink a cup too.

'It hurts,' I told her. Not the tea. Me.

The bruises on my chest and arms didn't really hurt that much, I realised. They had earlier, but maybe it was because I had looked down and seen what I looked like. I bruised easily. I still do. I go black and blue, which looks way worse than it is. But other bits of me hurt. Like between my legs. And the black hole inside my head terrified me.

249

I was very close to my family, but still there were things we didn't say. I knew all the things girls are supposed to know growing up. What I didn't learn at home I learned in school where there were classes explaining everything, and we were given pamphlets which I read. But it's like getting your period – even though you read about it, and understand the biological facts, it isn't until you actually get it that you can comprehend it. It's only then that you know that your life has been changed – moved on, I suppose. That what is happening to you now will happen every single month, bar pregnancy, for thirty-five years or more. I suppose it is the same with pregnancy – you know the facts, but it is the experience alone that clarifies it or makes it real. I think it must be like that with rape too. But because of the blank inside my head I couldn't get around the darkness to reach the place where I could realise or identify with what had happened.

I had been penetrated. I could feel the after-effects but my knowledge of the act was absent. I wanted to ask Mum about it, but I didn't know how. Because there were things we talked about and things we didn't, even though we were a very close-knit family.

Something was niggling at me. I had thought of something and I didn't know what it was. I tried to re-run the thoughts I had had.

'What is it?' Mum asked. I realised my hand was squeezing hers tightly. I was afraid.

Pregnancy.

To be made pregnant unawares. To carry some

horrific progeny from this event.

'What if I'm pregnant, Mum?'

'It's all right, darling,' she said. 'They're going to give you something to make sure that doesn't happen. It'll be all right.'

They had already thought of that. There was nothing they didn't know or think about. Except how to open my mind and release memory into the void.

'Promise?' I needed so much reassurance. I needed to hear her using my name or endearments like *darling* or *my child* so that I'd know I was still her daughter, that in her eyes I was not damaged as her offspring.

'I promise,' she said. 'I promise.'

'What'll happen to me?' I asked.

'Nothing will happen to you,' she said. Then she paused as if considering my question. 'What do you mean?' she asked.

I meant ... but I didn't know what I meant. I didn't know what I was supposed to do. How I was supposed to feel. I didn't know anything.

I didn't answer. I didn't know the answer. I didn't know the question.

Within several hours I felt 'normal'. Of course I didn't know what normal could mean after being raped. But I felt completely reconnected with my arms and legs. Even the dull woolliness in my head had eased. But while all of those bits of me had returned, with those normal sensations something new had arrived and it wouldn't go away.

It was sheer unrelenting terror.

I had been afraid of things in the past – of Dad not coming home, of something happening to Mum, family things ... afraid of something happening to the structure of our family, of pain or loss to one or all of them. But those fears were ones you managed to live with. You told yourself not to think about them, not to dwell on them because otherwise how could you get up in the morning and go to school? But what I was feeling now was a different kind of fear – it had to do with darkness and the void in my head, to do with what had happened to me, what had been done to me, and my lack of knowledge as to how that had come about, and what it entailed.

I wanted to think of nice things. My mind drifted and I could imagine the aromatic smell of the pine cones on the fire, and the Dumpling all dressed up in her new Christmas clothes playing with the present I had made for her. I had bought a bag of pasta and sprayed the contents with gold paint. When they had dried I had painted little green leaves and holly berries on them. It had taken me ages and they were awfully pretty. I just knew she would like them. The berries were scarlet, and the leaves dark green, and when they had dried I had varnished them. I was going to suggest to her that she put them away with the decorations when Christmas was over. She liked keeping things in boxes and going and finding them later. I knew she would like the idea of that. She kept all these empty boxes in her bedroom and she looked inside them as if she could see things we couldn't. I knew she would like my idea. It would be like the crib. When we were little, both Daffers and I hated it being put away after Christmas, but oh, the joy when it was taken out the following year. It was like coming on it anew. I just knew the Dumpling would get that joy again in a year's time when we took down the box and she would find her Christmas pasta all over again. It would be like another present.

I hoped I would get home in time to give it to her myself. I didn't want to spend the night in hospital.

I thought of Ronnie Fields. I wondered what he was doing, and if he was out walking WC, and if he would take him just once round the block, or go for a really long walk. I had hoped we would go for a walk together and maybe he would kiss me while we were out. Maybe up in the park, or if it were getting dark, maybe under a lamppost with that dull yellow light shining through the mist that always seemed to be present on Christmas night. And he would hold my hand...

Chapter Fifteen

Maria's Tale

I don't do guilt, as Grammer says. I don't believe in it. And yet while George and I sat outside the hospital room where our eldest child was being treated for rape and serious assault, I wondered over and over again how I could have prevented this from happening.

Had I been too busy in bed with George that I didn't hear something in her voice when she called good night? But George said no, adamantly no. It was the first time I ever heard him sounding like his mother.

'Don't do this to yourself,' he said. 'Once you start casting blame or taking on guilt you won't be able to find a way forwards.'

He admitted though that he was having the same problems as me, although he was sure that we would have picked up something from her voice had the assault already taken place at that time. The police said the same thing. They said that they were sure she must have left the house again.

And yet Plumpet was not a sneaky child. She was not the kind to slip out of the door when she thought you weren't looking.

'We have to think rationally,' George said. 'We have to find a reason for her to have left the house again.'

The only reason I could think of was to meet Ronnie Fields. And yet ... why would she have done that? She had just been with him. We had trusted her to be with him, and him to be with her. In fact, I was delighted when I met our new neighbours, pleased at how like us they were – normal, decent, with similar values. At first glance they were ideal. And for Plumpet to have made a friend so quickly and so smoothly with such a nice boy was a relief. She had no close friends at all. She preferred to be at home. She liked reading. She was happy with her own company but she liked family around. And she was categorically not the kind of child to pretend she was going to bed and then to slip back out of the house.

I said this to the police, but I could feel them thinking that this was a typical parent's reaction. And I know that if Delia said that about her daughter Daisy, I would think 'don't be so naïve' – that Daisy would be the first to find an escape route out of the house if that was what she wanted. And possibly Daphne too.

That was difficult to think about. It was difficult to take on the idea that one of my children might do something like that – and yet, if one were likely to do it, it would be Daphne. And then if Daphne were a candidate for such action, was it not possible that Plumpet might be too?

The fact was, as the police said, Plumpet had left the house.

There was too much to think about. There were these diverse events, which somehow inter-connected and the result was that our daughter was now lying in a hospital bed, covered in bruises, raped and drugged. And she had left the house in order for that to happen.

'Could someone have broken in and forced her to leave with them?' I asked.

'We're not ruling that out,' I was told. 'But it is not likely. You were awake. There are two other children – no one heard anything.'

'The Dumpling doesn't speak,' I said. 'She couldn't have said anything.'

'But,' George interrupted, 'if Dumpling is concerned about something, she goes for assistance. Like this morning – she was the one who got you out of bed to go into Plumpet.'

That was true. And Dumpling had been awake the previous night. I knew that. I wanted her to be asleep because I wanted George to myself after the girls had gone to bed, but I knew that Dumpling had been awake in her cot, passing time until she either fell asleep or thought it was close enough to morning to come in to us.

Of course, it was possible that she had been asleep, but she is such a light sleeper – she once even heard the mousetrap in the kitchen spring at about three in the morning, and had dragged me downstairs. It took me a few blurry-eyed moments in the kitchen to realise what had happened and that the trap had sprung. Fortunately the mouse must have leaped clear of the device so I didn't have to deal with any contents, dead or otherwise, but the point is that the Dumpling has supersonic hearing. Therefore it confirmed my suspicion that Plumpet walked out by herself. Otherwise the Dumpling would have picked up on something.

Between the emotions I was experiencing – my distress for Plumpet, my heartbreak at what had happened to her, my fear for her – the rational part of my mind was struggling to find an explanation. What would cause a girl of her age to slip back out of the house so late on Christmas Eve?

I wanted George to go back home and ask

Ronnie Fields outright for an answer, but he wouldn't. He said we had to wait. He said that his place was in the hospital with Plumpet and me. Pretty rich I thought, coming from him. I mean, I thought his place was overlooking paddyfields in Cambodia or somewhere. I could feel the frustration rising in me. It was as if I was bottling up a thousand emotions and I had no way of airing them. With Plumpet, when I was brought in to her, which was at regular intervals, I could hardly speak. I knew that what she needed was reassurance, but I was so distracted and all over the place that it was all I could do to sit beside her and hold her thin hand in mine and say, 'It's all right, darling,' when it quite clearly was anything but all right.

She looked so frightened and so lost. Outside the door when George went to get coffee I kept trying to put myself in her place, to try to imagine what it was like – that kind of violation and the total absence of memory.

And the awful thing was that I kept thinking that at least I could help her, whereas if it were me lying in there in that bed, I would have no one to help me. Which was ridiculous, but that is what I was thinking. I would normally have had Grammer, but Grammer was George's mother, and I was having these terrible feelings of anger towards him, and I started to feel anger towards her for having a son who insisted on working as far away from his family as possible. Now and again I would pull myself up short and think, Well, I did know he was going to work abroad when I married him – but then the other thoughts would surge in, and I was thinking if he hadn't come home the previous evening I might have been more in tune with what was happening, and somehow I might have prevented this.

My poor Plumpet.

Because it was Christmas, the hospital was down to the essence of its staff only, but they did everything they could for us. The woman from the rape centre came and talked to George and me. She talked about counselling for us, counselling for Plumpet, counselling for everyone until I wanted to scream out, 'Is there not some way we can move out of this? Is there not some way we can put the clock back or put the clock forward and move from these moments in time?'

The doctor came – a young woman who looked like she hadn't slept in a month or more, but whose gentleness with Plumpet was astounding.

The police came. Again it was a woman who spoke to Plumpet while her partner talked to us. We went over the previous evening until I felt it was written in blood that I was too busy being fucked by my husband to hear what was going on in my own house. But later it transpired of course that nothing *had* happened in the house – that Plumpet had left. But why? And how?

Eventually the doctor and the young policewoman whose name was Margaret came and talked to us again. Because of the shortage of staff and the labs being virtually closed there was a certain amount of guesswork going on.

'Mr and Mrs McHarg,' said the doctor, removing her glasses and sitting on a chair in front of us, 'this is what we are surmising, although we won't be sure until tomorrow or the day after when the lab checks Plumpet's blood: we are almost sure that Rohypnol, or something similar is what was used to drug your daughter.'

'Rohypnol?' George and I were now in totally unfamiliar territory.

'It's a brand name for Flunitrazepam. Flunitrazepam is a benzodiazepine, you see. That is to say it's like a tranquilliser – very potent.'

'A tranquilliser?' I was like a parrot.

'Like Valium for example, but many times stronger.'

'How was it given to her?'

'In tablet form – probably in a drink. As I said, it causes sedation. It has a lot of side-effects, and these include amnesia, muscle relaxation, the slowing down of the psychomotor responses.'

I couldn't speak. I sat there listening to her, wondering if any of this was going to make sense.

It was George who started asking the questions.

'Could she have taken it deliberately?'

'It's always possible,' Margaret from the police said thoughtfully. 'I mean, if it were handed to her she might have put it in her mouth and taken a drink to swallow it. But no one would willingly take it. It has these terrifying side-effects. We don't come across it much here, but in the United States it is rather better known. It's called "roofies" for short, and it is, to all intents and purposes, a date-rape drug.'

I sat there. In a way there was no surprise – I

259

mean, we had been told that Plumpet had been drugged and then raped. We knew she had no memory of it. So it all made sense – and yet it was outside reason. This was our daughter. Our child. Such things weren't supposed to happen to one's child.

'If it didn't happen in our house,' George said, 'and I'm understanding from you that at this stage you are absolutely confident that it didn't, then how did our daughter get back home suffering from all these side-effects?'

'We think that some kind of instinct got her home,' Margaret said.

Like a wounded animal.

I thought of Plumpet, bruised and sore, somehow crawling home to her own bed and waking ... and I wanted to scream again. Oh, the anger, the pain, the frustration. They rose in waves in me, and I sat there wringing my hands.

'How do we treat her?' I asked.

'How do we catch the perpetrator?' George asked.

'What do we do now?' I asked.

There were questions, which came and went. And there were answers, which sometimes made sense and later made none.

Our child needed to be cared for, to be made to understand that our love for her was unchanged. Apparently she might feel guilt, especially as it looked as if she had walked out into this situation.

'Why should she feel guilt?' I asked. 'She did nothing.'

Part of the problem was that she had no memory, which meant that she couldn't even be consoled with facts. We could say to her that it wasn't her fault, but she might have a problem in believing this. And added to all of this, there was no trace evidence. It looked as if she had been cleaned afterwards.

'Cleaned? How would cleaning get rid of the evidence?'

I wanted to die as it was explained what had been done to her. She had been raped. She may or may not have been penetrated by the male organ – that was totally unclear. But she had definitely been penetrated by some implement, which is what had done the more serious tearing and explained the blood in her bed. The so-called positive side of that meant that hopefully she wouldn't have contracted what was called an STD – a sexually transmitted disease. But tests would be run, both now and later to ensure that she had not caught anything. Even after she had been bathed (because they said she would not have been able to bath and shower herself) she would have gone on bleeding.

'So might there be blood at the scene of the crime?' asked George, suddenly in the role of Perry Mason or Detective Ironside.

By now I was crying. George wanted to move away from me to talk to these people without me because as he said, my weeping wasn't helping. But I had to know. I had to be there even if I could only take in part of what we were being told.

'It depends,' said Margaret. 'Whoever did this

261

to her even washed her hair. The thoroughness involved in sending her home clean would imply that wherever it happened was left clean too.'

'Explain,' George snapped. Even his nerves were now fraying.

'Whoever did this knew to leave no traces. He left none on her. I imagine he left none anywhere. Other than the tearing and the bleeding.'

'But you will look?'

'Yes, of course. We have already looked. We will continue to do so. It may or may not be the way of catching the person.'

'The boy next door,' George said.

'Ronnie Fields?'

'Yes. From the point of view that he was the last person we know she was with, he seems the most likely culprit.'

'And from any other viewpoint would you come up with him as a possibility?'

'I've been away,' George said. 'I'm not in a position to assess the situation properly.'

They looked at me. By now there was just Margaret and some other detective. The doctor had gone, and the woman from the rape centre was back in with Plumpet.

I shook my head. 'I only met him briefly,' I said. 'If he did do it, then I just don't understand. He's so...' I searched for a word. 'Boyish,' was what I came up with. 'He's so unlikely to be a rapist,' but maybe that's what a good rapist is – unlikely.

They nodded.

'In our opinion, whoever did this, possibly did it before. Or else he had it very well planned. And in order to plan it, he would have had to be sure that Plumpet would leave her home – so he would have had to have made an assignation. But as her memory seems to be unimpaired up to a point, it seems unlikely she left by appointment.'

'I don't follow.'

'Well, she can remember everything up until about ten forty-five, and after that it is blurry or just gone. And seeing as she saw only Ronnie Fields after ten forty-five, it seems impossible that she had arranged to meet someone later because then she would remember who it was.'

On and on it dragged as they went over and over the options with us. It now transpired that Plumpet didn't remember saying good night to us, but Margaret said that with Rohypnol that was not that unusual. Plumpet could remember being in Theresa Carmody's with a glass of Coke and a bowl of salted almonds, and Ronnie Fields, it appeared, was absolutely clear that he walked her home.

The detective who was with Margaret had been interviewing Ronnie Fields. He took out a sheaf of notes and said, 'Ronnie is adamant that he kept calling the cat but it never appeared. Then he and Plumpet washed the glasses and left them to drain on the sink. He looked again for the cat but there was no sign of it. They left the light on in the hall, and the cat locked in the kitchen. Then he walked Plumpet home – right up to her front door. She let herself in and then he went home.'

'Maybe he didn't go home,' George said.

'You mean, waited outside until Plumpet came

263

back out?'

'Yes.'

'According to his parents, he came in and sat down with them for about half an hour before they all went up to bed.'

Ronnie was but a boy, and as these pieces were taken out and put together, it became clearer and clearer that a ruthless and cunning mind had been behind the assault. Someone with experience. Someone who knew what they were doing.

They gave Plumpet a local anaesthetic and then they stitched her. We took her home in the late afternoon. At first they talked about keeping her in. There are other side-effects to Rohypnol about which they hadn't told us. As the day wore on it transpired they were monitoring her for things like respiratory depression. Someone let slip the fact that people have died from the drug when it has been combined with other drugs or alcohol. I kept thinking thank God Plumpet had not drunk anything other than Coke.

It did occur to me briefly that we as a family were not unique in going through this, but it seemed a sort of exclusive situation, and there was a feeling of isolation attached to it, a feeling of being locked into it and not being able to see any way out of it. I tried saying this to George, but he just said, 'Nothing is unique.' Maybe it was a rational way of viewing the world, and maybe he was right, but I felt that I was trapped, and I hated the idea that Plumpet was feeling that too.

George drove the car and I sat in the back with Plumpet. At some point George had gone home and collected fresh clothing for Plumpet, which Grammer had put together. He said that the police had 'done' her room and had removed any garments which she might have worn the previous day, but by that stage we both knew that whoever had done this to her had been very clever.

He had even washed her hair. The police cut a lock of it to see if the shampoo could be identified in case it would assist in convicting the rapist later.

Plumpet had been bathed and showered again in the hospital; now her hair smelt of apple shampoo and her face looked slightly scrubbed. She was dressed in dark grey trousers with a pale green polo-necked sweater. She leaned against me on the back seat. She is slightly taller than I am but it didn't seem like it that day. She appeared smaller and thinner than she actually is. I wondered if that was because of the frailty which had been exposed in her by this attack. The back of her hand was bruised and punctured from the intravenous drip to which she had been attached in the hospital. I had seen it before they slipped a plaster on it. She looked at it a couple of times and I knew that she was taking in the darkening colour of the bruise, which was emerging from the sides of the bandage. We both knew that the bruises on her body were going through similar changes. They were getting worse as bruises do, before they change and start to fade.

Because of the stitches she sat uncomfortably beside me. I held her hand tightly.

'I'm scared,' she said as we approached our road.

'Tell me what you're scared of,' I said, 'and I'll do my best to stop it from happening.'

'I'm scared...' She shook her head and then bowed it. 'I'm scared of people knowing. I'm scared of how they'll look at me. I'm scared because I'm scared.'

It was as if she were caught in a cycle of fear. I don't know if she had ever been afraid of anything before in her life.

'First of all,' I said, 'no one need know. Just us. Just your family. And we love you more than anything.'

'But people will find out,' she said.

'No, they won't,' I said. 'It can stop right here.'

'But the Fields...'

'We'll talk to them. They won't tell anyone,' George said.

'Your dad is right,' I said. 'They won't want anyone to know either.'

'Ronnie,' she said, and then she stopped.

I didn't know what she was thinking. I tried so hard to put myself in her place, to be her age with all that vulnerability and innocence and hope about life, and to work out what she was feeling. I had no idea.

I tried prompting her, but I couldn't get her to continue.

Home was muted. Grammer and Waldorf were doing their best but I realise now that I was in a state of shock. It was all too much. We came in and settled Plumpet on the sofa, feet up, shoes off, two pillows behind her head. The Dumpling, who would usually be all over her, was frantically trying to get George to pick her up. At first he didn't seem to even see her, until Daphne said, 'Daaaa ... aaad,' in a loud and penetrating voice.

'What?' he said. I knew he had a lot on his mind. Didn't we all?

Daphne went and picked up the Dumpling and handed her to him. 'She needs to be cuddled,' she said to him.

It was all very unlike Daphne.

'Can I get you something?' she then said to Plumpet. 'A drink or something?' Plumpet shook her head. 'I'll bring you down your stocking,' Daphne said. 'You haven't seen it yet.' And before Plumpet could say yea or nay, Daphne had gone haring up the stairs to retrieve Santa's presents.

I looked at Grammer, who made a slight headshake at me. Sometimes she can be quite sensitive. Actually, I'm not being fair. Grammer *is* sensitive, if in an eccentric and unusual way. But I was angry that day. Angry with the lot of them. Except of course the girls. My girls.

Daphne sat beside Plumpet on the sofa and encouraged her to go through her gifts. Waldorf had brought his camera and he took photos of them. He took photographs of everyone, but I know that he took photos of the two of them together because it was such an unusual moment. There was real concern from Daphne, and a muted sadness from Plumpet, which she endeavoured from time to time to disguise.

'Dumpling,' said Daphne, 'come and sit with

267

your sisters and Waldorf can photo the three McHarg girls. Won't you, Waldorf?'

He patted my shoulder at some point, and he said very quietly so that only I could hear, 'You know, Maria, you have every reason to be proud, even on a day like today.'

It was a kind thing to say, and distraught and all as I was, I could see the truth of it. And I *was* proud. I was proud of the three of them, each in their own way, and Daphne was coming up trumps. George retreated behind two large gin and tonics, and I suddenly thought of Martin Garner and wondered what he and his wife, the mother-in-law and the turkey were up to. I knew that if he were here, and if this awful, awful event hadn't happened – how could I even use the word event? It should be crime. This awful, awful crime. But if Martin were here, or I were there, or we were just somewhere else, I could imagine the laughter in his eyes, and hear him saying, 'Fancy a stiff one, Maria?' And we would both have laughed.

Instead I watched George knocking back the second stiff gin and tonic and I wished I were somewhere else.

Evening came, dinner was eaten, crackers were pulled – everyone was doing their best, but there was this dreadful sense of expectancy, and yet there was nothing to be expecting. Plumpet clearly needed bed early. She was sitting between Grammer and me, and from time to time I watched her hand going out to Grammer and being held on Grammer's gold and black-skirted lap. Grammer would hold her hand with one hand and stroke the back of it with the other. Then Plumpet would take her hand back and retrieve her fork and stare at the piece of food speared on the end of the prongs.

George suggested to her that she went to bed after we had picked at the plum pudding, and Plumpet's eyes widened in fear. She opened and closed her mouth and Daphne got up and came to her and put her arms around her shoulders and said, 'It's okay, Plumpet.'

'Perhaps a different bedroom, m'dear,' Waldorf said. It was unclear whom he was addressing, but it struck me as being a very good idea.

'We can move your bed into our room,' I said.

'Or mine,' said Daphne.

The Dumpling waved her spoon in the air and tapped her own chest firmly.

'Or we could move her into the spare room in my apartment,' Grammer said.

'So many offers,' George said to his eldest daughter. 'What would you like?'

What would she like? What a stupid question. What would she like indeed? She'd like the clock put back. She'd like to have a real Christmas without having been raped. She'd probably like Daphne to be slightly whiny and complaining that everyone had got nicer or bigger presents than she had.

What would she like?

I looked at George, and I suddenly wondered what *he* would like. I asked myself, Did he even know what he wanted out of life? Was this it? To come home once every six months and to have all these women from three different generations dancing attendance on him, and worshipping the ground he walked on? Four different generations, I realised as I thought of his grandmother in her nursing home. He calls her Grandam. I wondered, would he go to see her while he was here? He hadn't gone in quite some time – not since she had accused him of constructing the aeroplane in which his father, Dirk, had nose-dived into the South China Sea.

I also wondered how long he was planning on staying, because I knew that it wouldn't be for very long. You see, George did not like it when things weren't completely smooth in his private life. That was probably part of the reason he spent so much time abroad – it meant he did not have to deal with the rough and tumble and the ups and downs of everyday existence. I only realised that while I was sitting there watching him. But the girls loved him, you could see it in their eyes. Plumpet looked at him, and she said, 'I don't know, Dad. So many great offers,' and she gave the tiniest of smiles.

Daphne and I started to clear the dishes from the table and Waldorf said that he still hadn't given Plumpet her present and would she come with him into the sitting room. George lit a cigarette and stared at the ceiling, while the Dumpling played with his lighter.

'George,' I said as I could all too clearly imagine the coloured paper from the crackers igniting under the Dumpling's fumblings.

'Mmmm?' he said vaguely.

'Your lighter,' I snapped. I knew I sounded like a shrew. George was away so much and I was so unused to having to draw his attention to something, that when I did, I was terribly conscious of being a nag. And yet I know from other couples, Sam and Delia for example, and clearly Martin Garner and his wife, that some women nagged or cajoled all the time. It's part of their relationship – but it was not part of mine.

And then, to compound matters, he looked around the table and said, 'What lighter?'

I could feel my lips going into a tight line. 'The lighter our youngest child is about to use,' I said icily.

The Dumpling, totally unused to hearing me speak like that, dropped the lighter on the table and her lip quivered.

'Dumples,' said Daphne as the fat lip quivered even more, 'up you come,' and she lifted the child from her chair. 'We're going to go and look at that doll Santa brought you. I think it looks a bit like Plumpet, don't you? And I think we should tie its hair up just like Plumpet does hers. What do you think?'

The Dumpling nodded as she thought about that, and the lighter and my angry voice were forgotten.

Grammer looked at George and her face was fierce. I retreated from the dining room with the remnants of the plum pudding as I heard her say, 'When you're here you'll make an effort, George. Understood?'

I suppose he was doing his best.

Chapter Sixteen

Dumpling's Tale

My new Barbie doll looked only a little like Plumpet with long hair. And she was not furry and soft, but hard and skinny. Pink Pig was squishy. My Plumpie doll was not. Her knees did not bend. Daffers and I took off her clothes, peeling back layers of satin with tiny fasteners difficult for Dumpling fingers. Shiny lace knickers, hold-up stockings. More like Mum than Plumpet.

'Look at her hair,' said Daffers. 'It's just like Plumpet's.'

It was shiny and soft. With Barbie's hair brushed out, Daffers made two plaits and asked, 'Dumples, is it nicer like this or tied up?'

Dumples was her new name for me. She christened me that Christmas Day. It was a dark day with no light other than the fire and the twinkles on the pine tree. Flickering twinkling glimmering shinely.

My Plumpie doll had no hips. Plumpet had bones over which her trousers sat. There were lots of clothes for the Plumpie doll.

'How will we dress her?' asked Daffers. She picked up jeans and sweatshirts, a tight leather skirt and red sweater, black trousers and a hoodie. We chose the black trousers and hoodie.

'Christmas Day isn't usually like this,' Daffers said to me.

I looked at her, waiting for her to tell me more.

'Today something bad happened to Plumpet,' she told me.

Dumpling saw the pain in Plumpet's eyes. There were marks on her neck and chest. Plumpet hurting.

Mystery Man came home and Mystery Man was Dad. I think. He slept in bed with Mum. Dumpling left in her barred bed alone.

Dumpling hurting.

I heard voices in the night.

'Good night, Dad. Good night, Mum.'

Plumpet going to bed.

Silence on the landing. Plumpet's bedroom door opening. Half a creak, not a whole creak. Why not? Silence. Then Plumpet's feet on the landing carpet, quietly going back downstairs. Creaking sounds from Mum's bedroom where Mystery Man was. Front door opening and closing. Silence. Plumpet gone out. It's dark out there, Plumpet. Come back. Silence. Silence. Silence.

Santa coming?

I heard the sound of a car on the road. Not going up the road. Stopping. Santa coming by car, not reindeer. I knew the sound of that car. I had heard it before. It must have been lent to Santa.

Dumpling snuggled down under the covers to wait for the arrival of a large red man with a sack of surprises. Surprisingly sacked. Silence.

Sleepy times slipping in. Thumb in mouth. Waiting for nighttime noises. More creaks from Mum's bedroom. Silence.

Sleep.

Someone hurt my Plumpet while I slept.

The Plumpie doll in trousers and hoodie looked more like Plumpet. We tied her hair back, so that she was all neat and clean like Plumpet.

'Did you get presents you like?' Daffers asked me.

I nodded. Colouring pencils. Markers. Paper. Kiddywink scissors, as Grammer called them. Jigsaws. Plumpie doll. Gunkey. Lots and lots of fun. A ball. A tape. New stories. Lovely shapes in gold decorated with holly leaves and berries.

Lucky Dumpling.

But no lighter for Dumpling. Snap went the Mystery Man's fingers and fire shot out of the silver cuboid. Mum used matches to light the fire. Grammer used matches to light the candles. The Mystery Man, now Dad, used a lighter. Instant fire at the flick of his fingers. Flickering instantly fire.

I wondered, did Plumpet go out to meet Santa?

Santa in a car not on a reindeer with a red nose.

Chapter Seventeen

Plumpet's Tale

I sat in an armchair opposite Waldorf.

'You, m'dear, are just worn out,' he said. 'Too much to take on board, I think.'

He was right. I could hardly move for tiredness.

'Do you want someone else to make the decisions for you at the moment?' he asked.

He sat there and suddenly he seemed to be the only person who was making any sense. He seemed to know that I wasn't up to much.

I just nodded.

'Time enough tomorrow or the next day to start thinking,' he said. 'But for now, I think the best idea is if your father and I move the three beds into the one room. Yours, Daffers's and Dumpling's. How about that?'

That sounded fine. I didn't want to be by myself, but I felt that whoever I agreed to sleep with I was going to end up rejecting someone else.

'What about Grammer? And Mum?' I asked.

'What about them?' he said. 'They want what's best for you. And best for you now is bed with your sisters.'

He was right.

I sat there while he went and got Dad and the two of them went upstairs to switch the furniture around.

Grammer came in and sat on the arm of my chair. I had the feeling I was going to cry again. It was all so awful.

'Waldorf is right,' she said. 'You need bed now, and you're not to think about anything.'

'It's a bit difficult,' I said. I mean, how could I think about nothing, when there were a hundred questions in my head, and no answers. And there would probably never be any answers. That's what they said in the hospital.

'We can talk tomorrow. Or the next day, or whenever you like. And if you don't want to talk to us about what's happened, we'll find other people for you to talk to,' she said. 'But right now, you're going to bed, and the only thing you are going to think about is your presents.'

Grammer could be very firm when she gets a notion.

'Do you think I could bath again?' I asked. I saw her looking at me and I wondered what she was thinking.

'Yes, of course,' she said. 'Come on upstairs. Mum said that the hospital said you're to have salt baths for the next few days, but I'm going to put a little extra something in right now to give you a good night's sleep.'

She ran the bath for me, putting in some lavender oil, which she swore by. She always said it was the best thing for helping you sleep. She put some on my pillow too. And then of course the Dumpling wanted some in her cot, and Daffers said, 'Are you leaving me out, Grammer?' But do you know something funny? I didn't think Daffers was being serious. It was more like she was parodying herself. Even the Dumpling looked at her and then gave me a funny sort of conspiratorial smile. It was really nice.

Waldorf and Dad had put the Dumpling's cot and my bed into Daffers's room. Not because Daffers's room was the biggest, but I think because Waldorf felt I'd be better out of my room altogether. Daffers's and my beds were sort of side-by-side, and the Dumpling's cot was at the foot of them. She lay on her side so that she could see us through the bars. It was sweet in a way that she still wanted to sleep in a cot. Mum had suggested getting her a bed, but the Dumpling had held tightly on to the bars of her cot and shaken her head. She was so tiny anyway that she still fitted into Daffers's and my old cot.

'We're a bit like the Waltons,' Daffers said.

There was a lot of, 'Good night, Mom, good night John Boy,' and then we settled down.

More than anything I wanted to see Ronnie. And yet, more than anything I was afraid of seeing him. More than anything? I don't know. I just knew that I wanted to be near him and to make sure everything was all right between us. And yet I was so afraid that he would hate me for what had happened to me. Or that he'd hate me because he undoubtedly had had to answer questions about the previous night. Then I remembered Grammer saying not to think about anything but my presents, and so I thought about the nice clothes which were down in the sitting room, and the paints with all the nice names on them – burnt umber, and maroon ... lovely

277

words, and jade green. And that made me think about the green ring Dad had brought me home from his last trip, and I reached out and touched it on the bedside table and I knew that it had not been on my finger the previous night. I didn't know what that meant, but I knew it was important. I'd had this funny feeling during the day that there was something to do with the ring, but I didn't know what it was. I thought of getting out of bed and going down to tell Mum or Grammer, but before I could, I had fallen asleep.

I woke to hear the rain pelting against the window. Daffers's room seemed so different from mine. I could differentiate her breathing and the Dumpling's if I listened really carefully. As quietly as I could, I got out of bed and went and stood at the window. Lifting the curtains I looked out at the darkness. It took a while for my eyes to adjust and to see beyond the rain. The beating they were getting from the heavens obscured the trees. After a while the rain eased, and as the clouds shifted, the moon appeared and I could see the bare branches of the trees down in our small orchard. I could also make out the shape of the gigantic Buddha on the patio, but the green lights were switched off. The wall between our garden and the Fields's was just about visible. Bit by bit I identified various things in their garden. It took several minutes before I realised that their kitchen light, or some downstairs light was on and that was why I could see more of their garden. I wondered who was up next door and what they could be doing. Was Ronnie still up, sleepless like me? From Daffers's window you couldn't see Theresa Carmody's garden at all. I stood there until I was almost too cold to move and then I slipped quietly out of the room. In my own room I got my slippers and dressing-gown and I went downstairs. I wondered for a moment if I could be sleepwalking, as I seemed to be moving in a sort of dream. I wasn't sure where I was going. A bit of me thought of just opening the front door and walking out and maybe finding out what I had done the previous evening, but in the hall, I turned towards the kitchen and went in and switched on the light. The room was still warm and I made myself a cup of tea.

It was all so incredibly dreamlike, as if it wasn't me at all, but another girl in my nightclothes coming down in the night for some kind of comfort. I fetched my presents from the sitting room where they were in a pile. I had to get two plastic bags to put them all in so that I could lug them back into the kitchen. Sitting on the sofa I went through them again. I had the feeling that I was one of the luckiest people alive but that I was blighted.

Grammer said girls shouldn't indulge in excessive introspection. Daffers said that that was rich coming from Grammer, but I didn't think Grammer went in for introspection. She was a sort of pick-up-the-pieces type of person. When I think of her I think of one of those old-fashioned ships which has the head and bust of a woman at the prow. Grammer was a bit like that, head held high, at the front of the crowd, determined, facing the wind. She sometimes did things which were a bit embarrassing, like at the school play when you feared the enormous feather on her hat was blocking the vision of at least five people in the rows behind her, or when you sang your solo and you could hear her voice above the clapping calling, 'Encore, encore!'

Mum said that she was to be admired enormously – that she had handled disaster in her life and that she was an icon for many of her own generation.

I took out my little tubes of paint and wondered where they had been bought because I'd never seen any like them before. They had the most wonderful colours. I am going to study art when I finish school. Ronnie said he was too. I hoped we'd get to the same college but we hadn't even discussed that yet. There had seemed to be so much time. I tried telling myself that there was still time, but once I started thinking like that I felt that there was no time at all.

When I thought about Ronnie I could almost feel his hands – he had cupped my breasts. It was the loveliest feeling imaginable at the time. Now when I thought about it, I couldn't feel that exciting tingling sensation. In fact, I couldn't feel anything except a sort of horror. I pulled my mind back from it and squeezed some of the Furious Fuchsia out of its little tube. It was a real Dumpling colour. She looked lovely in strong colours. Her jacket, which had this white fur around the hood, was a lurid lime green. My ring looked like an emerald. I knew it hadn't been on my finger the previous night. I went and got a paintbrush from the press in the corner. Both Grammer and I kept our art things in there. Dumpling kept all her toys and gadgets in a box, but her colouring pencils and markers are on the bottom shelf in the press. Grammer said that girls learn by example and that Dumpling was the living proof of that.

When Ronnie kissed me the first time, I just lifted up my face to his. I wondered, did I do that by instinct or was it something that I learned off the television? He was awfully gentle with me. Lots of little kisses, and asking, 'Is this nice?' 'Do you like this?' When I listened to the girls in school talking about those kinds of things it all seemed to be to do with how long they are kissed for, or how far down their throats the boy's tongue went. I had always found the idea of someone else's tongue down my throat a bit frightening. I mean, how did you breathe if your nose was a bit blocked with a cold? Or how did you swallow?

He wouldn't want to kiss me now. Ever. He would have been told what had happened to me. Maybe he'd think I asked for it. After all, I only knew him a little bit and I let him kiss me. And then I walked out of our house in the middle of the night and someone got me and did this awful thing to me.

I had not washed my palette the last time I used it. Criminal, Grammer would say if she knew. I smiled at that as I rinsed it under the tap, and dried it on paper towels. Grammer says, leave things as you like to find them. This refers not just to one's palette but also to the bathroom, one's hairbrush and the shelves in one's wardrobe. Daffers paid no heed to this advice except for the bathroom, of course, because both Grammer and Mum insisted.

I painted a bowl of almonds on a table, and two glasses. I would have liked to paint Ronnie's legs because when I thought of the table I could see his legs quite clearly. They were very long and he was wearing dark trousers and black socks. I liked men's ankles. You didn't get to see them when they were standing, but when they sat you could see the anklebones just below the end of their trousers. I also liked men's necks, and the way their collarbones ended in a bumpy bit and then there was a tiny hollow. Female necks are like that too but they're not as interesting. I got out some of Grammer's charcoal and I drew a few necks and throats.

Then I painted a green ring in a gold setting. And all of a sudden I thought of what had been done to me and I wanted to paint something that would describe it, and the only thing I could think of was to use the charcoal and draw a face that was screaming. For a few moments I knew exactly what Munch was expressing when he painted that picture *The Scream*. We were doing Munch in class the previous term, and I could quote from his diary. It was January, 1892 when he wrote about how he had been walking with some friends and he stopped and leaned against something and the sky was blood-red, the clouds were flaming over this blue-black fjord, and he *stood there trembling with fear*. He wrote that he *sensed a great, infinite scream pass through nature.*

Well, that infinite scream passing through nature – I knew what that scream was. That scream was me.

The door opened suddenly and Grammer came in from her apartment. 'Darling,' she said when she saw me. 'Oh, darling.'

I looked up in surprise.

'You look very tired,' she said to me. 'What are you doing?'

I said I was just drawing and painting a bit because I couldn't sleep. She looked at my artwork. I didn't really want her to see it, but I couldn't hide it without smudging it, as it was either all wet or all charcoaly.

'Are you all right, darling?' she asked. Then she slapped her forehead with her hand, and said, 'Of course you're not. How could you be? Waldorf suggested I came in to check that you weren't up and prowling. I told him not to be ridiculous, that you'd be out for the count. But I was wrong, wasn't I?'

I didn't reply. Apart from anything else, it was the first time Grammer had admitted that Waldorf stayed over. I was glad she had said that. There was something nice about her sharing it with me, even though she had not meant to. I suddenly felt so tired and my body just ached and ached.

'We need to get you back up to bed,' she said. 'I'd take you into my apartment but if one of the family woke and found you gone they'd be so frightened – so let's just get you back up to bed.'

But my body wouldn't move. It was like lead.

She removed all the paper and paints from around me and put them in the dining room, then she fetched a pillow and quilt from her place and tucked me up there on the kitchen sofa. Dimming the lights she sat on a chair beside me and held my hand.

I heard her saying, 'Oh, Plumpet. It will be all right,' and then I was asleep.

I dreamed I was walking in an orchard, but it wasn't our orchard. It had fruit trees with lemons hanging on them. I tried to reach for a lemon because Dad had said he wanted a slice of lemon for his gin and tonic, but every time I reached up at the down-hanging fruit, even though they seemed within my grasp, I discovered that they were further away than they seemed. I looked down at the ground thinking that I was walking on soft long grass only to discover that the ground was covered in slime and my feet and legs were getting dirtier and dirtier. As I walked my feet became heavier and heavier and I found I could hardly lift them from the muck. I thought I could hear voices calling me, or maybe it was someone singing a song. I stopped struggling so that I could listen to the words. I wanted to call to the voices to ask them to come and help me but I didn't know which track between the trees they were coming from. A wind started to blow and the words and sounds were carried away in different directions, and I moved slowly and weightily between the rows of lemon trees trying to find them. I think they were the sounds of children, because from time to time I could hear laughter – like the chuckling and giggling of children, and all I wanted was to find that laughter so that I could be part of it. When I woke it was morning, and all I could think about was having a bath. My dream was so real that I thought my feet were covered in mud.

I was still lying there wrapped up in Grammer's spare duvet when the family appeared.

'Let's have that cooked breakfast we planned for Christmas morning,' Mum said cheerily, having bent to give me a kiss. 'Why don't you get up, Plumpet, and dress and come back down. It'll all be ready by then.'

'I just need to have a bath first,' I said.

'Another one?' she asked. She seemed surprised. 'Are you sure?'

'I feel mucky,' I explained.

She pursed her lips.

'Oh, let her,' Dad said. He sounded slightly exasperated.

I withdrew under the duvet, as I didn't quite know what to do. There's usually no problem if we want to shower or bath. I wondered if it was because he thought there might not be enough water. After all, some of the places he stays in sometimes don't even have running water, let alone hot water.

I know he had said, 'Oh, let her,' when Mum protested, but it sounded more like something else, more like, 'If she wants to be irritating, then let her be irritating,' or something like that.

I looked at them both, not knowing what to do.

'Go on,' he said. 'Go on up.'

I eased myself off the sofa. I still hurt.

Dreadfully. Between my legs where they had stitched me hurt even more than the previous day. Daffers, who was carrying the Dumpling, said, 'Dumples, you sit down here and play while I go up with Plumpet and run her bath. Didn't you say Plumpet is supposed to have lots of baths with salt in them, Mum?' she asked.

Mum, who was now pulling out frying pans, said, 'Yes,' in a clipped voice.

'Well, then,' Daffers said, 'surely that's the best way for her to start the day?'

Daffers reminded me of Grammer then. 'A bath a day helps you work, rest and play,' she quoted to me happily. I could hardly walk but I didn't want them to see that, as both Dad and Mum seemed to be in a funny mood.

On the stairs I had to hold the rail and I was almost pulling myself up.

'Are you in awful pain?' Daffers asked me.

I wanted to tell her then about the stitches and how much it hurt, but instead I told her about the dream I had had and the lemon trees and the mud and slime and how I had to have the bath because I felt so dirty and she kept saying, 'Oh, Plumpet, oh God, Plumpet,' and her voice sounded shocked.

I said, 'What's wrong, Daffers?' because I didn't know what she was reacting to. And she put her arm around me and we lumbered up the stairs together and when we got to the bathroom and she started the bath and asked me how much salt to put in I could see that she was crying but she was trying to hide the tears.

'What's wrong?' I asked her again.

She tried to say that she had got salt in her eyes, but she hadn't even picked up the carton so I knew it wasn't that.

'Please tell me why you're crying,' I said. 'I don't know what anyone is thinking and it's a horrible feeling.'

She said, 'I'm crying for you. I'm crying because I can't bear what they've done to you.'

'I'm all right,' I said. 'Really. Just sore. They were kind in the hospital.'

'I don't mean that,' she said.

So I suppose she was talking about the rape and stuff.

'Do you want me to stay with you while you bath?' she asked me.

I hadn't been naked in front of her since I was about seven and we used to bath together sometimes, so I didn't really know what to say.

'I won't reach in and splash you,' she said, referring to the last time we had had a bath together, when she had all but drowned me. She filled up the bath and then she put in a dollop of Grammer's lavender oil, which Grammer had left on the windowsill.

'Better not put in too much,' I said.

'It'll do you good. It's good for all kinds of things,' Daffers replied. 'Not just sleeping, but also soothing. It'll be good for your skin.'

It was like hearing Grammer's voice. This was such a different Daffers. Not one I'd encountered before.

I got undressed slowly, and lifting my legs to climb into the bath hurt big time, but once I was sitting down it was all right. The hot water both soothed me and made me feel clean again. I just liked being in it. I wondered how long I could stay there before someone made me get out.

Daffers sat on the bathroom stool trying to look out of the window. But I had seen the expression on her face when I took off my nightclothes and I knew that she was trying not to stare at the bruising. I sat with my knees pulled up and my arms around them with my head resting on them, and I could feel the steam from the water cleaning my pores, and I thought, If I can just stay here, it will be all right.

After a bit, Daffers asked if she should go and sort something out for me to wear. I thought of saying to her that I didn't really want to get out of the bath, but I had the feeling that if I said that, then she would go and get Mum, and I really didn't want Mum coming up.

'Did you ever think of being a nurse?' I asked Daffers to delay the progress of events, because the longer she sat on the stool, the longer I could stay in the bath.

'Nope,' she answered. 'I'd never have the patience.'

'Patients?' I smiled.

She laughed. 'Nope, not patients.' She emphasised the 't' at the end of the word.

It was nice hearing her laugh. The bathroom was all steamy and there was condensation on the mirror and on the speckled glass of the window, and there I sat in the bath, turning the hot tap on and off to top up the heat, and Daffers sat with perspiration appearing on her forehead, and bit by bit her curls started to droop, but she sat there chatting.

Well, not exactly chatting. More making observations, and then taking peeks at me. I hadn't really looked in the mirror so I did not know how bad it was. In fact, it wasn't until I got out of the bath and wrapped myself in a towel when she went to get my underwear, that I took a proper look at myself through the steamed-up mirror. It looked bad enough that way through the steam that I didn't see any point in going into Mum and Dad's room and looking in their long mirror. Why upset myself further?

If I ever really wanted to know, I could ask the police because one of them, Margaret, had taken all these photos, which I suppose they put on my file. She had even measured some of the bruises.

Daffers and I went downstairs. Dad must have thought I was still in the bath because he was in a really bad mood, and I heard him saying, 'I don't know why you bothered with the cooked breakfast. It's not Christmas Day, so why pretend.' And I felt awful, because I felt responsible for ruining everyone's Christmas Day.

I hovered in the hallway, but Daffers pushed the kitchen door open really hard so that it banged against the shelving behind it, and said, 'Let's pretend it's Christmas morning. Maybe it'll make Plumpet feel a bit better.' Grammer was standing there and she looked fit to kill. And I didn't know who was cross with whom, or why any more.

I wanted to cry but I was afraid I would make it worse. And then Daffers said, 'That smells good, Mum,' and she pulled me by the arm into the room.

She pushed me over to my place at the table, and she put the Dumpling sitting beside me. The Dumpling was in a funny mood too and she banged on the table with a spoon, and put one finger to her lips as if she wanted quiet. We three girls sat in a row, and Dad got up and left the room, letting the door bang behind him. Mum was putting bacon and eggs on our plates when Waldorf appeared and said in the direction of the frying pan, 'Who's been reading my *Beano?*' and then Daffers and I laughed, and I thought it might be okay.

Daffers asked me if I wanted her to cut up my breakfast for me, and I said, 'Now you're really being the nurse,' and she and I laughed again at the joke we had shared in the bathroom, and I kept thinking, What's going to happen now? I mean, after we finished breakfast the rest of the day just stretched ahead into infinity.

Then the doorbell rang, and I could hear Dad talking to Ronald Fields in the hall, but he didn't invite him in or anything. I could not hear what they were saying through the closed door, just the sound of their voices. I couldn't even work out what kind of things might be being said. Grammer looked at Mum and then at Waldorf. I saw her biting her lip and I couldn't work out anything that anyone was thinking.

Mum said, 'Would you like a scrambled egg instead?'

I looked around to see who she was talking to, and then realised that I was the only one not eating; she meant me. I shook my head and tried to eat the food on my plate, but I couldn't swallow.

'Should you go back to bed?' Mum asked me.

I shook my head again. I didn't know what I wanted to do or where I wanted to be.

Chapter Eighteen

Millicent's Tale

You tell a child it will be all right and yet you know it won't be. I sat there beside her watching her sleep in the dimmed light in the kitchen for a long time during the night. Her face looked gaunt and there were shadows under her eyes. This was the same child who had been laughing and joyous and full of joie de vivre just thirty-six hours earlier. I hoped her dreams weren't troubled – and yet how could they not be?

I used to dream terrible dreams after Dirk McHarg disappeared. I dreamed of his return and that trollop of a secretary of his, Anne Pollock, long-legged with a face like a basin, sauntering into our house after him. 'We're home,' he'd call in this dream. And I, believing I was awake, could see him throwing his bags in the hall. 'Thank God we're back,' he'd say. 'Anne, my love, come and meet Millicent.' And I'd have to meet this girl again. A girl I had once quite liked – in the years before my nemesis. She wasn't particularly bright, or particularly good-looking, but she obviously had that certain *je ne sais quoi* which turned old Dirk on. I had been ironing his shirts in my dream just in case he might return.

Getting rid of his things had been quite odd. I mean, you're told your husband has gone down in the sea and won't be back, and there you are with a wardrobe full of his clothing. So what do you do?

I left it until after his memorial service and then I put everything of his in bags and left them out for the refuse collection. I kept a pair of cufflinks for George – well, there wasn't much point in keeping anything else. All Dirk's good clothes would be passé by the time George fitted them and I didn't want them around anyway. I filled his wardrobe with new clothes for me – I still hadn't found my new style. That took time, error and practice. I would grow to like bright colours but I didn't know that then. I learned to like leather and silk and the feel of feathers. Hats? Oh yes, there is little I enjoy more than shopping for hats.

Sitting there beside Plumpet I wondered what one could do to get her through this and out the other side. It's all very well for a young widow to take to buying hats and learning to write novels as a way of recovery from her husband's betrayal and death, but that hardly applies to a teenage girl who has just been raped. Drugged and raped. Please don't get the wrong idea and think that it was all plain sailing for me, a woman in her mid-thirties suddenly exposed and alone, but somehow I had managed to get it all back together. Being an adult helped. Having an understanding of what had happened to me, of what Dirk had done and how he had died – well, that helped too. I just had to get my mind around it, and then work out what to do. But this was a child – and seventeen *is* still a child. Plumpet was really just a little girl. She had no experience of the hard side of life. She was sheltered and protected, cared for and loved. But to be drugged and raped? Well, I could think of treats and distractions for most things, but not for this.

The following day, after Waldorf had got the fire going in the sitting room and she and I were in there alone, she kept looking at me and opening her mouth as though to ask or say something, but then she would close it and stare at the fire or out of the window.

Eventually I said to her, 'You know, Plumpet, you can say anything to me. Believe it or not, I can handle anything, and I might even have some answers for you.'

After a bit she said to me, 'Grammer, losing your virginity is supposed to be exciting and wonderful, isn't it?'

I see, I thought. And I did see. That precious commodity which I had once kept for my marriage bed, and which later generations, going by what one heard and read, kept for a second date at best, was on my granddaughter's mind. It was then it occurred to me that in a sense she had not lost her virginity.

'Plumpet,' I said, 'sex for a female is ninety-five

per cent from the neck up.'

She looked puzzled.

'You have to trust me on this,' I said, 'as one who knows. It's all to do with what is happening in your head. The turn-on is to do with your brain. You'll hear people saying that men think with their penises – and I'm pretty sure that most of them do. Not all though. I cannot categorically say that they all do.' I mean, it would be unfair to dismiss the lot of them like that. I haven't slept with the entire male half of the world's population, so there may be the odd exception. The very point of statistics is that there is an exception.

'What I'm saying, Plumpet, is that if sex for a female is in the head, then it involves participation of some sort – so a violation is not sexual for her. It is a crime, a crime of violence – but the victim is not participating so she is giving nothing. It is a crime of such extreme violence and invasiveness that no punishment is great enough to cover it, but from the viewpoint of the violated she has given nothing. She has not given her virginity – that is still intact.'

'But Grammer – that's all gone. Whoever did that to me, took my virginity.'

Waldorf had told me to talk as straight to her as possible. He said that at her age there would be terrible inhibitions about talking about such things, and that it was up to me to break through those barriers so that I could reach her and so that she would know she could be reached. I said to Waldorf, 'But her mother?' He just looked at me and said nothing. Waldorf, as he put it himself, had been to the school of legalised buggery. 'It was part of the system,' he told me once. I was shocked, which is rare for me, but as he said, he survived. And I suppose that is what counts.

So I persisted with Plumpet. 'Darling, your virginity is in the head as well as being physical. The person who did this to you has not touched that at all. That has not been violated.'

'Do you mean because I have no memory?'

'No, I don't. I think it helps because you have no memory, but I don't think that is the overriding factor. I think you have to see this as a crime of violence. I know that it was a sexual act for the man who did it, and I know that it was a crime against your sexuality. But when you've recovered physically from it, you will see that you are still intact. That when you come to "give your virginity", that when you are a participator and are giving something freely and willingly, that it is in the best sense for the first time.'

'But I feel savaged. I was savaged,' Plumpet, bruised and sore, cut and stitched, protested.

And she was savaged, and she felt savaged – and how can you bring someone beyond that? It's fine at my age philosophising about virginity and states of mind, it's quite another thing when you are Plumpet's age and you know you have been brutalised, and you are overcome with the devastation of what has been done to you. And you also know that the magic of love, to which you aspired, has been destroyed.

Do we learn patience as we get older? Or is it the difference in years between the vulnerability of a grandchild and one's hardened approach to life that gives us the energy to persist? I don't know.

All I do know is that over those few days and during the conversations I had with my eldest granddaughter, I didn't want to let her slip away. I could see how it could happen. At times I could see her mind closing down and her face blanking and I tried so hard to hold on to her.

George was useless. He was absolutely and utterly useless. I have no idea what he was thinking, or how his thought patterns were developing. I wondered if that was part of the problem – that maybe I had not talked sufficiently to him when he was a youth, that maybe it was a generation thing. That the time we put in with our own children is but practice for when we have our grandchildren. In which case God help those who have no grandparents.

Maria, lovely sweet Maria, did not seem to have a clue how to make proper contact with Plumpet. I worried if that was my fault too, and said so to Waldorf in the privacy of my apartment. 'Is it possible that because I am so close to the girls, and because they spend so much time with me, I have intruded on their relationship with Maria?'

But he said no. He said that children need relationships with all their relatives, and that each of those relationships is different, regardless of whether it is with parent, grandparent or sibling.

'Did you ever try to stop one of the girls from being close to their mother?' he asked.

And of course the answer was no. The truth is that parents and children form their own alliances, their own special bonding and their own way of speaking to each other.

Maria excused herself the day after Christmas Day and went for a long walk. She did the same the following day and the day after, and then said that something had come up at work and that she had to go in for a few hours.

In the meantime George spent a lot of time reading old newspapers and looking at the television.

'I don't like what's happening,' I said to Waldorf.

He just said that I should try to keep my own bonds intact. 'You're the force in the family,' he said. 'Hold on tight.'

Looking back, I'm pretty sure he was right, but at the time I was caught in this dilemma – my need to help Plumpet and my concern about separating her from George and Maria.

If you had asked me a week earlier if I thought she was close to her mother, I would have said yes. But it was clear that I had got that wrong. Waldorf says, 'There's close and there's close.' And he was right.

'I think she should be allowed to see Ronnie Fields,' I said to George and Maria the day after Christmas.

George shook his head.

'For God's sake, George,' I admonished him. 'Do you really think that Ronnie Fields did this to her?'

'I don't know,' he replied.

'Well, do you, Maria?' I asked my daughter-in-law.

'I fluctuate,' she said. 'At first I thought it had to be him, and then I knew that it wasn't – and backwards and forwards my thoughts go and I just don't know.'

'It isn't worth the risk,' George said.

'But if Ronnie didn't do it – and I'm only putting in the "if" out of deference to you because I don't think now for one moment that he did do it – wouldn't it be better for Plumpet to see him? He might be able to help her. It's not as if he doesn't want to see her,' I said firmly.

And it was true. He had called on us twice, both times with his father and both times George had sent them away. The last time I had overheard Ronald Fields telling his son to return home because he wanted to speak with George alone.

'George,' he said when Ronnie had gone, 'look – I sympathise. I know this is the most appalling situation, but Ronnie wasn't involved in it, and he wants to be with her. Maybe he can help her.'

'No,' George said, which was pretty ripe coming from someone who wasn't doing much himself to help.

'Listen, George.' Ronald was clearly bracing himself for another attempt. 'I can imagine how you feel–'

'How dare you!' George responded. 'How dare you? How could you imagine how I feel?'

'What I was trying to say is that my son wants to be with your daughter – and maybe she needs him at the moment. A friend...'

'Waldorf,' I said, 'what is wrong with George?

298

Why won't he and Maria see outside this, outside themselves?'

Waldorf didn't have an answer. All he said was that he thought persistence was the best option and with a bit of luck George and Maria would come around.

'When? When Plumpet has withdrawn so far that they see Ronnie Fields as a possible option to her being catatonic?'

But George was being stubborn, and no amount of reasoning with him went anywhere. These things must be genetic. He reminded me of Dirk and the good old days when I would be trying to get him to come to some function – and of course I realised much later that he had reasons of his own not to want to go. I suppose it cut into his screwing time. Or maybe it was embarrassing going to a dinner with one's wife, when one has screwed the hostess and at least two of the other guests. Who knows? Maybe he was just tired and wanted to put his feet up, knowing that if he went to the party he would probably give the term homo erectus its real meaning. George did not want Plumpet seeing Ronnie Fields, despite the chance that it might do her some good. She asked him. Begged him, in fact, but he stuck to his line: 'Your mother and I feel that it would be better for you not to see him.'

'Parents know best,' I said to her at one point. But she looked up at me wildly and said, 'Do they? How do you know they do? How could they know what's best for me?'

'You could text him on my mobile,' Daphne

said. Her mobile phone had been confiscated for most of the term in school, but had been returned to her on the last day before the holidays. Plumpet didn't have a mobile phone. She said that she did not have that kind of friendship with people that she would want to send them one-line messages or receive one-liners from them.

I pretended not to hear when Daphne made her suggestion. I mean, I did not overtly want to go against her parents' decisions.

'I don't know if Ronnie has a mobile phone,' Plumpet said.

'He does,' Daphne said quickly and almost with glee. 'Look, I got the number from Raleigh,' and she handed her phone to her sister.

I was about to say, 'I didn't know you had seen Raleigh,' but then I reckoned I would be better off playing the role of a couple of the three wise monkeys, and so I said nothing and pretended not to hear.

Plumpet took the mobile from Daphne. I must say I thought Daphne was coming up trumps. She showed Plumpet how it worked, and Plumpet sat there toying with the gadget.

'I was just thinking,' Waldorf said, lifting his head up from his book – he was immersed in Michael Fry's *The Scottish Empire* – 'that I'd rather like to buy you girls each another present.'

George and Maria were both out. Maria had gone into the office, and George had taken the Dumpling with him to get milk and the papers and the four of us were sitting round the fire in the kitchen.

'Goody,' said Daphne. 'Like what?'

Straight to the point, is Daphne. Wastes no time, and yet subtle when need be. A strange new subtlety, I might add, that had not been there a few days previously.

'I was thinking that you could have a new case for your phone,' he said to her, 'and that I might get Plumpet her own phone. Could be useful.'

It could be very useful if Plumpet was going to start text-messaging Ronnie. Really, Waldorf sometimes has his finger right on the button.

Both girls looked at him in surprise.

'Brilliant,' said Daphne. 'I'd like one with smiley faces on it, or there is a new one with cute little pink sheep – all woolly.'

'I bet the Dumpling would like the sheep,' I said.

Plumpet just said, 'Thank you, Waldorf,' and then looked back at Daphne's phone in her hands. The concept of a phone of her own seemed suddenly to galvanise her into action. 'I wonder what I should say,' she said, looking down at the mobile.

'Just say hello,' Daphne said. 'Ronnie just wants you to make contact with him.'

'Were you talking to him?' Plumpet asked, her eyes all large in her pale face. All large and hopeful.

'Well, not really,' Daphne said. She didn't need to add that she was just covering her back. 'He sort of sent a message through Raleigh that he wants to know if you're all right.'

It sounded lame, but Plumpet started texting him. 'I'm just saying that I'm okay, and how is he,' she said. 'How does that sound?'

Under the circumstances it was as good as it could be, I thought.

'Tomorrow,' Waldorf said, 'if you find that text-messaging is fun, Plumpet, you and I will go shopping, and we'll get Daphne her woolly sheep cover.'

Plumpet got the hang of text-messaging faster than you could spell *water buffalo*. Her message to Ronnie Fields got responded to immediately, and her face lit up with joy. I caught Waldorf's eye and we both just nodded to each other. Plumpet's white sad face had a smile on it.

'Look,' she said, 'he's fine and ... oh.' Her smile was still there but she did not finish the sentence.

'Oh, look,' said Daphne, peering over her sister's shoulder. 'He sends you a kiss.'

'Oh Daffers, stop it,' and Plumpet gave Daphne a swipe with a cushion and I suddenly thought the sooner we can recreate normality, the better chance Plumpet has of being normal.

'What are you texting him now?' Daphne asked her.

'I just said that I missed him,' Plumpet said. She looked quite shy when she said that. I thought how sweet she was, and how innocent. And I thought of all the girls in all of the world ... why our sweet Plumpet?

Time was hanging heavily on her hands. You could feel it. Where once she had been busy, she now was just lying around the place. Of course she did not feel up to much, I know that, but the old Plumpet would have been painting or reading

302

or playing with the Dumpling. This Plumpet lay on the sofa staring out of the window or sitting in the bath, so to see her busily using Daphne's mobile, or smiling at her sister was wonderful.

I did a lot of thinking about George in those few days, and I reckoned that children grow into one or other of their parents. It was the only conclusion I could come to. He did not quite have the ability to completely close off from things he didn't like, whereas Dirk had had this talent to just shutter down. But nonetheless both showed their disapproval over anything they couldn't handle. There are no rules I'm sure, for how one handles what had happened to Plumpet but I could see from Waldorf that not all men reacted the same way as George. Waldorf was so gentle with her, but at the same time he was being more than astute. I tried talking to him about it, but he said, 'Millie, m'dear, I'm not Plumpet's father, so maybe it is easier for me in some way.'

'But you're shocked too,' I said.

'Yes, I'm shocked and I want to kill whoever did it to her,' Waldorf replied. He said it both firmly and grimly.

It was very unlike Waldorf to make such an extreme observation. I suppose it was then, in some subconscious or remote way, that I got the idea that removing from the face of the earth whoever had done this, might be the best way to assist Plumpet in putting it behind her.

I spoke to George again later that day.

'Have you any idea how much pain Plumpet is

in?' I asked him.

He crumpled the newspaper he was reading, unfolded his legs and looked at me. 'They said she would be over the pain in a couple of days,' he said.

'They did, did they?' I replied. 'And who are they, might I ask?'

'In the hospital – the doctor, the nurses.'

'And you don't suppose they were just referring to the physical pain?' I asked him.

'What else would they have been referring to?' he said.

'George,' I said as evenly as I could, 'you of all people have seen things that shouldn't happen, but that do. You've seen the results of war and famine and flood. You rescued the Dumpling. You've seen her mother hanging by the neck from a gibbet. You've seen horrors... For heaven's sake, I'm not talking physical pain. I'm talking what's going on in Plumpet's head. That is as real as physical pain. That's torment and torture and it doesn't go away lightly. You of all people must know that.'

He scowled.

I thought of Waldorf saying that maybe as a father it is too difficult to countenance, but for fuck's sake...

'Listen,' I said. 'God knows you've done some wonderful things in your life, but you've also done some dreadful things. And don't think I don't know, because I do.'

Well, I did know. I knew exactly what he and that bitch Marjorie Whelan had been up to over the years. Why else had I tried to run her down in her own driveway?

'What are you getting at?' he asked.

Well, I had no wish to go down the Marjorie Whelan pathway – what can I say about a woman who balls both father and son? So I reverted to the topic of Plumpet.

'Plumpet needs your support.'

'She has it.'

'No, she hasn't. You may think you are giving her support, but you are not. She's feeling alone and hurt and frightened, and she is also feeling rejected.'

'Rejected?' He seemed genuinely surprised.

'She needs to feel that you love her.'

'Of course I love her!'

'Then show her,' I said. 'Get out from behind your newspaper or the television and let her see it. Put your arms around her. Hug her. Make her feel special. Listen to her.'

Chapter Nineteen

Plumpet's Tale

We text-messaged each other until Daffers's phone ran out of credit. Then Waldorf gave me his. Ronnie was really great at putting in loads in the short type of words that Daffers used when texting. We had started with little short messages and then moved on to other things once we both felt that contact was really happening. From the tentative to the banal in a way. I wrote things like *I got paints for Christmas. The Dumpling loved her painted pasta.* While he said things like *WC 8 stuffing b4 bird stufd.* Those kinds of things really made me smile. *Raly got crikt bat & wants to chop down trees in gardn.* Every text-message ended with lots of *xxxx.* Everyone seemed to understand that this was all making me feel a bit better except for Mum and Dad, but they were out and Grammer said it was okay.

Ronnie said we should meet but that we shouldn't tell anyone. I couldn't see how we could do that, but he said that if Daffers and I went out for a walk he and his brother would catch up with us. He asked me if there was any way I could slip into his back garden, because down at the end, past their trees they had a small area with seats and a brazier, and we could go there if I liked. He said there was wood and charcoal to burn in it. It sounded fun, but I was afraid that Dad or Mum might see me going in his gateway. I just wanted to talk to him properly. The messaging was great but once we had made contact like that I just wanted more and more.

When Mum and Dad came back – Dad had been out with the Dumpling, and Mum had had to go into the office for a bit – I got Daffers to suggest that she and I went out for a walk. She said to Mum that we were going to go up to Herbert Park. Dad said he would come too, but Grammer said, 'Now, George, maybe a bit of fresh air and the two girls alone could be the best thing.'

Mum said, 'What if I come too?'

But Daffers said, 'Mum, just me and Plumpet. We'll go up to the park and it will be nice, just the two of us.'

And Mum, knowing how we two don't usually get on, thought for a minute and then said yes.

It was fearfully cold and we wrapped up with jackets, woolly hats and scarves.

'What if she follows us?' I asked Daffers as she closed the front door behind us.

'She won't. Grammer will keep her there,' Daffers said firmly.

We had promised to be back in an hour. I slipped my arm through Daffers's and she said, 'Are you afraid?'

I wasn't afraid – not at that moment. I felt safe with Daffers, and safe because I was going to see Ronnie. Daffers asked me why I didn't feel afraid and I told her, and she said, 'There. See? That proves it.'

'Proves what?'

'That it couldn't have been Ronnie,' she said, adding quickly, 'not that I ever thought it was. But if it had been, even though you can't remember anything, you'd feel afraid. So therefore it wasn't.'

It was real Daffers logic, but I went with it. I knew it wasn't Ronnie, but I could see that other people might need proof.

Despite the cold, it was lovely to be out. The icy air bit into our faces, and there was white haw on the bushes, and snowy frost frozen onto the windscreens of the parked cars.

'We should have brought bread for the ducks,' I said.

With a grin, Daffers reached into her pocket

307

and pulled out two heels of bread from a sliced loaf. It was most un-Dafferslike to think ahead. I was terribly impressed.

'Clever, aren't I?' she said. 'I told Mum to give me some so that you could feed the ducks.'

The poor old ducks looked like they were stuffed when we reached the pond. Clearly we weren't the only people who had thought of them on that frosty frozen day. They ignored my efforts to attract their attention as we walked round by the pond.

'Where are we meeting Ronnie?' I asked.

Daffers pointed ahead to the children's playground. It was abandoned now because of the cold, but two figures emerged from the other side. Ronnie and Raleigh.

Ronnie came over to me while Daffers pushed off in the direction of Raleigh. I stood there looking up at him as he approached. He looked much the same as the last time I had seen him. He was wearing black jeans and a bomber jacket in black and grey, and he was smiling as he came over. I didn't know what to do. I stood there wondering what was going to happen, but when he reached me he just put out his arms and wrapped them around me and I stood there enfolded in the synthetic material of his bulky jacket. I put my arms around him and held on tight. If there was a moment of real happiness, then that was it.

'You okay?' he asked.

I just nodded my head. I was too welled up with emotions – fear, joy, love and sadness – to say anything.

'I missed you,' he said.

I nodded again against his chest. I had missed him. I had only known him such a short time, and I had missed him terribly.

'It'll be all right,' he said. He released me from his embrace and took my hands in his. 'My poor Plumpet,' he said.

I liked him saying that. Well, not the poor bit but the word 'my'. I wanted that *my* again and again. I wanted to feel the safety of it. It contained no rejection, no uncertainty, and no reservations. It was all that I needed.

'Let's walk,' he said, 'so that you don't get cold. Raleigh and Daffers are on the swings.'

I looked back at the playground, and there they were, side-by-side on two swings clearly trying to see who could get the highest fastest. I smiled. It was a lovely image, a wonderful moment.

'She's not the kind to give in easily,' I said. Then I heard my words and I quickly tried to give them direction, in case he thought that I was implying that I was the kind to give in easily – to give away precious parts of myself easily. 'I mean, Daffers ... you know ... she won't want Raleigh to get higher than her. On the swings, I mean.'

'I know what you meant,' Ronnie said. And I knew that he knew that I had been afraid he would misunderstand the meaning of my words.

As we started to walk back towards the pond and the fattened ducks, I put one hand in my pocket and Ronnie was about to put my other in his pocket when he must have felt something because he looked down at it and said, 'Oh, I see you got your ring back.' Then he slipped my hand

and his into his pocket for warmth.

I thought about that sentence for a moment, and then I said, 'What do you mean?'

'Remember?' he said. 'You left it in Theresa Carmody's.'

'Did I?' I asked.

'Yes, you left it on the kitchen sink.'

I thought about that for a bit. I felt very tired. It was almost as if it was too much to think about, as if it was opening a door that was too heavy to push and I didn't want to go through.

'Don't you remember?'

I shook my head.

'Plumpet,' he said, 'Dad said that when I talk to you, I should follow up on anything that is odd or that doesn't make sense.'

'I don't remember most of what happened that evening,' I said.

'I know. Dad told me. I don't want you to think that I'm prying and stuff, it's just that...' His voice trailed away. I looked at him properly. He looked tired and pale. Drawn – that's what Grammer would say. She says that about people who are stressed or sick or worn out.

'You're not prying,' I said. 'I want to know what happened too. I can't get away from it all without knowing. Grammer says I'm better off not remembering – that it's less real that way. But I'm not sure. I don't think she's right.'

'I want to know for your sake,' Ronnie said, 'but I also want to know for mine. Dad said you need protecting more than I do, but you know that I've been questioned. I think they believed me, but I won't feel comfortable until we find out the truth.'

310

So there we were talking about this awful thing, and it wasn't like at home where I didn't feel safe with Dad's anger towards me, and Mum looking like I'd let her down and the Dumpling playing with her pasta and shivering when she looked at Dad, and Daffers being as nice as pie, and me with a pain inside that wasn't just physical but also the biggest headache you could imagine right in the middle of my stomach. I looked up at Ronnie, and I thought this must be what it was like to be with someone who loved you – like Ronnie's parents. I thought of Ronald and Maureen and how they had danced together and were so comfortable around each other.

So I said, 'I don't know. I don't remember what I did with my ring, but I remember in the hospital being surprised that it was on my finger, but I didn't know why.'

'You took it off,' he said.

'Why? Why would I do that?'

He asked me what the last thing was that I remembered, and I told him about sitting on the sofa and the glass-topped table and the bowl of almonds.

'And the drinks? Do you remember we had two glasses of Coke?'

I nodded. One of the ducks, a male one with a lovely shiny green head, waddled off the path and launched himself into the pond as we approached.

'And what did we do afterwards?' he asked.

'Afterwards?'

'After we were sitting on the sofa...'

'I don't know.'

'We went out to the kitchen and you started to wash the glasses, and then you took your ring off. You said that's what your mother and grandmother always did. They took their rings off if they were going to wash something.'

I thought about this. It was true that that was what Mum and Grammer did. And I suppose we do copy our parents and I could imagine myself doing that and even saying it, although I didn't remember it.

'And then after we left, and I walked you to your front door you realised that you had left your ring behind. I said we could go back and get it but you said it could wait until the following day because we were going to go back to look after the cat. We had to find it on Christmas morning.'

That made sense. I nodded again.

'Plumpet,' he said suddenly, 'supposing when you got into your house you changed your mind. Supposing you thought you ought to go back and get it? Is that a possibility?'

It was. It certainly was.

'It's possible,' I said. 'You see, Dad had only just given me the ring, and I don't think he'd have been too pleased if I had just left it somewhere straight after him giving it to me.'

'Would you have gone back alone? Wouldn't you have been scared?'

'Scared of going in next door? No. It wouldn't have bothered me at all. I go in and out of Theresa Carmody's all the time. We all do. Even the Dumpling. She goes through the hedge to Theresa's.'

312

'But at night? Would you really have gone in there alone like that? In the dark?'

I thought about that. My brain seemed to be working very slowly, as if I couldn't really decide what I would have been likely to do.

'I don't think it would have been an issue for me,' I said. 'You see, in the past I've looked after Cat before for Theresa when she went away. I would have gone in by myself before.'

'So all you had to do was to go back out again, after I'd left,' Ronnie said thoughtfully.

'But Mum and Dad said that I came up and said good night and that I was fine.'

'Okay. But suppose that after you said good night, you changed your mind about leaving the ring behind, and went back downstairs and let yourself out.'

'And then?'

Ronnie didn't say anything. He held my hand and we walked around the far side of the pond, and the sky started to get dark even though it was only about three o'clock, and the wind whipped up so that the pond rippled madly and the ducks headed for the little islands in the centre. The pathways leading in all the different directions with their ivy-clad posts and their gnarled old trees looked like something in a fairy tale. Not one of the nicer fairy tales. More like one by the Brothers Grimm. You know, where there is something lurking, or something evil waiting in the forest.

'You remember nothing?' Ronnie then said.

'Nothing. Not until I woke up in bed in the morning and couldn't move. I don't even know how I got there.'

'Dad says that the drug used on you has amnesia as a side-effect.'

'How does your father know so much about all of this?' I asked.

'It sounds silly to say that he has inside information,' Ronnie said, 'but he said he won't rest until this is all properly explained and until whoever did it is caught. Even though he's on holidays, he's been in and out to the office checking up on what's been happening. He's on the phone the rest of the time.'

It sounded both very safe and very determined. It also sounded more positive than how my dad was reacting, but I didn't like to think about that. When Dad looked at me I felt sort of dirty and I didn't like the feeling. It was bad enough to feel the way I was feeling without that as well.

'Dad has worked on cases like this before.'

I thought about that in silence, until Ronnie said, 'What are you thinking?'

'I find it odd – not nice or something – being a case,' I said.

'You're not a case,' Ronnie said. 'I meant he has dealt with crimes like this one before, but this one is different. It's me and you.'

'Does he hate me?' I asked.

Ronnie seemed really surprised. He stopped walking and, turning me towards him so that we were both just standing in front of each other on the pathway, he looked at me. 'Hate you? Why would he hate you?'

'Well,' I hesitated, trying to put it into words. 'I was afraid you'd all hate me. I mean, you just moved in next door, and the next thing you're being questioned about a rape. And it's all my fault.'

'Why is it your fault?' he asked. He really did seem puzzled, as if the idea had never crossed his mind.

'I don't really mean *my fault*,' I said. 'I mean more ... well, because of me, I suppose.'

'Dad said that you are a victim.' Ronnie squeezed my hand. 'He also said that guilt often goes with that. You know, like if someone is mugged, afterwards they feel angry with themselves for letting go of their bag, or stupid for having had so much money on them, or whatever. I don't mean that what happened to you is like being mugged – I just mean some crimes carry awful penalties for the victims. Dad says that guilt goes with what happened to you, and that that is terribly unfair.'

This was amazing. It was also so ... reassuring. I *did* feel guilty. In some way I felt that I had walked into the situation that ended up with me being raped. And also there was this fear, because I couldn't remember what had happened, that maybe I *hadn't* been raped, but that I had done something willingly. Even though I knew that it didn't make sense. I mean, why would I let someone willingly do that to me? Like cover me with bruises, and tear me so badly that I had to be stitched?

'What are you thinking?' Ronnie asked again.

'Ronnie, please, can you tell me all that again – what your Dad said, I mean. I need to hear it once more.'

315

So he said it again, all those things about guilt, and how unfair it was that someone who had been so violently hurt should then carry guilt on top of that. I told him how uncomfortable I felt with Mum and Dad, and that it was Grammer and Waldorf who were being much more understanding. He said that maybe it was more difficult for parents.

'But your parents are being very supportive to you,' I replied. And although I was glad for him, it made me feel sad for me.

'It doesn't mean your parents love you any the less,' he said. 'It's just their way of reacting.'

Well, I didn't think much of it. They had tried to stop me seeing Ronnie, and yet meeting him was so comforting. It was the best feeling I'd had over the past few days, the first time that I'd felt even remotely hopeful. Hopeful about what? I don't know. Maybe just about the possibility of there being a tomorrow.

In a sense I felt lucky at that moment. Taking it as a fact that I had been raped, I was lucky that there was a boy around who seemed to care about me. Another boy might have just left me, or not known how to talk so openly. Ronnie was good at that. It was like a gift. I tried saying it to him, how I liked the way he just talked and there was nothing hidden, how he was so upfront, and straight. But all he said was that I was like that too, so it made it easier. This made me smile. In school everyone says that opposites attract, but Ronnie and I were very similar. I didn't know what that meant – if anything – but it made me feel better.

'Okay,' he said, 'let's assume you went back for your ring, and then there is the big blank. Do you remember coming home the second time?'

'No.' I had no memory of that at all. 'They said in the hospital,' I explained, 'that I must just have headed home at some point. Somehow. I don't know.'

It sounded lame. Grammer had said to me that wounded animals go back to their lairs, and that somehow or other I must have done that too. I had this image of a fox with an injured hind leg limping painfully homewards in the dark. It was difficult to think of that fox as me.

Ronnie had his arm around my shoulder now and we were heading back in the direction of the playground. In the distance I could see Daffers and Raleigh still swinging away. Daffers's giggles were carried on the wind and it made me laugh. Ronnie laughed too. 'See?' he said. 'It'll be all right.'

Raleigh said hello to me and slowed down on the swing until it was vertical. Daffers did not seem so keen on stopping until Ronnie pointed out that it was cold standing there, and then she got off too. We walked together back towards home with Daffers playing the fool.

'Catch me if you can,' she shouted at Raleigh as she set off at a high pace. She's a good runner, but she hadn't taken the Fields's long legs into account and Raleigh must have caught her somewhere among the trees, because there were these squeals of outraged indignation ahead of us.

'What will we do now?' I asked Ronnie,

meaning what could be done, how could we utilise the information about the ring.

'I don't know,' he replied. 'I'll tell Dad. By the way, I wonder if the cat ever came back?'

'I suppose so. I think Waldorf has been looking after it.'

Daffers and Raleigh were back with us now.

'Oh, the cat is fine,' Daffers said. 'Waldorf has been feeding it and letting it in and out.'

'That's good,' Ronnie said. 'Remember we were concerned that it hadn't come home on Christmas Eve?' He said that to me. Of course I didn't remember, but I just nodded. I was thinking about Theresa Carmody and wondering when she was going to get back. She had been gone for days.

'The cat was in,' Daffers said to no one in particular.

'In when?' Ronnie asked her.

'On Christmas Day. The cat was in Theresa Carmody's when Waldorf went in. He fed it and let it out.'

'Are you sure?' Ronnie asked.

'Yes,' Daffers said. 'I remember someone saying something about it.'

'That proves it then,' Ronnie said.

'Proves what?' I asked.

'The cat was not in when we left, and it was in the following day. So someone let it in.'

'But maybe it was me. Maybe I let it in when I went back for my ring,' I said.

'You should phone Dad and tell him,' Raleigh said.

We were only about twenty minutes away from

home, but Ronnie took out his mobile and phoned his father. I could just hear parts of the conversation, the bits about my ring and about the cat being out on Christmas Eve, and in the next day when Waldorf called.

Then Ronnie said into the phone, 'What? When? Oh. What will we do?' He listened while his father spoke, and then he said, 'But Plumpet's parents don't know she's out with me. We don't want to make it worse.'

When he hung up, Raleigh, Daffers and I were standing there looking at him, waiting for him to tell us what had happened.

'We're to come home,' he said to us.

'Why, what's up?' Raleigh asked.

'Dad went into the office and looked at the file to see ... to check up, I suppose. And he saw in it that the cat was in the house on Christmas Day and he remembered me saying that the cat hadn't come home the previous day, so they've got a search warrant for Theresa Carmody's.'

'Are they allowed to go in without her knowledge?' Raleigh asked. These must be the kinds of questions the sons of a detective might ask. Certainly it would not have occurred to me, or to Daffers.

'Theresa Carmody is back,' Ronnie said. 'They're there now.'

'We can't go back with you,' Daffers said, 'in case Mum or Dad see us. There'll be war. They told Plumpet she couldn't see you, you know.'

'I know,' Ronnie said. 'Dad said we could either say we had bumped into you, or else to just go up our road separately.'

I told Ronnie that Waldorf would be buying me a mobile phone the following day, and he was really pleased.

'I'd like a grandfather like that,' he said.

Daffers laughed. 'He's not our grandfather,' she said. 'He's Grammer's boyfriend.'

'Boyfriend?' I said. 'It's a funny word for him. He's just Waldorf.'

As we walked back, and we couldn't go very fast because of me, Ronnie told us about how his and Raleigh's bedrooms were all finished, and about the little patio at the end of their garden with this outdoor fire and how his father had put the barbecue down there and they had planned on having a small party and were going to ask us and Theresa Carmody – a kind of garden warming, he said.

'Imagine,' Daffers said, 'we've lived next door all our lives, and I had no idea that you had a patio at the end. You know, we've never been in your back garden. Grammer didn't like the neighbour and she told us to steer well clear of her, so neither of us have ever been in there.'

'You'll have to come in and see it,' Ronnie said to us both.

'We can't at the moment,' Daffers replied. 'It's Mum and Dad who want us to steer well clear of you now.'

'I'm surprised you never tried climbing over the wall,' Raleigh said to her.

'I would have,' Daffers told him, 'only Grammer put wire up on our side just under the top of the wall to discourage us from such thoughts, as she told us.'

As we crossed the bridge over the River Dodder, I heard Ronnie telling Raleigh and Daffers about my ring and how I must have gone back to get it, and Daffers said, 'So you did go back.'

'It looks like it,' Ronnie said. 'Otherwise, how else did she get the ring back?'

And Daffers said, 'Oh,' and her voice sounded slightly strangled.

'What's up?' Raleigh asked her.

'Nothing,' she said. 'I just need to think.'

And Ronnie said, 'Share it, Daffers.'

But she said, 'No. I really have to think. There are all these things... I need time to think.'

Now Daffers did not usually do much thinking at all, but I was too tired to wonder what she meant. I stopped for a moment on the bridge and looked upriver where the sun was setting and the sky was streaked with yellow and crimson fire, and I thought about Munch looking at the light above the fjord and how the sky reflects itself in different ways the whole world over. I tried not to think about *The Scream* but it was difficult because I didn't feel like the others felt. I don't know how to explain it, but they seemed to be so solid, and they seemed to be able to think, and I felt like something had ripped me apart and it had torn my mind asunder. Ronnie held my hand until we got to the bottom of our road.

'You and Daffers ought to go on ahead,' he said. 'It's easier for everyone.'

But then we saw all these cars outside Theresa Carmody's and I didn't want to walk up the road without Ronnie. I just did not want to pretend that I was not with him, so the four of us went up together. Theresa's car was parked outside her house. Her driveway is as long as ours but the entrance isn't wide enough for a car, so she always parks in front of her gateway. There were three other cars behind hers. One had just pulled up, and Margaret, the detective who had interviewed me in the hospital, was getting out of the last one.

'Hello, Plumpet,' she said to me. Then she greeted Daffers, Raleigh and Ronnie all by name, which surprised me because I hadn't thought that she might have met them. But she clearly had, because they all called her by her name.

I looked up the driveway to Theresa Carmody's house and I shivered.

'Go on in home, Plumpet,' she said to me. 'It's cold out here. Bring her on into her house,' she said to the others.

I stood there stock still, staring up at Theresa Carmody's and I tried to tap into something, anything, tried so hard to find some memory of going back for my ring, but there was nothing. There was just that big gaping hole in my memory.

'C'mon, Plumpet,' Daffers said to me, pulling me by the arm.

'Why don't I remember?' I said. I was asking no one in particular, just putting the question on the icy wintery air.

Margaret placed her hand on my shoulder. 'You won't remember, Plumpet,' she said. 'It's the side-effect of the drug. That part of your memory won't come back. That is just a fact. If you like,'

322

she added, 'I can come in and talk to you about that later. So you understand.'

The way she said it was really nice, as though she understood. And I liked the idea of talking to her about it. I nodded. 'I'd like that,' I said.

'Then I'll come in to you later,' she said. 'When we're finished in there,' she nodded her head at Theresa Carmody's house, and I wondered what, if anything, they would find in there.

'You know,' Ronnie said to her, 'that Plumpet left her ring in there that night, but she had it on her the following morning?'

'I didn't know that,' Margaret said. 'I only just got a call to tell me to come over. Nobody has briefed me. Are you sure you left it behind you?' she asked me.

I explained to her the peculiar feelings I had had in the hospital, and how I had been surprised to find the ring on my finger and I didn't know why I had been surprised. Then Ronnie told her about how I had taken it off to wash the glasses, which he had then dried and put away.

'You didn't think of putting the glasses in the dishwasher?' she asked us.

'No,' Ronnie said. 'We just wanted to leave the place the way we found it.'

'So either someone gave you the ring or you went back,' Margaret said thoughtfully. 'Good. Go on in home. I'll be in later.'

Someone gave me the ring? Was this a possibility? I had not thought of that. I pondered it as Daffers and I went into our house.

No, it didn't seem likely. If someone came to

323

the door and rang, everyone would have heard the bell. No, although I continued to think about it, I knew that that was not what had happened. I also knew with awful clarity that I had definitely gone back to Theresa Carmody's. And with that same clarity, I knew that what had happened to me, had happened in Theresa Carmody's house.

Chapter Twenty

Daffers's Tale

It should have been me.

That was all I could think once I knew that Plumpet had gone back to Theresa Carmody's. Of course I don't mean it *should* have been me, I think I mean more that it *could* have been me. It *might* have been me. It could so easily have been me. Except it wasn't – it was Plumpet. And once I got that idea into my head I couldn't get away from it. I couldn't articulate even to myself, let alone out loud the way my thoughts were going. But in that instant I knew who had done it to Plumpet. I had no doubt, but I knew not to say anything aloud until I had worked it through.

Grammer always says that I speak without thinking and I wanted to blurt it out, but I was afraid that if I did, I wouldn't be able to explain how I knew. I was afraid that I would forget all the bits that made up the puzzle, and I felt that if I said nothing until I'd worked it out then I could tell them and it would be all right.

No, it would not be all right, but bits of it would be. I just needed to think and remember all the things that had happened. I'm not like Plumpet – my brain doesn't work all quickly and logically like hers does. My mind comes around corners, and bumps all over the place until I can see something. Even the Dumpling sees things quicker than I do. But Grammer says we're all different, and we all come at things our own way, and that we shouldn't try to rush things, because then they won't make sense to us, or to anyone else, and if someone like me has to do things slowly, then I should just do them slowly. She says I'll get there in the end, and what's the rush anyway.

Sometimes, in fact mostly, I think there *is* a rush, because who wants to sit working out some mathematical puzzle when you could be doing something more fun, and then I try to rush and rush to get to the end, and it takes twice as long, if not more. But with this puzzle I wanted to put the pieces together, because even if I was so sure what had happened, I wanted to be able to see it clearly.

When Plumpet undressed and got into the bath, I saw the bruises on her and they reminded me of something, but I couldn't think what. I wanted to see those bruises again – there was something about them that had made me think of something else. And then there was something to do with the Dumpling, but I couldn't quite remember what.

So Plumpet and I went home and as we reached

the front door, it opened and Dad appeared. He looked furious. 'Where have you two been?' he said angrily.

'You know we went out for a walk,' I said. 'We told you. We went to Herbert Park.'

Plumpet looked like she was going to cry. I don't know how he could be like that with her. Anyone could see that what she wanted was kindness, and for someone to tell her she was safe and that she would never get hurt again. Even if it wasn't true. Anyone could see that, but not Dad.

'You've been gone longer than you said you'd be,' he said, slamming the front door behind us as soon as we'd stepped in.

'We bumped into that detective, Margaret – you know, the one who was here on Christmas Day?' I said quickly.

'So?'

'We could hardly tell her we couldn't talk to her,' I said.

'You could tell her to come and talk in here, rather than out on the street,' he said.

Street? Since when was our road a street? But I thought it better not to ask him. He had a habit of saying, 'Are you giving me cheek, Miss McHarg?' To which the correct answer was probably yes, but I always said no anyway. With my fingers crossed.

'We did say to her to come in and talk,' I only partially lied. 'She's going to come in when she's finished in Theresa Carmody's.' I thought I'd distract him by telling him that she was in Theresa Carmody's house, but either he already

326

knew or he wasn't interested, because he wasn't about to be diverted.

'You can't be trusted,' he said.

Silence as both Plumpet and I looked at him. It was unclear if he meant Plumpet or me or maybe both of us.

'We weren't doing anything,' Plumpet said sulkily.

I thought, Grammer, where are you when we need you? The hall seemed icy cold. I needed to say something quickly before he said anything else. All I could think of was the brutality of what he might come out with.

'We fed the ducks in the park,' I said frantically.

'The ducks?' He seemed really surprised.

'I took bread with us,' I said. 'The Dumpling loves feeding the ducks. So do I. Remember, Dad, when we were little, we fed the ducks on a lake in Switzerland. Was it Lake Geneva, Plumpet?' I asked. It could have been Lake Chihuahua for all I knew, but I knew that Geneva was in Switzerland. At least I thought it was.

'Oh, I remember that,' Plumpet said. 'We took rolls from our breakfast to feed them, but then we couldn't find any. Ducks, that is,' she added.

'And do you remember how there was a little tiny bar of chocolate on our pillows at night?' I asked.

'And the carpet in the room was so thick that you said you might sink.' Plumpet tried a laugh.

It didn't really work as a laugh but Waldorf suddenly appeared in the hall and said, 'Well, hello there. And has anyone seen my *Beano?*' He had a real Waldorf look on his face. He looked like this actor called Leslie Phillips. He sounded like him too. 'George,' he said, 'I was thinking, isn't it time for a G and T?'

If I were an author like Grammer and was writing a book, I'd call it *Waldorf to the Rescue*. If I had a grandfather I would rather like him to be just like Waldorf.

Plumpet and I headed upstairs and I said that to her, and she said, 'Who needs a grandfather? We have Waldorf just as he is.' And she was right.

If I were going to write a book, I'd write one about someone like Plumpet. She's more like a real person than a character in a book, if you know what I mean. Her hair is like a real person's. In a book you'd read *she had thick wavy hair that flowed over her shoulders*, and you'd think of someone with thick wavy hair. But the real Plumpet, the one who is my sister, well, she has thick wavy hair that falls over her shoulders when she leaves it loose, and she has this heart-shaped face that isn't like something you'd read about. It's more real. *She* is real. A real person with feelings and kindness and stuff. I don't know how you'd write about that. I don't know how you'd be able to describe her properly so that the reader would understand that she is a really good person. Not some wonderful heroine, just a really decent kind person.

In my room she pulled off her jacket and threw it on her bed. My room looked funny with all of our beds in it. Like a three-bed dormitory in a story or something. Well, two beds and a cot.

'Plumpet?' I said, as I unzipped my woolly hoodie.

'Mmm?' she said. She was just standing there not really looking at anything. Just standing. And anyone looking at her would know that she was such a nice person. I kept thinking that. 'What?' she asked.

I didn't know what to say. There were too many things to say, and I didn't know how to say them.

'Dad doesn't mean to be like that,' I tried.

'Oh,' she said.

But she was hurt. I knew that. He had hurt her by not trying to understand. I thought about that. It was sort of difficult because it was an awfully big thing to try to understand or to think about. There she was and she had been hurt like human beings aren't supposed to be hurt. I mean, you're born and you live a life – whatever kind of life comes your way, I suppose. And in the one that came our way we lived in comfort and warmth with Grammer and Mum, and we had apple tart and cream, and roast beef and things, and we went to school and tried to learn what we were supposed to learn, and we were expected to grow up and then do things that would keep us in comfort and warmth with more apple tart and cream, if you follow me. But something had gone wrong.

Like worms in lemons.

And there was poor Plumpet, and it was bad enough what had happened to her on Christmas Eve without Dad being mean to her.

'Plumpet...' Suddenly it didn't seem the right time to ask her to show me her bruises, so I stopped.

But she had her own thoughts on her mind

because she didn't ask me what I was going to say. Instead she said, 'I think I'll have a bath.'

I thought that was a bit odd. She seemed to be having an awful lot of baths.

'Maybe you should wait. After all, Margaret is coming in and you don't want her to visit you in the bath, do you?' I said.

I had missed the opportunity to go with her and take another look at the bruises, but I reckoned that I could do that later. With the way Dad was behaving it was no wonder she wanted to lock herself in the bathroom, and I could just go with her. We had done it once, so there was no reason why I couldn't go in the next time, and then I could take a good look at the bruises.

'Oh, I'd forgotten about Margaret,' she said. And she really had. You could see it in her face. She had totally forgotten.

We lay on our beds for a bit. I think she might have fallen asleep because I was just staring at the ceiling and after a bit I realised her breathing was all quiet.

'Are you all right?' I whispered. There was no answer, so I turned and looked at her. She was lying on her side, with her legs pulled up and one hand in a fist at her mouth and her eyes closed. Her hand looked all bruised, green and blue it was, from the drip she had had attached to her in the hospital.

I swung my legs very quietly off the bed and went and took a closer look. You could see the puncture mark from the needle in the centre of the bruising. I thought about that for a bit. She'd been given an intravenous drip – that's what it's called, I think – on Christmas Day, and it was really clear today. You could now see that there was a needle prick and lots of bruises, whereas a few days ago all you could see were the bruises. Well, there had been a bandage on it so maybe you could see the prick.

I wondered what I should do. If Margaret arrived and I tried to tell her what I was thinking, maybe it would look silly, or maybe Dad would tell me to keep out of it ... or maybe Plumpet would be even more upset. I thought about telling Raleigh, but he's just like me and he wouldn't know what to do, so then I decided to tell Grammer or Waldorf. I left Plumpet asleep and went downstairs.

On the way down I thought about Raleigh. Apparently the original Raleigh had something to do with potatoes, and he plonked his cloak on the ground so that Queen Someone-or-other wouldn't get wet feet. And when he was about to be executed he wrote to his wife, *I am but dust*, and she carried his head around with her for the next eighty years. Or something like that. Raleigh told me about it when we were on the swings in the park. Could you imagine me having a conversation like that with Daisy? Okay, about the head maybe, but not the rest. At the rate I was going I would be getting full marks in my history exam. Raleigh was full of facts, but they weren't boring like when you were taught history in school. He knew about the interesting side of things, which made the person real. I told him how I was interested in volcanoes and scree and ox-bow lakes and things like that. He didn't seem to know much about those sort of things, so I was able to tell him about Krakatoa, which had erupted in 1883. The explosion was heard over four thousand miles away, and thirty-six thousand people died as a result of it. From lava and tidal waves and things like that. Anyway, after everything had settled down again, two thirds of the island was gone. It had disappeared. And to the north of the island, there were all these new little islands. I found that amazing. So did Raleigh.

Then I said to Raleigh that our family was a bit like Krakatoa. 'Before Plumpet was raped,' I said, 'we were like a big solid island. And now we're more like bits of islands instead.'

'Like satellites around a moon?' he asked.

I wasn't sure if that was what I meant, so I said that it was as if we were all broken up and not one unit any more.

He said that the opposite had happened in his house. That his dad said they had to keep talking and to piece it all together. He said something about the family who talks together stays together. His mother had cried and cried, but his father said it was going to be all right, that he wasn't going to rest until he sorted it out. He was as concerned for Plumpet as he was for Ronnie. Raleigh said that his father had told them that no matter how awful it was for the Fields, they had to remember that it was many times worse for Plumpet and her family.

I thought that was pretty generous of him. I know he was right and that it *was* worse for Plumpet, but it showed a sort of unselfishness, I think. In our house our dad wasn't behaving as if something bad had happened to Plumpet. He seemed to feel that something bad had happened to *him*, or that it was because of Plumpet. And it jolly well wasn't her fault.

They were all in the kitchen, with the Dumpling on the floor doing something with a geometry set – mine probably, as I didn't have much use for it – and a piece of paper. Grammer was on the sofa as was Dad, and Waldorf was propped against the worktop. They were all drinking. Mum was in the cooking area with vegetables everywhere.

I went over and said, 'Hello, Dumples. And what are you up to?'

She looked up at me and grinned, showing off her little rows of even white teeth. I wondered how I could get Grammer or Waldorf out of there because I really did want to tell one of them about Plumpet's bruises, but they were all having a drink and I couldn't see how I could say, 'Hey Grammer, can you come out of here for a minute while I tell you something I don't want anyone else to hear.'

I looked at Mum, who had started to chop onions and there were tears burning her eyes. I offered to help her and she peered at me in surprise.

'Yes, please,' she said. 'Ratatouille,' she added as if that wasn't clear to me. There were several aubergines, some courgettes, onions and tomatoes all over the place. Usually she was really tidy when she was cooking, but that day she wasn't.

I opened a newspaper to use under my

chopping board. Years ago, Mum taught us to do that. She said that when you've finished, all the bits you don't need are already there in the paper ready to be thrown out – so much easier than picking them up later. All right, I know. I wouldn't usually care where the bits ended up, but it seemed to make sense that day. Theresa Carmody said we should use a compost heap, but Grammer said the fumes add to the ozone problems. At least I think that's what she said. I wondered what was happening next door in Theresa Carmody's. And I wondered why Mum was behaving so oddly. She had a sort of a half smile on her face, and it wasn't connected to the vegetables.

I cut the aubergines up into cubes – a little bit larger than bite-size, because they shrink when they're cooked. I thought I'd quite like to be a vegetable grower when I grew up, or maybe a chef. It must be nice to watch your own produce growing out of the ground, and then preparing it and serving it up. Sometimes it was random though – I knew that from watching the fruit in the orchard. You could not tell a year in advance what the next year's crop was going to be like. We had two plum trees, and some years they were so overladen with fruit that they could hardly stand up, and other years you only got enough for a few pies and a couple of fruit salads. It must be a bit difficult if you did not know what you were likely to produce.

Theresa Carmody grew tomatoes in her con-servatory. They smelled so wonderful when they appeared in the summer. Plumpet said that the smell was better than the taste, but I didn't agree. Plumpet saw things in her own way – differently to me anyway. I liked the taste of something, whereas she liked how it looked. She is always searching for the right word to describe something. She is very good at art. She had painted a still-life in oils and I swear you'd think it had been stolen from an art gallery. She had the light on the fruit just perfectly done. And she had painted a silver pitcher and tumbler at the back of the table, and you could almost feel the weight of them, so brilliantly had she done them. Actually it was a goblet, not a tumbler. I remember Grammer correcting my vocab and saying it was a goblet, but a short while later she had written a book called *The Pitcher and the Tumbler*. Of course her editor changed the title of the book. It was about two acrobats, I think, and an Olympic Games. And one of them did something on the highwire – I don't really remember. Anyway, Plumpet is really brilliant at painting things. You just have to look at them and you could see what she was saying in them. Plumpet had painted a picture of a face with a scream on it. It was in the dining room on the table. The face looked so like Plumpet's, even though I'd never seen her screaming. I wondered did she scream when...

The doorbell rang and I got such a fright that the knife slipped on one of the aubergines and I cut my finger and let out a yell.

'What is it now?' Dad said crossly.

I didn't know if he meant who is that at the door, or what are you yelling about now? I didn't answer him. No one did. As Mum held my hand under the tap, Dad went out to answer the door and I kept saying, 'It's okay, Mum. It's only a tiny cut,' because I wanted to get out to the hall so that I could be there when Margaret talked to Plumpet, but Mum insisted I kept my hand under the tap while she got a plaster.

Dad came back in after a few minutes and said, 'That was Margaret. She wanted to talk to Plumpet alone. What do you think of that?' He said this to Mum.

'Where are they?' Mum asked.

They were already in the sitting room and there was no way I could slip in there.

'Why does she want to see Plumpet on her own?' Dad asked.

'Didn't you ask her?' Mum said.

He hadn't. I watched all their faces as Mum dried my hand, and got out antiseptic ointment from the drawer.

'Do you think I should go in and be with them?' I said. 'I mean, I could keep Plumpet company...'

'Be quiet, Daphne,' Dad said.

Huh, what did he know? I needed to tell Margaret or someone, anyone, what I knew before Plumpet's bruises changed any more.

I looked at Grammer and her mouth was in a tight line, and I didn't think it would be a good idea to try to tell anyone in the room. Then Grammer went and got her coat, saying she was going out for a blast of fresh air.

With the plaster on my finger I hurried through the rest of the vegetables, a bit clumsily I must admit, but I wanted to get them finished and to

336

get out of there as fast as I could. Grammer had disappeared and I really wanted to tell someone. I decided that if I couldn't get Margaret before she left, I'd go over to see the Fields. Raleigh's father would know what to do.

I tried hovering in the hall, and that sort of worked for a bit because I could hear the murmuring of voices in the sitting room, and I felt reassured at the tone of Plumpet's even though I couldn't hear what was being said. But then when Margaret came out, Dad and Mum appeared immediately from the kitchen and I was ignored. I couldn't even catch Margaret's eye. They all went back into the sitting room to Plumpet and I thought of going into Waldorf, because I had abandoned the idea of telling Raleigh's father, but the Dumpling was in there, and even though she didn't say anything, there were some things she shouldn't hear. I mean, you never knew what might be going on in her head. Then I decided I would go and tell Ronald Fields so I got my coat and I was about to slip out the front door when Grammer suddenly appeared on the garden path.

'What are you up to?' she asked me.

I shuffled a bit because I didn't know what to do. 'I know something,' I blurted out, 'and I need to tell someone before it is too late.'

'Will you tell me what it is?' she asked.

I said yes.

Then she said, 'Come on into my apartment and tell me now.'

So I did.

Chapter Twenty-One

Theresa Carmody's Story

I came home from my Christmas break in The Four Seasons, which was only down the road I know, but I was full of appropriately seasonal joy, satiated with sex, but ultimately bored. Tony Fonzetti was a dab hand in the sack, and lovely to look at across a dinner-table, but there was zero going on between his ears. I didn't realise this at first: I never do. I always suspect it with potential new lovers, but it is not until I have actually experienced it that I really believe it.

We stayed away for four days, most of which time we spent in bed which, as luck would have it, was just as well. For me, I mean. As I was doing all the paying, I was the one who signed most of the room-service dockets, and this gave me a regular alibi for the four days.

I drove home and parked the car outside the gate. I only had a small overnight bag with me, as I had not intended to stay so long away, but what I had with me was sufficient to see me through. What do you need when you're spending most of the time in bed anyway?

I came home, opened the front door, checked on Cat who was out on the prowl and not to be found, and then I took my bag into the kitchen to put my few items in the washing machine. I was surprised to find that the machine was full and had run its cycle; it doubled as a dryer, and the dryer too had been run. So there was a load of dried clothing to take out and fold. I didn't remember running the machine. My recollection was that the drum had been just over half full, but then it was several days earlier, and it's not the kind of thing you usually recall. The dishwasher too had been run, so I supposed that maybe Plumpet had done all of that.

I pulled the clean clothing from the washing machine, and let it fall into a plastic laundry basket, and then I put my dirty bits and pieces into the machine. I had just got upstairs with the now nearly empty bag when the doorbell rang. I took a quick look in the mirror in my room. I had to admit that I was looking well – four days in bed, no matter how active they have been, brightens your eyes. I fluffed up my black curls a bit, and ran a wetted fingertip over my eyebrows. The thing about shagging a man is that you do get to sleep in between shags, and I felt that I looked both rested and glowing. I licked my lips and smiled happily at myself before running back downstairs.

Outside the door were a variety of men. They showed me IDs in plastic cases and I tried to take in what they were saying. One, who identified himself as Michael Fogarty, said they had a warrant to search my house. I was having a real problem taking all this in, and I looked from one face to the next trying to work out what was going on.

Michael Fogarty asked if he and I could sit

down and have a chat, but he also made observations like, 'Your cooperation would be
appreciated,' and I got the definite impression
that if I didn't cooperate *I* might not appreciate
it. I tried to think what to do. I wondered for a
moment if this could be some wild practical joke,
but I couldn't think of anyone who would play
such a joke, or what it might mean.

'Come in,' I said.

I brought them through the hall to the living
room. The room was dark so I switched on the
lights and then realised that the curtains were
closed, so I went to open them, and then realised
that it was already evening outside, so I left them
the way they were. I was a bit disorientated time-
wise from having spent so much of it horizontal
over the previous few days. Day and night blend
somewhat when you're hard at it.

'What is this about?' I asked.

'A crime has been committed,' said Michael
Fogarty, 'and we have reason to believe it may
have happened on your premises.'

I wondered what he was like in bed. He was
wearing a leather jacket, and his hair was sleeked
back. He had sharp eyes, which took in every
aspect of the room while he was addressing me. I
glanced around too. It looked much the same as
when I last had been there.

'What kind of a crime are we talking about?' I
asked.

'My men are going to take a look around the
place while we're talking,' he replied. He had
already shown me the search warrant at that
point; I had duly perused it, even though it

340

meant nothing to me.

'So,' he said, settling back in his chair, 'you've been away?'

Statement or question, I wasn't sure. I nodded. 'Can you tell me what this is about?' I asked again.

'I will,' he said, 'but first of all, just outline to me where you've been and who you've been with.' He had taken out a notebook and pen, and I watched while he scribbled something down.

'Do I need legal representation?' I asked him, as it suddenly occurred to me that whatever this was about, he really did think it had happened in my house and that maybe I was under suspicion.

'Not unless you think you do,' he replied, which of course could mean anything. 'If you would like to organise representation, we can put this conversation on hold.'

It wasn't said in a threatening way, but I wasn't quite sure where it left me. Anyway, as far as I knew I didn't have anything to hide so I said, 'Look, I'm quite happy to talk to you, but I would like to know what is going on.'

'I'll get to that in a minute,' he said, 'but before I do, can I clarify this – you've been away, isn't that right?'

'Yes,' I said. 'I'm literally just back. I got into the house maybe five or ten minutes before you arrived.'

'So, on an initial glance, did you notice any-thing different? Anything out of place? Anything not quite the way you left it?'

'No,' I said. 'Well, almost no. Someone seems to have run the dishwasher and the washing

341

machine, but other than that... And the cat is not here, but he wasn't here when I went away. The neighbours were coming in to let him in and out. Cats ... you know – territorial,' I explained, in case he thought I had been careless in just leaving the cat to fend for itself. 'Nothing has happened to my cat, has it?' I asked in sudden consternation.

'Your cat?' He seemed very surprised. 'No. No, nothing has happened to your cat that I know of.'

The doorbell rang again. 'Shall I get that?' I asked.

'Yes,' he said. 'I expect it is Margaret Mc-Gregor.'

So I went out to the door, and indeed it was Margaret McGregor – a pleasant young woman, about my age or maybe a little younger with a kind face. She introduced herself and asked if Michael Fogarty was there, and I brought her in and they nodded to each other.

'Should I offer you coffee or something?' I asked them.

They both said, 'No, thank you,' as one, so I sat there and waited.

'Where have you got to?' Margaret asked.

'Ms Carmody was telling me about the changes she found on her return from her Christmas break,' he said.

'And nothing has happened to my cat,' I added. It was a bit of a non sequitur where she was coming from, but it was the most significant thing I had learned to date.

'So what changes have there been?' Margaret asked me with what sounded like gentle curiosity.

'Nothing really,' I said. 'I'd left the house in the neighbours' charge, and I suppose they tidied up a bit.'

'Tidied up?' she asked.

'Well, run the dishwasher and the washing machine. For both of which I am grateful, I might add,' I hastened to say. 'You can imagine what the dishwasher would have smelled like!'

Margaret nodded. 'Any other changes? Anything out of place? Even the tiniest thing,' she suggested.

'Well, I'm only in the door,' I said. 'I haven't really looked around. I wasn't looking for anything, so I suppose I didn't really notice.'

'Would you like to take a look around now?' Margaret asked. 'We'll go with you. Tell us if anything seems out of place – anything at all.'

'I think it's time you told me what this is all about,' I said. 'Have I been burgled?'

She looked at Michael Fogarty with a surprised expression.

'We hadn't got that far,' he explained.

'I did ask,' I said. 'Mr Fogarty hadn't got around to explaining.'

He nodded at her as if giving her permission to supply the required explanation. I sat and waited.

'Well,' she said, 'one of your neighbours was seriously assaulted and at the moment we're trying to work out where it happened.'

'Millie?' I asked. I was really shocked. I don't know why I thought it was Millie, but I did. 'Is she all right?'

'Millie is fine,' Margaret said. 'But could we take that look around and see if there is anything

343

out of place.'

We got up and went from room to room. Downstairs everything looked much as I thought I had left it. We went through to the conservatory, and then back into the kitchen where I noticed again the pile of clean laundry in the basket. Then we went into the hall and upstairs. The bedrooms and bathrooms all looked the same. The three men who had come with Michael Fogarty were looking in drawers and on the beds. Other than that I didn't get the impression anything had been touched.

'It all looks as I left it,' I said, 'other than the laundry. There are a load of towels which have been washed that I don't remember using, but that's the only thing.'

'Towels?' Michael Fogarty said.

'In the kitchen. Someone ran the washing machine – at least, I think they did. I don't remember running it before I went away, though I suppose I might have.'

'And the dishwasher?' Margaret reminded me.

'Yes. The dishwasher too,' I said.

'What would have been in the washing machine that you recall?' she asked.

'I'm not sure,' and I wasn't. 'I'd had a drinks party so there would have been tea-towels, and I probably put in some underwear and maybe my bath towels before I went. I don't know. I don't really remember. I probably just did what I usually do,' I added. 'I may even have run the load and just don't remember doing it. I thought it wasn't full, and I don't usually run it on a small or half load. Waste of money...'

'Let's take a look at the items in the basket,' Margaret said, 'and perhaps you can tell me what you're sure you put in.'

This was all very uncomfortable. Who likes the idea of having someone go through their underwear? I felt a bit unwilling to go and look in front of them but at the same time, the sooner I did what was asked of me, the sooner this would be over.

We went back to the kitchen and I emptied the basket on to the kitchen table. There was an assortment of coloured knickers, a pink bra, a black lace slip, a couple of pairs of tights and four tea-towels, all of which I was reasonably sure I had put in the machine.

'And this towel,' I said, pulling out a full wine-coloured bath towel, 'and probably this one too,' as I pulled out a matching hand towel.

'And all of these?' Margaret asked, gesturing towards the other towels.

'I don't remember using them,' I said. 'As far as I know, they were in the airing cupboard, but I can't be sure.'

'They are your towels?' Michael Fogarty asked, as he looked through them. There were four of them.

'Yes,' I said.

We went back into the living room.

'Please tell me about Millie,' I said. 'What happened to her? And how is she now?'

Margaret and Michael looked at each other.

'Millie is fine, as I said,' Margaret replied.

'As fine as she can be under the circumstances,' Michael Fogarty added.

I still didn't realise that they were covering up.

'I've to go inside to the McHargs',' Margaret said to me. 'I'll tell them you're back.'

'May I come with you?' I asked.

'It's not a good time,' she said. 'I need to see them alone. But I will tell them that you're back. I'll leave you now, but I'm sure we'll talk again.'

We shook hands and she left me with Michael Fogarty, who started asking me about my relationship with the neighbours. I explained the good terms we were on.

'I'm terribly fond of them all,' I said. I sounded a bit gushing and I knew it, but I *was* very fond of them all, and I enjoyed their company. 'They're a bit like an extended family,' I said. 'I live here alone and I really like them, all of them, both as neighbours and as friends. There are the five of them – oh, George is home at the moment, but as a rule there are the five females and they are great company.'

'Do they come in and out by themselves?'

'How do you mean?'

'I mean, do you enjoy a relationship with them individually or is it always in a group?'

'Individually,' I said. 'The girls often come in separately. The baby, the adopted child, Dumpling, she just slips in through the hedge if she wants to visit. They got a scare once when she disappeared like that, so I always let them know when she turns up. Though in winter she is less likely to come because if I'm in the house and the back door is locked, she has no way of telling me that she is out in the garden.'

'And the others?'

'I probably see Maria least of all, even though we're closest age-wise, but then she is out at work most of the day, and I suppose she's busy in the evenings. But Plumpet and Daffers might pop in and out, sometimes just for a chat. And I see Millie all the time. I write too,' I added. Well, not like Millicent McHarg – I haven't been published yet. I just haven't really found my niche. Millicent McHarg is phenomenally successful. I admit I'm waiting for some of her success to rub off on me, but it hasn't yet happened.

'Now, can we go through where you've been,' he said.

'You mean over the last few days?' I felt a bit uncomfortable, because I'd been in bed, bar one visit to the hotel dining room. The rest of the time had been room service only. 'Do I have to say?' I asked. 'I wasn't here, and I can prove it, but I'd prefer not to get into this if I don't have to.' Normally I wouldn't care who knew what I was doing or with whom I was doing it, but this was different.

'You don't have to say at the moment if you don't want to,' he said. 'It just might make it easier for everyone if you did.'

Put like that, what could I do? So I explained about this new boyfriend and how we spent Christmas in a hotel down the road.

'Is that unusual?' he asked.

'Unusual?'

'Going off with a new boyfriend, and not being with your family?'

I explained that I didn't have much in the way of family. 'There's really just my sister and myself.

Everyone else is a bit distant – you know, cousins and people. No parents, no one else close. And Polo – she's my sister, she does her own thing. So for me to spend the few days like I did really wasn't that unusual. Christmas can be quite a lonely time,' I added. I guess I was looking for the sympathy vote.

'Who else has a key to your house?'

'Other than myself and my sister? I had left a spare key with the McHargs.'

'And that's it? No other keys?'

'Well, there is one which I usually keep under a stone in the front garden, for emergencies. You know – in case I lock myself out or whatever.'

'And who else knows about that key?'

'Lots of people. It's a bit of an open house.'

'Who in particular knows about the key?' He was so persistent.

'I don't know.' I tried to think of people who knew about it. 'If someone is coming to stay and I'm not going to be here I tell them where it is.'

He made me go out and check that the key was there, which it was but he wouldn't let me touch it. He called one of his men who lifted it with tweezers and put it in a plastic bag.

He took details about the hotel where I'd been, and about Tony Fonzetti, even though clearly it couldn't have been Tony who had committed this crime. Michael Fogarty and the others stayed about another hour going through everything, then they asked me to phone them if I noticed anything else amiss. I thought they would never leave. By now I was tired and I wanted to call Millicent to check that she was all right and to ask her what had happened. I couldn't understand their reticence.

To my absolute consternation they went through the laundry in the kitchen with a fine-tooth comb. They took the filter of the washing machine out and put revolting-looking dredges into a plastic bag, which they then sealed and marked. On one level I watched with interest as this had the makings of a great story, but as I couldn't work out what they were looking for, I was a bit in the dark. They also seemed very interested in what I might have cleaned before I went away.

'Did you wash your bath?' Michael Fogarty asked me.

'When?' I could feel myself being both surly and curious at the same time. Did I wash my bath? For goodness' sake!

'After the last time you used it?'

'Oh.' I thought about that. 'I had a shower in it on the morning I went away,' I said.

'And did you wash it after that?'

I didn't think so. I have a woman who comes in and does for me a couple of times a month, and while I rinse the bath out I am inclined to leave the big scrub to her. I found myself explaining this and wondering if I sounded like a slut.

'So you didn't wash it after your shower that morning?'

'Well ... no.'

'And was your cleaning woman due in that day?'

'On Christmas Eve? No.'

'Might she have been here since?'

'Definitely not. She's gone away to her daughter

349

in the north for a week or so. I don't expect her back until after the New Year,' I said.

'When was she last here?'

I had to check my diary for that one even though I was pretty sure she hadn't been here for at least a week before Christmas. My diary proved how accurate my memory can sometimes be, and I was quite pleased with myself when I was able to give him the actual date – ten days before Christmas.

'So you haven't cleaned the bath as such since then?'

'As I said, I live here for the most part by myself, and no I haven't had anyone staying since then, and no I haven't given it a thorough clean since then.' If I had known there was going to be such interest in my household hygiene I would have cleaned it every day, but I hadn't.

It was at that point that I said that I wasn't actually sure that I *had* put my bath towel and hand towel into the washing machine; I couldn't definitely recall doing so. He noted that down too.

By the time they left and I took another peek at myself in the mirror I no longer looked quite such a sexually satisfied would-be author – more like a tired and rather worried one. I was about to get my coat to go into the McHargs' to find out how Millicent was and what on earth was going on, when the bell rang again, and I opened the door to find Millicent standing there looking remarkably like when I last saw her – no signs of bruises or muggings or whatever.

'Millie,' I said with relief, 'come in. They wouldn't tell me what had happened to you. I was just about to come over to the house.'

She came in and dumped her motheaten fox furs on the hat-stand. She says they belonged to her grandmother and that it is sufficient that her grandmother has turned to dust, and that she is going to mind those furs as a souvenir of a bygone era. Anyway, in she came, dumped the furs and said, 'I've been waiting to come over. I'm glad you're back. I held on until I saw them all leaving.'

'What happened to you?' I asked. 'Are you all right?'

'Of course I'm all right,' she said. 'Why wouldn't I be?'

'Then what's going on?' I asked. 'I understood you'd been attacked.'

'Not me,' she said, striding into the living room. 'Plumpet.'

'Plumpet?' I was completely startled. 'Plumpet?' I repeated. I almost asked her if she were sure, but she clearly was.

'To protect her,' she said, 'we're keeping it quiet. She doesn't want anyone to know, which I'm sure you can understand, but I need to talk to you.'

'You and all,' I muttered. 'Look, Millicent, I wasn't here. I don't know what's been going on...'

'I know that,' she said, 'but it looks like it must have happened in here. I'm sure you gathered that from your recent police visit.'

'Oh yes,' I said. 'I had gathered that. But I thought something had happened to *you*. I think

351

you had better tell me what did happen,' I said.

Since I moved in next door to the McHargs, and yes I will admit that the fact that Millicent McHarg lived one house up was a selling point for me, she and I have been friends. She is a big-hearted woman, generous to a fault, humorous, quick-witted, wonderful company, and an asset to one's social circle. She has sat and listened to me talk about plotlines for my novels, has passed work of mine to her publishers, who to date have not bitten, but as Millicent says, 'Keep at it, Theresa, it will happen yet.' She has shared the little they know about the Dumpling's back-ground, and has drunk tea or gin with me and talked through her worries about George managing to get official identification for the child to ensure her safety in this country. She has teased me unmercifully about my sexlife, and has shared in parlance some of the funniest bedroom stories you would ever hear. But she would not tell me what had happened to Plumpet other than to say that she had been assaulted.

'Why won't you tell me?'

'It's not for me to tell,' she said. She was bottled up in some way. It was difficult to put my finger on it but although she appeared as usual, wonderfully dressed in deep rich colours, and her head tilted at a determined angle, there was something different.

'We always talk,' I said. 'We've always shared, even in the short time we've known each other.'

'I know,' she said. There was sadness in her voice. 'I can't talk to you about the details.

Plumpet is under age and we, the family, have decided to try to keep it as quiet as possible. More than anything, that is what Plumpet wants.'

'But if the police find out who did it,' I argued reasonably, 'it will come out then.'

'Plumpet will be protected,' she said firmly.

And knowing Millicent McHarg the way I did, I should have believed her.

'It's enough for me to tell you that she has been seriously assaulted,' she said. 'And we're really trying to put the pieces of it together because she remembers nothing.'

I assumed she had got a bang on the head. A bad one.

'Poor Plumpet,' I mused. 'I'll get her flowers.'

Millicent always gives people in trouble a gift. It's such a lovely idea. When my uncle died shortly after I moved into this house, Millicent sent me a case of champagne, and a smoked trout. Apparently I had referred to him as 'the old trout' at some point. In a kindly way, of course.

So Millicent sat in the living room and I poured us each a Slippery Nipple, a drink designed by the gods if concocted by man. We knocked them back while I told her about Tony Fonzetti and his bedroom abilities. We fell around the place laughing about my hairpiece being stuck in his shirt at the McHargs' party. Then she asked me about the visit from the police, and I told her about the search warrant, and how I had cooperated in every respect.

'Not that I liked them looking through my underwear,' I said, 'or asking me about how often

I washed the bath.'

'Tell me,' she said. 'Tell me all about it. What on earth were they up to?'

'I have no idea,' I said. And I explained about the bath towels that I hadn't put in the washing machine, and how the police even took the filter from the machine and removed the most awful amount of hair and gunge.

'You wouldn't know what they were up to,' she laughed. 'Would you?'

So we had another Slippery Nipple and I told her all about their interest in my house keys and how Polo had one, and how dozens of people knew that I kept one under the stone inside the hedge at the end of the front garden.

'My goodness,' she said. 'You are trusting.'

'Not really,' I replied. 'A house is just a house, and only friends know about the key.'

She looked at her watch, and then checked the time on the clock on the mantelpiece and said she really had better get home.

'Ratatouille and couscous for dinner,' she said. 'Mostly prepared by Daphne, so I ought to get back.'

Another time she would have invited me and I half expected her to ask would I like to join them. Instead she said, 'You've probably got unpacking to do, so I won't ask you in tonight, but I'll come and see you tomorrow and maybe we can talk a bit more.'

I was quite unsteady on my feet as I showed her out.

Chapter Twenty-Two

Millicent's Tale

I arrived back home from Theresa Carmody's and dinner wasn't quite ready. After the richness of the Christmas food, which we had been picking at for days, the vegetarian meal was going to make a pleasant change.

'No stuffing?' Daphne asked when we eventually got to the table, but she was joking. This was a new girl imitating the older one.

Plumpet grinned at her. She said, 'Maybe WC got it.'

An in-joke, which brought a smile to the Dumpling, Waldorf, Daphne and myself. George, who was having a serious humour bypass, said, 'Stop complaining, Daphne. It's perfectly good food.'

She looked at him. The old Daphne would have said that she wasn't complaining. This Daphne just looked at him and said nothing. When he turned to reach for the bottle of wine, she winked at Plumpet.

Role reversal, I thought. The younger child was becoming the elder. It was strange. I needed to think, but with everything happening at the table it was quite difficult. I needed to think about what Daphne had told me, and I was trying to work out how to handle Theresa Carmody, and at the same time keep an eye on proceedings.

Waldorf said, 'Lovely meal, m'dear,' in the direction of both Maria and Daphne.

Daphne looked pleased although Maria gave the impression of not having heard him. I wondered what was on her mind. It was clear that things weren't great between her and George and hadn't been in days. I suspected that something else had happened. I still had not managed to speak to them since Margaret had had a chat with Plumpet earlier, and then both George and Maria had gone in together to the drawing room. Whatever had gone on between Plumpet and Margaret had done her no harm at all. Plumpet looked brighter than she had been in days. I knew I had been right in encouraging her to slip out to see Ronnie; even if I had not said it, I felt I had been the driving force behind that, although Daphne had definitely played her part there too. And Waldorf.

The Dumpling was spooning couscous into her mouth with her customary dedication.

'Isn't that child old enough to use a fork like everyone else?' George asked irritably.

'For goodness' sake, George,' Maria suddenly said. 'Can no one do anything right when you're around?'

The Dumpling put her spoon down, and picked up her fork and started to use that instead. Her bottom lip was wobbling and I knew she was trying not to cry.

'My fault, Dad,' Daphne said. 'Dumples was imitating me.'

I looked at Daphne and saw that she had quickly replaced her fork with her dessert spoon;

she smiled at George and put the spoon down. And somehow the moment passed.

'I'm planning a trip to the city tomorrow,' Waldorf said, apparently addressing the wine bottle. 'Fancy coming with me, Plumpet?'

The Dumpling banged her fork on her plate and looked up hopefully at Waldorf. You could see her thinking, Me too, and the bottom lip had most definitely stopped its wobble.

'I'd love to,' Plumpet said, her face actually lighting up further.

'I think that there is a little Dumpling at the table who might like to join us,' Waldorf said. 'What do you think, Plumpet, m'dear? Would she cramp our style?'

Plumpet smiled at the Dumpling. 'Want to come too, Dumpling?' she asked.

The Dumpling looked at Daffers as if to include her.

'Shall we make it an expedition for three young ladies?' Waldorf asked.

'Don't indulge them,' George contributed unhelpfully.

'Indulge them?' Waldorf said. 'I wouldn't know how. They'll be indulging me by escorting me. What more could a man want?'

Maria said, 'That sounds lovely, girls. I've to go into the office for a couple of hours again tomorrow.'

'Again?' George asked.

'There's a contract to be ready for the day after New Year's Day,' she explained. 'I've no choice really.'

'I don't remember you working on previous

Christmases,' George said.

'This one is different,' Maria answered, and then she added quickly, 'because of the workload at the office, I mean.'

'Plumpet has an appointment at the hospital tomorrow,' George said.

'But it's first thing in the morning,' Plumpet said quickly. 'I should be back by ten, Waldorf, so I can definitely come with you.'

'And who is going to take her to the hospital?' George asked, as if his eldest daughter had nothing to do with him.

'I am,' Maria said. Her voice sounded angry but her expression was quite benign.

'But I thought you were going into work. I thought that was your priority this Christmas,' George said peevishly.

'I'll go in after that,' she said.

'Can I come with you to the hospital?' Daphne asked.

'Will you be up to going into the city afterwards?' George asked Plumpet, ignoring Daphne. Then he added, 'It may take more out of you than you imagine.'

Flying fucking helicopters. What was the man thinking of? Two Slippery Nipples or not, I was going to have this out with him as soon as dinner was over.

We had fruit salad for dessert and then Plumpet asked to be excused, saying that she wanted to have a bath.

'I'll come with you and sing to you,' Daphne said.

'Sing?' Plumpet said. Everyone laughed, because

358

Daphne most certainly can't sing. Not a note in the poor child's head.

As the two girls left to go upstairs, I looked at Waldorf and discreetly nodded my head towards the Dumpling, at which he suggested that the Dumpling and he played a game of Ludo. She was down off her chair like a rocket, a piece of pineapple in her hand and a big smile on her face as she went to get the box of Ludo.

'Let's play it in the drawing room,' he said to her, 'beside the Christmas tree. That's what we used to do when I was a child.' He can be quite a nostalgic man sometimes.

'George,' I said, when they were gone, 'for someone who trades on sensitivity, you can be the most insensitive human being imaginable.'

'What are you talking about?' he asked.

'Just take a look at yourself. You spend your life in a helicopter searching for disasters and then relaying those tragedies around the world in what I have always found to be a courageous and sensitive way. You have changed the lives of thousands of people for the better by homing in on catastrophes and calamities, but in your own home where real devastation has taken place, you are doing nothing to help.'

He looked at me in amazement, as if he had no idea what I was talking about.

'Grammer is absolutely right,' Maria said. 'If I hadn't seen your behaviour and your reactions these last few days with my own eyes, I wouldn't have believed it. You show a million times more sensitivity when you're out on some battlefield.'

'I just do my job,' he said. He looked completely mystified as if he really did not understand.

'You do it with compassion.'

'I don't,' he said. 'I do it with detachment. That is the only way you can live.'

That's the only way you can live. *Live?* Detached? Now both Maria and I looked bewildered.

'You weren't detached when you rescued the Dumpling,' she said. It wasn't a question, more a statement of fact.

'An aberration,' he responded.

'What was an aberration?' she asked. 'That you let your detachment slip for a moment or that you rescued her?'

'Both,' he said.

'Do you regret rescuing her?' she asked sharply. Her face looked shocked.

'No. But I regret letting my detachment slip.'

'But you gave her life. You gave her hope. And we love her. She has...' Maria struggled to find the words.

'She has enriched our lives,' I helped her out. 'She has an existence which she never would have had. And so have we.'

'Every day I see children like her,' George said. 'I have no right to interfere in any of their lives. No matter who they are.' He sounded terribly moralistic.

'By filming them, by relaying their despair around the world,' Maria said, 'you are "interfering" as you put it, in their lives. And it is that interference which gives them a modicum of hope. It is because of what you do, that aid arrives in the right place, that their suffering is seen, and... I don't understand you,' she said. 'I just don't understand where you are coming from. You almost sound as if you regretted bringing the Dumpling to safety.'

He didn't answer her. He just took another drink of his wine.

'What's going on with you?' Maria asked.

'I'm tired,' he said. 'I've been out there for a year, and bar the odd few days, I've worked non-stop. I came home for a peaceful Christmas.'

'You are a selfish, selfish man,' she said, standing up angrily, pushing her chair back behind her so that it fell over. 'Do you think any of us asked for this Christmas to be like this? Do you think that Plumpet asked to be drugged and raped? Do you think this is easy for any of us?'

I hadn't thought that Maria had been doing a particularly good job of handling this crisis, but by comparison with George she was light years ahead. She was tuned into the randomness and the unfairness and the cruelty of what had happened.

'This isn't about you not having a relaxing Christmas,' she said. 'This is much bigger than that. This is a tragedy just like those you report on. Oh, I know it's not on a grand scale – it's just your daughter and your family who are affected. I pulled out the stops for you last summer when you needed me. I went out to you and we cancelled our summer holiday for you. But if you can't pull out the stops for us, if you can't behave like a normal person, if you can only do detachment – then maybe you shouldn't be here.'

I had never seen or heard Maria so angry or so articulate. She started bringing dirty dishes out to the kitchen and stacking the dishwasher noisily. George reached for the bottle of wine and poured himself another glass.

'Perhaps you could give your wife a hand with the dishes,' I said icily.

He ignored me and took out his cigarettes again and lit one.

I got up and left the table. I couldn't believe how like his father he had become. I wondered if it was because Dirk had been around for his formative years, and that was why the influence was so strong. Or could it be that this behaviour pattern was trapped in his genes? I could not understand how my son could be so selfish, and not be able to see his selfishness, or be able to see how destructive he was being.

I went back to my apartment where I lay on the bed because I was feeling a little woozy. I thought about what Daphne had told me earlier when she and I had come through here to have a quiet talk. She had lain on the bed and I sat in my armchair at the window.

'What did you want to tell me?' I asked her.

She hummed and hawed, and I guessed that it was going to be difficult to get it out of her unless we managed to bypass all her natural inhibitions.

'Darling,' I said to her, 'you can tell me anything. Anything at all. There is probably nothing I haven't already heard.'

'Mmm,' she said doubtfully.

'At my age...' I began.

'Plenty-nine?' she said with a wry smile.

'Yes, plenty-nine. Believe me, at plenty-nine I think I've heard it all. All the things to do with life and sex. All the various aberrations of the human being.'

'Aberrations?' she asked.

'Deviations, abnormalities. All the strange things that people do. And believe me, they do do strange things.'

'Oh, I believe you,' she said.

I glanced at her face. She was lying on her stomach, her head propped on her hands, and she was staring down at the quilt. It's a lovely silk patchwork quilt, in shades of purple, navy, wine and dark green. The threading is in gold and pink and sky blue. I picked it up in New York the first time I went there. I could only see her profile the way she was lying on it.

'Of course,' I continued, 'when I was your age, I was constantly surprised at things that people did. I had had a very sheltered upbringing and it wasn't until I was much older that I realised there was nothing in the world that is new.'

'How do you mean?' she asked.

'Well, when I was your age, I would never have imagined that someone could do something like this to Plumpet.' I didn't know what details she actually knew, and I wasn't sure how to lead her to what it was that she wanted to tell me. 'It wasn't until I was married that it dawned on me that there is nothing new in the world. There are always bad people, and all crimes have been committed before. There is nothing new.'

'But what happened to Plumpet...' she began.

I waited. Silence. She went on staring at the quilt.

'What happened to Plumpet,' I said after a very long pause, 'has happened before in life, and sadly will happen again. What we have to do is to help Plumpet. That's all we can do. We can help her by understanding her. By listening to her. And maybe by putting the pieces together. And I don't just mean by putting the pieces of Plumpet back together, but also by putting the pieces of information together and maybe helping to work it all out.'

'Like Humpty Dumpty?' she asked.

'No, I didn't really mean like Humpty Dumpty,' I said. 'After all, he was an egg. You can't heal an egg.'

She smiled. I could see the corner of her mouth.

'Also,' I said, 'by putting the pieces of information that we know together, we can work out who pushed Humpty Dumpty off the wall.'

'Didn't he just fall?' she asked.

'Maybe someone put him sitting on the wall knowing that he would fall,' I said. 'Or maybe someone crept up behind him. Some bad man...'

'Or woman,' she said.

'Yes, or woman,' I said. 'But more likely to be a man, I think.'

'What if it was a woman?' she asked.

My sixth sense or woman's intuition, call it what you will, told me to tune in fast and not to let this pass.

'It could have been a woman,' I said, trying to

keep the doubt out of my voice.

'And if I said that it *was* a woman who had done that to Plumpet, what would you say?' she asked.

I had not thought of this being a possibility at all; it had quite simply never occurred to me, but I knew to encourage her gently to see where it would lead.

'I'd say you're a very clever girl, Daphne, so tell me more.'

'I'm not clever,' she said.

'You've got intuition,' I said. 'And you're astute when you want to be. You're a whole lot more intelligent than you like to let on. It suits you to hide that. So tell me more.'

'It was Polo Carmody,' she said. Her voice faltered and she looked over at me to see my reaction.

I kept my face impassive as I tried to digest this. 'Polo,' I said. 'I see. Now tell me about it.'

And she did. Out poured a story that took me a while to digest as well as to sort out.

'They're bitemarks on Plumpet,' she said, 'all over her chest and neck. You saw them Grammer, didn't you?'

'The bruises?' I said.

'Yes. They're from bites.'

'Yes.' I nodded at her. I had assumed they had been caused both by the force of fingers and of a mouth. So I followed that all right. I could see that it had been a shock for her to connect a mouth with them. That had not been something within her imagination.

'Yes, you're right,' I reassured her.

'Polo did that,' she said. 'The Dumpling told me that Plumpet had gone back out. I know we know now that she *had* gone back out, but we didn't at first, and the Dumpling told me – she told both of us, but we didn't get it. I didn't get it at first, did you? And then there was the car and that was Polo's car. I know it was. And Polo did that.'

She had lost me.

'The Dumpling told us?' I didn't get it. I could see that she was absolutely sure about what she was telling me. She was confident of her facts but I needed her to start at the beginning and tell me it slowly so that I could put it into sequence.

It transpired that on the night we had been to the pantomime and afterwards went into Theresa's house, Polo had spoken to her in the kitchen and made her feel uneasy. After that, Daphne had apparently hidden behind the curtains in the living room at the back of the house, from where she could see into the conservatory and there she saw Polo doing something with a man. She couldn't remember his name.

'You know who I mean, Grammer,' she said. 'The man with the purple eyes.'

'Yes,' I said thoughtfully. 'Christian Holt's brother, Gervaise.'

'Yes, that's his name,' she said. 'And then while they were doing this thing – you know, this thing they were doing...' She couldn't say what it was. All I could work out was that it wasn't the Full Monty but it was obviously something odd.

366

'You've seen sex scenes of one sort or another on the television and in the cinema,' I said. 'Was it a bit like that?'

'Sort of,' she said.

'Then what happened?'

'He put his finger in her mouth, and she must have bitten it, because afterwards, remember he came into the living room and was being introduced around – or introducing himself, remember? Well, there was a bitemark on his hand and it was bleeding.'

Yes, I did remember. He had taken a handkerchief from his pocket and dabbed at it. At the time I had thought he must have been cutting up food in the kitchen or something.

'Did you actually see the bitemark?' I asked her.

'Oh yes. Polo has very small teeth, sort of pointed – and you could see the mark of four teeth and one of them was bleeding. One of the marks, I mean. One of her teeth is slightly longer than the others.'

Okay, I thought. So Gervaise stuck his finger in Polo Carmody's mouth while they were doing something unmentionable in the conservatory. And her teeth were so sharp, or she bit him so hard, that she marked him and actually cut through the skin.

'Connect this with Plumpet,' I said, although I was now beginning to get the connection all right.

'Yesterday, when she was having a bath, I saw the marks on her. The bruises are starting to lighten and you could clearly see where one tooth had bitten into her skin. All over the place. I mean, in loads of different places.' She paused. Then she shook her head. She was clearly trying to get it as right as possible.

'I'm sorry. That's not completely true. I didn't see that – it's what I think is there. I *think* that's what I saw. Remember when she first came back from the hospital, how all you could see was the bruising on her hand, and now you can see the mark from the needle? Well, I think that now the bruising is fading on her body we'll be able to see that there are toothmarks there. I think that's what I saw when she was in the bath, only I didn't know what I was looking at...'

It all came out in such a rush. It was Daphne trying to tell me what she was sure of, together with her surmises – facts and fantasy mixed. But I could see why. And she was right about Plumpet's hand: you could now see clearly where the intravenous drip had been inserted, whereas on Christmas Day all you could see was black and blue bruises and a swelling.

'You do believe me?' she asked suddenly. 'Grammer, you do believe me?' Her voice was worried and insistent.

'Yes, Daphne,' I said. 'I most definitely do believe you. Now, let me think.'

She laid her head on the bed and her body relaxed as she waited for me to work out what to do next.

'One of us needs to take another look at those bruises,' I said. 'And ideally in a way that doesn't alarm or upset Plumpet.'

'Next time she baths,' Daphne said, 'I'll try and

go with her.'

'Right. And the way she is having baths at the moment, she will undoubtedly have another one this evening.'

'Is it odd that she is having so many baths?' Daphne asked me.

'I think she was told to have salt baths,' I explained to her. 'Until the stitches have healed.'

'Stitches?' She looked truly horrified. 'Stitches, Grammer?'

I had not meant to say that. I just was not thinking or maybe I assumed she knew.

'Grammer, what stitches?'

There was no way I couldn't explain to her. She was sitting bolt upright on the bed.

'I'm sorry,' I said. 'Whoever did this to her used some implement and it tore her so that she needed to be stitched.'

She looked at me with her eyes wide open as my words slowly penetrated her mind.

'Why would someone do such a thing?' she wailed. 'Why would someone ... how could someone...?'

How indeed? The word evil doesn't begin to encompass the wickedness and iniquity to which some people aspire. I put my arms around her. You cannot protect children – you can only try to. She started to cry. I could hear the word Plumpet through her muffled sobs.

After a few minutes, I said, 'Daphne, listen to me. If you're right, and I think you may well be, we need to work together. We need to help each other. Plumpet needs us all on her side.'

'But I am on her side, Grammer!' she cried.

'I know you are, darling,' I said. 'I have no doubt about that at all. But dry your eyes now, and talk to me about the Dumpling, because I didn't understand that.' I handed her a lilac lawn handkerchief to blow her nose and wipe her eyes. I buy white ones and dye them. After all, we all need a little colour in our lives. And white lawn dyes so well. I spray them with vanilla musk – it has a very soothing effect.

She dabbed at her nose and eyes, and said, 'Nice smell, Grammer,' and I knew she would be all right.

Then she sat with her back against the headboard and reminded me what the Dumpling had done on Christmas morning. I say reminded, but in fact I had no memory of it at all. I suppose too much had been going on.

'I'll get her to do it again,' Daphne said. 'And I'll ask her questions. You'll see.'

'No, don't do anything,' I said. 'Not yet. Just do Plumpet and the bruises. That's enough for now. I need to think about the Dumpling. I don't want someone later saying that we drilled her.'

'How do you mean?' she asked.

'I mean that if you practise this with her, it might look like a set-up or something,' I said. 'Just leave it for now. Leave it with me. Promise?'

'I promise.'

'Right. Now let's go into dinner.'

I had already been into Theresa Carmody's at that stage, and encouraged her to knock back the Slippery Nipples – there's nothing like a Baileys and Sambucca to give you a kick and to loosen the tongue. She gabbled away and I started to get a picture of what might have happened. But I had not made the connection with Polo. It just had not occurred to me. But all those towels – carefully washed, and the police were obviously on to something if they had taken the hair from the filter in the washing machine.

I found that reassuring.

Now, dinner over, I wondered how Daphne was getting on in the bathroom with Plumpet, and if Waldorf and the Dumpling were still playing Ludo. He had said he would like to teach her how to play chess, which I found a wonderful idea. And I wondered how George and Maria were sorting out their differences. I couldn't see how that was going to resolve itself – at least not at the moment.

I made myself a cup of coffee and contemplated my next move. I would try to see Theresa Carmody again the following day, and play that one by ear. I wondered if I should phone Margaret with the information Daphne had given me, or whether there was a better way to use it. I thought of Plumpet upstairs in her bath and I pondered the difference between physical and emotional suffering. The bruises were undoubtedly already fading and in due course would heal, the hospital would no doubt say that the tear was healing too, and then where would that leave my eldest granddaughter? Would she walk away from this? Would she move on? Would she be able to move? What would happen if it could be proved that Polo Carmody was the perpetrator? What would

371

it all mean to Plumpet? Would she be able to accommodate that in her mind and in her life? Was she better off not knowing? Was she better off knowing?

It's odd how things are so much clearer when they relate solely to oneself. Or maybe that is not even true. Maybe we all just see things in different ways, and one is armed better when it is oneself. Or is it just that the armour is different?

Chapter Twenty-Three

Plumpet's Tale

Someone had put the heater on in the bathroom, and so it was warm. I think Daffers must have turned it on earlier. While I was getting undressed and into the bath, she went and got me a fresh towel from the airing cupboard, and clean pyjamas and my slippers from my room. I couldn't believe how kind she was being. I think I must have lost weight because I could feel my ribs. I didn't look down to see because I didn't really like the feel of them and I didn't want to know if I was right. I promised myself that I would eat more the following day. And I didn't want to see what I looked like. I hated my body. I hated and hated it. But somehow I didn't want Ronnie to hate it.

I kept thinking about Ronnie and what it was like walking in the park, and how the ducks all looked contented even though it was so cold, and how he held my hand, and how all the bad things did not seem so important at all while I was walking beside him. There were so many things I did not want to think about – like Dad, and how annoyed he seemed, and how nothing I did seemed right, and about the big empty hole in my head and how I didn't want to look into it, and how I kept forgetting and then remembering things, and how the food tasted like nothing at dinner, and how I felt that I had ruined Christmas.

But whenever I thought about Ronnie I felt all right.

I kept trying to think around him – wondering what he was thinking. I felt that he really did like me. That what had happened to me didn't change that. That was reassuring. I knew he must have an agenda of his own – like, his Christmas must have been ruined too. My brain told me that. But inside me, where my heart is, where my feelings are, there in that secret place, I felt that he did care – not just for him, but for me too.

And it was that knowledge which gave me hope.

Daffers came back into the bathroom and plonked herself down on the floor. 'You okay?' she asked.

She gave me hope too. I don't know why, but somehow the kindness or kinsmanship I felt from her made me feel that I wasn't a bad person. Waldorf was a bit like that too, but differently so.

'Yeah, I'm okay,' I said.

'Can I see the bruises?' she asked.

I thought, Which bruises? These on my neck and chest? Or the ones no one can ever really see which are inside me? When I thought that, I suddenly realised that no one need ever see the bruises inside. I'm not talking about the other physical bruises, about the hurt between my legs, about the rough feeling of the stitches, or the funny feeling of swollen jelly inside me. I meant the bruises inside my head, which only I would ever really know about. I know she was sitting on the floor waiting for me to show her the bruising, but I kept thinking, This is important, this is vital – if you really want, no one need ever know. It seemed an idea that I should hang on to, that I should remember. I told myself not to forget that, but I was afraid that I wouldn't know how to recall it.

I let my hand trail over the side of the bath so that she could see the bruises on it.

'I've seen those already, Plumpet,' she said. 'I meant the ones on your front.'

Your front! I almost smiled. My front was my neck and chest, my small breasts, my now bony ribs. I looked at my hand which I had just shown to her, and I knew that she and all the family must have seen those bruises change from black to purple and blue over the last few days. I closed my eyes and turned slightly towards her.

'Do you mean these?' I asked.

I had the feeling that she was moving in closer to take a look, and I couldn't imagine why. I felt a sort of violation. It wasn't to do with her peering at me. It was to do with what had been done to me. It was to do with the fact that something had been taken from me, and it was, fleetingly, characterised in those passing bruises.

I waited for absolutely ages before opening my eyes, and when I did, she was still there, looking carefully at my chest.

'Daffers,' I said, 'they're just bruises. Leave it.'

'Have you looked at them?' she asked.

I shook my head. I was aware of them though. I mean, when I put on my bra and half glanced down, I was aware that there were these marks. And they were sore. I could see them out of the bottom of my eyes, but I deliberately turned away from them. In a sense they almost did not matter to me. They were really a representation of something else. That they hurt was not really relevant. Does that make sense? What really hurt was what was in my head and in my heart, not the feeling of the stitches, nor the pain from the bruises.

She didn't say anything, so I looked at her face to see if I could read something there.

'They're bitemarks,' she said.

I wanted to scream. I wanted to scream and scream. And inside my head, I think I did. I wanted to say, Does it matter what they are? Are they of any importance whatsoever? Who cares that they are bitemarks? All these things in my head, and no words to say them.

'I don't care,' I said. 'I don't care.' I pulled up my knees so that she couldn't see. I didn't want anyone to see. They would go away, I knew that. Bruises and things like that go away. I only had to wait, and then they would be gone. Gone for ever.

'Plumpet.' Her voice was so gentle, it didn't sound like Daffers at all.

'What?' I said. But I didn't want her answer. I didn't want to know. I wanted it all to go away. I wanted the water to wash everything away, and then for it all to go down the plughole, with the grime of a bath, and the soapsuds and the pain. All to go away.

'Plumpet,' she said again. 'I think it's important.'

'What's important?' I asked. 'Nothing is important. I just want to get away from this time and this place, and either to go back to before Christmas Eve, or to go forward to a place where this doesn't matter.'

'Don't you want to know who did this?' she asked. Her voice sounded puzzled, but kind. Like someone who really wanted to understand, and who was asking me to help her get to that understanding.

'I don't know that I do want to. I mean, if I know who did it, then I have to handle that. And I can't handle anything,' I said. I know my voice sounded funny, but I couldn't help it. 'I can't even call that person a person, because what kind of a human being would do this to another?' I felt cold. Completely and utterly frozen inside. It was like coming to an understanding – a realisation of something that had been somewhere deep inside my head and that I didn't want to acknowledge.

'And yet,' I continued, 'what other word can one use – instead of person, I mean?' I tried to find the words. 'I can't say that the person is an animal, because I don't think that animals would do this to each other. The person who did this – I don't want to know. It's all I can do to handle *me*, Plumpet. To get up in the morning, and try to pretend that I'm me. That I'm the same person I was before Christmas Eve. That there is a chance I may be that person sometime again in the future. That's all I can do. Nothing more. No, I don't want to know who did this. I thought I did. But I don't.'

Daffers just said, 'Oh,' and I wondered if she understood.

'I mean it,' I said. 'I really don't want to know. At first I couldn't think anything at all. But when I could think, I thought I had to know, that I had to find out who was responsible. I thought that was really important. But now, now I don't want to know. I don't want to have to confront him in any way. Tell me you understand, please,' I begged her.

'I'm trying to,' she said. 'You see, I thought it was really important that you found out, so that the person could be brought to court and sent to jail, and stuff. I thought that that was the way you would feel better. And then you'd know they couldn't do it to someone else.'

When she put it like that, it seemed that maybe she was right ... but I didn't like the idea of court, and having to 'confront' whoever it was.

I glanced down at my chest. There were loads of these bruises, and I could see what she meant about teethmarks – they were there all right. You couldn't see them before because I was all swollen and black and blue, but you could see them now all right, as the bruises were lightening and going a sort of greenish shade. I closed my eyes. I didn't want to see them. They would pass soon enough and then they would be gone.

'You know you're going to hospital in the morning?' Daffers said.

'Yup?'

'Well, I think you should show them to someone,' she said, quite firmly for Daffers.

'Why?'

'Look, okay you don't want to know who did this – at least not right now – but if they are some kind of evidence, then someone should see them.'

She could be right, I thought. But I pushed the whole idea away. I really didn't want anything to do with it.

'Can I come with you in the morning?' she asked. I think she had asked that at dinner, but I don't think she had been given an answer.

I nodded, eyes closed, as I tried to let the bathwater wash away the bad feelings.

In the morning I bathed again, and when we got to the hospital Mum asked the doctor should I be having so many baths.

'If they make Plumpet feel better,' the doctor said, 'then that's what counts. And certainly the salt in the bath helps the wound to heal.'

This was after I had had to sit in this horrible chair with things which kept my legs apart, and the doctor checked the stitches and inside me. I tried to think about stuff like Ronnie in the park, and how Waldorf was going to get me a mobile phone – nice things – but it was difficult to concentrate on them, really difficult to keep my mind off what was happening to me.

'Looking good,' the doctor said. 'I'm going to book you in for an ultrasound so that we can see that there is no lasting internal damage. And in a few weeks' time you'll have another blood test.'

I didn't ask what for, because I didn't want to know. Daffers and Mum were sitting outside waiting. I did want to ask what an ultrasound was, but I was afraid of the answer. But the doctor seemed to have guessed what I was thinking, because she explained that it was a bit like looking through me, that they would smear some kind of jelly on my stomach and then the radiologist would run a kind of ball over it, and he would be able to see on a monitor what I looked like inside.

'It doesn't hurt. You just lie there and you can watch the monitor if you like,' she said.

'Do you think I'm pregnant?' I asked her.

'Absolutely not,' she said.

'Do you know what drug was used?' I asked her.

'How do you mean?'

'When I was drugged and raped,' I said.

'I'm going to get your mother in so that I can talk to you both about that,' she said.

I was helped down from the chair, and I dressed and waited for Mum to come in. She sat beside me and held my hand.

'We're as sure as can be that it was Rohypnol,' the doctor said. That was what Margaret had said the previous evening. 'However, the problem, if that's the word one can use, with Rohypnol is

379

that it often leaves no traces in the body. It usually flushes straight through the system. So the lab tests showed up nothing.'

'Is that good or bad?' Mum asked.

'It makes it difficult to prove that Plumpet was drugged. I know you were drugged,' the doctor said as if to reassure me, because my mouth had opened to protest – and I do think she knew that. 'It's just that if this ends up in court, there will be no lab reports to confirm what was used.'

'It's not going to court,' I said. 'There is no way that I'm going through that.' I could hear my voice, but I was unsure if I sounded petulant or determined. I just wanted them to know that that was simply not going to happen.

'I'm sure when the time comes,' the doctor said, 'you would be allowed to give evidence privately – that you wouldn't have to go into the courtroom to do it. They would take your age and your state of mind into account.'

'I'm not going to be giving evidence,' I said. 'I don't have any to give anyway. I remember nothing, so how much use would that be?'

'Don't you want the person who did this to you to be put away for a long time?' the doctor asked me gently.

I tried explaining as I had done with Daffers earlier. I tried saying that at first I felt I couldn't live knowing that that person could be someone I knew, or even someone I didn't know, but that if they were out there on the loose I would always feel scared.

'But now I don't feel that way,' I said. 'Now I don't want to know. I just want to move on from

380

here, and as soon as I'm physically all right, then I have the chance to do that. But if there is a court case or something like that, it'll be one more thing connected with what happened to me, and I don't want to have to face that.'

'You may feel different later,' the doctor said. 'You're going through such emotional and physical trauma at the moment – the shock of what you've experienced is ... well, it's dreadful. And you are doing very well. But as you work through it, you may find later that you need closure. And closure may be in the form of having the perpetrator put away.'

I didn't think so, but I didn't bother arguing.

At that point the detective called Margaret McGregor arrived, which surprised me considering she had come to the house only the day before. She had been so kind then, talking about the drug and how it was perfectly normal to feel as shocked and as frightened as I did about the missing hours, and how it was normal for me to have further memory lapses. A nurse had knocked on the door and said that she was outside, and would like to see the doctor.

I sat with Mum and waited. Looking out of the window I saw that it was snowing.

'Are you okay?' Mum asked.

I said that I was, but that I hoped the snow wouldn't put Waldorf off going shopping as it sounded like fun.

'He's great, isn't he,' I said. I wasn't really looking for a reply. It was more of a statement, but Mum said tightly, 'Yes. It's nice to know that men aren't all a waste of space.'

I didn't say anything to that, because what could I say? I wished she hadn't said it though, because I felt she was getting at Dad, and I didn't want her thinking or saying things like that.

Before I could think of anything to say, Mum was asked to come out and I sat there watching the snowflakes drifting slowly down. They sort of melted when they reached the glass, and then they dribbled down to the bottom of the pane where they built up an ever-increasing dam of sludgy-looking ice. I wondered if the ducks in the park liked the weather like this, or if they even noticed. I reckoned they would probably like a visit today with some bread, as not too many people would go out for a walk. I wondered next if there would be any chance to see Ronnie. I wished Mum knew that I had met him the previous day, but I couldn't see any way to tell her that would not end up in a row.

Margaret came in with the doctor and said hello to me. I smiled at her. She was really very nice.

'I just want to take a look at those bruises on your chest,' the doctor said.

'They're fading,' I said, hoping that would put a halt to that. I didn't really want to undress again as I had thought we were just about finished.

'We measured them the day you came in,' the doctor continued, 'and it seems a good idea just to see how they are progressing.'

I wondered if Daffers could have said something about them, but I didn't think it was likely. Margaret had turned up unannounced, so it wasn't as if she could have been called in. I assumed it was just the end of the procedure.

I took off my sweater, and unbuttoned my blouse. I think Margaret had been there on Christmas Day; she might have been around when they had measured the bruises that day, but I wasn't sure. It all seemed very long ago. The doctor was reading my file while I was getting undressed, and Margaret just said, 'Don't mind me, Plumpet. Just see me as part of the furniture.'

'Can you slip your bra off too,' the doctor said. So I did. I didn't look at either of them; instead I just watched the snowflakes falling and wondered what Ronnie was doing. I wondered what it would be like having Ronnie see my breasts, but I couldn't really imagine it, and the room was so sterile that it didn't lend itself to thoughts like that. But I did like it when he had touched them. I knew that.

'Yes,' the doctor said. 'They're fading nicely.'

'I'm just going to measure the marks,' Margaret said, 'and then I'm going to photograph them.'

I looked up in dismay.

'It's all right,' she said. 'It's normal procedure, and your face won't be in them.'

'I don't want you to find who did this,' I said to her. 'I want all this to go away. I don't want to have to give evidence or anything.' I felt like I was whinging, but I didn't want this to go on any more.

'Plumpet,' she said, 'no one is going to do anything without your permission. I'm only doing this for the file, so that later on if needs be, we'll have a full record of everything to do with the crime.'

So I sat and watched the snowflakes, aware of what she was doing, and seeing the flash of the camera, but paying no attention.

'There now,' she said. 'All done.'

I looked down then at myself. The tiny pinprick marks were even clearer than the previous evening when I was having the bath.

'Are they teethmarks?' I asked.

'Yes, I think so,' she said gently.

The doctor nodded. 'I don't think there is any doubt about it,' she said. 'They're all virtually identical.'

I was aware of the two of them looking at each other, and feeling that they were part of a conspiracy of some sort – some scheme from which I was excluded, although I knew that if I wanted to participate, all I had to do was to pursue the questions that were lying somewhere in my mind. But I didn't want to. I wanted the questions and the answers to go away. So I said nothing.

When we were leaving, Daffers slipped her arm through mine as we walked down the corridor. I wondered briefly if she had betrayed me, if she had told them about the marks, but then I didn't want to know the answer to that either. I knew that to see it in terms of betrayal was unfair, and yet I couldn't see it any other way. Going back to the car I really just felt like going to bed, not going into town or anything.

Daffers chanted in a conspiratorial voice, 'We're going shopping, we're going shopping.'

I nodded. I wondered if I could get out of it. A

bath and bed was all I wanted.

'I suppose Waldorf wouldn't mind if we went tomorrow?' I half suggested, half hinted.

'Oh, don't be like that,' Daffers said with excessive enthusiasm. 'Think of the poor old Dumpling who is as excited as anything. And think about your new mobile,' she added in a whisper.

That was fair enough. I mean, the Dumpling was excited, and all going well I would get the mobile, and then I could take it with me to bed and either text-message or phone Ronnie. The idea of that was quite exciting and reassuring, so I nodded my agreement.

'It'll be great,' she said. 'And I bet Waldorf takes us somewhere brilliant for lunch.'

Food. Ugh. The very thought of it made me feel ill. Then Mum suggested we stop for breakfast on the way home. I was scared that Daffers would agree, but she didn't. I think she was looking forward to the trip with Waldorf so much, that she didn't want any more delays.

Mum seemed relieved too that we didn't want to stop.

'You don't usually work over Christmas, do you?' Daffers asked her.

'Oh, it's just one of those years,' Mum replied vaguely.

'I don't ever remember you working before,' Daffers persisted.

The snow had stopped, and it hadn't settled anywhere, but the sky was dark and I was sure it would snow again.

'Oh, don't ask,' Mum said lightly. 'Contracts,

contracts and more contracts – and deadlines. Things you don't have to worry about.'

'I know all about deadlines,' Daffers said. 'I hate them. They always creep up on you.' This comment led me to believe that she probably had some project for the start of term, but as Grammer said, you could bring a horse to water, but you couldn't make it drink.

Mum dropped us at the gateway and drove off quickly and the two of us went up to the house.

'Where's Grammer?' Daffers asked Waldorf. It was odd how she didn't ask Dad, but I suppose it's because we're not really used to him being there. However he did look up from his paper and said hello, but then retreated behind it again. I thought he would ask how I had got on, but he must have forgotten. I didn't really mind, because it meant that I didn't have to talk about it. Not that I would have known what to say.

'Oh, she's gone out,' Waldorf replied. 'Which is what we're going to do girls, as soon as you're all ready.'

The Dumpling went off to get her little jacket, and Daffers reminded her to get her mittens, as it was so chilly outside, and then the taxi arrived and we set off. Waldorf had done his homework, as he said, and he directed the taxi to the top of Grafton Street, because there was a selection of large phone shops all within walking distance. It was brilliant fun choosing the mobile. There was nothing that Daffers didn't know about them, and special offers on calls, and and and ... she knew it all. She got the new cover she wanted, and I got a sleek little phone that slipped easily into my jeans pocket, and then we went to get the Dumpling something because Waldorf said, 'You're all my dears and I'm not having one of you left out.'

In the toyshop, the Dumpling pointed at different things and we showed her and explained to her what they were. She laughed when Daffers showed her how a yo-yo worked, and she pointed at Waldorf who didn't seem to get the joke. And then she looked at dozens of different furry toys, and boxes of jigsaws, and finally she settled on the yo-yo and insisted that it wasn't wrapped or put in a bag or anything. She put it in her pocket and patted it, and you could see she was as pleased as could be. She hugged Waldorf, and he just said, 'I would have bought you anything, you know, m'dear. Anything at all.'

And I think he would have.

Chapter Twenty-Four

Maria's Tale

I went through the motions that Christmas, trying to pick up the pieces as they fell around me. It was indescribably awful.

People gather strength from different things – sometimes from other people, sometimes from events. In my case I seemed to be diminished by the minute. I didn't seem to have whatever it took to get through it. It was like childbirth in a way, when you are so swamped by pain that you can't get outside it, and you keep wishing it would end, and if it cannot end, that maybe it could start over so that you could have a second chance at it, so that you could keep on top of it.

It all seemed to have happened too fast, and there was no time to draw a fresh breath. George became more difficult as the days slipped into each other, and I didn't seem to know how to cope with him either. I kept wondering if the problem was that I wasn't used to having to deal with him. He had never been there for the general trials and tribulations of parenthood, and now that he was there, he was so clearly out of his depth. Not that there were any guidelines for what we were going through, but whatever maternal instincts, or woman's natural reactions that I would normally fall back on, he seemed to thwart them each step of the way.

Two days after Christmas, I bailed out. This was not in the sense that I was abandoning Plumpet in any way. I felt guilty enough for having been preoccupied while she was being attacked, and I knew that I was lashing out in an effort to reduce my own sense of culpability, even though my rational self was claiming that it was not my fault. But I felt that there was fault somewhere, and I was ready to blame anyone.

In an effort to distance myself slightly so that I could cope better, I went for a walk, and as a result of that walk I phoned Martin Garner at home, and without giving him any inkling of what had happened in our house, suggested that

I might have to do some work on the January contracts. Just to get on top of them, of course. He seemed to think it was a good idea, and made some comment about how he would assist me, that it was all mothers and mothers-in-law in his house and a case of too many women on his case.

His observation did make me think, albeit briefly, that maybe that was what it was like for George, but then I dismissed that idea. After all, George was definitely responsible for himself. It was his choice to work overseas, and his to come home at the last minute. And surely it should be his duty to muck in, as a father should. And yet he chose not to.

Getting out of the house was a relief in itself. During termtime the discipline of routine makes everything so much easier, and although I certainly never had anything to hide before, I realised now how I could have done anything and no one been any the wiser.

I'm not sure how conscious I was of what that phone call to Martin Garner actually meant. I convinced myself that I just wanted contact with someone outside the claustrophobia of home, and he was the ideal person as I had got the feeling that he might not have been in for the most enjoyable of Christmases himself. But of course, that was just my way of covering up what I was really about to do. Phoning Martin Garner was tantamount to inviting him to sleep with me. And he had a wife ... so what did that make me?

Not a very nice person, is what it made me.

I justified it in different ways. One was that I simply wanted to go into work – but why then was I phoning Martin, other than to get him to come in too? Another way was my saying to myself, we are each responsible for our own actions, and if Martin chooses to come into work as well, that is his choice.

Of course Martin would not have thought of coming into work, if I had not phoned him. I was the equivalent of Eve in the Garden of Eden. A temptress. Not a word I had ever applied to myself before. I tried to just close off the thoughts of his wife and her Christmas, telling myself that they were nothing to do with me.

I met him at the office. The caretaker let me into the building, and I thought that I had arrived first, and that I would be sitting primly at my desk when Martin arrived.

I sat down and pulled out the contract which was genuinely on my mind – although the deadline was the end of January, not the beginning. I was turning the pages of it when I became aware of his presence. He was standing in his office doorway watching me, and I had no idea how long he had been there. I tried not to look flustered, though my heart did a complete loop and a somersault.

'I didn't realise you were already here.' I tried not to stutter.

'And there was me thinking that you were just playing it cool,' he said. One side of his mouth was smiling. It was a most beguiling look, and I wasn't sure what to say. I had been practising being nonchalant for when he came through the outer door – I had just got my timing and the door wrong.

'And how was the McHarg Christmas?' he asked.

I knew then that I was not going to tell him. Any ideas I had had about offloading everything simply evaporated, and I made non-committal comments like, 'Oh, you know. Food, drink, crackers – the works.' I didn't want to get into the other thing.

He nodded. My observation clearly rang a bell.

'And a surplus of family?' he asked sympathetically.

I smiled grimly.

He came over and looked at the contract lying on my desk. I could feel his breath on my ear as he moved closer and we both stared at the document as if it was the most important thing in the world. He leaned further forward, and I think his cheek touched my hair as he reached down and turned the page.

'Is it more interesting than the jokes in the Christmas crackers?' he asked.

I looked at him and our faces were so close that I could see the length of his lashes, long, dark, thick – totally wasted on a man, I thought, but not on him. Grey eyes, tiny laughlines at the side of them, large pupils, smooth cheeks, freshly shaven, a waft of aftershave – something spicy, quite tantalising. It was different this time to the previous time. It was like a moment caught and elongated as we examined each other's faces, and our mouths came closer and closer. Our kisses were hungry and demanding. I didn't want him to stop. I just wanted to be immersed so totally in passion that everything else would be blotted out. He kissed all around the outside of my lips before pressing his firmly on mine. I could feel his tongue flicking against my teeth and edging further in. I did not want him to stop. Still kissing me, he put his hands under my elbows and lifted me up from the chair.

'Did you lock the door when you came in?' he asked.

I shook my head.

We locked it on the way in to his office. He had already cleared his desk, and I noticed that the receiver was off the phone and both were placed on the floor. He saw me taking this in, and we both smiled at the memory of the reason he had done this, as he started to undo my clothing. It was not like the previous time although it was just as intense. In some ways it was slower and more equal, a little more gentle, but just as exciting. He was an expert lover if one can describe someone like that. There was no fumbling, no pauses, no stagnation in the momentum of his movements. He took me on his desk, he standing leaning over and into me, and me, with my bottom on his blotter and my legs wrapped around his waist. He thrust into me rhythmically and smoothly, and with each thrust I detached further and further from the problems at home, until I could think of nothing but the movement of his body as we lifted on to some other plane where mind and body interconnect so intensely that there is neither one nor the other, just the composite.

I hated the feeling of him withdrawing, hated when it was over even though I felt a level of satiation. I could not bear what was out there, outside the office, back in our home, where I knew the white face of Plumpet would greet me, and the faint annoyance of George.

The next time was different again, as was the next. I refused to think what it would be like when this 'silly season' was over and we would return to work. I did not want to think about what it would be like meeting him on an ordinary day with the others in the office, whether this would be sustainable in any way, or if there would be embarrassment or frustration. It was not relevant. All that mattered was that I could forget for short periods the awfulness of home, my inability to put the clock back and to save my eldest child. Going home after that first time, I did not feel any guilt or shame. I just felt relief, both physical and mental, at having had time out.

I wondered how I would feel if George had done the same thing. And then suddenly I thought that I did not care.

I was definitely able to give a bit more when I got home. After I had showered of course, after I was sure there were no traces of a spicy aftershave on my face and throat and breasts. I told myself not to think about what I had been doing in the office – at least not while I was in the girls' company. That way I could give more of myself than I had been able to before. I tried to stop casting blame in my head – there was no one by then whom I did not hold responsible, but I think that was all a reaction to the fact that deep down I blamed myself. If ... if only ... all the *ifs* which make up our lives, and with which we have to live.

The doctor in the hospital said that Plumpet was healing nicely, but that they would do a couple more tests before giving her the all-clear. She asked me how Plumpet was handling things on an emotional level.

'She's quieter,' I said. Plumpet was always the quiet one, which is just as well because Daffers made enough noise for two if not more. 'A bit withdrawn, and maybe not eating very well.'

'Does she have friends who rally around?' the doctor asked.

'Well no, not really. She's a bit of a loner.'

'So there is no one there for her among her peers?'

'She doesn't have any special friend,' I said, and as I said it I wondered if her short acquaintance with Ronnie Fields could be called a special friendship.

'That's a pity,' the doctor said. 'It's often the peers who bring normality back to a situation. And it is usually with one's peers one can talk most freely.'

'But she can talk to us,' I said, and then a bit of me realised that she had not talked to us – at least not to me.

'And is she?'

'I would like to say that she is, but I'm not sure. She's not talking to me anyway – at least not much.' I hated admitting that, but honesty seemed to be the best way to help Plumpet. 'She's spending time with one of her sisters, and she's very close to her grandmother.'

The doctor frowned. 'As long as she is talking to them it will be of assistance to her. And you have the number for counselling – it can be helpful. It reduces the feelings of isolation and alienation.'

I made a mental note to talk to Grammer about it. After all, she was the one on the shop floor, so to speak, the one who spent the hours with the girls while I was out at work. She might be a better judge of the situation. I wished I had suggested her coming to the hospital too, and I decided that for the next appointment I would ask her along.

Just as I thought we were free to leave, Margaret McGregor turned up in the hospital. That added another half hour to the visit, but eventually we got the all-clear and Plumpet came out, pale-faced and muted.

After I dropped the girls back home for their day trip with Waldorf, I drove to the office, but when I got there I didn't feel like the rendezvous which was ahead of me. It had been different over the past few days – a relief from home and responsibilities, a break from the deadly intensity of what was going on around me, a respite from the bleakness of this Christmas.

When I pulled up outside the office and was about to go into the underground car park I realised that I simply could not go through with the assignation. I phoned Martin Garner on his mobile and said I couldn't make it. I could hear a mixture of disappointment and concern in his voice.

'Are you all right?' he asked.

No, I am not, I thought. I'm upset and feeling guilty and I don't know what to do about it.

'I'm just bogged down with family,' I said.

'So why are you sitting outside the office car park?' he asked.

I glanced in the mirror and to my horror I realised that his car had pulled in behind mine, and he was sitting there. He got out and came around to my window, which I duly opened as I sat there looking and feeling sheepish.

'What's going on?' he asked. He had such a kindly and concerned look on his face and I thought, I am going to start crying if he is nice to me. I just sat and looked at him, afraid to open my mouth.

'Pull into the parking lot,' he said, 'and we'll go and have a coffee down the road.'

Drinking a cappuccino with a cigarette between my shaking fingers, I shook my head when he asked me if George had found out.

'No,' I said, 'though George is part of the problem. Things aren't great at home at the moment. A lot of tension.'

'Tell me about it! There's nothing I don't know about Christmas and tension and too much family.'

I suspect this is something you won't know much about, I thought. I didn't know how to even begin and yet I wanted to tell someone – someone outside the situation.

'Something happened to one of my daughters,' I said. 'On Christmas Eve,' I added.

He didn't say anything. He sipped his coffee

and waited while I tried to find the words.

'Something bad.' That was the best I could do.

'Is she all right?' he asked.

I nodded, even though I knew that of course she was not all right. We sat while I stared at my cup. The froth on top was speckled with chocolate powder.

'Is that why you phoned me the other day and suggested coming into the office?'

Again I nodded. 'I was trying to escape from the home front for a bit,' I said.

'And did it work?'

'Yes.'

'But now?'

'Now? Nothing. Now I can't think. I've just come from the hospital where she was having a check-up – she had been injured, you see. And I felt...' Again I was lost for words.

'Guilt?'

'Maybe, I'm not sure. More like, it's fine for me – I can walk away from it and come in and be with you. And she can't get away from what has happened.'

'Guilt,' he confirmed.

He was probably right.

'Well, you shouldn't do something that makes you feel guilty. So if you need to go home to be there, then that is what you should do. I'm not going anywhere – the holidays are over in a few days, and I'll still be the same person in the office. And I'm there for you if you need me.'

He seemed so understanding, and I got this feeling that maybe every man other than George knew how to handle difficult situations, and that

I was the only woman who had managed to find and marry the single solitary man on the planet who didn't have a clue.

'You're awfully understanding,' I ventured.

'That's not what my wife would say,' he said. And in that comment was the possibility to look briefly into the window on his private life, and I thought maybe all marriages end up the same – habit being a great deadener. His voice was not bitter, but it contained something akin to it. Sadness, maybe. Mixed with resignation. Or maybe wryness tinged with acceptance.

That's what happens, I thought. We try our best, but some things, like the heady early days of courtship, are not sustainable. But then, who would want that excitement to last for ever? We grow with it, into someone else – a husband and a wife. We try ... I swear I tried. Girl becomes woman. Boy becomes man. We change and grow into other people who may or may not be compatible.

I was moved by Martin's kindness as well as his honesty. I wondered if marriages in people our age contained these qualities. Clearly mine did not. Clearly his did not. And yet kindness and honesty were qualities in him because he was showing them to me, sharing them with me. It seemed awfully sad. We sat there with his hand over mine and there was such an air of understanding and gentleness between us that I savoured it just as it was.

On the way home I drove the long way around through Ringsend and Sandymount, for no other reason than to prolong the thoughts in my head and because I was now in no rush to return to the house. The girls were out with Waldorf, and I wasn't sure what I was going to face on my return.

And so it was that as I drove along the seafront I saw George and a woman coming out of the gate of a house overlooking the sea. At first I thought it couldn't be him, that it was just someone who looked like him, but as I passed them I had no doubt that it was my husband. I was tempted to stop and wind down the window and let him see that I had seen him. But I drove on and away from the moment, trying to retain in my mind all that I had observed.

He had had his arm around her, pulling her in close to him as they walked and there was something about her which rang a bell. It wasn't until I drove up our road that I realised who she was: Marjorie Whelan – our previous neighbour whom Grammer had nearly run over when she had driven inadvertently up the Whelans' driveway.

Marjorie was older than me by a good ten years if not a little more, a woman whom I had never particularly liked, especially since Grammer had told me that Dirk McHarg, George's father, had had an affair with her during their marriage. Parking the car in our driveway, I thought about that, and about Grammer's comment the previous summer that losing her driving licence was well worth it. 'Well worth what?' I had asked. At the time it had seemed to me that thirty years after Dirk McHarg had disappeared was rather late in the day for her to try to avenge herself on

Marjorie Whelan.

George had been due to come home in July, but in mid-June something happened, something that upset him deeply and so I went out to be with him instead. I was only gone a week, long enough to be there with him over those difficult days, and yet not long enough, I later felt. He had had a lot on at the time and a week was all I really could spare as Grammer said that if he was not coming home, I should take the girls away for a holiday. Normally when he came home in the summer it was for a month. And during that month we'd have two weeks at home, and then we would take the girls somewhere for the other two weeks. It was very difficult at the time and I was trying to balance everything and keep everyone happy. Anyway, while I was away Grammer had had the incident with her car.

'Oh, just seeing the look on Marjorie Whelan's face when I drove into her car and porch. You should have seen her move!' Grammer was gleeful.

Marjorie had been just outside the porch at the time. She had been away for a week and was only just home, and according to Grammer she virtually took a nosedive into the porch.

'But your licence!' I said. 'Your wheels ... your freedom.' Clearly my car meant more to me than it did to Grammer.

'So?' she said. 'What odds? I have enough money to use taxis, and I've always been interested in public transport.' Whatever that meant.

I said no more. After all, Marjorie had slept with Dirk, her husband, my father-in-law whom

400

I had incidentally grown to like, and Grammer believed in a sort of earthly justice. 'To err is human,' she often said. 'To forgive, divine. And God knows I'm no deity.' Which was true enough.

As a result of that accident, Marjorie Whelan sold up. She said she had been planning on moving anyway, that the house was too big for her, and that she bore Grammer no ill-will.

I was there when she said it, and I remembered thinking, It may not be ill-will that you bear, but there is something. She had never been much of a neighbour; really, her only interest in us had been when George was home.

'We're old pals,' she would say to me. 'I was there for him when his father died.'

He had been twelve, and she in her twenties. I thought about that now. And suddenly I was not quite so comfortable with it. Seeing them walking together like that had not struck me as being necessarily the walk of two mere friends. And the more I thought about it, the more I started to put small pieces together, and what I was coming up with took my breath away.

Grammer was not in the house when I returned. The place was empty. I made a sandwich and sat in the kitchen staring at it, telling myself that I was being fanciful as images came up of George home on leave saying things like, 'I'm just going into Marjorie to catch up.' Or 'Marjorie's boiler needs replacing – you don't mind if I take her to the hardware shop, do you?'

And I, who had never warmed to her, nonetheless said nothing, because she was an old neighbour of George's from his childhood, and I felt I had no right to pull wifely rank. I don't believe in wifely rank. I've watched Grammer over the years, and listened to her tales from her early days of marriage, and I've often felt that you cannot change the tide in the fortune of man. That if it is going to ebb or flow in a particular way, why rail against it? If the price you pay to make a marriage work is to pull rank on your partner, to expect them to do as you say, to police them as you move through life, who wants that? Either they want to be with you, or they don't. And I could now, for the first time, see clearly that George did not want to be with me in the conventional sense of the words.

And did I want to be with him?

My actions over the previous week seemed to give a particular answer to that question. He was no longer the man I had married. And I was no longer the woman with whom he had proclaimed to want to spend the rest of his life.

My head started to ache. I put my sandwich in the bin, took a couple of painkillers and went to lie down. Of course the bed was not made, so I plumped up the pillows and pulled up the duvet before climbing in under it. I couldn't see any way forwards.

And I couldn't see any way back.

Chapter Twenty-Five

Dumpling's Tale

Up and down went the yo-yo when Daffers spun it. I didn't know how to make it do that for me.

'I'll put you standing on a chair,' Daffers said. 'Then you'll have more length.'

But Waldorf said it was better to keep that until we got home. I think he was worried about my snowy shoes on the hotel chair.

I had been in this hotel before – with Grammer and Purple Eyes. This time we went into the dining room. Stiff white napkins on the table and lots and lots of silver cutlery. Silvery cuttle.

'Melon without the port for Dumpling,' Waldorf said to the waiter. 'In small pieces. Easier.'

The knife was so heavy that I was glad it would be cut up for me.

'Fish off the bone...'

Boneless fish. Fishless bones.

Everything came perfectly designed for a Dampling, tasting soft and smooth, textures like clothing, looking so pretty.

Purple Eyes was there again, sitting at a corner table by himself. I kept my eyes on my plate. No one saw him, but he saw us. He watched us while he drank his wine. The candles on the table sat in silver holders and the flames flickered. Flickered and flickered. Waldorf moved them a little to one side so that he could see each of us. Plumpet had the same food as me but she didn't eat as much. Daffers ate everything – pâté and melba toast, steak and little potatoes like mine, lots of different vegetables, and crème caramel.

'I'm stuffed,' she said. She would not say that if Grammer had been there. Waldorf laughed.

There was stuffing in the goose on Christmas Day. It was stuffed. You can say that all right. One of my potatoes rolled off under the table.

'Leave it where it lieth,' Waldorf said.

Plumpet had a glass of wine, which the waiter poured her.

'Do you like it?' Waldorf asked her.

Plumpet had little black shadows under her eyes. 'You're so good to us,' she said to Waldorf.

I knew she was thinking about her new mobile phone. I patted my pocket where my yo-yo was sitting close to me. It was made up of two halves – smooth and circular, jammed together with the string wound up the middle. One side was red with blue swirls, and one side blue with red ones, and when Daffers let it fall from her hand, the red and blue spun round and round so you almost could not see which colour was which.

Waldorf had rabbit to eat. Not like the rabbits in my books, but more like white chicken on his plate.

'There's a hare on my plate,' he said to Daffers.

She peered at his food. 'I can't see it,' she said.

Plumpet and I laughed and laughed. Waldorf had not meant a 'hair'.

Daffers giggled when Plumpet explained.

404

'Dumples,' she said, 'you got the joke, and I didn't.' But she found that funny too and she went on laughing.

Dumples was a good name. It had Mum, and Plumpet in it, and it had dimples too. I have dimples. Grammer said they are an endearing feature. Feat. Feet. I don't have two feet like Daffers and Plumpet have. I have one real foot and one pretend. But I don't mind because I don't remember ever having two so I can't compare. Two look easier though. But when it is very cold like it was that day, I only have cold in one foot. That is a bonus.

Grammer says, 'Count your bonuses and your blessings.' I have five toes. Only five to get cold.

Once I heard Daffers saying to Plumpet, 'Hey, Plumpet, if you could have anything in the world, what would you have?'

And Plumpet said, 'A real foot for the Dumpling.' That was my Plumpet.

If I could have had anything in the world I'd have had the shadows go away from under Plumpet's eyes, and snow that wasn't cold, and a rabbit – but not to eat – and Dad all laughing like the night he came home, and a place in bed with him and Mum, and a sunflower that grew in winter.

But I loved my yo-yo. I loved my yo-yo best.

Chapter Twenty-Six

Millicent's Tale

After Daphne and I had talked in my apartment, that evening before dinner, we had left things so that she would go with Plumpet when she next had a bath. And that morning, the one when Plumpet went into the hospital for her check-up, Daphne confirmed that the bitemarks were now clearly to be seen on Plumpet's chest, with one toothmark longer than the others. The moment they left the house in the morning I phoned Margaret McGregor and told her that the bruising was now such that actual puncture holes, clear and definable, could be seen and, as I suggested, measured.

'Where's Plumpet now?' she asked.

I explained about the early morning check-up in the hospital, and she said she would get down there right away. I did not mention Polo Carmody.

I was reminded in a way of writing one of my novels. There are all these strands of thought, ideas, plots and so on, which you have to tease your way through to bring the story forward. And then every so often, far too often in fact, in come other thoughts and ideas as the characters take on their own life. Somehow you have to contain them all as you work towards the end, to bring about a denouement which will leave the reader satisfied and you with your characters' integrity intact.

I didn't know what would happen now. Clearly Margaret would look after the marks, measure them I suppose, and then what? Would I suggest to her that she should measure Polo Carmody's teeth? Would she legally be able to do that? There was also the niggling thought that Daphne had said that Plumpet didn't want the case pursued. The more I thought about that, the more I could understand and relate to it, although I was not sure that other people would see it that way.

When Dirk, my darling Dirk McHarg, went down in the South China Sea together with his pilot and his floozy, I did not want, could not bear in fact, the publicity attached to it. It was enough to deal with his demise, enough to waken in the morning knowing that he was never going to come back, enough to know that I had to pick up all those pieces which make or break a marriage. To have to deal with shame or humiliation on top of that was completely beyond me, and so I found ways of handling the fact that he had died with another woman, and that he had been unfaithful to me for the best part of fourteen years.

And here was Plumpet wanting to keep her privacy and her anonymity intact, not wanting to face in court what would have to be faced. I could understand that. It was enough that she was physically hurt and emotionally scarred, that she was damaged by the attack in ways that were all she could handle – if indeed she could handle

them. Why should she have to face her perse-
cutor? If that was something she could not bear,
why should she, who was the victim, have to face
further torment?

I at least was a full adult when Dirk disappeared, and that was hard enough. If Plumpet
could not handle this, then she should not have
to. But I was loath to leave it at that. How could
I leave it at that? What if it happened to someone
else, another of my grandchildren for example,
and I had been able to prevent it? I could not
prevent what had happened to Plumpet, but
there was the future to take care of.

I balanced all these thoughts in bed that night
– the night before Plumpet went back into the
hospital.

Waldorf said, as we were drinking a last
nightcap, 'Millie, m'dear, do you have something
on your mind?'

Well, I usually do have something on my mind.
I mean, how can you live without always having
something on your mind? Like the plot you're
working on, or your next interview, or the price
of hats ... of course there is always something on
my mind.

'No more than usual,' I said to him. But I said
it kindly. He was a boat I did not want to rock,
and the fact that men think of nothing as a rule
did not necessarily apply to him.

'More than usual, I think,' he said.

'Just something Daphne said to me,' I said. 'I'm
thinking about it.'

'Would you like to tell me, m'dear?' he asked.

'Not quite yet,' I said. My best planning is

always done in silence.

George was still in bed when Maria set off with Plumpet and Daphne to the hospital. 'I wish you were coming too, Grammer,' Plumpet said.

We were alone in the kitchen. I think what she meant was, she wished she were not going there at all. She looked awfully wan, and I hoped that Maria would be properly focused, because she struck me as having a lot on her mind as well as on her plate, and what Plumpet needed was to be at the top of her supporters' agenda.

As soon as they left and the Dumpling was busy with her porridge under Waldorf's watchful eye, I donned my hat having put the eagle's feather on it, and I set off. At the gate Ronnie Fields shot past being pulled along by the elephant.

'Good morning, Mrs McHarg,' he called.

I would have said, 'Millicent, for heaven's sake, call me Millicent,' but he was gone. Mrs McHarg indeed! She was Dirk's goodly wife, who had searched the back of the washing machine for missing socks, and folded his underwear neatly before placing it in the chest of drawers for him to pull out, wear, and deposit on someone else's bedroom floor.

I walked up the Fields's driveway. It was quite some time since I had been there, and last time had been while driving my car. I recalled the look on Marjorie Whelan's face as I hit her wheels and then the porch. Stupid woman. 'You could have killed me,' she said. Of course I could have killed her, I just chose not to. Bad enough her bonking Dirk, but five years after he passed on to a piscine world, she moved in on George. Women who style themselves on Mrs Robinson, Mrs Robinson from the film *The Graduate* I mean, have a lot to answer for. I had worked hard to get George to go and work overseas, all in an effort to detach the tentacles she had inserted into him. And even my bringing Maria into our home – an ideal choice, I always thought, Maria being kind, malleable and very alone – had not managed to unclip the link between Marjorie and George. Ah well, I thought as I stood in front of the re-vamped porch, shoddily revamped I might add, but I suppose she just did a patch-up job on it so as to sell the house. Ah well, indeed. She had finally pushed off and I had thought that that would stabilise George with Maria. I seemed to have got that one wrong.

I rang the bell, and Ronald Fields came to the door. A combination of being guarded and pleased to see me is how I would sum up his demeanour.

'Will you come in?' he asked.

I had every intention of coming in, but I could understand the enquiring way in which he asked me. After all, his reception in our house since Christmas Eve had not been particularly welcoming.

He took me into the living room, which I'm glad to say bore no resemblance any more to the way in which Marjorie Whelan had kept it. Gone were the kitschy little ornaments and the floral carpet and heavy drapes. The Fields appeared to have a more minimalist approach to décor, although I could not work out when they had had

410

the carpet fitted and the curtains hung. Everything looked new and clean, with sharp lines.

'Will you have coffee?' he asked. 'There is some percolating in the kitchen.'

'I'd love some,' I said. I hoped this would set the tone right as I needed to assess where he stood and then to ensure that he was firmly on Plumpet's side.

'I'll tell Maureen you're here,' he said. He paused in the doorway. 'Shall I ask her to join us, or do you want to speak to me alone?'

He's on the ball all right, I thought. He too is assessing this carefully and wants to get it right.

'I do want to talk to you,' I said, 'but I'm happy for Maureen to be in on it if you would like her to be.'

He nodded. I sat and waited and looked at the paintings on the walls. After a few minutes Maureen came in. I stood up.

'Oh, Millie,' she said. Her eyes were large in her neat-featured face. 'Oh Millie,' she repeated as she came towards me. And in those words we were allies on the same side in a war against the wounds of Plumpet and the damage inflicted on Ronnie by association. We held each other's hands and I thought of the misery she must have been going through. Her relief at my being there was evident. And I felt relief at her response.

We sat beside each other on the sofa, and she said, 'I'm so glad you've come in to us. Ronald and I have felt so helpless. Even though we understood your family's reaction to our trying to make contact, it just made us feel so awful ... so powerless. And Ronnie, Millie, poor Ronnie –

411

he's an awfully good wee lad. He'd never hurt Plumpet, not ever ... and he likes her so much.' She was almost in tears.

'I know,' I said. 'I know that. I think we needed time to work through things our end – and Plumpet, you know...'

'Of course I know,' she said. 'How is she? Please tell me how she is.'

'She's ... quite fragile,' I said. I wanted to reassure her, but it was difficult to find positive things to say, because how do you really know? 'She's back in the hospital this morning.'

She nodded her head. 'Poor Plumpet,' she said. 'Such a gentle, tender wee girl.'

Ronald came in with the coffee on a black veneer tray, with art deco cups – a lovely splash of colour. Nice style, I thought. Lump sugar with silver tongs, some Christmas cake ... elegance and homeliness combined. I liked it.

He poured out the coffee, putting sugar in his wife's cup and stirring it for her, towering above her as he placed it in front of her on the table.

'Will you have cake, Millie?' he asked me.

It seemed churlish to say no, even though I had just had my breakfast. Normally I would not think of the possibility of the presence or absence of churlishness, but in this instance I wanted to get it right, so I took a piece.

'Plumpet is in the hospital this morning,' Maureen said to him.

'I know,' he said.

'You didn't tell me! Why ever not?'

'It's on a need to know basis only,' he said to her. His voice was serious, but not dismissive.

'Because of his work,' Maureen turned to me, 'he has a certain amount of access to what is going on – he's been keeping an eye on things, both for our Ronnie's sake, but also for wee Plumpet.'

We did not ask each other how we had got on over Christmas, or waste time on the weather, which suddenly appeared to change as snowflakes drifted past the window. We were all focused on one thing only.

'Margaret McGregor has gone into the hospital,' I told them.

'Oh?' Ronald sat and looked expectantly at me.

'I phoned her as soon as Maria set off with the girls.'

'I see.'

And then I told them both about the teethmarks, how distinctive Daphne said they were, how one toothmark was deeper than the others.

'Very distinctive,' I said with a certain pointedness in my voice. 'Daphne was very specific about that.'

'I see,' Ronald said thoughtfully.

I waited to let him digest that, knowing he was astute enough to realise there was more.

'Where does that lead to?' Maureen asked. 'I mean to say, can the police pull every dental record in the country to match them up?'

Ronald was watching my face and he ignored Maureen's questions.

'And did Daphne have anything further to say on the subject?' he asked carefully.

'Yes,' I said. 'She was very sure of her facts. Girls can be remarkably observant, you know –

shrewd and perceptive in ways that one might not necessarily expect.'

'Are you going to tell me the rest of this?' he asked.

But I did not want to just say it – I wanted him to arrive at the same conclusion, but to get there by himself. I thought that would be safer. I am not sure why I felt that, but I did. And my instincts are usually sound.

'I wondered if perhaps later today – I can't tell you yet exactly when, because I need to make sure that the Dumpling is back and that George and Maria are out of the way – but I think it would be best if you came in, maybe for a drink, and then let the Dumpling tell you the rest of the story.'

'The Dumpling?' They were both surprised.

'Just because she doesn't talk,' I said, 'it doesn't mean that she doesn't notice things.'

Maureen said, 'I know. There's a whole lot going on in that wee girl's mind. Anyone can see that.'

'Should Margaret McGregor be there too?' Ronald asked.

'I don't think so,' I said. 'You see, there is a bit of a problem.' And I explained how Plumpet did not want to know who had done it.

'She may feel very different later,' Maureen said. 'She's still dealing with an awful lot – the sense of violation must be enormous.'

'Combined with the lack of memory,' Ronald added.

There was silence as he sipped his coffee. 'What do you want?' he then asked me.

414

'I want this sorted,' I said. 'I don't know how, but I want it sorted in such a way that it doesn't happen again – that Plumpet and the other girls are safe from this person – but I don't want Plumpet to have to go through another ordeal.'

'The only way that can happen is if the person is caught, prosecuted and put away,' Ronald said.

'Are you sure that is the only way?'

'How do you mean?'

'I don't know,' I admitted. 'I suppose at the moment I want to be sure that Daphne is right about who she thinks it is.'

'Yes, first things first. We need to ascertain that – and then proceed from there.'

'Tell me about Rohypnol,' I asked him. 'Where one gets it, what it looks like.'

'Ronald brought a couple home from work to ask wee Ronnie if he had ever seen them before,' Maureen said.

'They come in bubblewrap,' Ronald said. 'The real name is Flunitrazepam, and they're very common in the States. On the street they sell at less than five dollars a tablet. They act like a Valium, but are about ten times more potent. You can imagine their effect – rather like a massive sedative. I hadn't come across them before, although I had heard of Rohypnol, but as you can imagine I've read up on the subject this last week. I think the drug has to have come from the States. You see, it used to be available across the counter in Europe, but no longer. Its use is restricted to hospitals now.'

'Hospitals?'

'Yes, as a sedative or to help someone to sleep.'

'How do you suppose it was given to Plumpet?'

'I don't know. It's usually put into a drink. And it's usually given with alcohol, sometimes taken with heroin.'

'Plumpet hardly ever takes a drink. She's more of a soft fizzy type of drinker,' I said.

'Okay,' Ronald said. 'I know you've more to tell me, and I can see you don't want to go into that now. So after the Dumpling has told her story, we'll talk again. But let's suppose Plumpet went back next door to get her ring...'

I waited while he thought a moment.

'And then she meets this man next door, whoever he is, and she has a drink – perhaps out of politeness, perhaps because she can't see how not to.'

I nodded. I wanted to say, 'Or perhaps it was a woman,' but I did not want to feed him information. I knew that he would get there in due course.

'She is slipped the Rohypnol, and the damage is done,' he continued. 'And in due course, she gets herself home and comes to in the morning, memory gone but clearly very badly injured.'

'She had had a bath or shower,' I told him.

'I know. It's in the report. So whoever did this to her, cleaned her up before she went on her way.'

I hadn't thought clearly about that. The idea of Polo Carmody getting Plumpet into the bath, cleaning her up, washing her hair, leaving her with no evidence on her, bar the teethmarks, had not really occurred to me; now it seemed to me that Polo Carmody, physically strong but slightly

416

built, might not have had what it took to do that. And then I thought of the towels in Theresa's kitchen. All clean. Lots and lots of towels. There had to be two people, I decided. Not just Polo. She wouldn't have had the strength to get Plumpet in and out of a bath.

'I'm sorry,' I said. 'What were you saying?'

'I asked if that ties in with what you've been thinking?'

'More or less,' I said, but I was not completely sure.

'Don't worry,' he interrupted my thoughts. 'We just need to piece it together – sometimes other aspects become clear later.' His voice was strong and reassuring, and I felt that he was placing some kind of trust in me, and that he was quite prepared to go with what he possibly could only see as my intuition.

Ronald left Maureen and me while he went to make a phone call. I would have liked to ask him if the call was connected with the case, but I didn't. He was letting me proceed with things my way without forcing me to fill him in. I therefore gave him the same leeway.

Maureen reached for my hand as soon as he was out of the room. 'Men,' she said slowly, 'don't always see things the way we do.'

'No,' I said. 'They don't.'

'You know, if I can help you – if there is anything I can do, I will do it.'

I liked her even more in that instant. I knew that somehow she understood. Understood what? I nibbled on my slice of cake as I thought about that. I think she understood that Plumpet might not want to proceed along normal police lines.

'Thank you,' I said. 'I'll bear that in mind.' The inkling of an idea was germinating somewhere in my intellect. 'I wonder...'

'Yes?'

'It might be too much to ask,' I said.

'Anything,' she said. 'Just ask. I want to help. I really do.'

'I wonder, I just wonder if perhaps I could see the Rohypnol – you know, you said Ronald had brought some home to see if Ronnie had ever seen it or anything like it. It's probably too much to ask.'

She was silent for a moment, and I knew that she was looking through what I had asked her, looking for what was hidden behind my words.

'I think,' she said, 'that that could be arranged. But right now might not be the best time.'

We smiled at each other. I had no doubt that she had understood me.

I did not want a mere look at Rohypnol.

I wanted some.

Chapter Twenty-Seven

Theresa Carmody's Tale

I didn't sleep that night. After Millicent left – of course she had always told me to call her Millie, but I did like the name Millicent, and that was how she was known to the public and I loved being able to introduce her as my friend Millicent, and people would immediately know it was the Millicent – I had another drink and sat there in the sitting room staring at the glass-topped table. Then I went and made myself a cup of coffee.

I was sitting in the kitchen drinking it when Polo let herself in.

'You're back,' she called as she came into the hall. 'I saw your car.'

'I'm back indeed,' I said. 'Did you miss me?'

'Oh, I rang every day,' she laughed.

'I've been so busy since my return that I quite forgot to check my voicemail,' I said. 'I must do that later.'

'Oh, it's probably all just me, ringing to check if you're around.' She stood beside the kitchen table and started to fold the towels, which were lying in a heap exactly where the police had left them.

I was about to say, 'You'll never guess what's been going on...' but she interrupted me by saying, 'I ran your dishwasher and washing machine while you were away. I knew they'd smell to high heaven by the time you got back.'

And I suddenly thought, But no one knew I wouldn't be back for days. I had said I would probably return on Christmas Day. I got up to pour her a cup of coffee while I thought about that. After all, I had been due back on either Christmas Day or the next day – it just so happened that I had stayed on. Why would she run the washes? Normally we share everything – well, most things – but I was puzzled and knew if I asked her outright that she might clam up or that I wouldn't get the truth, so I just laughed and said, 'I didn't think the washing machine was full enough for a cycle.'

'Oh, I put in some towels from your airing cupboard,' she said. 'I reckoned they could do with a freshening.'

Now I was really puzzled. She doesn't usually look out for me like that and the contents of my airing cupboard would no more interest her than the contents of my dustbin.

'When did you run them?' I asked.

'A couple of days ago,' she said vaguely. 'Why?'

'Oh, I just wondered. How did you know I wouldn't be right back?'

'I didn't,' she smiled. 'I just thought it would be nice for you to come back to a clean house.'

'Thank you,' I said. 'It did seem cleaner. Even my bathroom was immaculate. I'm almost sure I didn't leave it like that.'

'Call it a Christmas present,' she said as she finished folding the towels. 'I'll put these up in the airing cupboard,' she called as she left the room.

I wished I had not drunk the three Slippery Nipples because I couldn't think straight, but I knew there was something wrong.

My sister, Polo, had a key to the house but I hadn't emphasised that with the police. After all, she was my sister, and why shouldn't she have a key? It was all the other keys I had been thinking about, not the one Polo had. Now this terrible feeling of unease crept through me. This was my sister – how could I be thinking such things about her? And what was I thinking?

I tried to clear my head. She was upstairs for ages and I started to think about how she liked playing around with drugs. She had been at it for years, I knew that. Once I had caught her snorting coke in the conservatory and I had said, 'Not in my house, Polo.'

And she had said, 'Don't be so tight-arsed.'

And I said, 'No, I mean it.'

Drugs scared me. And even though I knew I would never try them or take them or whatever one did, I was afraid of her doing it in my house. I could get caught by implication. Drugs could be found on my property and I would be the one to carry the can. Polo, you see, was not the kind to clean up after herself. Oh, she kept her own place clean enough, but she was not given to cleaning up in mine. She never washed a dish, and seldom put anything in the dishwasher.

My feeling of unease increased. I wanted to say something, to ask her what was going on, but the three drinks had blurred my clarity, and I thought it would better be kept until I had slept them off and could have a straight conversation with her.

I could hear her upstairs at the airing cupboard. All those clean towels. So unlike Polo, even as a Christmas present. What a peculiar notion, I thought. To give me new towels, maybe ... but to wash all my old ones? And now to fold them and to put them all away: this was not my sister Polo.

Polo was given to odd bursts of generosity, but she was first and foremost very selfish. And she seldom thought beyond the moment. This had been clear at school when she had got into trouble over that girl who had created a fuss. I had known the girl in question, and even if I were inclined towards lesbianism, which I'm not, I would have been very careful about making overtures of any sort with someone unless I was sure of my ground. Polo never seemed to think about things like that. When she had been living in New York, she had got involved with some unsavoury sorts. Daddy had told me that on that fateful trip of his to try and pick up the pieces – the trip on which he had died. But I sort of knew that anyway. She had always got involved with people who brought out the bad side of her.

There – I had thought it: 'the bad side'. That was like admitting out loud that there was a bad side to her.

I've never been given greatly to introspection. I've always found it rather self-defeating. Actually, that may not be completely true, now that I think about it. You see, as a child I think that I did do all the internal-thinking bit that people do. But then Polo got expelled from the school in Switzerland, and I had to leave with her because Daddy said she needed someone to keep an eye on her, and of course he was too busy with work. He said it would give me a fresh start too, although I did not want a fresh start. I hated leaving that school. I had lots of friends in my year; I had got used to being there. It had been difficult to start with, when we first went there. Of course, Polo and I had been brought up in boarding schools, so it wasn't that that was so difficult. It was more the whole cultural thing, the language, the mixing with new girls, new companions, and the time it took to make friends. But after we left there, I think I stopped the introspection bit, and just got on with things. I didn't have any choice. I was cross, both with Polo and Daddy and maybe with the school too, but I couldn't do anything about it. One day we were boarders in one school, and the next we were in a different school altogether.

I remember saying to Polo, 'Now look what you've done,' and her replying that it wasn't her fault. She said they had just been messing around, but I saw the girl who had made the complaint, and I didn't blame her for complaining – she was badly bruised on her neck, and she couldn't stop crying.

Daddy said to Polo when we were in the taxi going from that school to the next one, 'You have to think of the consequences of your actions,' but Polo never seemed to. She would say things like,

'How was I to know?' But we did know. At least I did. I knew that if I didn't have my homework done, I'd be in trouble. And if I spent all my money on a Monday, I'd have none for the rest of the week – actually, that's not quite true, because we had unlimited resources. Unlimited is not the right word, but we always had plenty of pocket money: our 'allowance' as Daddy called it. I often had to lend money to Polo, but I usually got it back, some time later. I don't think I knew the term 'the consequences of our actions' back then. It was a term that Millicent McHarg used, and when she did, I always related it back to our schooldays.

Someone should have told Polo about those consequences. Spelled them out to her. I've spent the rest of my life trying to make friends but also trying not to be too intimate with anyone, and I think that is because of my school experiences. I had learned that if you get too close to people then they get taken away from you and you have to start again, so instead I make lots of casual friends, I fill my house with people and laughter and fun, and am careful not to get too close, so that I don't get hurt. It's how life works, isn't it? We learn by experience, and if the experience is tough, we learn a tough lesson.

There was a day, not long after the Dumpling arrived next door, a summer's day, and I was sunbathing in the garden, drifting between waking and sleeping in the heat of the day. Polo was there with me. She was not a great sunbather – I think she found it boring, whereas there was little I liked better. Suddenly I woke to hear Maria McHarg calling through the hedge, asking if the Dumpling was in with me. And of course I said no. Anyway, it turned out that she was, and by the time I found her she was in the kitchen, trying to open a drawer, bless her – it was where I kept a bag of jellies, just for her. Maria came to the front door, and she was so upset because the Dumpling had disappeared. She retrieved her daughter and hugged her and said of course she understood that I hadn't realised that the child had come through into my garden... This story would not be remotely interesting or relevant, except that afterwards when I went back out to the garden to lie down again, Polo was sitting there watching me with a smile on her face. I explained what had happened and that somehow the Dumpling must have slipped past us.

Then she said, 'I know.'

'What do you mean, you know?'

'I saw her come through the hedge.'

'So why didn't you say something? Maria was worried sick! The Dumpling is only a tiny child – how could you not say something?'

She shrugged – Polo style. 'It was interesting to see what would happen,' she replied.

The incident left me with an uncomfortable feeling. That Polo had known implied that she was too callous for words. I didn't like thinking that, so I just tried not to dwell on the event. Later, I almost told Millicent about it, and about how it had made me feel, but in the end I didn't, because I was afraid it would reflect badly on me, and I didn't want the Dumpling, or either of the other McHarg girls forbidden from coming into my house or garden.

You see, I loved having them around. They were so guileless, and straight and different. These are just words. They were so much more than that. They were so much more than the mere content of those words. The Dumpling did have guile – so sweet, so little. I loved her shuffling in to visit me. I loved it when she started to appear regularly through the hedge. I put a little collar and bell on Cat's neck, because Millicent said that the Dumpling was worried about the robin being trapped by him. Once I watched the Dumpling sitting on the grass, and the robin came right up to her – and you should have seen the look on her face. It was full of curiosity and childlike innocence. Daffers was different. She was a noisy child. Of course the Dumpling was completely silent. Millicent said that she had been traumatised as a baby. It was a horrendous story, how George McHarg had seen this bundle lying under a gibbet, the child's mother swinging there, and she left lying beneath. They came in on a helicopter and George and some other man got out to look. Millicent said that they didn't film it, that they just acted very fast. Within seconds they were back on board and they had the Dumpling with them. They had to take her regularly to a physiotherapist, and they did exercises with her all the time to strengthen her legs, and she saw a specialist every few months. The poor thing only has one foot. No one knows why her mother was hanged, but I wonder if perhaps in ignorance people thought that

426

because the Dumpling was not whole, that maybe she was seen as a blight on their community, and because her mother had borne her, maybe she was blamed. Who knows? Millicent said they would never know, that it could have been because the mother was not married, that that was what George had said. But the important thing was that the Dumpling was safe.

I really had drunk too much. My thoughts were going all over the place. And I kept forgetting what it was I was trying to think about. Polo reappeared in the kitchen and said she'd see me soon, and that she'd be back the following day, I think, and then she left. I sat there for ages, just thinking about the McHarg girls, and how much I liked Millicent, and how I hoped that Polo had had nothing to do with whatever had happened to my friends next door.

Chapter Twenty-Eight

Dumpling's Tale

Diddle Diddle Dumpling – that was what my dad said when he saw me. He was not like he used to be when he was the Mystery Man – when I only remembered his feel and smell, and how his arms held me close, and he blotted out the memories of before.

Now he was just Dad. He read the paper all the

time, or looked bothered as he glanced around at Plumpet, Daffers and me. He looked puzzled and angry when he looked at Mum, and he avoided Grammer.

Daffers said that his other home was far away and that he was only here on a visit. I wanted to make him smile but it didn't seem possible. I showed him my yo-yo and he took it from me and looked at it carefully. 'Yes,' he said. 'I once had one like that. But mine was yellow.'

He handed it back and I tried to make it spin up and down like Daffers did, but I was not able to. It hit the floor and rolled until I pulled it back with the string. Then he smiled.

'Let me show you,' my dad said. He slipped his finger through the loop and let the yo-yo fall and it spun down towards the ground and then back up towards his hand. I smiled up at him. I wanted him to show me how to do it. I looked hopefully at him.

'It's practice, Dumpling,' he said. 'Like most things in life, it's just practice. You'll learn. Give it time. My father showed me how to do it, and that was a long time ago.' He was thinking about things – things from before me, and before Plumpet and Daffers. From a time when there was just him, his father and Grammer. Up and down went the yo-yo, and back and back he went as he thought of a time and place where his yo-yo went up and down. Yellow. Rolling yellow. Yellowing roll. 'Our father got your papers sorted just after we found you,' he told me. 'We'd been looking for you for days.'

Now he was gentle and kind. I looked at his

428

face and I tried to remember. There was something here that I was not certain about and I was not sure what it was. People felt different when they held you. Grammer was all bosomy. Mum curled on her side in bed and when I held on to her, even if I was asleep I knew it was not Grammer. My dad held me on the plane; first his face was soft, but after the long journey his chin became rough. Back, back before that I tried to go. There was something. Something there. I didn't remember.

I took the yo-yo from my dad and I went up to my room. In my wardrobe were all the boxes. They held my memories. Some I knew without looking. I pulled them out. One by one. This one. That one. In one of them was the memory I wanted to look for. I lifted the lids off them. One by one.

In one box was the memory of the jelly Plumpet had made for the day I arrived. Plumpet's arms holding me.

'She's here to stay?' Plumpet asked.

'Yes,' said Mum.

'Yes,' said Dad.

'Hummmph,' said Daffers.

I closed the box. In the next one was Theresa Carmody in a bikini on the rug on her grass. 'What a Dumpling,' said Theresa Carmody. She laughed and smiled. 'You're always welcome in here. Come and sit beside me on the rug.' Theresa smelled of perfume. Her laugh tinkled. I put the lid back on.

In the next box were all the shapes I had ever seen or thought of. I pushed it aside. Then there was an empty box. I opened it and let flow in all the nice memories of lunch with Waldorf and the heavy knife, and Plumpet smiling at her new mobile. A nice one to look in later.

But now, I needed to find the one that belonged to long ago. Go along. A long long time. Ago. Go.

There was a wine-coloured box at the bottom. My hand hesitated on the lid. I knew it was in there. I eased the lid open slowly, and as I looked in I could remember the Mystery Man. He had curly black hair. He had a wide forehead like Dad's. A birthmark on his forehead. But he was not Dad, no. He had grey hair. It was curly like Dad's. It was curly. Same hair. Same feel. It was black. It was grey. Not one man. Two men. Two men. Both with birthmarks. One was my dad. The Mystery Man was not my dad. Beside them in my box of memories was a woman. Smaller than Grammer. Smaller than Mum. Thin like Plumpet, but smaller. Straight black hair. Eyes like mine that tilted at the sides. Not round eyes like Plumpet and Daffers had. Smooth face. She looked at me. She smiled. I could smell her enveloping me. Long ago. The sun scorched the earth. There was no wind. On the plane Mum had called Dad the Mystery Man. She said he was full of surprises. I had mixed these men up. The woman loved me. Once long ago. I was hers. The woman loved me.

And the other man.

I closed the lid. I had seen the faces so clearly, like looking in a photograph. The graph of faces. There was Dad and he was Mum's Mystery Man. My Mystery Man was gone. Somewhere

430

hot where the sun scorched the earth. Where the rain was heavy. Where night was sizzling and damp. A man with curly hair who loved me with the woman. A man with curly grey hair who held the woman in his arms. Who came sometimes and loved us. A man with grey curly hair who ran beneath the propellers of the helicopter. A man who arranged my papers. 'Our father got your papers sorted just after we found you,' that's what my dad had said. Oh, the mysteries. All mixed up in one box.

It was snowing outside now. Real snow. Lots and lots of it. There was no snow in places where it was always sunny. There was another place and there I was lifted from the ground by a man who I think was Dad. He carried me in his arms and then hid me. Dad and Dad's Dad.

Mum came. They brought me home to Grammer, Plumpet and Daffers. What did I leave behind? It was a bad place, but I didn't remember it. It was not in any of my boxes. It was a place left long behind. Time to go. Time to leave. A place left. Left. Behind.

I put the box away and closed my wardrobe door. Daffers called me. 'Dumples!' she said.

I scooted across the floor, as she opened my door.

'Come downstairs and play with me, Dumples,' she said. 'Dad and Mum have gone out with Plumpet for a while. You will come down and play with me, won't you?' She lifted me up in her arms and I put my yo-yo back in my pocket, and down the stairs we went, tee-tum, tee-tum. Daffers hummed.

'We're going to play a special game,' she told me. 'You and me and your pasta quills. All right?'

I nodded.

The lights on the Christmas tree were twinkling, and the fire was lit. My box of pasta shapes was sitting on the floor waiting for me. Grammer was sitting with a drink. And there was the detective, Muscle Man, Ronald Fields sitting by the fire. No Butterfly. No dancing Butterfly.

'Hello Dumpling,' he said to me.

I think he had been waiting for me to arrive.

Chapter Twenty-Nine

Daffers's Tale

Grammer suggested to Dad and Mum that they take Plumpet out for a while. 'A little special time with her,' Grammer said.

Plumpet didn't look too keen, as special time with Dad and Mum usually meant a meal out, and Plumpet was off her food.

'We had a really big lunch out with Waldorf,' she said.

'Just have something light then,' Grammer said to her. 'You don't have to have a three-course meal.'

I knew what was going on. This was part of Grammer's plan. She needed the house clear of parents, and of course Plumpet, because she had told me that she had invited Raleigh's father in and that I was to get the Dumpling to tell her story.

Grammer could talk anyone into doing anything, and so the three of them left and I went to get the Dumpling. Ronald Fields was in the drawing room by the time we came back downstairs. Grammer moved fast when she wanted to. Which was most of the time.

Waldorf came in with a drink for the adults and I sat down on the floor with the Dumpling.

'Dumples,' I said, 'remember Christmas morning? Do you remember how you put the pasta on the floor?' I reached into the box and took out her container of quills. 'Lay them down the same way,' I said to her.

The Dumpling looked at me and then at the quills, and she started to put them in rows. They formed the same pattern as the last time. Three quills side on side, then a break and a further three, then fourteen, then seven.

'Is that the staircase, Dumples?' I asked her.

She pointed towards the door into the hall, and she nodded. I fetched her Barbie doll, which she had got for Christmas and I handed it to her. 'Pretend that is Plumpet,' I said to her.

She took it in her hands and kissed it.

'That's right, Dumples,' I said. 'That's Plumpet. Do you remember she came home on Christmas Eve? Did you hear her?'

She nodded.

'And then what happened?' I asked her.

She put the Barbie doll standing near the first set of quills and then she mimed her going down the stairs.

'Did she go out?' I asked her.

Again the Dumpling nodded.

'Had someone knocked on the door? Is that why she went out?'

She shook her head.

'Good little Dumples,' I said to her. 'You hear everything, don't you?'

She nodded her head vigorously up and down.

'Did you hear anything else?' I asked her.

She went to the treasure box and took out one of her little cars, and she pushed it across the carpet.

'Did you hear the car?' I asked her.

There was even more vigorous nodding of her head.

'Do you know whose car it was?'

She looked at me and nodded, then she dipped her head downwards and would not look up.

'I wonder whose car it was,' I said thoughtfully. 'Was it Mum's car?'

She shook her head.

'Was it a taxi?'

She looked doubtful.

I was trying to get there slowly. 'Was it Theresa Carmody's car?'

Again she shook her head.

'Was it Polo Carmody's car?'

And then she nodded.

'You heard it on the road?'

She nodded after each question.

'Did it stop?'

'Next door?'

'Did someone get out?'

She put up two fingers. Two? I stopped my

434

questions as I digested that. I hadn't expected that. I looked at her. She was watching me with her dark brown almond eyes.

'Two people?' I asked.

Again she nodded.

'Do you know who they were?'

She shook her head.

Two people. I had not thought of that. So Polo had had someone with her. I thought of the man with the purple eyes whose name I couldn't remember and wondered if he was the other person. I glanced over at Grammer and at Ronald Fields. Both were sitting forward on their chairs, engrossed in what was going on.

Grammer nodded at me. There was encouragement in her nod. She looked at Ronald Fields and he nodded too. Then he made a slight shake of his head, and I felt that the session with the Dumpling was being brought to a close.

'I wonder if you'd like to play a game of Ludo with Waldorf?' Grammer asked the Dumpling.

Dumples got up immediately and went to get the box of Ludo.

'Shall we play it at the table in the kitchen?' Waldorf asked her. She nodded and reached for his hand.

'Dumpling,' Ronald Fields suddenly said, 'did you hear Plumpet come back in later?'

She shook her head, and closed her eyes, dropping her head towards her shoulder.

'You were asleep?'

She nodded.

'Did you hear anything else?'

She shook her head and looked up at Waldorf,

and they went to the door.

'You're a very clever little girl,' Ronald said to her. She beamed happily at him.

I started to tidy away the pasta.

'You're a very clever girl too,' Grammer said to me. 'I saw her laying out the pasta on Christmas morning, and I didn't see any pattern.'

'I didn't see it at the time,' I admitted. 'I just thought there was something vaguely familiar about it. You know the way you count the stairs as you go up and down them sometimes – I just didn't see it at the time.'

'Would she really have heard the car from her bedroom?' Ronald Fields asked thoughtfully.

'She hears everything,' Grammer said. 'During the day she hears Mum's car as it turns the corner down the road. At night, there would have been no noise at all.'

'And she was probably busy listening for Santa,' I added.

Ronald agreed. 'As a child,' he said, 'I could hear way better than I do now. I must admit that familiarity with a place does increase your awareness. I haven't got used to any of the noises on the road here yet, but when you do get used to them you can identify all kinds of things without even realising it.'

'So there were two people,' Grammer remarked.

'I bet the other was the man with the purple eyes,' I commented.

'Gervaise Holt,' Grammer said to Ronald Fields by way of explanation. 'You met him in Theresa's at her party,' she added.

'I recall,' he answered slowly.

'Did you tell him about Polo biting Gervaise's finger?' I asked.

Grammer said that she hadn't but that she would now. And she told him what I had described, and Ronald Fields said that he remembered Gervaise dabbing at his finger and that it was bleeding. He said he had wondered what the man had done to cause that to happen.

I sucked my bottom lip and didn't say anything. It was one thing telling Grammer what I'd seen, but I couldn't tell Raleigh's father.

'You had better say how it happened,' Grammer prompted me.

It was odd how I couldn't wait to tell Daisy about it, but I certainly did not want to tell Ronald Fields. I thought that would be quite an interesting thing to think about later – how it was easy or fun to tell one person, but how there was absolutely no way you could tell someone else.

However, Grammer had other ideas and I ended up having to tell Ronald Fields what I had seen in the conservatory. A very edited version of it. I left out the shorts and all of that.

'Hmmm,' said Ronald Fields. 'Did I get that right? Polo Carmody walked into the conservatory and stuck his thumb in her mouth and she bit it?'

'It wasn't quite like that,' I admitted. I was sort of caught, because if I didn't tell the truth then he wasn't going to believe me, and I needed him to believe me. So I told him a bit more of the story, with Grammer prompting me now and again.

'And it was his finger, not his thumb,' I said.

'I see,' he said. 'I'm beginning to get the drift of what you are telling me. He was playing with her?'

Playing? I certainly hadn't thought of that being the word to describe what they were doing.

'I don't think it was a game,' I said a bit reluctantly, as I didn't really want to get into this with him.

'An adult game,' Grammer said helpfully.

Of course that was a different way of looking at it.

'Are you sure of who the two people were in the conservatory?' Ronald Fields asked.

I explained that I couldn't see the man's face, but that I had seen his jacket, and it was the same one that Purple Eyes was wearing, and the bite corresponded to what Polo had done.

'Right,' he said. 'Now, Daphne, I don't want you talking to anyone else about this. With your grandmother, of course that's fine. But I'm going to need to get a statement from you.'

A statement. I hadn't thought of that. A statement meant lawyers – and lawyers meant court. And court was the one thing that Plumpet most definitely did not want. I didn't know what to do.

'Grammer,' I said. 'Plumpet...'

'I know,' she said. 'I know.' Her mouth was in a tight line.

'Plumpet?' asked Ronald Fields.

'She doesn't want this to go to court.'

'I know,' he said. 'I understood that from what you said when you came to visit. But it'll have to go to court. We're dealing with something – with

438

people who have to be put away. We'll explain that to Plumpet. I'm going to fill Margaret in on this – Margaret McGregor, you know. She said that she and Plumpet get along quite well – she'll handle this.'

'What if Plumpet can't handle it?' I asked.

'We don't want this to happen to someone else, do we?' Ronald Fields said to me.

Of course he was right, but the thought of Plumpet having to endure anything more was awful.

'Does Plumpet have to be involved?' I asked.

'I'm afraid so,' he said.

'Can't it be done without her?' Grammer asked.

But it transpired that it could not be done without Plumpet, because she was the victim.

'What will happen now?' Grammer asked him.

'I'll go into the office right now and we'll see. I need to report on this and we'll take it from there.'

I looked at Grammer and tried to read the expression on her face.

After Ronald Fields had left, Grammer said that she was going out for a while.

'You've done your bit, Daphne,' she said. 'Leave it for now. Plumpet will be back soon and just keep her company.'

'If it's not too late, do you think we could go in and see Ronnie and Raleigh? It might do her good.'

'Play it by ear. See how your parents are, gauge the mood,' she said.

I could see she had something on her mind.

Chapter Thirty

Millicent's Tale

I waited until I heard Ronald Fields's car pull out of their driveway and down the road. My hearing might not be as good as the Dumpling's, but I can still pick up on the things I am listening for. It seemed best to go into Maureen Fields's immediately even though I did not think I was going to get the opportunity to use the Rohypnol straight away. But I had this feeling of time running out.

'I have them for you,' Maureen said as soon as she saw me.

'Will he miss them?'

'Probably. I'm just surprised that he left them in his jacket pocket. It's not like him. I thought he would take them back with him this evening,' she said, as she handed me the little bubblewrapped packet.

I took it from her. There were two tablets in it, and I thought how innocuous they looked. And yet with just one of those tablets my darling Plumpet lost a night of her life and changed the rest of it. I felt through the foil side and they were round – I was sure I had pills the same shape in my bathroom.

'Thank you,' I said.

'Do you know what you're doing?' she asked

tentatively, her small hands open in a gesture of something I could not identify.

'No,' I said. Then I decided to change tack. 'I just wanted to see what they looked like.' I peered at them again, and we chatted about the weather and how she was settling in, and then, as if we had both tacitly agreed that I had forgotten to hand them back, I left with the tablets in my pocket.

'Oh,' I said as an afterthought as I went out of the porch door, 'Can you tell Ronnie that Plumpet is out with her parents but should be back soon if he wants to call her?'

'Will that go down all right?' she asked.

'It will with Plumpet,' I said. 'And that's all that counts.'

And that was all that counted with me. That Plumpet would come through this as intact as possible. That was all I cared about.

I went back home and with one fingernail – I kept my nails long and exceptionally well manicured – I slipped the two Rohypnol tablets from their casing and replaced them with two other round tablets. Of course they were not identical. They did not have the maker's name on them, nor the number 2 which the Rohypnol sported. Nor were they quite as slim. The Rohypnol were really quite flat. The Rohypnol I slipped into my pocket and back I went to Maureen Fields next door.

'I forgot to return these,' I said to her, passing the tiny packet back.

She took them from me, saying not a word.

'I was thinking,' I said thoughtfully, 'that maybe

if you put them in a trouser pocket of Ronald's and then accidentally washed the trousers, forgetting you had put them there...'

We exchanged a look.

'I must run,' I said.

'So must I,' she replied. 'I've a wash to put on, and a day's work to put in.'

'A woman's work is never done,' I said encouragingly. I briefly thought that might be a good title for my next book. It could be about a conspiracy between two women ... neighbours. Well, maybe not neighbours – it's better to steer clear of the blatantly obvious. An interesting plot was unfolding in my mind. I'm always thinking of plots for my books at the most unlikely times. This could be about three wives – all of whom had been married to the same man... But I was digressing and I knew I had to get a move on.

'I must fly,' I said.

We smiled at each other and I went home.

What occurred next I did not mean to happen. Not then. Not the way it happened – if at all.

When George, Maria and Plumpet came back from their dinner, Plumpet looked even more wan than she had done earlier.

'Are you all right?' I asked her as they came into the kitchen.

She didn't answer, which was most unlike her. I despised myself for the banality of the question, but what else could I say?

'Come and sit down here,' I said to her. She looked as if she had been crying. I didn't ask her anything more. I just sat beside her and she leaned against me. Maria and George both went out of the room. I could hear them on the staircase.

'Dad's going back to work,' Plumpet said to me in a small voice.

We'll see about that, I thought. But aloud I said, 'I know, darling. They've been pressuring him to get back – the way they always do, but more so this year.'

'Really?' she said doubtfully.

'Really,' I said firmly. I was not having this child taking on any guilt over the adults' behaviour.

'He and Mum rowed over dinner,' she said.

'About what?' I asked.

'I don't know. About everything, I suppose,' she said.

'Like what?' I asked persistently but gently, trying to sound casual.

'Oh, like why Mum had to work while he was home. And she said that he was so busy watching the television and reading the papers that she was surprised he'd even noticed she wasn't there.'

'Adults do row,' I said to her, 'even in the happiest of marriages. And obviously it is difficult when he is away for such long periods of time.'

'But before, they were always so pleased to be with each other. This time it's different,' she said sadly. 'And it's because of me.'

The poor child. Didn't she have enough on her plate? Didn't we all have enough on our plates without them sharing their arguments in front of her? Oh, I tried reassuring her. Over and over.

And then she said that they had also argued with her because she didn't want to find out who had done those awful things to her. We talked about that for a bit. She was so afraid of having to face whoever it was. She said they were insistent that the culprit had to be found and put away. But she was afraid. She was afraid of everything. She feared finding out. She feared people knowing. She feared a court case. I found myself thinking about the women Dirk McHarg had screwed, and the horror I had experienced on finding out who they were. I tried telling her that knowledge is strength – but it was so easy for me to say. I had been an adult when I had faced certain facts about my life, and compared with what she was talking about, my realisations seemed quite trivial. As an adult you can deal with these things better. I had managed to arm myself when everything fell apart in my life, but I was in my thirties, not a mere child like Plumpet. And if she was afraid of dealing with some things then I knew that we, the adults, had to find a way to deal with them for her.

'Plumpet, Plumpet,' I said. 'You are to stop worrying. Your dad and mum and I will deal with everything. We'll make this go away.'

Or at least *I* would make this go away. That is what we grandmothers are for: to fix things for our grandchildren, to give them the benefit of our experience and our years – and heaven knows I had chalked up some experiences.

I comforted the child as well as I could and became strengthened in my resolve.

Next step was to talk to George and Maria – separately or together, I didn't care. George was so locked up in his own problems and his own perspective that I wasn't sure that he understood what I was talking about. I would say, 'That's men for you,' only it's such a gross generalisation and I certainly couldn't include Waldorf in it. Although there is always the possibility that Waldorf is the one and only exception to the rule.

I tried talking to them. But they had both clammed up. It was extraordinary.

Chapter Thirty-One

Maria's Tale

Of course we should not have argued in front of Plumpet, I knew that. But somehow things between George and me had got out of hand.

When we got back from our meal with Plumpet, which had been a total disaster, she not eating anything and insisting that she wanted everything to do with the rape dropped, George and I went upstairs to the bedroom, which once had been a room enveloped in love, but now seemed cold and empty and reflecting the way our marriage had become in the last few days.

'George,' I tried again, 'please listen to me. I need you. The girls need you. And yet you are not here at all.'

'I am here,' he snapped.

'You know what I mean,' I said. 'Please know that I feel so much sympathy for you over your father.'

Dirk McHarg, whom Grammer had thought drowned some thirty-three or thirty-four years earlier, had in fact only died the previous summer. It was the reason George had not come home during the past year. He knew that he would not be able to hide this fact from his mother, and the last thing he wanted, having kept his father's survival a secret for over twenty years, was to finally let it slip when Dirk was really dead. Grammer did not need to know. She had done her grieving many, many years earlier, and why should she be made to suffer this now?

When I first met Dirk McHarg, on my honeymoon, I was not altogether sure that I liked him. He had abandoned his wife and his son and forged a new life for himself in a distant country. George, of course, had sworn me to secrecy all those years ago. He had, in fact, gone out there straight from college with a film crew on his first job, and tried to find out where his father had disappeared in the sea. I think he was looking for somewhere to grieve or to make his peace ... I don't know. Something like that. And then, by one of those strange quirks of fate, he was having a drink in a bar one evening, and who did he find himself standing beside? He had not seen his father in eleven years at that stage, but he recognised Dirk McHarg immediately.

I too recognised him immediately when I first met him. He looked like his photographs, which Grammer had shown me. And he looked remarkably like George – the same high forehead, same curly hair, although more grey than black. A hard man, I thought at the time, although over the years, as I got to know him a little better on my frequent visits out there, I started to see some of the attributes of which Grammer had spoken. He was undoubtedly very intelligent, just like George. He was attractive-looking, given to flirting, very charming and, as it turned out, quite a kind man. He had made the most of the opportunity which came his way when his chartered seaplane had gone down in the sea, complete with his secretary, but without him on board as he had been running a fever that day and had decided at the last minute not to go.

'An accident,' he said to me. 'An opportunity given to me by chance – and I took it. I felt guilt over abandoning George, I suppose, but Millicent made a success of her life without me.'

I didn't tell him what his wife had said about him. Apart from the positive things, she also said that behind every great man was an even greater woman, and sometimes the disappearance of the great man gave the woman the opportunity to become herself. I didn't like living a lie, knowing about Dirk's existence and not telling Grammer, but I had promised George – and what was the point in rocking the boat anyway? Both Dirk and Millicent had new lives, and both were quite content without the other. So I kept my counsel and said nothing, although at times it was incredibly difficult given my close relationship with Grammer.

The one time I really wanted to tell Grammer

was when we brought the Dumpling home. It had been Dirk who had lifted her from the ground, and Dirk who had moved mountains to get her the paperwork so that we could adopt her.

I was sorry when he died. In many ways he had made good his life. He had created a sound relationship with his son. I think that as a woman, I might have felt a certain amount of rancour if my father had run off and I found him years later. But George was not like that. His finding his father was a complete bonus for him. As he said to me, 'I was looking for a place to throw a wreath in the water. How could I not have rejoiced?'

When Dirk died the previous summer, I went out to be with George. We told Grammer that something had come up with work and that he couldn't make it back. She of course was a little cross with him, because she sometimes felt that he preferred to be away than at home. But it was difficult for him. He had been living two lives, and trying to keep the other one completely separate from his mother – who was a most astute woman.

But while I sympathised greatly with him at the time of his father's death, and in the subsequent months, I felt that he was not making a good enough effort with the girls. I could see that he simply did not know how to handle what had happened with Plumpet – but then neither did I. None of us did. It was new territory, and it was not bringing out the best in either him or me.

And of course there were all the added complications – the fact that I was having an affair with my 'boss' as Martin liked to call himself. And now, having seen George with Marjorie Whelan, I felt that it was all too much. I was afraid of bringing up the Marjorie Whelan thing with him. I was afraid of what it might unleash. And who was I to say anything? I was having an affair too – if that was what he was doing with Marjorie, and I certainly felt that it was.

It was all too much. I felt crowded by events and circumstances, and I knew that I was letting Plumpet down at a time when she needed me more than ever before. I felt I was letting everyone down, including myself. I think my affair was already over, and I felt that Martin and I would settle for friendship, but it was difficult to look ahead. It was difficult to see anything clearly – there was just too much happening.

Some time later that night we reached a place where there was a certain degree of honesty between us. George said he was aware that for us to get through this period, he was going to have to change his career. The time had come for him to get a contract in Europe as opposed to the Far East. Then we would have more time together to work things through. I asked him if this had anything to do with Marjorie Whelan. I just had to. It seemed that if I didn't, she was going to be like a ghost in my life.

He seemed surprised. 'Marjorie?' he said.

'Yes. I happen to have seen you with her. I was driving home along Strand Road in Sandymount, and I saw you both,' I said lamely. I didn't want him to think I had been spying.

'She was an old friend of my father's,' he said.

An old lover, I thought – of both your father and of you, but I didn't say that. I kept it to myself.

'I needed to see her,' he said. 'To say goodbye. To tell her that it was over.'

'Over?' I queried. 'That your father had died?'

'No,' he said slowly. 'She did not know that my father was still alive. He wanted no one to know. I never betrayed him on that front.'

I was about to ask him what he meant when he said it was over, when suddenly I did not want to know. I did not want it spelled out. If it was over, then what was the point in us discussing it? Either it was or it wasn't – time would tell. And I did not want to know any details

Everything seemed out of kilter, and I couldn't see any way of moving things forward if I dwelt on the present or the past. So I thought I'd just say nothing other than to encourage him. After all, what I wanted was my family back – my husband as mine, and my children safe.

Isn't that all any woman wants?

Chapter Thirty-Two

Millicent's Tale

I owed Theresa Carmody a visit. I had said that I would be in to see her, and so after I had tried, unsuccessfully, to talk to George and Maria, I decided the time was right. All right, I did notice that her car was not there and that Polo Carmody's was. I thought I'd drop in, pretending that I had not seen the car situation. I'd just go in – maybe have a chat. It seemed an appropriate moment, and as the young ones say, you go with the flow. And so I flowed on up Theresa's path.

I rang the bell and gave it a good hard knock at the same time, and as the door opened, without looking at who answered it, I just stepped into the hall, and said, 'Theresa, darling – coffee. I need coffee.' I was in the hall before I made optic contact with Polo Carmody.

'Polo,' I said, appearing marginally flustered but not too much as I am not given to being flustered, and a flustered person could find herself outside the door before she knew it. 'Polo, I'm in need of coffee. Is Theresa in, or would you be an angel and make me one?'

And we were in the kitchen before she knew it.

She looked as she always did. Straight blonde hair, badly cut I might add, trailing down around her slightly elongated face. Unsmiling and unsympathetic is how I would describe her. She appeared slightly spaced out, one moment staring at me, and the next blinking repeatedly and then looking carefully at me as if perhaps she could not see me clearly.

'Where is Theresa?' I asked as I settled myself on a chair.

'She went out,' she said briefly, as she spooned coffee into a pot. She spilled quite a lot of it on the table, but did not seem to notice. It was as if her coordination was off.

'Shall I get the cups?' I asked her, thinking there was a pretty good chance she might drop them on the floor.

But she got them herself and put them on the table.

'How was Christmas?' I tried to keep the momentum going because she was such a tricky customer and I knew from the past that silences prolonged when she was around. I couldn't help but wonder if she had been drinking. There was no smell of alcohol, but she was behaving very oddly.

'Much as usual,' she said.

Hah! I thought. Much as usual. Is that how you'd describe it? You drug and rape my granddaughter and you describe it as 'much as usual'.

I think it was that phrase that galvanised me into action. Up until that moment, I was not completely clear on what I was going to do, or if indeed I would do what was at the back of my mind. But I found my hand touching the two tablets in my pocket, and when she poured the coffee and went to get milk from the fridge, I slipped them into her cup. I briefly thought of just putting in one, as I suspected one was enough, but I didn't know what effect the hot coffee would have on one tablet, whether it might diminish or dilute its potency, so I popped in the two.

'Nothing like coffee to warm the heart,' I said, although I would much have preferred something stronger to drink. I kept my hands around the cup to warm them as it had been freezing outside.

'Are you out of coffee in your house?' she asked – somewhat rudely, I might add.

I nearly lied and said yes, but my mind was moving ahead of me and I feared that later she or someone might somehow find out that there was no dearth of coffee in the McHarg household and that somehow my lie might catch me out.

'No, indeed,' I laughed. 'It's just that some-times an old grandmother needs to escape from all those children.'

'How many are there?' she asked.

And I thought, You bloody bitch, you don't even know. You randomly chose one of my grand-daughters and look what you did to her. And I thought then how it might have been Daphne or even baby Dumpling and that this woman would not care. There was something about her that had always left me feeling cold, and now I felt hatred in my heart, and the only relief I got was from the knowledge that when the Rohypnol took effect, she would be as helpless as Plumpet had been. And knowing how traumatised Plumpet still was by the loss of memory, I thought, Fitting revenge that this woman will feel that trauma too. Let the police deal with her later, but she will have had this punishment. Let her feel the fear.

I think that's what I thought. I think that's how I sold myself what I had done.

I drank my coffee slowly and I chatted about the seasonal weather, a book I had just finished and about the book I was about to start. After some twenty minutes I finished the rest of my coffee, which was now cold, and I left her sitting at the table.

'Don't get up,' I said to her. 'I had better go back and face the fray at home.'

That was the last time I saw her.

During the night Theresa Carmody must have come home, because I woke to the sound of banging doors, and looking out of the apartment window I could see the blue light of an ambulance flashing on the road outside.

'What's that?' Waldorf asked me, as he lay with his head on the pillows beside me in my kingsize bed. I must say he had a very nice profile and it looked exceptionally good when lying on his back like that.

'I don't know,' I said. And I went back to sleep.

The following day there was silence from the house next door. None of the family mentioned the rumpus on the road during the night and so I said nothing. The Dumpling played on the floor with her pasta shapes, and I noticed that she got out her little cars and pushed her ambulance around a bit. George and Maria seemed to have reached some sort of equanimity, because there was no sniping between them.

'I'm going back to work tomorrow,' George said to me at about lunchtime.

'Are you? Already?' I asked.

'Yes. I've a six-month stint to do on the present contract, and then I'm planning on coming back. The six months will give me time to sort out my things abroad. I've also got to train someone to take over from me, as I want to leave everything in order when I chuck in the present job.'

I was surprised. I've always felt that there was something keeping him so far from home, and it seemed amazing that at a time when he clearly could not cope with family life, he would decide to return.

'And how does Maria feel about this?' I asked.

'Why don't you ask her?' he said.

All right. All right, I thought, I will ask her.

A little later I had time on my own with Maria.

'It will give us six months to work out what it is we want,' Maria said to me. 'It is not as straight-forward as George may be implying. I think we both need time.'

Time, I thought. Isn't that what these two have been doing all along? Passing time apart? I did not know. I tried not to interfere.

'Anyway, I don't think he is planning on getting work right here on our doorstep,' she said. 'More like somewhere in Europe.'

That made more sense, and sounded more like George.

'We need to have a talk on another front,' I said to Maria.

'Any time you like,' she said. 'I want to talk to you too. I've something I need to ... share, I suppose.'

'Now's the time,' I said. I was not in a particular rush to tell her what was on my mind, but I was very interested in what she might have to say to me. We went into my apartment for a little peace and quiet.

'You first,' she said.

'No, no,' I insisted. 'After you.'

And then, horror of horrors, she told me that she had been up to something she shouldn't have been up to – I swear she was that obtuse – but of course I could read her like ... well, like a daughter-in-law.

A little something in the office. I wasn't surprised.

'It's human nature,' I said to her.

'I'm thinking I should tell George,' she said.

'You're *what?*' I said. She jumped. I had shouted, although I didn't mean to. 'Maria, my dear,' I said to her, in my firmest tones, 'under no circumstances are you to tell George anything of the sort.'

'But I want our marriage to work, and honesty–'

'N. O., I said. Follow me? No. Don't do it. You have no reason to tell him. Keep your own secrets. It won't help anything.' Honestly, why on earth would she want to share an affair with her husband?

'But I know things he has been up to, and I feel that I should come clean.'

She didn't know the half of it, I thought. I felt

the Marjorie Whelan affair would not be a very nice thing for a woman like Maria to know about. It was dirty, sordid. It would make her question her entire marriage. And God knows, it was enough that she suspected he had been having affairs abroad. Maybe he was, for all I know. That's what men do, isn't it?

'Listen to me. You are armed and strengthened by whatever you have been up to. You can tell me about it if you want, but I'm no fool and you've been under terrible pressure. Is it over?'

She nodded.

'Then keep it to yourself. George is the kind of man who likes to think that you are as pure as the day he married you. That's the way it should stay. Men who wander always assume they are the only ones who do, and they like to think of the little wife being completely loyal.'

'But...'

'You want him to trust you, don't you? Then don't tell him anything to undermine that trust.'

I finally got her to see sense, although it took a while. I knew what I was talking about – I had been around the block a couple of times by then, and I was absolutely sure that if she wanted her marriage to work, if she wanted stability in her home life, then silence was the best policy.

'What did you want to tell me?' she asked.

I had almost forgotten, but not quite. I filled her in on the story Daphne had pieced together. Maria was torn between distress that Daphne had not told her, and complete fury directed at Polo Carmody.

'Now, you listen to me again,' I said, trying to

calm her down. 'Daphne didn't tell you because you've been too preoccupied, and as long as Daphne told someone, it doesn't matter whom. And with regards to Polo...'

'I want to kill her,' Maria said. She was talking about Polo, of course.

'Revenge,' I said, 'is best served cold. The police are on to it. I'm quite sure something will happen today.'

'My poor daughters,' she said. 'I've neglected the three of them.'

There was a noise and we looked up, and there was the Dumpling on the floor just inside the door. I wondered how long she had been there. She came over and put her arms around her mother's legs, and Maria lifted her so that the Dumpling was sitting on her knees.

'They love you,' I said to Maria.

And they did. And that is what mattered.

I did wonder on and off during the day how Polo Carmody was doing. In a state of terror, I hoped. At least, that is what I told myself I hoped. It was evening before I saw Theresa Carmody's car was back outside her gate.

'I'm going in to say hello to Theresa,' I said, to no one in particular.

Plumpet was lying on the sofa pretending to read, but every so often she took out her mobile and sent a text. The Dumpling was busy with a chess set. As far as I knew no one had taught her how to play, but she seemed to have grasped the basic moves. 'Well done,' Waldorf said to her, and she looked up at him and smiled. Daphne had taken herself off to Plumpet's room – a project for the start of term had suddenly occurred to her. I must say I was impressed, as she would usually leave something like that until the last night before going back. George was having a G and T, and Maria was reading.

I put on my grandmother's fur, and went next door.

Theresa answered the door, looking very bleak I might add.

'Oh, Millicent,' she said. 'Thank God it's you. Come in.'

'Are you all right?' I asked her, divesting myself of the fur in her hall. She shook her head.

'Millie,' she said, 'Polo is dead.'

Whatever I had been expecting, it certainly was not that. I did not think it would be that simple. It transpired that Polo had died of respiratory failure – coke, alcohol and a variety of other drugs were in her system.

I sat Theresa down in the kitchen, and made us both coffee, then I went and got the brandy and poured us each a double. She was very shaken, but then so was I. I cannot honestly say that murder was what I intended. Yes, I admit I had thought about it – I know that at some point during those past few days I had thought that if the person who had done this to Plumpet were off the face of the earth, then my granddaughter would not have to handle anything more. But I had not meant to kill her. I had wanted to teach Polo a lesson, that was all.

I think.

'Run that by me again,' Waldorf said later in my apartment.

'She went and died. Fell off her perch. Popped her clogs. I don't know how to explain it better than that.'

'And you had slipped her a Rohypnol?'

'Two, as it happens.'

He was silent. I could see he was trying to digest the fact that Millicent McHarg, corseted and famous, had managed to commit murder.

'But there were a load of things in her blood,' he said thoughtfully.

'Probably no more nor less than she was used to,' I said, 'except for the two Rohypnol.'

'They won't be able to identify the Rohypnol,' he said.

'I know,' I said. 'But that's not the point. I did it to her.'

'Well, you didn't mean to,' he said reasonably. 'Now did you?'

No, I had not meant to. Not really. Not definitely.

'And it means that Plumpet doesn't have to deal with her in a court case, doesn't it?' Goodness, but he was being very reasonable. 'And,' he continued, 'if you were thinking of coming clean, I'd be very inclined to think again. First of all there are the Fields who will be implicated in that they supplied you with the pills. Then there is the fact that it would be in the papers – oh, I know there is no such thing as bad publicity when you're a writer, but... It would come out why you did it, I suspect, and there will be Plumpet

460

involved again whether you like it or not.'

I started to feel a lot better.

I quoted from the Bible, 'Vengeance is mine, said the Lord. Not of works, lest any man should boast.'

'Hmmm...' said Waldorf, rather sceptically, I thought.

'Oh, all right,' I said. 'Vengeance is mine, said Millicent McHarg.'

We went to bed. I must say, death is a great aphrodisiac.

And I slept better than I had since Christmas Eve.

Chapter Thirty-Three

Daffers's Tale

We went back to school, Plumpet and I. I would have walked with her but she was going with Ronnie, so Raleigh and I cycled together, and I had my project done and in my bag – a first for me. Dad had gone back to wherever he goes to, with a promise that he would be back for Easter and that everything would be all right. Mum seemed pleased to get back to work and to have us back at school.

'I love the routine,' she said.

Polo Carmody's funeral took place the day before term restarted. I went to the funeral with Grammer and Mum. Plumpet stayed at home

461

with the Dumpling. I was glad Polo was gone. Theresa Carmody looked lovely in black and she didn't seem terribly upset. She didn't cry or anything like that. Grammer said I was not to think about it any more. She said the only reason she was bringing me to the funeral was so that I could have a sense of closure, whatever that was. She said that all that was important now was to get Plumpet healthy again. She had told Plumpet that Ronald Fields would be dealing with the case, and that Plumpet need not ever face anyone in court, but that if she ever changed her mind, there was no problem, but for now we must just reassure Plumpet that it was all over. Plumpet certainly seemed relieved when Ronald Fields told her that he had the matter in hand and that she need never go to court. She had at least two baths a day and I didn't think that was normal, but everyone else just said that it was good for her. And she had lost an awful lot of weight, but for some reason no one really seemed to notice.

It seemed a wonderful end to that awful Christmas, Polo dying just like that of a drug overdose. Grammer said that there was a lesson to be learned there for us all: 'Don't meddle with drugs,' she said to us. There did seem some sort of justice in Polo snuffing it. I thought we should tell Plumpet that Polo had done it, but Grammer said that Plumpet just couldn't take any more shocks at the moment.

'What about Purple Eyes?' I asked Grammer.

'What about him?' she said.

I didn't like the thought of him still out there.

'He's gone back to the States,' Grammer said.

He had not been at the funeral. Grammer said that the police were looking for whoever had supplied Polo with the concoction she had taken. She spoke about a drug underworld, which sounded very seedy.

'But Purple Eyes,' I persisted.

'He'll get caught,' she promised me. 'His past will catch up on him.' She said it in such a determined way that I felt she was right. 'I've to go to the States next month or in March,' she said to me. 'My publishers want me to do some publicity there.'

'You stayed in his house the last time you went,' I said. I felt a bit worried. I didn't like the idea of him at all.

'You're not to worry,' she said to me.

'I could come with you,' I suggested. 'I've never been to the States and I'd love to go to New York.'

'You'll go to school,' she said. 'That's what you'll do. And you'll watch out for your Mum, for Plumpet and the Dumpling while I'm away.'

'Will Waldorf go with you?' I asked.

'I haven't suggested it to him yet, but he probably will.'

I didn't think Waldorf would miss out on a week in the metropolis. That's what Grammer called New York. The thought of which made me picture Grammer as Batman and Waldorf as Robin.

'You won't stay in that man's apartment this time, will you?' I asked anxiously. Grammer said that she wouldn't. She said that she fancied the Carlyle.

'But you'll be seeing him, won't you?' I persisted.

'He's with my New York publishers,' she said, 'so I won't have much choice. But you are not to worry. There is absolutely nothing for you to worry about. I know exactly what I'm doing.'

I didn't doubt that. It was just that I was frightened of the idea of that man with the purple eyes.

Grammer said that she was going to post him a copy of her new book, and that he would come down and see her in the Carlyle – she was already fancying a drink in Bemelman's Bar and dinner in Café Carlyle – and then they would take the train back uptown or downtown or something. She went back to looking at the newspaper and I peered over her shoulder to see what was attracting her attention.

'Oh, look Grammer,' I said. 'It's you.'

There was a very nice picture of her at Polo's funeral. She was wearing her ostrich feather in her felt hat. It was the most dramatic of her feathers and only came out on occasions when Grammer felt triumphant.

'Not too much chin showing?' Grammer said.

'No chin, Grammer,' I reassured her. 'You look wonderful.' And she did. She always did.

'I hope to goodness no one thinks *I* had anything to do with her death,' Grammer said.

'C'mon, Grammer,' I reassured her again. 'Why would they? They've just photographed you because you were at the funeral and Polo was an heiress or something. And there is no such thing as bad publicity, as you always tell us.'

Grammer laughed. 'Too bloody right,' she said. She once told us that a critic is like a eunuch in a harem. That's a place where there are loads of women all wearing floating see-through clothes in purples and pinks. She said that someone called Mr Wilde pointed this out once a long time ago. The eunuch sees it done every night and knows how it's done, but can't do it himself. When I asked her what that meant, Grammer said, 'When you're old enough to understand it, it will make sense to you. But in the meantime don't let the critics knock you.'

And we held hands as we looked at the newspaper. The article said that Polo Carmody, heir to the sausage empire, had been cremated after the funeral. Good, I thought.

'Burned to a crisp like an overcooked sausage,' Grammer said.

That made me laugh.

'Divine justice,' she added.

I quite liked the idea of divine justice. I couldn't help thinking that Grammer herself was a bit like the living version of divine justice. She always managed to sort things out.

Chapter Thirty-Four

Plumpet's Tale

Polo Carmody died of a drug overdose. I never realised that she took drugs. It hadn't occurred to me. I felt sorry for Theresa because Polo was her sister, and I could imagine how I would feel if something happened to Daffers or the Dumpling. I couldn't really remember the last time I had seen Polo. I supposed it was at one of Theresa's Christmas parties.

She was cremated the day before we went back to school and I stayed at home and minded the Dumpling. Grammer and Daffers went to the funeral. I think Waldorf went too, I don't really remember. But there are things I do remember about that day.

After they left – Mum must have gone into work I think, and Dad had already gone back to work too – Ronnie Fields came in with WC and we sat around listening to music and I read the Dumpling one of her new Christmas books, and Ronnie and I talked about going to art college the following year.

Some of the time I didn't feel real, and other times it was as if I had forgotten for a few minutes what had happened, and I just loved sitting there with the Dumpling on my knee and Ronnie beside me.

I hated the fact that Dad and Mum had been arguing all the time over Christmas, and no matter what anyone said, I knew it was my fault. They'd never argued before, so obviously what had happened to me had been the cause of it.

Ronnie said that what had happened had brought his parents closer together. I loved going into their home. There was always coffee bubbling in the percolator in their kitchen. When something happens, like it happened to me, it changes people. Daffers was different, for one thing. She sort of grew up over those ten days. And she became very like Grammer. If I had been able to find anything funny to laugh about, that would have been it. The idea of two Grammers was really a daunting prospect. Grammer knew what she wanted in life. Lots of people don't. They just do what they've been programmed to do. But Grammer says that we have choice.

That evening, after the funeral, we were all sitting looking at the fire, with music playing in the background. Mum was reading the newspaper and the Dumpling was sitting on the floor playing with something. Daffers had been given a diary for Christmas and she was actually writing in it. Waldorf put his head around the door. 'Has anyone seen my...' he paused.

And just like that the Dumpling, not even looking up, said, 'Yo-yo?'

There was complete silence in the room for a moment, except for Mozart's Piano Concerto No. 21 playing in the background, and one by one we turned and looked at the Dumpling. She put her hand over her mouth and looked up at us.

Behind her hand I could see that she was smiling.

'Say that again,' Mum said to her. But the Dumpling looked back down at her jigsaw and said nothing.

'Did you hear that?' Mum said to the rest of us.

We had. We just sat, speechless, looking at our silent Dumpling. Grammer came into the room after Waldorf and found us all just sitting there. Even Waldorf had collapsed on to a chair.

'What's going on?' she asked.

'Dumples spoke,' Daffers said. 'She said "yo-yo", didn't you, Dumples?'

'And about time too,' Grammer said.

Which of course was true. Apart from seeing specialists and physiotherapists because of her missing foot, the Dumpling had been to hearing specialists and speech therapists in an effort to get her to speak. Grammer had always said that she would talk when she was ready, but Mum had been worried because it had been impossible to work out why the Dumpling had never said anything when every doctor in the country said there was nothing wrong with her.

'Say it again, Dumples,' Daffers encouraged her.

But the Dumpling had returned to silence and chose to say nothing.

That was definitely the nicest thing that happened at Christmas. It was even nicer than Ronnie Fields kissing me again earlier that afternoon when we took WC for a walk – and that had been very nice indeed. I had thought that that was as good as it could get.

I think we learn everything from our parents,

and that's why Ronnie behaved like his father and was so kind to me, like his father was to his mother. I think I might be a bit too much like Mum. She's very acquiescent and I think I am too. Daffers isn't a bit like that. Daffers has got more and more like Grammer over the last week or so.

And of course the Dumpling is like no one – at least no one we know.

Six Months Later

Chapter Thirty-Five

Plumpet's Tale

'Well, Prunella McHarg?' Dr Walmsley said to me.

I was sitting in a chair in his room. It swivelled slightly and sometimes I turned it so that I could look out the window. His room is three floors up in the hospital, and the view from the window is really just of the sky. But by looking at the sky you could tell all kinds of things about the day.

Sometimes I didn't swivel the chair. I just sat with it facing him. He wears glasses and he has a thin ascetic face. The lines on it are kind lines. Sometimes I make him smile and that makes me feel good. I know that I only swivel the chair when we are touching the bad things. I suppose that because he is a psychiatrist he knows that too. But I don't have to hide anything in here. He told me that. I can tell him everything. Everything is safe within these walls.

I smile at him. 'Well, Doctor Walmsley?' I say.

I feel good today. I can joke slightly, and by repeating his words and his tone of voice I know that he knows that I'm on top of things.

'So how was last weekend?' he asks.

'It was good,' I tell him carefully as I sometimes am not sure which way he is going.

'And are you ready for this weekend?'

I look down at my hands. The right one is resting on the left one, on my lap. They are sitting quietly.

'Yes. I think somehow that I am. I'm scared,' I say, 'but I know that that is to be expected. And last weekend – that was my fourth weekend at home – well, it was fine, really. And it was the first time that I wasn't really dying to get back in here.' *Dying*. The words had been flowing very quickly and they suddenly dry up as I think about what I'm saying. I look down at my hands and they are tightly clasped.

'That's progress,' he says. 'I know that on other trips home you've been very keen to get back in here, into the safety of the hospital. So that is good progress.'

'It is, isn't it?' I say. I can hear the childish hopefulness in my own voice. 'Grammer says that it's a slow process to get back on one's feet. She says that even after I leave here this weekend, that I'll still be coming in here now and again.' I say this because I want to hear him confirm it. It's safe in the hospital. There is no pretence.

'You will still be coming in once a week for a while.'

'I know. But I don't think I really need to,' I add, because I want him to tell me that it is nothing to do with needing to come in. I just like the idea that he will be there for me.

'It's the right thing to do,' he says. 'I'll be here to talk with you or to listen to you – just like it's been over the last few months.'

'Grammer says it's a bit like a back-up support system,' I try. 'And that I've got to go with it. She

474

says coming in here to you will help ease my way back into the real world. The real world...' I listen to the words I'm saying and I wonder what they mean. *The real world.* 'It's as if I've been in an unreal world – is that how people see it? And yet it's been real for me. Grammer says that I've done very well.'

'You have done very well,' he says. 'You have come a long way.'

'It's been six months.' I know that it is six months even though I don't remember the days or the details of those days as they passed. 'A whole six months...' I can feel my voice trailing away. Those six months have slowed up my life. Is that good or is that bad? 'I've missed my exams in school.'

'And how do you feel about that?'

'I don't know,' I tell him. 'I'd been so looking forward to college next year, and now I have to go back and repeat.'

'Your mother says that you'll be going to a different school.'

'Yes. It makes more sense. It's one of those finishing colleges so it is more like a university. I feel good about it. I'm just sorry I'm not starting in art college this year.'

'Why are you sorry?'

'Mainly because of Ronnie. He and I were both going to apply for the same place. We still are.' I think about this for a little. A bit of me knows that if I had managed to hold things together this last year and had passed my exams and gone into college, that maybe what happened would have happened anyway. But I don't want to talk about that so I try to distract old Walmsley.

'He's taking a year out,' I tell him. 'Ronnie, I mean. He's going to bring in WC later today and we're going for a walk.'

Then there is one of those silences that sometimes happen when I'm talking to Dr Walmsley. I swivel the chair and I stare out the window. I don't mean to, but I find myself pushing up the sleeves of my sweater and looking at my wrists. When I look back at him he is watching me.

'I'm going to be all right, aren't I?' I ask him.

'Yes,' he tells me. 'You are. Would you like to tell me what you're most afraid of now?'

'Outside? Do you mean outside?'

He does not answer. He just watches as I slowly swivel the chair back so that I am facing the window again. There are white puffy clouds and they are moving quite fast. The clouds are coming from the south so the wind will be warm.

'I suppose I'm most afraid of...' I seek the words. I want to tell him. 'Most afraid of ... well, of breaking down in class again.'

'Would you like to talk about it?'

'About what happened? About why I broke down in class? Or about what happened when I broke down in class?' I swivel back so that I can look at him, as I want to see his face. But he doesn't answer. He is just watching me and waiting.

Back goes the chair to the window so that I can see the clouds.

'That day in class,' I hear myself saying. 'That awful day. We did talk about this before, didn't we? Sometimes I'm not sure if I've talked about something with you, or if it has just happened in my head.'

'That day...' he prompts.

I let my mind go back to the start of term just after Christmas – last Christmas, awful Christmas. Daffers's carrot superglued on to the snowman on the window. Frost everywhere. Dad gone back to work. Normal days and routine, Mum said. She said that that was what I needed. At first it seemed all right. I would get up in the morning and Ronnie walked with me to school.

I loved that. It seemed to launch me into the day, and it was something to look forward to as I tried to eat breakfast. And during the day when I couldn't concentrate in school I could look forward to finding Ronnie standing outside waiting for me when I came out. The days sort of passed like that. Then came the day about six weeks into term when I was in a practical art class. The blackness in my memory seemed bigger than me that day. Oh, it was there all the time – this big gaping hole, but for some reason it suddenly seemed to be larger than the whole of me that day. There had been mornings when I was so shaky and nervous that the only thing that got me out of the front door was Ronnie standing on the step smiling at me. But that day ... that day was the worst.

'Ronnie walked me to school,' I say. It's difficult because I think that it was just another day. At least early in the morning, that morning, it seemed like just another awful day. I didn't want Ronnie to leave me when we got there, but of course I didn't say that.

'We had practical art. I always liked that,' I tell Dr Walmsley. 'I was about to start making a candlestick. Part of my final project.'

Sometimes Dr Walmsley says nothing. He just waits. It hurts thinking about it. I want to tell him what happened. But it hurts.

'I screamed,' I tell him. 'I just screamed. Not out loud. Inside my head, I screamed and screamed.'

I remember this scream building up inside my head as suddenly tiny fragments of memory came and went and came again. I couldn't hold the memories. But they were there, like flashes. They were bigger than the hole in my mind. They were bigger than me. I needed to get away from them.

'I needed to escape them. The thoughts. The things in my head. I ran...' I had run to the door and I briefly saw the faces of my classmates looking at me in amazement and I needed to get away because I thought they all knew what had happened. I thought how could they not know.

'I don't remember after that,' I try, because I want to stop thinking.

'What is the next thing you remember?'

'Being in here. In the hospital. In the secure wing. You know, where you first found me.' I could hear the words I was using. Of course Dr Walmsley did not find me. Presumably he was assigned to me. But I like to think he found me. I like to think he took me from the secure wing under his wing. A more secure wing. There is safety there.

'Do you want to tell me what really happened?'
Dr Walmsley asks.

I could tell him. He would like that. I may
already have told him. I'm not sure.

'The candlestick,' I hint. 'You know. The
candlestick.'

There is silence again in the room. The clouds
drift slowly by. The wind has dropped. I swivel
the chair back to him.

'I knew then. I knew that day. It came back –
bits of it. The candlestick. I've told you this
before, haven't I?'

'Yes, you have.'

But I'm going to tell him again.

'I remembered then. You know – I remembered
then what they had done. Not all of it, but some
of it. And I saw her face. I saw it clearly.'

'Polo's face?'

'Yes, Polo's face. She's dead. She can't do it to
anyone else,' I say. 'That's the good thing. That
had eaten me up. Since it happened, I mean.
Since Christmas. That had just – it had sort of
killed me. Not that it was Polo, because I didn't
remember who had done it. It was the guilt thing.'

'The guilt?' He prompts so well.

'Yes. I felt such guilt. No, no,' I tell him quickly,
'I don't mean guilt about what was done to me,
because I know that was absolutely not my fault.
I know that now, even if I wasn't sure about it
back then. But I felt such guilt because I didn't
want the police to pursue the matter – and
everybody else *did* want me to pursue it.'

'Tell me about the guilt,' he prompted me
again.

'Because I didn't want it pursued, I felt later that there was the possibility that he ... they ... she ... might do it again. To someone else, and it would have been my fault.'

'The police would have pursued it anyway,' he says. 'They didn't simply because Polo was already dead.'

'Yes, but I didn't know that,' I say. 'And that's why I felt so guilty. And then when I remembered, that day in class, when we were working on candlesticks – then I suddenly knew it was Polo, and I remembered the candlestick, and I knew what had been done to me ... it was awful. I think it was worse than not remembering.'

I recalled running from the room and someone taking me to the nurse's office at the school, and I lay there for a while, waiting for Grammer to come and collect me. They had phoned her. But I could not find the words to say that Grammer didn't drive anyway and couldn't collect me. I pretended to be asleep so they would leave me alone. I could remember Polo and the candlestick and I suddenly knew that Polo had not been alone. At first I was saying to myself, *Polo is dead. It's over. I know what happened – well, roughly what happened. And it's over* – and then I suddenly knew that Polo had not been alone.

'I hated my body,' I try telling him. 'I hated it so much. It felt vile. I thought if it no longer belonged to me, and it didn't feel like it did belong to me any more, I thought if I could just leave it behind – move away, you know.'

I got up off the nurse's couch and let myself out into the corridor. I went to the craft cupboard in the Art Corridor where I knew the sharp cutting knives were. I held the knife in one hand knowing that I could finish things, finish everything there and then. I felt surrounded by blackness, as if I had fallen into the hole in my head. And then I couldn't do it. I couldn't do it. I don't know why. It wasn't as if light suddenly penetrated the emptiness of me – it wasn't that. It was just that I couldn't do it.

'I couldn't do it,' I said to Dr Walmsley. 'I just couldn't do it. I don't know anything more. That was it. I had no redress. I...' I find myself looking at my wrists as I'm telling him all of this. They are unmarked. I remember the blackness, the silence, the scream inside my head. But they are part of the past. I'm almost sure they are part of the past.

'I'll be all right now,' I reassure Dr Walmsley. 'You know that, don't you?'

I feel him watching me so I swivel back towards the window.

I thought about Gervaise Holt. I had never told anyone that I was sure he had been there that night.

'Did I ever tell you about Gervaise Holt?' I ask him. 'He had purple eyes.'

'In various sessions I had with other members of your family, his name did come up.'

Dr Walmsley has such a calm voice. It is difficult to tell from it what he knows.

'I think I was in here before I put it together.' These are things that I try not to think about. 'I don't really remember him being there that night although I recall very clearly now going back up

481

to the door of Theresa's house to get my ring. Clearly? No, that's the wrong word. I recall it as though I know it must have happened, and sometimes I think I can actually remember letting myself out of our front door. The ring ... Dad had just given it to me, and I'd left it on the draining board by the sink. It all comes and goes in flashes.'

There is another long silence.

'I don't remember any of this in colour. Or even in black and white. It's more like shapes and feelings. It's so intangible and yet I know it happened. I had let myself into the house when Polo suddenly appeared in the kitchen just as I slipped the ring back on.'

I got such a fright when the kitchen door swung open, as I didn't realise that anyone else had come in. And there was Polo Carmody standing in the doorway.

'What are you doing?' she asked me. Her eyes were narrow and she made me feel like I was doing something wrong.

'Theresa asked me to look after Cat,' I said. 'I left my ring here and I was just putting it back on.'

'Have a drink with me,' Polo suggested.

'I ought to get back home,' I said. I could think of nothing I would like less than having a drink with Polo Carmody.

'It's Christmas time,' she said. 'Stay and have a drink with me,' and I did not know how to say that I really did not want to. I kept thinking that if I were Daffers, I'd find a way to say no.

'Just a glass of Coke,' I heard myself saying in

my polite voice.

We took our drinks into the sitting room and I sat again by the glass-topped table with the bowl of salted almonds.

'I remember her looking at me,' I tell the doctor. 'I remember hearing the ticking of the clock on the mantelpiece and looking through the glass table and seeing the toes of my shoes. I remember thinking about the Dumpling's shoes and how her little finger traced the hearts stitched on them. I remember looking around and thinking that there was someone else there ... and then there is a blank. I couldn't move. There is a moment in time in which I saw Polo and a candlestick and I knew she was about to do something terrible to me. I think I was naked. It was as if I was weighed down...

I can still remember the feeling of sluggishness that had slowly and completely overpowered me. I remember a moment when I could clearly see the ceiling and then Polo's face looking into mine, and the look on her face terrified me. Then in between the blanks I know I was being raped, that something terrible was being done to my body and that I was powerless to resist it.

'I wanted to scream,' I say. 'But I could make no noise. It was here in hospital when I went over and over it in my head and I remembered them telling me that I had been bathed, that I was clean when I was brought to the hospital on Christmas Day, and I knew then that Polo had not been alone. She could not have bathed me. She was not that much bigger than me. And then I thought of Purple Eyes. He had stared up at my bedroom window one night with Polo and I knew that someone had been with her.'

'Could you remember him being there?' Dr Walmsley asks me.

'No, I can't categorically state that I do, but I know that it was him. I could remember his eyes at some point while I was lying there unable to move. Not as being purple, more as shapes that were uniquely his purple eyes. I wonder, though...' So many things that I wonder.

'What do you wonder?'

'I wonder how they thought they'd get away with it.'

'If they had used the drug before, they would have known the side-effects, one of which is amnesia.'

'But bits of it came back to me,' I said aloud.

'Not enough for you ever to have been able to stand up in court and point a clear finger,' the doctor said. 'And they knew that. There were no witnesses. No evidence. There was only your impaired memory, which might never have come back. They knew you would remember virtually nothing, and anything that was there would be vague and elusive. And with Polo dead the police simply could not find an accomplice.'

'I wonder, did they even question Gervaise Holt?'

'I gather he left the country when Polo died,' Dr Walmsley explained. 'And they had no grounds for connecting him with the crime.'

'In a way I came out of this quite well,' I told him. 'I mean, it's over and as Grammer says, it's my choice as to how to cope with the past. She

484

says that we can choose to be victims, and that she will help me to ensure that I am not a victim for the rest of my life.' Grammer can be very adamant when she decides something.

'Indeed,' the doctor said dryly.

We then had another one of our silences. After a bit he said, 'So you go home at the weekend?'

'Yes. You know Dad works in Europe now? Well, we're going to the Continent for two weeks to spend time with him. He's planning on moving home in September when Maya starts school. The Dumpling insists that we call her Maya, which actually seems to suit her now. She's grown in the last few months, and she's very excited about school. Grammer says that she is more than ready for it, especially since she started talking – and she's walking so much better. Mum says she needs lots of company to keep her stimulated. Grammer says the Dumpling is going to go places. She sees the world differently to the rest of us – the Dumpling, I mean. Grammer says her perspective is unique, as is her use of language. We all call our father "Dad", but once the Dumpling started to talk, she insisted on calling him "Brother".' I laughed as I told him this.

'Brother?' the doctor repeated.

'Yes, Brother,' I said. 'It's sweet, isn't it?'

He looked at his notes, and then wrote something down. 'Do you know where Gervaise Holt is now?'

The funny thing was that I did know. I found myself fidgeting with my hands again as I really preferred not to think about Purple Eyes. Eventually I nodded my head.

485

'Would you like to tell me?'

I didn't really want to tell him because I didn't know what to say. I did know what had happened to Gervaise Holt. I knew it by chance as I happened to have been sitting in Dr Walmsley's waiting room for a half an hour before he was ready to see me and there was a newspaper lying on the table. I supposed they would have told me sooner or later.

'I read it in the paper this morning,' I said.

Chapter Thirty-Six

Millicent's Tale

I knew what I had to do. I had planned it months earlier, but Plumpet's breakdown, as we choose to call it in the family, rather postponed things. She needed me near her so I put it on hold, but as the day approached when Plumpet would be coming home I knew that I could put it off no longer. I did not want to put it off any longer. It was time. High time.

I had quickly got over any problems I might have had with Polo's sudden demise, and once I had properly taken her death on board it had occurred to me that if I had any regret, it was to do with the fact that Polo probably did not know that we had cottoned on to her. And that gave me reason to pause. I like to think that she had a sense of consciousness up until she died, and that maybe it dawned on her that I had slipped something into her coffee. But of course I can't be sure. And it was for that reason that I had done a bit of serious thinking about how to proceed.

Ronald Fields said that there was no overt reason to believe that Gervaise Holt might have been involved in the drugging and raping of my granddaughter, although the police were definitely of the opinion that Polo Carmody had not done it alone.

'Ronald,' I said to my neighbour on the day of Polo's funeral, '*I* know that Gervaise Holt has to have been her accomplice.'

'Knowing it isn't enough, Millicent,' he said to me. 'We need proof. Something we can use to bring him in. And we have nothing. He has an alibi for the night in question. He was staying in the Shelbourne Hotel. He was seen in the bar. He signed chits for drinks ... and the doorman who knew him well by sight, says that he did not see him leave.'

'But if we know that it was him–'

'Plumpet can't identify him. Polo can't be questioned because she is dead. We have nothing to link him with the crime.'

Well, always look on the bright side, Millicent, I told myself. Plumpet did not want this to go to court. I did not want this man to get off scot-free. Two and two made four. Ergo, I would just have to don my avenging angel's cloak again. Or should I say wings?

I knew what I had to do, but I wanted to do it in such a way that he would know that his number was well and truly up. I wanted that knowledge for him before he joined Polo in what I hoped was some form of eternal inferno.

My plans were, as I said, put on hold because of Plumpet being committed to hospital. But when Plumpet came home for her fourth consecutive weekend, and was due to be released during the following week, I knew that I was running out of time. When she left that Sunday afternoon, I went straight to the airport. Thanks to the time difference I was in New York not long after I departed from home, if you follow me. I left Waldorf behind to keep the household running and to make sure, in case anything went awry, that he was there to hold the fort.

Eagle feather in my hat – my predatory feather as I like to think of it – furs on my neck, business class all the way, and by New York nightfall I was ensconced in the Carlyle. With two Manhattans under my belt – well, under my corset I should say – I checked the train times, sorted my paperwork and rang Gervaise Holt.

'Gervaise, c'est moi,' I said to him, enthusiasm and warmth dripping from my tongue. He seemed surprised to hear from me, but not disagreeably so, and agreed to meet me in the bar the following day for a drink and a chat and to escort me to my publishers.

It was a very warm day, and I was glad that I had brought some linen ensembles. Not to mention my hatbox. It was really too warm at that time of year in the metropolis for felt on one's head. I removed a very nice cream stiffened linen hat with a little netting, which just partially covered a portion of my forehead. I pinned one of my dyed coque feathers to it, and checked my lipstick before heading down to the bar.

He arrived shortly afterwards, looking much the same with his purple eyes, and a smile on his lips that stopped short of the rest of his face, and that lived-in look, which made me want to throw up. All over him, I might add.

I had with me my new novel, which was to be published first in the States. I had called it *Three Sheets to the Wind*, but undoubtedly my editors would re-title it. I also had with me the detailed synopsis of my book *Revenge* that no one would ever read other than old Purple Eyes, as Daphne had named him. I pretended to him that it was a work of fiction but that I had used the names of real characters in it.

'They can be changed later,' I said. 'I just thought it would be fun to write it from the perspectives of people I know.'

'How interesting,' he said as he sipped a Pernod.

'Theresa was asking for you,' I said.

'Theresa?' He appeared genuinely puzzled.

'My next-door neighbour, Theresa Carmody – Polo's sister.'

'Ah, Polo,' he said.

During the silence that followed, I ate two olives and watched him as he started to read the synopsis of *Revenge*. I allowed him three pages before I said we had better be off.

'It reads well,' he said thoughtfully. 'How much of it have you completed?'

I patted my briefcase, a very nice dark wine-coloured leather bag, which coincidentally matched my blouse, implying that it was all there, although indeed it was *Three Sheets to the Wind*, which was in it in loose manuscript form. *Three Sheets to the Wind* did not make as good reading as *Revenge*, although there was a very good scene in it in which the heroine who finally succumbed to the purchase of a tumble-dryer has sex on top of the aforementioned dryer, discovering that the vibrations from the dryer added magnificently to her orgasm. The moral of which is, always be prepared to try something new.

I digress.

I had timed it all to perfection and I smoothly removed the synopsis from Gervaise's hands as we stood to leave. 'We authors, you know,' I said with a coy little smile. 'Terrified of someone stealing our ideas.'

We walked to the subway as I said I was in need of a breath of fresh air. He seemed deep in thought as we progressed through Manhattan.

'So far,' he said as the throngs went past us, 'I have picked up the characters who are loosely based on the members of your family.'

Loosely based? I almost snorted.

'I was just getting into the main part of the plot. What is the crime you allude to?' he asked.

We were on the steps going down towards the platform when I explained that a rape took place, and that ultimately this was a story of revenge.

'A rape?'

We were easing our way through the people gathered at the edge of the platform.

'Well, the girl is drugged and raped.'

490

Another long silence as he digested this. I kept an eye on the clock on the wall as I really was going to have only one chance to do this right.

'This is a bit of a change from your usual novels,' he said.

'I know,' I said. 'The extraordinary thing is that it was Polo Carmody's death that has empowered me to finish what must be done.'

He looked puzzled. His eyes turned sideways to me and they seemed to narrow slightly. Then he stared at the tracks as if considering my words.

'Here,' I said as I passed him the last page of the synopsis. 'Take a look.'

I could hear the train now and there was that inevitable surge of bodies as people struggled to take their positions. I saw him glance at the few lines on the page and I know, I am absolutely sure that he took in what he read, because he half put out a hand as if to steady himself against the inevitable, and then the train whooshed into the station.

Somewhere, someone gave a scream. It sometimes echoes in my head but with that scream came a wonderful silence in my mind, and all the fury I had felt for Polo Carmody and Gervaise Holt disappeared with him under the train.

The sheet of paper fluttered from his hand as I gave him the push and I stuffed it into my pocket to dispose of later. I just know that he read the words: *After Polo Carmody dies from the double dose of Rohypnol which Millicent McHarg slips into her coffee, Millicent goes to New York to push GH under a train.*

491

Epilogue

There are still days when the gaping hole in my memory is larger than me, and during those days it is difficult to find a foothold of any sort. I come back to the basic things I know and they are that I am Prunella McHarg and I am one of three. I know dates and facts of events in both my life and in the lives of others.

Grammer says that we are defined by the events in our lives but that we can choose whether to be the victims or the survivors of those happenings. She says there is a randomness in life about which we can do nothing, but that there are times when we can take matters into our own hands; there are times when we are controlled by events and then there are times when we can do the controlling.

My life is still in front of me and I have choice.

I have seen the randomness of events, the chance coincidence of being in the wrong place at the wrong time. I have seen Dad watching floods and famine and telling the world so that the world can help the victims because those victims are trapped in their circumstances. Grammer says I was born lucky, born in a place and to a family where I have known such love and such support. I have been given time out in this hospital where I can piece myself back together. I am learning both to confront the terrible images in my mind and then to put them aside. That is where there is choice for me. There are days when I know that I am strong enough to override what happened to me. I will always be a girl who was drugged and raped on Christmas Eve, but that does not have to be what defines me. My big fear that I would have to go to court and confront the monsters who did those things to me, that fear is gone, and the monsters are gone too. They cannot do those things to anyone else ever again. When I read in the newspaper that Purple Eyes was dead I felt that I might be safe again. There was such a nice picture of Grammer in the paper as she had been with him at the time, and she always manages to attract publicity. The report said she was in a state of shock, which doesn't sound a bit like Grammer, and she was quoted as saying 'God is good'. I don't imagine she was very shocked. It's the kind of thing they say in the papers. Anyway, Grammer will overcome such things. I know that. She flies home today.

My strengths will come and go and come again. Dr Walmsley says that each time I will be a little stronger. I am going to pass my exams this coming year and then I am going to art college. Ronnie Fields is taking this year out because he wants to wait for me so that we can study together.

I go home tomorrow.

I am Prunella McHarg and I am one of three.